S0-ADY-852

How Did That Sun Get Out

PS
3552
.U72485
H69
2001

How Did That Sun Get Out

A classical novel

Roger Burkholder

GOSHEN COLLEGE LIBRARY
GOSHEN, INDIANA

Writer's Showcase
San Jose New York Lincoln Shanghai

How Did That Sun Get Out

All Rights Reserved © 2001 by Roger Burkholder

No part of this book may be reproduced or transmitted in any form or by any means, graphic, electronic, or mechanical, including photocopying, recording, taping, or by any information storage retrieval system, without the permission in writing from the publisher.

Writer's Showcase
an imprint of iUniverse.com, Inc.

For information address:
iUniverse.com, Inc.
5220 S 16th, Ste. 200
Lincoln, NE 68512
www.iuniverse.com

Epigraph translated by Bernard Frechtman.
Used by permission of Philosophical Library, Inc.
Front cover illustration *Word* © 1998 Roger Burkholder
Back cover illustration *What May Be Saved* © 1997
by Pamela King and Roger G. Burkholder

ISBN: 0-595-00257-9

Printed in the United States of America

To those who make constructive their legitimate disgust toward the sort of mentalities displayed by members of the Federal Bureau of Investigation of the United States in their unspeakable efforts to torment Dr. Martin Luther King, Jr. into suicide.

Silence itself is defined in relationship to words,
as the pause in music receives its meaning
from the group of notes around it.
Jean-Paul Sartre, What Is Writing?

Contents

PART I

1
Solo Delivery

1

'All of the markers, except for one, in rows. Giant, circleless, and broken. Dominoes.'

Summer was ending with a wave of wrenching heat. The rustlings of leaves were tinged with the fibrous cracklings of a brittle introduction to the dawning autumn, and currents of warmth already were beginning to rise within a chill of early morning.

Throughout the city, doors for employees were being unlocked. Hands were fumblingly searching for indoor light switches. The infrequent hums of solitary speeding automobiles had almost ceased and soon would be replaced by the steady murmurings of daily traffic. Some of the drivers, nudging their patiences toward fluid internal protections against cacophony and disarray, already were closing windows and carefully reaching toward dials of air conditioners.

Few pedestrians as yet were anywhere in sight. One, a lanky teenaged boy, stood rigidly on a suburban sidewalk beside a high, black metal fence. Crinkling his eyelids together to block out most of the sunlight, the boy peered, as he often had, through the ribbed bars of the fence at an aged ovoid stone adjacent to a mound of earth.

I wonder, the boy thought, if they'll hear the snow falling over them and hope it's only the leaves or the wind in the grass.

'Not hear. Experience somehow.

'I don't know how to get at what it's like there to them.

'If it's like anything at all. I'd be afraid of the sounds of snow, though.

'But maybe they're not afraid. Maybe snow makes them something like warmer.'

Because he had been getting a crew cut practically every weekend for as long as he could remember, the boy seldom needed a comb. Once, he had allowed his tawny hair to grow for a month in order to have it trimmed into a flattop, but he had found the grease and the twice-a-day training sessions too much trouble and the next week had requested the barber to shave his head back into his customary quarter-inch style.

'The fence is made of iron or steel. No matter how many times I look it up in the table, I never can remember which one FE stands for....

'I still think the words are on the other side of the stone. Even though it looks a little like they used to be on this side.... But I don't see how they would've worn away so soon. I can't think of reasons for the stones unless the words last. A stone would only mean someone, but the words get at who....

'I used to be hardly able to see over this mound. Now, it's as high as my knees. I mean my knees are as high as it. Because it sunk as much as it will a long time ago. And now I've grown as tall as I'm going to....

'Maybe it's that they lie here getting ready for when the earth over them has settled, and then they somehow leave. So that what's left doesn't have anything to do with them anymore. What's left is for us. To remind us...

'I'm sure it's a mass grave.

'It has to be.

'But the stone looks older than from the violent revolution here.

'So, maybe it's a family all died together from hunger. Or from a disease, more likely. One of our first plagues. Their first plagues.

'Or it could've been used for criminals. Putting all the ones together when they died who didn't fit in when they were alive.

'Or maybe there weren't even any such symbols as I'd know on the stone at all. Put up way before Boston. Maybe the settlers took over even the lands of the dead.'

Impulsively testing his readiness for discovery, for certainty, the boy knelt, stuck a hand through the fence, and solemnly touched the mound. During the other times he had been near it, he had done no more than wonder and stare and guess.

Feeling suddenly queasy, he bolted up and looked rapidly about him.

When he was sure he was still alone and unobserved, he leaned toward the sidewalk, lifted a paper sack from the top of which emerged two sticks, held it protectively against his chest, eyed the open gate to the cemetery, and slowly turned to face Massachusetts Avenue.

After meandering several steps to a crosswalk, he glanced at a signal light and, although it was red, nonchalantly wove his way through the traffic.

'The college isn't open yet. Not for another week. A university, too. I can't understand what the difference is. Maybe one is a part of the other. Or maybe it depends on where you are as to what you call it. Where I am. Maybe if you're inside it's one and outside the other....

'Always before, I'd be in school by this week. Last year sitting looking out the windows. Watching the leaves change. Thinking about now. Thinking that now I'd be thinking about then. And now I'm doing it.

'I'll tell her tomorrow. I've got to figure out how. So that it'll be exactly right. I've got to get it right. For once I've got to talk something right. I'll tell her on the picnic tomorrow.'

While brushing his free hand over a rear pants pocket to assure himself he had his wallet, he noticed the rising warmth of the city air; and he unbuttoned the top two buttons of his jacket, a red and black plaid, cheaply manufactured to suggest the tempered strength of heavier garments worn in the mythic woodlands of magazine advertisements.

'There should be a wall. The markers are there because we're supposed to respect that the ones under them lived. It needs more apartness for that. We need, I mean.'

In less than a minute, he arrived at the entrance to a subway stop, where he hesitated, sighed, and impatiently ran his hand through his hair.

'It's disrespectful to have it so close to the street with only the metal fence. The street so close to it.

'Someday I'll go in and look at that stone.'

Tightening his cheeks to make them feel as they had when, gazing in a mirror, he had determined the pattern of muscle that would cause his oversized, fibroid nose to appear smaller, less imposing, he bounded down the subway entrance stairs and selected a waiting place amidst a crowd scattered throughout the station.

Quietly enough so that he was certain no one could hear him, he then started to hum, as he had been doing often lately, occasionally discovering what seemed to him to be original melodies among the many with which he was familiar. Sometimes words, too, would loosen in another part of his mind; and when that happened, he would playfully attempt to fashion them into silent lyrics, joining them to the humming without turning them into sound.

'A way can be found that nobody yet knows. Windows open on gardens, instead of slide sideshows....

'I've got to get it clear what I want to do. Settled. Not clear. Can't be clear. Settled. I've got to decide how much to tell her. It's the how-to-tell I've also got to get. This time I've got to talk it like I think it. Keeps sounding like I don't want it to. Except maybe I should tell her something different. Make it up. What I want to do first and as much of why as I can get and then how much to tell. I owe it to make sense, even if it's not going to be true.'

The majority of the people in the crowd were wending their ways home from the evening shifts of their various employments; they were nurses, cooks, janitors, and guards, the keepers of the demons of urban darknesses. All of them were weary; many of them were unkempt; most of them conceived of themselves as freer than people of the day, wilder.

'I didn't expect to get in. Nobody thought they'd admit me. She didn't. Much less say they'd pay for it. Only thing I have to do is be there four years. Except the why. I can't get the why of their paying. I can't even get at the who-they-are. It was those two tests. Paying because of them. Except what will I owe? Doesn't matter. Why the two?'

Crooking a hand behind him, he slipped his thumb around a small belt sewn into his shiny, gray chinos and hummed until a train howled to a stop. Inconspicuously he ambled away from the flow of people, moved toward a nearly empty car, stepped into it, and sat down by a window.

As if uncontrolled by human impulse, the doors clicked shut; and the train wriggled into hollow blackness.

Two other passengers were in the car.

A man—hatless, hair worried away, vested, shoes brightly polished, plump-wristed, lips pressed together in a jowled, noncommittal line, a briefcase and folded raincoat on his lap—turned through a few pages of an upheld newspaper, frowned, raised his eyes, and glanced across the aisle at the boy. Seeing eagerness, inquisitiveness, and alertness, the man said, "Stop reading my newspaper."

"I'm not reading it," said the boy.

"You were reading my newspaper. I didn't buy it for everyone."

"You were reading it. I saw you," said a matronly woman in a thin, nasal voice from the opposite end of the car. She was heavily rouged and lipsticked; the powdered slopes of her cheeks bulged into the fetid air; an artificial flower shaded her limp breasts.

"The headlines are so big, how can I help seeing them when he holds it up? That's not reading."

"Keep your eyes to yourself," said the man without acknowledging the woman's support.

"I wouldn't even buy that newspaper," said the boy.

"You shouldn't do that," said the woman. "Reading it. I saw you. Then saying you didn't. You shouldn't do that. A person has rights to privacy."

"The only rights aren't yours," said the boy, pleased the newly fledged lower tones of his voice had failed to break into a strident register.

A second stop was reached; and soon, a third. Hands clung to overhead rails in the now cramped car. Faces retained veneers of propriety, while apprehensive eyes pretended not to notice the distortions of normal posture being forced upon resigned, compliant limbs.

Facing a window, the boy readied himself for the next stop, where the subway would spurt out of its tunnel and permit him to re-experience the most encompassing view of Boston and the Charles River he had yet discovered. Leaving the echoing darkness occasionally reminded him of how it felt to float to the surface of a swimming pool after, lying on the sloping bottom, he had exhaled all his air. Sometimes he could see dozens of sailboats on the river; and he always looked forward to savoring their momentary, billowing evidence of the wind. The brief overview of the buildings had been a continual source of comfort to him; remembering it when in their midst had prevented him from being overwhelmed by their size.

Several times during the previous three months, he had attempted to explore the outskirts of the metropolitan community by using subways and buses, getting on and off randomly at stops foreign to him; but he had quickly learned that a stranger walking more than a block or two, whether in Newton or Jamaica Plain, was apt to be suspect and unwelcome. He felt uncomfortable anywhere except in the small part of the suburb of Arlington, where he was recognized, and in downtown Boston, which seemed to belong to everyone.

After the train had re-entered its tunnel, the boy smiled, hummed loudly, and sat in a satisfied daze until he heard a shouted, "Park Street." Standing then, he arched his arms elbows-forward and pushed his way out of the car.

As his feet touched the terminal floor, he was whistling complacently. A moment later, however, the train door snapped shut on the top of his paper sack, causing energy that was usually coiled dormant within him to surge upward from his belly and redden his face.

"You broke my kite stick!" he shouted to no one able to hear him. "Why didn't you stay for me? Why didn't you stay?"

Petulantly hardening his lower lip, he yanked the sack free and surveyed the terminal. Unable to find any sign that the legitimacy of his fury had been acknowledged, he then bowed his head, shuffled to the "Down" escalator and, bristling, glowering, climbed up it into the daylight.

'I'm no one. I'm not here.

'Can't fix it.

'Would've had to shorten it.

'Now it's too small.

'Have to wait for the stores to open.'

Yawning, he squirmed out of his jacket, folded it, stuffed it into the sack, and began to walk through one of the oldest parks in the United States, the Boston Common.

'Why do they say "nine-to-five" when they don't open until nine-thirty? Was because of the banks, but they're ten now. Maybe employees have to be there sooner. Whatever they do at the desks behind all the windows. Don't want that. Couldn't. Same after same. In, can't get out.'

As had been true for hundreds of thousands of others, many of the boy's impressions of the natures of rural environments had been contentedly gleaned from the ponds, the trees, and the rock formations of Boston Common; but recent ventures outside the city had made the park a less gratifying haven for him. He had become dissatisfied with the orderly growth of planted trees; and he strained, not with longing but with substantial curiosity, toward environments the forty-eight acres of parkland—rather than providing knowledge of—seemed now merely to be hinting at.

'If I were paying for it, I'd know why I was there. If it's better, probably is since it costs so much more, I'll know in a year what I want from it. I can't figure out anything from the catalogue now. Costs ten times more. Is it that much better?

'Always it's been the going with only becauses. It's whys I want now.'

Listlessly he passed an empty amphitheater, which had endured as an infrequently utilized remnant of nineteenth-century forms of communication. On other days he had heard people lecture from its tiny stage. Having been uncertain whether the preachers urging repentance, the warriors against communism, the supporters of disarmament, had been scheduled speakers, he had continued to suspect that anyone was free at any time to use the platform for the purpose of addressing whatever audience their words would prove capable of garnering.

'It's all I want is to wander, move on from that and find.

'A year full of Saturdays.

'I don't know if I'll even need the school. I'm not going this year, and that is for sure, and I have to tell her.

'I can't figure what they'd want from me. Unless it's to have some people there who'll get lousy grades, making the other ones who have money look good.'

Sitting down on a wooden bench which was positioned so that he could see both a duck pond and the subway entrance, he took off his shoes and let his feet play with the air, while he examined his shattered stick. Breathing throughout the city was becoming imperceptibly deeper than it had been an hour earlier. Hearts were beating faster. Urban smoke was graying the clouds.

'Unions. An apprenticeship. Don't need college for that. What help can it be? Except sometimes I get questions, and I don't know where to ask or how. But could I get into a union after the college? Because that's what school does. Is fit you for fitting in later. Except how fit? Where fit? Why do those tests matter so much when all the rest doesn't?

'Costs what we live on almost, she says...

'It must be so different setting things up in stores day after day from going in once every couple of months to shop.

'Cash register divides.

'I've got to get to where I can think. Today. I can't put it off. I've got to tell her tomorrow on the picnic...

'Nobody ever showed me the whys. I have to get at them myself. I wonder if there's a way to turn feelings into thinking. I wonder that. But I don't know where to ask or who. I wish I could remember what FE stands for. I should have it engraved on a belt buckle. When I want to know, I could look.'

Frowning, he broke the damaged stick into hand-length pieces, separated one from the rest, bent over, and tapped a stone as if it were a drum.

'Maybe it's not just that I can't talk what I want to say. Maybe I can't think right either. The difference is for sure. Thinking. Talking.

'I was going too fast before. I want to be more ready. That might sound right.'

He saw her boots first. They angled up beside him inches above her ankles and seemed to have been worn with the expectation that weather alone would care for them. The tongues were folded forward; the strings dangled; the fractured heels were caked with lumps of drying, ochreous mud.

Quickly he sat up and examined her misshapen, inattentive smile.

A black, felt hat sporting a green feather that jutted out over her forehead was attached to the red and brown curls of her hair by means of a giant, silver safety pin. A single-strand necklace of red spheres was coiled about her neck; and tied to the collar of her threadbare, fur coat was an intact, blue, Christmas-tree light bulb.

In one hand she held a bag of popcorn; frenetically she tossed kernels to pigeons.

Without looking at him, she said, "You know what a charity ball is."

"Yes," he replied.

"You've seen the pictures. You've heard the stories."

"Yes."

"She was dressed for a charity ball, and that is how she was dressed. She was. She said, to me, said, 'Do you know the way to Brookline?' 'Brooklyn,' I said, 'that's a long way from here. A far way.' 'No, Brookline,' she said. 'Do you know the way to Brookline?' 'I know,' I say, 'That's in another state. You'll have to ask someone closer.' And she was dressed for a charity ball!"

A parched laugh flew from her throat like a transparent balloon losing air. She had spoken leisurely and had altered the shapes of her sounds so frequently that her few words had invoked every neighborhood variation of a Boston accent with which the boy was acquainted and others unfamiliar to him.

"Brookline is a few miles from here," he said.

"Brooklyn is in another state," she replied, snatching the pieces of wood from his lap. "I said you'll have to ask someone else."

"Hey!" he cried out, disbelieving.

"They're not yours," the woman said nonchalantly.

"They are too mine. They're parts of my kite stick."

"Kite sticks are much longer. These are not kite sticks. They never were kite sticks. They are chopsticks. You took them from me while I was showing them to you. They were carved in Japan. I got them at dinner last night. I'm saving them for my granddaughter, who is six. Special presents."

"The subway broke it."

"You took them from me. They'll make my granddaughter happy. And I will not tell her about you."

As she pitched more popcorn to the bevy of pigeons girdling her boots, she edged her face so close to the boy that he could feel moisture from her breath on his neck.

"Do you like my disguise?" she whispered.

Trembling, making no reply, angrily he donned his shoes, got up, scampered across the grass, and, balancing the sack on his head with his fingertips, sauntered along a sidewalk that paralleled the southern border of the park.

'So what if I hold it on my head? People do that in Africa. Modern people. Right now. I wish I was there. I wish I was one of them.

'Us....

'Lost my breath running. Must be the air....

'It's why they are interested in me I cannot figure out. Why would someone give me all that? It is someone, not something. I fit in there like a piece the people who are putting together a puzzle can't see. All they know is the shape of the space. What is the shape of the me that will be?...It's the what-am-I-going-to-do-instead I've got to tell her.'

Making a right turn onto Washington Street, nimbly he strode past outstretched hands grasping for coins, past early morning leers, and past cafes where the air was redolent with stale donuts—not stopping until he reached the dilapidated facade of a small hardware store. Although the door was locked, through the window he could see a male clerk, dark-haired and brawnily short-sleeved, attending to a cash register; and confident it was almost nine-thirty, the boy rested the sack on the sidewalk, braced his right shoulder blade against the cornered windows of the entranceway, balanced one foot upon his other knee, and waited.

'Those tests, it's like they're making I'm better than school was.'

Hearing the door click unlocked, he reached again for his sack, turned, and hurried inside the store.

"Know what you want?" asked the clerk, running his words together. Middle-aged, he sat somberly hunched on a backless stool placed between the window ledge and a built-in counter upon which he leaned, supporting his head in his palms.

"Yeah."

"Seen it yet?"

"A kite stick."

"No kite sticks. People fly kites in the spring."

"Not everywhere. Today's the ninth day of the ninth month. That's a holiday for flying kites. In Indonesia and places like that."

"What is it you...?"

"A kite stick. Do you.... is...is there anything close?"

"Siding? Dowel stick? Dowel stick close enough for you?"

"I can't tell right off," replied the boy. "Where've...?"

Lounging from behind the counter, the clerk guided him to a horizontal case that contained rows of cylindrical pieces of wood of varying diameters and lengths.

"One of these do?"

"I guess so."

"Getting an early start on March, aren't you? Sure you aren't wanting to make an arrow?"

"A kite."

"How long a stick, then?"

The boy stretched his right arm out perpendicularly, lowered it with elaborate care a few degrees, and pointed to the floor.

"That's big for a kite stick," said the clerk, vaguely sounding condescending.

'Kinsuke flown to the dungeon roof, four-masted schooners, Malaysian wau bulans with baited hooks, a Kashira-gire, a Samurai servant's slave, Hargrove's four cells, Scott's unvented sled, a Marconi rigged second jib, Maillot's body-lifting diamond, Conyne's triangular box, Pocock's Charvolant, Alexander Graham Bell's tetrahedron, Kungshu Phan's three day wooden bird, Colladon's double line dirigible, Salmon's rhomboidal box.'

"I can pay."

"How about this one?"

"That's it."

"You want it?"

"How much?"

"Forty-five."

"Says thirty."

"Prices go up."

"Might break."

"Forty-five."

"All right," said the boy. While trailing the clerk to the cash register, surreptitiously he lashed his free arm toward a display of collapsible knives, grabbed one, and slid it into a front pants pocket. Facing the counter, he bowed his head and withdrew two quarters from his wallet.

"Want it wrapped for your car?"

"Don't drive."

"You mean to take it like it is?"

"Suppose so."

"I guess it's fresh enough wood for you. Might want to wet it some first before you cut it."

Holding the sack against his hip with one arm and the stick in his other hand, the boy replied, as he went out the door, "It's the winds, mostly, are important."

"'The winds,'" the clerk repeated. He sank back down on his stool. "Yes,…the winds."

'Got to disappear before he misses it. So what? It would've just sat there. Too many, anyway. Cross now here and maybe a ticket. So what?'

As the signal light changed to amber, he quickened his pace, turned, sidled a half-block between a row of parked cars and a released, oncoming line of traffic, and halted next to the front fender of a curbside taxi. The driver's partly bald head had fallen to the steering wheel. A burly arm hung limply out the window.

"Hey," the boy said, grasping the arm and shaking it.

Spitting and grimacing, the driver swung open the door and tore out of the car, fists upraised.

With the unsteady poise of a novice bullfighter who—mistaking skills for untrained ease—had leapt unannounced into a ring and been overtaken by fear that the quick insights allowed by the immanent confrontation might not prove enough to enable him to manage even a retreat, the boy inched backward, wielding the stick as if it were a saber.

"A ride. I just want a ride."

"Sorry, kid," the driver said, relaxing both hands and winking. Energetic and habitually immersed in all the details of his work, most of which he had learned to shape into what would please him, he was well past his sixtieth year. "I'm sorry. Can't be too careful. I was taking a nap before heading back to the garage. Nobody gets too many calls from this street…Don't be afraid. It's all right. Come on, get in. Get in."

"How much is it to the station?"

"Airport? Subway? Trains? Bus? Which one do you want?"

"The closest train."

"One-fifty from here."

"I need to hurry," the boy said, climbing into the backseat.

"You can sit in front, if you want. The union got that through. Couldn't before, but can now."

"The backseat's all right."

"Sorry I scared you," said the driver, locking his door. "Didn't mean to. Like I said, can't be too careful. Not on Washington. It's the worst street in Boston. The worst street. Everybody knows that. Everybody...."

"I haven't ever been in a cab before," the boy said quietly, as the car began to move.

Whistling and exhaling, the driver changed gears by hand and replied, "You'll remember this trip, then. Not many of the rest of them, though. That's what happens. Especially if you're behind the wheel...Gets the same after awhile...First ride. I'll shut off the meter."

"I can pay."

"Naw, listen, I'm stopping the meter. I don't mind. I shouldn't have jumped on you back there like that. Scaring you that way. Keep your money. I'm through for the day. Through.... I'll tell you, though, I was doing a lot of thinking before I went to sleep there. I was thinking about the President, see. I heard he reads three thousand words a minute, and the people around him do, too, not his wife and those, I mean the men he works with.... I bet what happened—You heard that about how fast he reads?"

"Yeah, I guess so."

"I'll bet what happened was that Eisenhower had left all these reports. It was Ike planned the Cuban invasion, after all. Kennedy didn't just get into it like it was a sailboat he'd built. So, they were sitting there reading like that—three thousand words a minute—telling each other they understood the plans. Because you can't make me think Ike would've set down for it to happen without even any backup.... Anyway, they sat there turning those pages, and the truth is it was them telling each other they could read that fast made them think they did. Right when they were missing most of it. Getting a few words here and there and looking at the rest, just at the blackness of it on the pages. Those stories people used to tell about him reading that fast, they didn't seem right; but then the same stories got on the news, so I couldn't help think there might be something to them. And now as I remember it, nobody has said anything about that reading since…. I bet one of these times it'll get said quietlike—it'll get said that was what happened. That'll explain about Cuba, it being the fault of the ones who were supposed to have taught him how to read so fast, the teachers. I bet that's how it'll turn out."

"I watch him, sometimes…in the afternoons."

"The press conferences, yeah. See, old Ike had so many secrets, so very many secrets. He had to, learned those ways in the war and couldn't change. But Kennedy just lays it out so a person can know where we're at. 'Let the word go forth,' like he said in his speech last January…. And what he does is, he answers those questions. Actually answers them. You couldn't find another place on this earth big enough to matter where whoever is on top would stand right there and answer questions with thousands of people tuned in, millions. Ike, now Ike would, especially after the strokes, he'd get up and stumble over those words in front of him, so you'd wonder back there three years ago…You probably don't remember that too well. How old are you?"

"Eighteen."

"Yeah, well, you probably don't then, back when you were thirteen, fourteen. Ike stuttering so bad made you wonder whether he'd understood what he was reading even. It got better. He did. But if Nixon had got in, I knew I'd have been sick for four years. Can't get away from them now with the set. They said it was his beard did him out of the job, but it wasn't that. It was *how* he stood up there saying we should trust him while his *whole* face was saying not to trust him. He's crazy. I'm sure of it. Crazy. Poor man. Suffering until it's arrested. Saying both things at the same time. Crazy like the head of Russia beating his shoes on the table at the

United Nations. All I could think last fall was, when it was settled, was, thank God, because get those two together, Khruschev and Nixon, crazy as starving dogs, there'd be no telling about the next minute. There never *is*, but then there *really* wouldn't be...."

"...He's...different...away from here.... Kennedy, I mean."

"Yeah," said the driver. "Changed so much this soon. All the responsibility. He's funnier now. Makes me laugh. None of them have made me laugh before. The Irish in him coming on more. I'll think of something he's said. Driving, I'll think of it. And I'll start to laugh. And then I have to tell what it was he said. Right while we're talking about something else, I'll laugh, and then tell it.... I think that about the reading explains it, though. They'll be saying that after awhile. There couldn't have been that stupid a plan. It was the fault of the ones who convinced him he could read three thousand words a minute. And it was because he knew how much he was going to have to do that he fell for it. Can't blame him for that...Here's the station right now.... I'll pull up into the space by the front entrance for you."

"Watch for my stick."

"Your what?"

"My stick...my..."

"Oh, yeah, I remember now. Good thing you reminded me. I thought it was a sword you had, or a machete or something, and that I was dreaming at first there. Are you making an arrow?"

"No, I...I'll pay."

"Nah, that's all right. You keep your money. It's on me. I've never been on a plane, see. That's the truth! Maybe something like this'll happen to me first flight I get! Fat chance! Fat chance!"

Brushing his hand through his hair, shutting the door, the boy grinned at the driver, then wedged the new stick into his sack and sprinted through the open entranceway of the terminal.

'Like a temple. To be here when no one else is so I could shout and hear the echoes falling on top of each other. But that's never. There's always people here. Probably hasn't been closed since it was built.

'Windows away. The gardens stay...

'Maybe I should put on a note instead of a hummer. But that might be too heavy. Unless I tear the towel for a tail. I could cut it now. And the patches will depend on what kinds of clouds there are.... No, a hummer. The clouds are right. Depends on the light.

'Decide whether to tell her what I'm going to do. Except what is that? I can't get to so far yet. I don't have it myself. It's a feeling. So how can I tell her?

'If it will fly.'

"The line," a voice behind him said close to one of his ears.

"What?" he asked, looking back.

"Your turn," said a pigtailed girl younger than himself. "You're holding up all the rest of us."

"Sorry."

'The way they look at me it's like catching thorns from their eyes.'

"What is one ticket for the ocean?" he hesitantly asked, uncertain how loud his words needed to be to travel clearly through a hole in the glass shield of a booth in front of him.

"This is a baggage-claim line. Ticket-purchase is any window to your left, numbers three to eleven. Round trip?"

"I guess."

"Will you be returning to Boston?"

"Yes."

"Round trip, then. When do you intend to return?"

"Only for today."

"The Local North schedule is on the board to the right of Gate Seven, directly to your left on the opposite side."

"Local North. But how much?"

"Decide your destination from the schedule and inquire at a ticket-purchase window. Next?"

'Round trip. Window seven. No, Gate. Board opposite. Schedule. Time. I forgot time. No, it's on the...'

"One way or round trip?"

"One way."

'Should've said, "Round trip."'

"Gate fourteen. Gloucester. Board at this time for an eleven o'clock departure."

"Can I get off somewhere before there and get back on later?"

"If you wanted a stopover, you ought to have informed me before purchase."

"But I could?"

"Simply request a stopover at time of purchase. Next?"

'I should've asked whether a stopover costs more. When I buy the ticket home. All I have to do now is wait until the end of the line without even counting the stops. Even with this sun, it'll be hot as it'll get there. Wonder what the tide will be. Walk with the light on my back. Follow my shadow on the beach. Will give me six hours. Should call now, but she'd.... Why does it take longer to get there than to come back?'

"This car or the next. Watch yourself. Find a seat. Have your ticket ready."

'For the ride.

'If there's enough wind, the patch tail will work with a hummer. I don't think I can carve in the train. All the stick needs is less. Oh, no, not...Yes. There's a knothole. No, it's alright. Scared me. Not all the way through. Cut it off.

'Not a whole knothole.

'Sometime I'll make a kite and flying it will be holding onto the sky so the light doesn't break...

'Good. Almost empty. They won't be looking at me. Why aren't the seats in the subway set up like this?...So what if I was reading his newspaper?...I should've said those press conferences always look like a quiz show.

Everything they knew, it turns out they didn't know. Memorized it for the program. Lying so well they could sweat for pretending. Questions weren't real. Started out a few caught, then more, and finally you couldn't trust any of them. So why should I believe the President? They'll do what they do whatever I think, anyway. So what? Doesn't affect me. I'm sorry I have to hear about him all the time. Them getting in a sailboat or riding horses. Playing touch football. At least before it was like they weren't there…

'All the while, what it is, is, I've been pulled along in a river, and I've been holding onto a log. I want to get to where my feet touch sand. So I can push some. Even if it's mostly the water pulling me. Some push of my own. Then I could figure out which way to push. Even get on the land…

'Gave me the ride and didn't want anything from me. So maybe they don't either. But the ride was to make up for…

'I won't know what I want to do until after I've done it. Doing it depends on not knowing what it'll be.'

Taking out the knife, he examined it, scraped off the crayoned price with a fingernail, ran the blade over his forearm, then shaved the price from the stick, closed the knife, and put it back in his pocket.

'I thought the windows wouldn't open, and they don't.

'Must be going as fast as it will, even though it's not past the city yet. Like a backbone that can't get out of its skin, pulled by a head until it stops dead.

'There's a restaurant car. They use knives and forks there. But what if the train jumped a little? Four holes in my throat. I couldn't anyway. Don't even have to look at the prices to know I can't afford them. I get so tired of that always there. Ever enough to buy what I want or stop wanting what I can't buy? Ever?

'How do they decide what number of cars to put on? Why would they keep a car for five of us? All that way. Maybe it takes more energy to get a car off than to pull it. Maybe it costs more. If there were too many people, though, they'd wait and put on another one…. Why is that backbone, when it's more than one bone?…If I had the figures, I could find out the cheapest way or the least time; and maybe they'd be the same. How would they know what number of people to plan on for each ride unless it averages up some-how? Probably this car stayed on from summer and'll get taken off soon. Unless the winter will make people take the trains instead of drive. Maybe it got put on for the snow.

'It used to be I could count up the people I knew who didn't drive like I could count up the people I've known who are dead. Now I don't know anyone else who doesn't have a car. But we don't need one. I could pick driving up easy anyway, so why spend all that when like this I can see the windows to look at with instead of to get past?...

'I never heard so much talk about a speech as about Kennedy's inaugural. "Burden." So what? How they say things fits together for awhile until I start to think, and then it turns out they must be lying or they're com-pletely crazy. One of the people from the television quiz shows should've become President because then everybody'd be sure he wasn't telling the truth...You used to be able to see people not wanting to be caught at mak-ing mistakes on those shows more than now when it's recorded...England wants this and Russia wants that, the news says, talking about countries like each one is a person, and really it's land and people on it somehow all together. Is it that after all this time the stone walls still divide the farms so they're sold the same way they were two hundred years ago? Or do the walls stay when the properties get divided? Countries kept getting formed, and we'd spell the new name, and that would be how it was. Nothing about the people, just the name, like it was a person. Making like corn isn't corn until it's picked and in the grocery store; and then it's corn, but only the package. It's the barbed wire I really want to see. As soon as I can. And the cattle. Because how do I know if I'll ever get a chance to again?...

'If I made a kite out of aluminum foil and flew it at sundown, the moon would be brighter than usual, reflecting the sunlight from the aluminum. Not so as you could see it; but instruments could be used or made that anyone could tell the little bit brighter of one ten trillionth or so by. Whatever it was, you could know it without seeing it. I'd be sure that little bit was there for awhile. From the numbers on the machines.

The truth is I don't even care whether the moon really would get brighter; but working on knowing would confuse them enough so I could sit and hold and fly the kite; and there'd be a reason for me being there that would settle them. They use machines like that to tell there's things so little they'd see an egg yolk like it was the sun. Maybe that's why called "sunny-side-up." Somebody thinking about all the things that small. I don't see how the sun can be on fire and the same size. Both at once. And what if it burns out? Or starts to? Clearly starts to? Billions of years from now. Could we light it up again? Set it to going? Keep it going? Send out what'll start the warmth again? The light again? Before there's cold or nothing? Or if it goes out, would the stars light up more than they do now? Move around? Some of them whirl together into a replacement sun? So how the sun went out would be just another matter for the history books? This sun come to be called "that sun"?

'I'd rather have ideas like this I couldn't ever tell a teacher than take tests asking questions I don't want to know the answers to.

'I need a year to decide what I want to do with my life. So that what college will turn me into will fit what'll come after. The time away is all I know right now.

'Can't tell her what, when I don't know myself.

'I might not be around Arlington much again. Or even at all. And until into last May, I was going to stay there all my life.'

Lifting his legs, stabilizing them upright on the seat in front of him, he rummaged through the sack for an orange, tossed it back and forth between his hands, peeled it meditatively, sectioned it, and ate it with dawdling fingers.

'I could have spent two hours weeding a garden and got enough to buy that knife. But it would've taken me years to make it, if I even could have. So many people, not just the ones in the knife factory, but the ones who drove the parts there, the ones who mined the ore, the ones who melted it down, all of them working at it, all apart, add it up and divide it and it's way more than two hours, so why would it be that to pay for one knife?

'It's like that with everything. How could they know how many knives to make and who would get them and where? The people who plan that out are different from the ones who do the work. College would let me do the planning, but then the making I couldn't do, not the touching. I don't think I'll ever figure out about the times and the prices by myself. Maybe some people really know those things, and they don't just guess. But it couldn't be more than a few people. Because most everyone wonders about it, and nowhere is there any explanation. It happened so fast all the books ever say is "Industrial Revolution, Assembly Line, Management, Unions." That's supposed to explain it. And it sort of does until I think about it.... One knife.'

Again he searched through the contents of the sack, retrieved a package of salted, unshelled sunflower seeds, bit it open, and sprinkled a few into his mouth.

'Swallowed a grapefruit seed once and worried about it a long time after. It starting to grow in me. They'd say it was cancer, only it would be a root and branches, then leaves out of my stomach. So many bugs inside us, they say, all the shots, so why not a plant?

'These wouldn't grow even in the ground. If you put a fresh one next to a cooked one, you couldn't tell them apart, the fresh one still waiting.

'Wonder if a seed is alive.

'Does the heat kill them?

'Or make it so they can't ever live from having been roasted?

'Maybe it's that they can't grow but are still alive, only no one knows.

'Cracking the shell kills oysters.

'An oyster isn't a seed, though....

'I could stay on a bus until I saw fields of sunflowers and stop and look and find out who owned them and where the factories, because they must be close after picking. When I know enough or am tired, or just feel like it, get on a bus again.

'That's how I want to be.

'Keep following my questions.

'If people won't let me work, because some things'd take years of skills, then watching, asking—asking any time there's a chance. That way I'd learn what the doing would be like....

'Ten minutes of digging weeds gets me these sunflower seeds. All the way from North Dakota. Cooked and salted and sold in plastic.'

He closed his eyes.

'String is in parts like a train. The parts are the fibers that can barely be seen in the threads. I'm a note on a string....

'Stomachs must be awfully hard because otherwise I'd be getting pieces of sunflower shell stuck inside like splinters...

'It all changes into me and out of me without my knowing....

'It's been one breath after another without heading anywhere. I'm bound to get caught in something, and before I do I want to know about what it's going to be.'

He lay his head against the pulsating window, and soon he slept.

2

With eyes red and bleary from Saturday morning drowsiness, Marianne Rongo noted on the way to her breakfast the laundry tied together in a sheet placed as usual in the hallway beside her bedroom door. It surprised her that a setting of dishes had been laid out on the dinette table, but she quickly assumed this was another of the small things her son had done to ready her for his upcoming departure. Though they were able to share breakfast only on weekends, she had become adjusted to his withdrawals and semi-trances since the letter of admission to Yale with a full scholarship had arrived the previous spring; and after glancing at the closed door to his room, she ate alone without any unusual concern.

He had been a quite taciturn child. With one exception, his high school record had been average: in a private conference with his biology instructor two years earlier, she had been told that her son's test answers had repeatedly been inappropriate but, nonetheless, had been composed in a manner that had indicated a grasp of essential scientific procedures, the basics of inductive and deductive processes and of predictive methods dependent upon mathematics. His experimental sketches had been too imaginative; yet he seemed to possess a rare and original scientific spirit, the instructor had claimed, which sufficient discipline might transform into distinguished achievement.

Marianne had almost entirely dismissed this as the delusion of a trapped teacher seeking justification for his collection of days; but her son's extraordinarily high, national test scores had confirmed the development of what previously had been largely undisplayed qualities. Though she had been aware that changes in college entrance policies had broadened income requirements since the time when continued education for herself had been impossible, she had filled out the necessary forms inattentively and had not fully appreciated such all-embracing scholarships were really offered until she had read the letter informing her son of his award; had she been thoroughly familiar with the possibilities of this variety of financial aid, there would have been little reason, she continued to feel, for her ever to have expected even his admission to Yale.

After washing the dishes with a habitual frown at water faucets that long had had "hot" mislabeled "cold" and vice versa, Marianne tied a scarf about her head, gathered together her own laundry, and carried both bundles to the apartment house basement. During most of the twenty years she had lived in the building, she had experienced inside its brownstone walls nothing with other tenants save the simplest of civilities, exchanging the same quick greetings with long-term neighbors as with those of a few months. Thus she was confident she would be uninterrupted, as she sat beside the whirring washers and dryers, reviewing the past week and anticipating the upcoming one, efficiently filing away within herself evaluations and expectations.

For nineteen years, she had been employed by a single law firm and had come to be regarded as virtually indispensable in maintaining the esprit de corps of the office. Following the enlistment of her husband in 1941, she had entered the concern as a secretarial assistant and, from the time of her husband's death shortly after the end of the war, had functioned primarily as a mediator among the attorneys, as a sounding board. Briefly in 1949 she had been in charge of all clerical personnel, but had been demoted (though officially the change had been termed a transfer of assignment and had been accompanied by a slight raise) when she had attempted to terminate a pattern later identified for her by one of the elder attorneys as "enduring weak link necessity." This had meant, it had been patiently explained to her in retrospect, she had been expected to hire a series of employees on the basis of neither their skills nor talents but, instead, because they could be counted upon to lapse in one way or another seriously enough to enable the rest of the firm to use them as scapegoats for varied hostilities and resentments. She had earlier recognized the phenomenon— the housewife grappling with overwork after a long interval in a residence, replaced by the recent, secretarial school graduate with poor grades who had been assigned tasks of such complexity that her failure had been unavoidable, replaced by the overeager, senescent widow who had been unable to comprehend the methodology of the new duplicating machines—but she had been unaware of its intentional nature. She had balked, been rebuked, and, after several days, finally acquiesced; and the procedure had become one of the many working conditions she initially had found repugnant but subsequently had been forced to accept in order to be certain of maintaining an adequate income.

The senior partners of the firm especially valued her for what had developed into a talent for accommodating fledgling, law school graduates, whom she had learned to soothe with informal recitations of projects in which they might participate and benefits of which they might partake, as soon as their careers had advanced into solidified reliabilities. Shrewdly and adroitly she fostered the young attorneys through boredom and distasteful assignments that left them drained, but not thoroughly so, left them malleable enough to be molded into accepting a history of agreements and clientele trailing out from the last century. Eventually, when time had severely limited their alternatives and fixed their responsibilities, they would find themselves fashioning arguments that would have appalled most of them in their first months of practice.

Back upstairs, Marianne saw that the door of her son's room was still closed. Suspecting he had worn himself out the night before laboring over a kite, another in a succession of kites he had been constructing since his tenth year, and that he had, thus, gone back to sleep, she turned on a television set in the apartment living room, manipulated the controls so there would be no sound, and quietly set about doing the ironing.

When all of the clothes had been pressed and folded, she went to her own room and changed into one of her other two housedresses. She was accustomed to having on hand only three of these and habitually put on one after completing the ironing. The dress she had worn for the start of her Saturday began the pile of the next week's laundry. The other two she interchanged, and her last waking gesture on Fridays was always the placing of that evening's dress in her bedside hamper.

Feeling refreshed and alert in the clean housedress, she stepped to her son's door, knocked, waited a moment, then opened it, and, smiling immediately, entered the empty room before her.

"Kites," she said aloud, putting a stack of clean clothes on the bed and reading:

TONIGHT LATE
I REMEMBER PICNIC

scrawled in green ink at the eye-level bottom of a narrow strip of coiled newspaper dangling like a broken spring from the ceiling.

Uninterrupted images of President Kennedy were flickering from the television screen, as she returned to the living room and sat down in its sole easy chair. Without the sound he reminded her of a zealous cheerleader. His inaugural rhetoric bespeaking the coming-to-power of a new generation had enraged her more than had anything since her husband's death; for it was her generation; and she was convinced that those belonging to it shared only a sense of loss. The outlines of her own life and the life of her husband seemed to her evidence enough that the opportunities of their contemporaries had passed away early, had already been betrayed. The President's vigorous style she regarded as a hollow mockery of what might have been; and his elaborations of the doctrine that two philosophies were struggling for global supremacy she adjudged simplistic and supremely dangerous. Two militaries, she thought, sighing. One wake, perhaps.

Irritably deciding to give the apartment a thorough cleaning, she stood, walked partway down the hall to a closet, and drew out a mop, a broom, a vacuum cleaner, sponges, and an assortment of polishes and waxes. As she angled her hands into a tight pair of rubber gloves, she cleared her mind of her workweek concerns and readied herself for a communion with a comforting array of memories to which she had often turned for sustenance, as to a photograph album, since calling them forth and arranging them a decade and a half earlier in 1946. It had been in the fall of that year when—late one evening leaning over her son's crib, watching him sleep—she first had determined that, henceforth, the essential events of her life could be experienced only in memory, that they had all occurred, that her most powerful, most loving feelings had all been felt; but it was to be the summer of 1947 before continual reviews of her memories had caused her to decide that this would have been true even had her husband lived on.

During the months preceding her birth, Marianne's parents had immigrated to the United States from Hungary, making a home of a Boston apartment smaller than her present one. It had rapidly acquired a combined odor of paprika dumplings and sauerkraut--an odor of which she occasionally could convince herself she found traces on her living room chair. Her father had been a jeweler, skilled in watch-repair, had hoped to establish his own shop in the new land, but had reconciled himself to an assistantship he had kept the rest of his life. His unfulfilled occupational plans had eventually changed into vague dreams of redistributions of wealth, property, and leisure time; the dreams had been kept afloat by multilingual pamphlets, both political and historical, he had received weekly in the mail. Although the family's economic level had proved to be no higher than it had been amid the circumstances they had abandoned, they had felt physically more secure in the United States; her mother, however, had never stopped treating their adopted nation as a foreign environment, all the while anticipating Marianne's thoroughly integrated adjustment within it.

Much of what her parents had shared with each other had been purposefully kept from her, for the two of them had excluded her from many of their conversations by speaking in a language she had not learned. She had approved of their attitudes of encompassing loyalty and predominant emphasis, and she continued to think it best that children be largely isolated from the relationship of their parents.

She had been sixteen when her mother had died and two years later at her father's funeral had considered it fitting that many of the inner and outer events of his life and of the life of her mother, as well, would always be mysteries to her. Lacking any means for storage, she had sold her father's tools, along with most of their furniture, and, keeping only the chair, cooking utensils, a picture woven of hair from somewhere in her mother's past, and those family documents that had been in English, had moved from the apartment to a rooming house nearby.

Securing a job in a clothes-making factory, she had seemingly sewn and cut identically patterned pieces of cloth unendingly, had returned nightly to her room, had curled herself into a bay window seat, and there had read the many of her father's pamphlets she had saved. Though she had known putting aside money for her enrollment in college to be a futile exercise, she had done it, nonetheless. She had lived partly on faith at that time, faith in a change in her life she had felt would be akin to the passage from purgatory into heaven.

Supported by restless yearning unattached to foreseeable possibility, she had become outspoken, had complained about wages to anyone who would listen, complained about working conditions, complained about the housing available to her; and she had watched many other young women, who had been well versed in conventions of submission, wear ruffles and floral designs into early marriages.

The collection of memories that was her solace had not, however, been selected from those times of solitary struggle, nor from the time of her childhood.

As she approached the unchanging assemblage that had absorbed her for fifteen years, she always remembered first the delicate, sweet, sharp smell of freshly cut cabbages, piled together as they had been on the kitchen sink of a house she had shared with her husband for nearly two years—the one house in which she had ever been able to live. The lot had been large; and together they had turned most of it into a vegetable garden, blithely but with a measure of impertinence, filling the front yard with cabbages.

It had been the end of February, the dreariest and most phlegmatic of months in the cities of New England, when winter offers a convincing argument that unrelenting grays demonstrate the fickle insubstantiality of blues and greens. She had been asked to a "gathering" (parties had been for the wealthy) in order to meet a young lawyer from Tennessee who had recently moved into the neighborhood, a young lawyer who had little practice but who had been speaking in nontechnical language from parlor to parlor of rights and obligations and legitimate demands. She had been jestingly advised that the two malcontents might profit from listening to each other and that in any case their conversations would release the word-weary ears of their respective audiences.

Guests had wandered throughout the cold, dimly lit house in a protracted dance, clinging and receding; the infrequent refrains of their muted laughter had been woven together by a trumpet player skirting the melancholy terrain of improvisational jazz. She had seen the lawyer from Tennessee standing in the kitchen, his back curved, his hands meeting his knees, but had not guessed his identity; for he had been dressed in the shabby garments of a day laborer, his hair a tangle of bronze curls, his eyes, glinting resinously and upturned to the ceiling, radiant without being fiery or agitated, reflectively poised between blinking and gazing.

"I asked him not to start in on one of his usual tirades, but he's gone all the other way and hasn't talked with anyone. Even so, he sticks out as much as ever. That's him. That's the man I told you about. Nick. Nick Rongo."

"But he looks as if he hammers in railroad ties."

"He does do something like that. Unloads trucks, I think. Go over and introduce yourself."

Nothing about him had suggested the formality she had associated with attorneys who, she had assumed, never were seen in anything but three-piece suits. She had tapped a finger against his back, had become flustered, and had said uncertainly, "Excuse me...I.... I was...;" and hesitantly she quietly had added, "Nick?"

He then had swirled to face her so swiftly she had nearly lost her balance. For an instant, his eyes had become fissured spheres of torment. "I'm sorry," he had said. "No one calls me that anymore."

"It's me who should be apologizing. I've forgotten your last——"

"It's Rongo," he had interrupted with quiet intensity, the glint having returned to his eyes.

"And I am Marianne Koslovsky," she had replied, surprised to find the surface calm of her tones shaped by an undercurrent of emotion undefined yet almost urgent.

"Yes, Miss Koslovsky...I have heard of you."

He had pronounced her name with a dignity so respectful she at once had apprehended she had been accustomed to hearing it said coupled with a demand for deference. The clarity of his tones had reminded her of a portion of the rotunda of the United States Capitol where one was supposed to be able to whisper and be heard only at a faraway point. She had been unable to think of anything to say, other than, "You might need to forgive me for asking; but, you see, I don't understand something that was said to me just now; and I can't help but wonder why it would be that...that a lawyer would work at...unloading trucks?"

"Wait," he had replied. "Excuse me for a moment."

His next words had seemed to carve a tunnel through the air to the trumpet player: "That's pretty good for a white man."

"What's that you telling me?"

"The best a white man can do with that music is to throw in a bit of the shame he's lived so as to mix it with the longings that died desperate."

"I don't play with shame, lawyer."

"I know you don't. But you should add some. Or you shouldn't play that kind of music."

"I have to've lived what went into the making of it? That what you saying?"

"You do with jazz. Or you have no account playing it. Unless you add in some shame. Otherwise you're using again what's not yours as if it were. That'll make those sounds mournfuller yet where they really come from, and already they depend on wondering how so much sorrow can make any sounds at all. You can't have known that much sorrow. No white man could have. The only way to play sympathetic is to put in a bit of shame. The sounds can't be imitated by us, grief and triumph that deep, but you can play with them if you loosen the notes with shame. That'd be aiming toward a music that'd be all the way decent human, 'cause it'd be composed paying mind to times that would be. Leaving aside the shame makes those times further off."

Marianne had expected disagreement; but the man with the trumpet had smiled and nodded, instead.

"If you see what someone's doing you can criticize, you owe it to let 'em know," Nicholas Rongo, in turning back to her, had said. "'Cause it's the finding you've noticed will let 'em be gratified, let 'em shift, maybe, too." During their years together, his salient characteristic had been a willingness to modify his views and to alter his actions accordingly; he had insisted on presenting his ideas so that truth, rather than his own reputation, would be at stake, had lacked ideological attachments, and had been so persistently rational that people had sometimes become angry when, changing his mind, he had accepted their lattices of argument.

The resinous glint having remained in his eyes, he had asked her if she wanted to take a walk with him in the open air. She had uttered a "Yes" she had come to regard as the first note of the prelude to her matured self. The stars had been white in a faintly overcast sky. "I often walk," he had said, "but rarely with anyone else." Experiencing her body's anticipatory efforts to give him warmth, to draw it from him, to bring it into being with him, she had replied without coyness, "You needn't feel more protective of me than I do of you."

With bitter regret Marianne was aware, while scrubbing the linoleum in the apartment kitchen, that there had been far too many collisions of social contexts during the previous two decades for conversations resembling theirs to take place anymore; their words had depended both upon a stability disowned in the course of the upcoming war and upon plans and hopes for a specified future that had not arrived.

"I am seldom paid for my legal advice because I want to bring about an end to practicing lawyers."

"Even with all that is wrong with the law, I expect we'd be worse off with an anarchy that would give us nothing on which to rely."

"It isn't law I want to end. It's the profession. I want to bring about a spreading of the tools of law. The lack of knowledge by the many benefits the few; or rather the few think of it as benefiting them, although their satisfactions can't be truly pleasing when so many people are being wrongfully taken advantage of. It's not difficult to set up a business and keep it running if someone has an understanding of the necessary forms and procedures, but lawyers' fees usually keep enough details hidden to lead most anyone into believing there's more to comprehend than there is. Our livelihoods frequently stem from vague relationships that leave us dangling between informal unilateral and bilateral contracts."

She had slowed her pace and had glanced at him quizzically.

"Those are ways of using time and exchanging money and skills and products," he had said. "Suppose I were offered a dollar to shuck a pail of oysters. If I did it, I'd get the dollar. That would've been a unilateral contract. But supposing someone said, 'I'll pay you a dollar to peel a bushel of oranges by eight in the morning.'"

"An orange marmalade factory foreman."

"Yes," he had replied, smiling. In later years, they had often turned legal precepts into whimsical stories, fables illustrating social principles. "I agree to peel the oranges by eight in the morning. He agrees to pay me. That's a bilateral contract. It's two-sided."

"And if you wanted three dollars or to be done by six you could say so?"

"Yes, that's right. The processes of negotiation let each of us know where we stand and what to expect. Contracts are the fabric of relation."

"People are often too desperate to know what they're getting into," she had said. "We live at the mercy of employers who can change guarantees when they want to."

"Most of us never got to know how to have a say."

"How do you intend to proceed, then?" she had asked.

"I'm not at all sure yet. I guess I'll run into a good bit of trouble. So far I've been getting by without really knowing what I'd do. The truck work, though, is for more than the earnings. I like the exhilaration. I can think better afterwards. I'd rather feel good from that than join a firm and be out on golf courses. Besides, that's work that matters, practically, more than a lot of law practice. I think we should divide up the things that affect us all, the routines, I mean, that embrace us. More of us should do the work of manufacturing and transporting. Then we'd have time to read and play instruments and plant gardens in the cities. We've got the means so that we all of us on earth can live comfortably. It's a matter of devising equitable patterns for sharing our resources."

The first broaching of a basic, though insupportable, hope is ordinarily accompanied by fear; but Marianne had been confident, poised, and very nearly dauntless when she had said, "I've been wanting to go to college."

"Do you live with your parents?" he had asked.

"My parents are dead."

"Were they——?"

"I'm incapable of talking of them," she had interrupted. "Separately they were too close to me for me to be able to do that. And together too far away."

"Well, much of college is a matter of developing an understanding of what to read. I'll manage that for you, if you want."

She had invited him up to her room. Smiling, he quietly had taken off his wet shoes and had left them outside on the hallway rug. She had lit a candle encased in glass.

"What of your family?" she had asked.

"My parents own a canning business. One of Roosevelt's Tennessee Valley Authority dams came in and took most of their land, covered it up with water. They had to move after being seventy years on the same spot, and some government officials asked them to make corrections in sharecropping and in factory processes. I'd just started practicing in Memphis, had time at last to figure out what lawyers do; and I'd supported the dam on the grounds that the reforms at the company were necessary. When my family found out about my views, they informed me I would not be welcome around them— or around 'ours,' as my father put it—again."

"Surely they'll change their minds."

"No, they will not do that. When ironclad gentility finds unacceptable dissension in its own ranks, the breaks are total and enduring…I'm amazed how different Boston is: it's a whole new branch of the human race. In Tennessee I knew the exploitation of the illiterates who maintain the earth; and in Massachusetts there's the exploitation of those who can read, but who are so crowded in together their connections with the sources of life are muddied over. It seems to me some kinds of illuminations ought to be reacquired here. I don't want to lose them, anyway."

"You have no contact with your people, then?"

"None."

"Why did you settle in Boston?"

"I figured I'd run into the lawyers who implement ideas in structures like the Tennessee Valley Authority. I guess Roosevelt has them tied up in Washington."

There had been a knock at the door followed by the aged landlady's withered, but piercing, tones: "I am obligated to remind you, Miss Koslovsky, that visitors are not permitted at this hour. I will wait here until you attend to this matter. We cannot be disturbed in such a fashion."

"It must have been your shoes," Marianne had whispered.

The tempo of her memories quickened, waxed staccato.

She had awakened early. It had been a Saturday then, too.

She had dressed hurriedly, had walked down the stairs without her coat, and in the entryway had paused, braced by the morning wind.

The next moment she had seen him, taller than she had thought, carrying in one arm a wooden basket, taking long slides on the icy sidewalk, his shoulders thrown backward and his feet tucked close together. As he had turned onto the rooming house pathway, he had started to wave, slipped on a patch of ice, toppled over, and regained his balance by grabbing an overhanging branch, which immediately had broken, causing him to stumble yet again.

"Good morning!" he had said at last. "I've brought warm donuts. Am I welcome at this hour?"

There had been no table in her room. Usually she had set a place for herself on the top of a bureau, had stood by it for her meals; but they had spread newspapers on the floor; and she had opened a can of orange segments, had made tea. Sitting upon folded knees, they had eaten their first breakfast together.

She had asked him if his eyes had often been remarked upon.

He had stiffened, "Why? Why do you ask?"

"It's as if you have two sets of them."

"What did you see? What did you see in my eyes?"

"The pain. I saw the pain."

"It *would* be the pain you'd notice," he had said simply, without hesitation.

In the basket had been a legal dictionary and a loose stack of pages handwritten by means of differently colored inks, the words interlaced with arrows and numbers meant to suggest relationships among legal principles, social frameworks, and theoretical situations that might be improved by the dissemination of knowledge of lawful procedures. She had puzzled through his hieroglyphic notations that day, using the dictionary, while he had patiently elaborated his intentions, explained his methodology, and answered her questions, so that by midafternoon she had been able to give body to his theory by citing an array of specific local realities she had long deemed unjust and humiliating. His last words that evening had been, "Thank you for not laughing about all these efforts of mine."

With few belongings to move and no relatives to consider, they had been married three weeks later and had rented a four-room, one-story wood-frame house, which quickly had become his office as well as their home. Soon· they had begun to sponsor seminars there and to organize informal discussion groups, wherein a neighborhood clientele had eventually discovered pertinent routes of self-representation and mastered techniques of pursuing for themselves helpful legal precedents. She and her husband had become searchlights into each other's dormant strengths, had learned to divine each other's thoughts well enough so that dialogues between them had often consisted of oral replies to the unspoken, had sanctioned one another in a union that had seemed destined productively to endure for many years.

Inbred chivalry had, however, caused Nicholas Rongo to be an early supporter of the entrance of the United States into the war, which with similar support from ever more people, was then unfolding over much of the earth. In 1941 he had weighed the possibility of immigrating to Canada and there enlisting, but in October of that year neither of them had thought it likely a national policy of isolation could continue through the following spring. He had seen her into the apartment, had put on a uniform, and had vanished, leaving her with the thirty-one months of memories from which she ultimately would cull a self-communing sustenance that would enable her to endure the solitude of her future.

A civilian perspective had at first allowed her to view the war as a temporary aberration, necessary in order to clear the way for the diffusion of technology and the global development of social structures founded upon self-evident human rights; but his initial letters from the European front had expressed dismay at the ideological fervor he had been encountering and a skepticism in regard to quick victory.

On a furlough in December of 1942, he had been in a state of dread: "I do not know how we could not have recognized that to approve of murder among members of separate countries is to approve of it within any of them."

She had meant to reply that she loved him partly because he could appreciate that some adults truly had neither approved nor joined themselves with any of the carnage but had, instead, unceasingly worked to lessen and prevent it; but he had interrupted her obvious intent to speak by showing her a book titled *Psychology for the Fighting Man*, which had been widely distributed among the troops. Scornfully pointing to its enormous list of authors, a spectrum of acknowledged authorities in human behavior who, unlike other such voices, had aligned their insights and therapeutic techniques with the purposes and procedures of war, he had said, "Those are the people we'll be expected to depend on when the war's over. We're not going to recover, but that won't be noticed. Because all of us are infected. The military everywhere habituates us to doing so many things we recoil from initially in decency, that we have no capacity left to follow our own wants. And we won't get it back. We've become unfit to participate in the way of life we're supposed to be protecting. It could all stop now. Everyone on both sides who has any sanity left understands that. But the momentum carries us on; for we know all we have is our guilt. That's all we'll ever have. There's no accomplishment that could give any of us pride again. And the worst of it is we convince ourselves we're fighting for the men beside us; we forget that true friendships do not result in the hatred of other people about whom we know nothing, save that they are as desperate as we are."

Gaunt and hairless, he had returned in 1945; abiding disgust had been all that had remained in the wavering focus of his eyes. His death a year later had been termed "due to pneumonia, with extended complications." Two months earlier they had learned that the Tennessee Valley Authority dam he had championed because of the humane improvements he had counted on its bringing to his homeland had been essential in constructing nuclear weaponry. Of their three-year-old son, he had once said, "I have forfeited every chance of deserving any affection from that child."

With the television set still radiating a procession of soundless tableaus, Marianne dried her supper dishes, filled her largest pot with water, put it on the stove, and turned on an electric burner beneath it. Then she removed a head of green cabbage from a drawer at the bottom of her refrigerator and was using a sharp knife and a cutting board to slice it into a pile of tiny shreds, when the telephone rang. Startled, she accidentally dropped the remaining uncut piece of cabbage to the floor, as, keeping hold of the knife, she stood and answered.

"Hello."

Wedging the telephone between her head and shoulders—"This is she."—she bent down and picked up the cabbage—"Yes, I'll accept."—and began to slice it into its own separate pile. "C. J., where are you?" she asked after a moment.

"The last train is gone."

"Where are you calling from, C. J.?"

"Gloucester."

"What on earth are you doing in Gloucester?"

"I'll wait on the beach."

"Do you have any money, C. J.?"

"I can get a ticket."

"Have you had anything to eat? Maybe I could telegraph you something if you went to a hotel."

"It's all right."

"But where are you going to sleep?"

"My things are in place."

"You mean you're going to stay outside?"

"The train left."

"Outside all night? We were planning on a picnic tomorrow. I'm making cole slaw right now."

"There's time."

"I think I'd better telegraph you some money to a hotel."

"I just wanted to say I'll be late."

"It's more than late. When will you be here?"

"Morning."

"But, C. J., should I count on the picnic?"

"...Yes."

"Do you have your key?"

"There."

"Do you mean here or with whatever you have on the beach?"

"Home."

"I'll stay in, then, and wait, C. J. I'll be here...Are you sure you're not going to get into trouble?"

"There's a cave."

"Are you going to be warm enough?" She stopped herself from adding, "I'd feel better if you went to a hotel."

"There's fine."

"Be careful, though...And call me again if you need to...What possessed you to go to Gloucester?"

"Thoughts.... The winds were...soundings..."

"You're certain you're all right?"

"It's not what I meant. I'm sorry I called."

"C. J., I'm glad you called. I would've been frightened in the morning."

"That I...had to call."

"Yes, of course. I...We'll have the afternoon together, anyway."

"Yes..."

"Good night, son. Be careful. Please do be careful."

After replacing the receiver, Marianne finished shredding the cabbage and put the pile made from what she had recovered from the floor into a colander, which she set within her sink for a thorough cleansing, simultaneously turning on a warm flow of water. Then, curling her back, her hands upon her knees, she asked herself aloud, "Did I think to ask about the rain?"

3

"I wish you could learn to start talking at the beginning and go right on through what it is you want to explain," his mother said.

"Grass isn't ever anything but even here," he replied. "Do they cut it at night?" Absently stroking his unshaven face, he stretched himself into the flexure of a hill at the muddy edge of the Charles River.

"You always combine the beginning with the end and skip back and forth so much with what's in between that attempting to follow you is like casting with a snarled line," she said, as she returned their dishes to a picnic basket.

"I have to do to know what it'll be," he said quietly but firmly.

"I can understand what you're intending for the year, C. J. I'm even glad about it. I don't know if college is the right thing for you. I can't know. You've got to decide that for yourself. I don't see any reason for you not to wander for awhile. I think it will be good for you. I'm even glad you've waited until now to tell me about it. I'm glad you went ahead and handled the arrangements by yourself. But you've got to learn to make yourself clearer or people are going to stop listening to you. I know you try, but I don't think you're aware how difficult you make it. Difficult for yourself and for everyone else."

Silently he raised his head, fingered a stone, skipped it across the water, twisted his lips into a makeshift smile, and lay back on the grass.

"Did you get any sleep at all last night?" she asked.

"The satellites. Gravity. There's a formula. The kite went toward them. They pulled each other more than the wind."

"You expect…to leave in a week?"

"In a week."

"We'll go out to dinner on Friday, then."

"On the train. I slept on the train…"

"Yes, I…C. J., I…there's something…there's something that's…Forgive me, C. J., I haven't been at all certain I would do this. Your father left it up to me. I didn't promise him. I want you to be sure to remember that…Your father wrote a letter for you, C. J. He wrote it in the weeks before he died. He expected you to have it at about this time, if I decided you should ever have it. I think you should have it now. I know what it says, and I know it's what your father thought." She took an unsealed envelope from her purse, handed it to him, and continued, "All I ask you to do is appreciate that your father's thoughts were his own. I'm sure it would be a mistake for you to regard his words as representative of anyone other than himself. And I want you to know I've never believed what he wrote you to be entirely correct."

Sitting up, he peered at her questioningly, and when she nodded, he opened the envelope, unfolded the one piece of paper it had contained, turned his back to her, and read the unfamiliar handwriting:

Our son,

Much of the civilization you might have enjoyed had been destroyed by the time of your birth in what began as an attempt to preserve that civilization. I refer to the quality of human relationships more than to the tools of mechanization. The momentum of the destruction continued past the time when it might have ceased because those of us involved in it on all sides had lost our capacity to partake of what was left of civilization. We had lost our self-respect, and we knew ourselves irreparably to have mutilated our own best impulses.

Many of us continued with the savagery, hoping we, too, would be killed by it so we would not have to live the guilt we knew had become all we could ever have again. There is only a little of what we originally sought to preserve and to enhance—with what proved to be impossible and terribly wrong means—left for you. Those who engaged in the mutual slaughter encircling the earth when you were born, those who live on, will seek to keep from you the truth of what they did; they will even increase the evil by glorifying it.

I want you to understand that they will try to delude you into offering them a respect you should never grant them. You must discern that they abandoned the decency of their futures, and you must offer them only a contempt based upon that discernment. Your contempt will be a form of respect, because it will be based upon a recognition of who many people my age truly are, the only form of respect you can possibly use in relation to a portion of those who reside in nearly every land on earth. Within that contempt will be an essential fragment of hope for the future of humanity. You must not ignore what we did. Neither should you expect yourself to forgive us nor to justify our actions. But you must bear in mind what civilization cannot allow again, and you must do this by maintaining your contempt. In staying firm with an awareness of what must not occur again and in preserving a contempt for what did, you in your innocence may sometime acquire a renewed vision of what life should and might be and a knowledge of the appropriate means for bringing that about. Oh, how I hope that you do.

Your father,
Nicholas Rongo

Partially affixing his gaze to a woman and three small children who were paddling a canoe down the shallow river, he refolded the letter, put it back in the envelope, and held it out to his mother.

"No, you keep it," she said. "Whatever you do with it...that is all there will ever be for you to have of him...I haven't been able to do much to create an environment for you, C. J. I've done what I could. You've had to do more than you should have had to. I haven't made a place for you to hide in; at least there's that. There's very little I can say to you now. There's usually very little anyone can say at the most important times in life. I don't think it matters finally whether you go to college or not. Ever. That's

GOSHEN COLLEGE LIBRARY
GOSHEN, INDIANA

not likely to affect what's fundamental. But I think there's more your father would have said, if he had been able to. I've got to do that myself.

"Life can be very empty; it can be very long. All that matters is finding someone to care about and be cared about by. Be respected by. I think your father would have said that if it seems to you there's someone you're coming to love, if passion strikes you, then follow it. You're old enough to hear that now. Love radiates outward from two people to others and to your own future, even if it doesn't seem to. I think that's what he would have said. Follow it even if it means censure and sorrow and regret. Even if it means social reprisals and economic upheavals. They don't matter as much as they might appear to.... But if there's a bit of love to share, C. J., then take it, take it while you can, whatever the cost. That's how you'll become truly alive. The earnings and the buyings are often done merely to pass away the years. Love can last for ten minutes and not ever come again, C. J. Sometimes a few words or a look will be almost all of love that a life has. You should seize moments like that and cherish them. Even if what follows seems to contradict what occurred so severely you come to doubt it happened. Even then it can have been enough to bring you through the time ahead. Memories are all a person really owns."

Shading his widening eyes with the envelope, he stared at her solemnly and asked in agitated, high-pitched tones betokening a tentative disbelief that was veering toward trust, "Ten minutes?"

"Ten minutes, C. J."

2 Solitary Notes

Journal of Colin Tsampa
(written by me only for my private readings—probably)
Do not damage.

July 10, 1945 Tuesday

It's as reasonable to think there will be a future as to think there was a past.

The past doesn't change; references to it should be made in ways that will be beneficial to our futures.

October 15, 1945 Monday

I feel relief that the uncertainty about war I have known for so long has ended. If I pass all my courses, I shall be able to graduate and to count on entering college next year. I have been allowed the chance to plan.

November 22, 1945 Thursday

It is untrue that teenagers can't have some wisdom older people may lack and need to be told about.

December 2, 1945 Sunday

Almost anyone, I think, knows science gives us the tools that improve our situations and that art gives us the meaningful beauty that makes a lot of the pain of life worth enduring. Yet lots of people assume that other people have no interest in either science or art. Why is this? Have we been numbed by war into being unable to convey to each other significant amounts of the realities of our concerns? Have we been made to want to appear in each other's eyes stupid and, therefore, blameless with regard to the broad range of dilemmas threatening our lives on what can come to seem every side at once?

May 16, 1948 Sunday

I didn't realize how much several years of separation would affect my relationships with those in Toledo. I have changed; so has home. I don't know how lasting my collegiate bonds will prove to be, but they seem stronger than those of boyhood friendships. I have lost a good deal of provinciality and have often become aware of its layers just as they were falling aside. I think I shall stay and work this summer in Chicago. Can probably find a routine lab assistantship even this late. It might continue part time through next year. That'd be good for me. I distinctly feel how limited my ties are with the world of work and how long it will be before I effectively join it. High school classmates already with children make me uneasy about the artificiality that's going to be my lot for so many years. I sometimes suspect that if schooling were taken from me I might be unfit for ordinary survival since time and distance have allowed me to identify aspects of employment that I know I'd now agree to only with great difficulty, with a kind of numbing of myself. Most people are hired so early that they accept many aspects of their jobs, I think, fairly unconsciously. But *perhaps* I am indefensibly arrogant.

August 28, 1949 Sunday

I suppose concerns for population growth could in some cases lead to exclusively homosexual patterns of living; yet when these patterns are without any concerns for children and future generations, I feel they may be motivated by urges toward death akin to those apparent in connection with various aspects of the ongoing stockpiling of nuclear weaponry.

September 4, 1949 Sunday

Lately I've been taking some schoolwork so seriously that I've been unable to decide whether to say "the arm of me" or "my arm" or "the portion of me that is an arm!" I don't want to be unduly conscientious in my linguistic considerations; and it's still worth suggesting that the verbal forms we ordinarily use in considering our personalities may make consciousness frequently appear to be an entity that *owns* all the other aspects of an individual organism.

December 18, 1949 Sunday

I have decided to attend medical school and to follow it with a psychiatric residency, instead of settling for graduate school and a doctorate in psychology. I think that physiological considerations are terribly important in approaching human behavior and that a thorough understanding of them will make me more effective in treating people as whole entities in order to eliminate suffering, or at least to lessen it, through a variety of physical as well as psychological-social techniques. Knowledge of ourselves is increasing rapidly, thankfully; and in one sense I'm planning on using the next four years to bide for time, while new techniques are developed by those now in research and practice. I shall probably be required to spend several years of my residency in the military; thus, I cannot count on earning a significant living for ten or even eleven more years. That will be 1959 or 1960. I will be thirty-one or thirty-two. On the one hand, some of my qualities may be seriously stunted by then; yet on the other hand, life will likely be long. I can wait for a family. One of the reasons I'm glad I'm a man.

February 5, 1950 Sunday

I am discovering that silent intonations when reading are awfully important; a written passage can often have many meanings that are dependent upon the contexts and upon the choice of "sounds" we make with and for our internal ear.

April 2, 1950 Sunday

I'm pleased I managed to do as well as I did in my science courses, since at three of my five medical-school admission interviews, I had to explain why there had not been more of them. I'm sure I offered a decent defense of my other selections, though, especially in talking about the American literature seminar of last term. Insights of some poets into behavior have been so astute that a part of their work must be viewed as a progenitor of current psychology. To substitute rigorously demonstrable knowledge, however, for the haphazard insight of the poet is a necessary goal. I expect that many people who formerly pursued solitary paths of artistic investigation would now choose to practice either psychology or psychiatry.

December 10, 1950 Sunday

I have so much less time than I had in college for a consideration of anything apart from school.

February 25, 1951 Sunday

Many problems now judged to be political will become medical ones in the future, as evidence is brought forth demonstrating what is healthiest for us all —evidence supplanting poorly reasoned briefs (for what is "best") that are based on national ideologies.

August 26, 1951 Sunday

I have just returned from a week's visit with my parents. It was difficult because they seek to treat me as I was when walking out the door at eighteen. My economic dependency probably influences this. We got into minor arguments, no, not arguments, but more into zones of tension over such matters as their referring to Toledo as my home, and my referring to it as their home. Although they say nothing negative about psychiatry, I know they are opposed to it as a profession, especially for me. They think it a kind of witchcraft, mumbo jumbo.

It's eerie to have been in the old neighborhood. It seems frozen in time, untouched either by the new towers on Huron and Madison or by the suburban spread over the fields on which I used to play touch football. Even though I know it is less a pocket of shipbuilders' homes than it was in times past, it all looks so much the same that when I'm there memories of these last five years slide away. I find myself behaving rather boyishly as the old responses come to the surface. I'm disheartened by the immaturity I displayed, even though Mother, Father, and the environment itself encouraged me to backslide. I shall attempt to prepare myself better for my next visit. I did anticipate the dilemmas this prolonged economic dependency might bring, but only in a general way. I hope in the future I can resolve them with more wisdom.

May 4, 1952 Sunday

I am surprised at the quality of psychiatric course work, thus far. I'm disappointed. The approaches are seldom rigorously defined, and no serious attempts seem yet to have successfully been made to relate them to our physiology. I'm beginning to fear that less is known than I'd thought. The pioneering work I'd assumed had been completed seems scarcely to have begun and likely will have to be done by myself and by my contemporaries.

May 5, 1952 Monday

Relapses alternating with remissions that become abatements, and then at last arrests and total recoveries—this I consider the path of treated mental illnesses, just as it is the path of what are thought of as various physical ailments.

June 6, 1953 Saturday

Now that we have announced our eventual fields of specialization, I am experiencing disdain from most of my fellow students. Few have acquired any respect for psychiatry. Always its findings have been presented to us as more tentative than those of any other discipline. Some classmates maintain that problems of human behavior are properly handled only within religious provinces, and others discount procedures of psychiatry on the grounds that they are too religious, i.e. too nonsensical to be respected.

January 17, 1954 Sunday

How I wish I had studied the philosophy of science: In matters of both knowledge and technique, far more is disagreed upon by experts than I had suspected. I have repeatedly seen cures in people who simply have assumed that we in the profession are confident of the value of whatever it is that we are doing, extraordinarily varied as our approaches can be. The uncertainties of biology are far less quantifiable than those of physics. Perhaps my generation can change that.

June 20, 1954 Sunday

I was more tired than I knew. During my final weeks here, I purchased a television set and spent many hours viewing the Army-McCarthy hearings. I deemed them at least as important as course work, in light of my occupational plans. It is obvious what tools I acquire over the next six years will need to be refined and adapted for a social situation such as this. Ill health can spread via our information mechanisms, it has become evident during the past months, as rapidly as measles in an uninoculated population. I am appalled by the continued psychiatric silence (professional lack of comment) in regard to this incredible display of pathology. Our capacities for careful thought have been diminished, our forums of public decision demeaned.

Can it be that actual work, when it finally comes, will carry with it this apparent obligation for political noninvolvement? It seems to me that a vigorous psychiatry would be of greatest use in the processes of settling public issues; for it is in determining our views of ourselves and of each other and in establishing social forms that health is created, encouraged, and even allowed. Social structures determine much of our individual psychological makeup. They ought to give us what it should be able to be demonstrated it is we need. Health and national adjustment can probably be quite different. Is it that until more is known I will inevitably be serving political ends? If so, how can I determine what they should be? Surely neither individual nor group health is being enhanced by the professional silence now prevailing. One can only hope the media will eventually disperse the antidotes of careful thought and conscientious reasoning. I do not see how I can fail to be involved in serious social critiques in the future, if I am to be effective in nurturing true health and in encouraging decency.

The postwar tensions between the United States and the Soviet Union are so pervasive hardly anyone is free of them. The stakes are great, could scarcely be greater. Indeed, so much of our budget is currently used for armaments it is accurate to think of ourselves as engaged in fighting right now, although the battlefield is diffuse, the casualty list difficult to determine, and the wounds hard to define. All the life-supporting tools of medicine may not be enough to save us.

August 15, 1954 Sunday

How astonishing is our manner of learning by indirection the manifold rules of living! Especially interesting are the behavioral forms we employ while we talk. Tonal patterns, styles of posture, hand gestures, and facial expressions communicate much that is relative to, or even in specific contradiction of, our speech. A father, thinking himself benevolent, says to a child, "Is there anything I can do for you before I go to bed?" What the child has understood might be translated as, "Get to bed now, because otherwise I, who have so much power over you, cannot sleep." The child will say, "No, I feel tired" instead of "Yes, I'd like you to order a pizza and bring me a pitcher of milk."

Much discourse similarly allows us to maintain complex illusions about our motivations and expectations. The person in difficulty will often have failed to appreciate the variations among words and intentions or for diverse reasons will be attempting to eliminate the contradictions between oral statements and their frameworks. The use of secondary forms of communication frequently depends upon shared patterns of camouflage. I shall begin to identify these as I encounter them and as they occur to me in reviewing my memories, attempt to determine their general nature, and then case by case and generality by generality evaluate them and see finally if I can develop or discover rules for judgment that would promote constructive behavior and both prevent and resolve harmful conflict. The whole matter is scarcely dealt with in print. I am interested in the help such clarification would provide rather than in getting credit for bringing it about.

October 3, 1954 Sunday

I am starting to understand how matters of economics are fundamentally related to hospitalizations. Even a brief stay here is apt to reduce possibilities of employment. In spite of the hospital conditions—company, food, and a sure roof over one's head often become preferable to solitude. Many people give up and return again and again. Too little is done to provide bridges back to life outside the hospital. This can defeat what progress there has been toward health.

December 3, 1954 Friday

How deluded it is to suggest that any one drama, no matter how ancient, could demonstrate the essential nature of being human!

December 5, 1954 Sunday

It is not that I consider mathematics inapplicable to studies of human behavior. I am convinced, instead, that concepts facilitating its use either for therapy or for research are inadequately formed as of yet. The mathematical mind functions similarly to the poetic mind, and I assume both disciplines will eventually prove valuable for my work. Awe and wonder are so integral to both. It's a pity much course work ignores these aspects of mathematics.

December 6, 1954 Monday

It's stupid to maintain that doctors and patients are necessarily adversaries. Disease is the adversary; it is held in common by therapist and patient. *Any person* is a good deal more than either a healer or a collection of symptoms.

February 13, 1955 Sunday

It is so obvious to me that experience is composed of that which is tentatively known, that which will be ultimately decipherable, and that which must be eternally mysterious and unknown in silence that I struggle to be other than arrogantly glad when people suffer crises of religious faith. The arrogance is a futile gesture toward maintaining *my own* spiritual health.

June 19, 1955 Sunday

I have been reading works composed six and seven decades ago by William James. His discussion of "the will," which he describes as a separate faculty that can determine who a person is by mediating between feeling and action, is intriguing. In our time, it is much more likely for feelings to be acted upon, whatever they are, without mediation. The mechanism of will was perhaps a social creation that is being discarded.

October 9, 1955 Sunday

I am amazed at the number of cases on the base that have a component of serious conflict in regard to racial relations. It is still difficult for me to realize how thoroughly segregated the armed forces were until 1948. I'm forced to challenge my conception of what the war that accompanied my youth was about; my thoughts as a boy that it involved the protection of a way of life have had to alter, somewhat, in the face of the knowledge that there really was little or no reality to that way of life for many who fought for it. Abstractions yet to be implemented. The European devastation still so evident in physical and psychic wounds and environmental wreckage continues not to be appreciated in the United States. One aspect of the gulf between civilians and the military.

July 20, 1956 Friday

I am ready to say that some attitudes I must help to preserve and strengthen in many patients in order to insure their successful adjustment here would be viewed as signs of severe maladjustments in civilian life. Under such circumstances, concepts of human sanity or even of a "sanity" present within the democratic institutions of western civilization are very nearly irrelevant, unless I am to come to the conclusion that I am involved in betraying them.

I'm not foundering; but I am, nonetheless, wondering to what degree my professional assumptions are reflections of the sorts of adjustments deemed socially-politically necessary in the United States. I would prefer to be able to make use of what genuine knowledge of the human situation there presently is. Watching recruits undergo changes in values that would be discouraged in civilian life can be unpleasant. Human health too easily can come to seem a matter of successfully accepting whatever cultural norms prevail. How destructive it is to list characteristics of sanity, then add, "save of course, for purposes of national defense...."

March 17, 1957 Sunday

Soon this portion of my training will be completed, and I shall be able to go back to the States. There simply has not been enough time to manage humanely all the dilemmas connected with the displacement of values that occurs here so frequently in what may be a kind of set of mental illnesses, somehow healable.

I have decided upon Boston for the completion of my residency. I do not expect to be ready for practice until I'm thirty-two.

November 27, 1957 Wednesday

Having returned adds special poignancy to tomorrow. The day also requires careful thought in regard to the President's sending of federal troops to Little Rock, Arkansas, and to the defiant governor's stance at Central High School. The President's action is proper; but since the separation of the races is maintained so thoroughly throughout the United States, I regret seeing the South once again being used as a scapegoat. Errors, iniquities, and inequalities are more widespread than is presently being officially recognized.

The ideas we learn to profess in this nation are so at variance with the lives we lead that much juggling of perceptions and conceptions is practiced in order that our images of ourselves and our actual selves not be experienced as in conflict. The divisively exploitive, black-white structures have been damaging to the health of us all. My profession is to be faulted for not having taken this into account. We have too rarely considered the nature of our shared social situations and have too often served only the wealthy. A greater emphasis upon environmental contexts would increase the meaningfulness, the value, of our work.

December 15, 1957 Sunday

It is getting easier for me to identify deceit, to divide lying from areas of more firmly held fantasy. Sometimes it is still necessary for me to do environmental investigation in order accurately to evaluate what can be extended verbal onslaughts. Otherwise, I find myself proceeding ahead having accepted radical distortions as descriptions of the actual situations of the patient's life. It is terribly difficult to learn to identify the truth simply on the basis of considering words without experiences to compare them with.

January 5, 1958 Sunday

I am very pleased at the relief I feel when a patient leaves the hospital or when clinic treatment has been completed. I had feared I might tend to make bonds detrimental to the patients. But I am finding the realms of therapy and friendship to be quite different. I have not yet faced the dilemmas of the one becoming the other.

February 9, 1958 Sunday

During my analysis, which is taking place as part of my residency, I find myself reporting elements of the past and present in terms of the particular theorist whose work I'm reading at the moment.

February 11, 1958 Tuesday

Hopefully soon to disappear is the silly and mistaken notion that if one regards oneself as behaving sanely, one is necessarily ill.

February 15, 1958 Saturday

Though we can't know each other's thoughts save as they are reported to us in retrospect, I have no doubt that thinking is a form of behavior. I am confident, too, that the closer acquaintanceships become to friendships, and the closer friendships become to love, the more we can somewhat sense—again, we can never know—what the other(s) is (are) thinking.

February 18, 1958 Tuesday

Alongside a new freeway yesterday I read a plaque referring to a pioneering designer of such highway systems as their "father." Comparisons of this kind are becoming widespread (as, say, a movie review reference to a "stillborn screenplay"); and I find them all vastly annoying. Such superficial equations of the processes of parenting with other activities, however constructive and difficult the activities may be, are confusing—especially so to young children—and demeaning.

The governmental powers of mayors and council members seem to me unfortunately disguised by allusions to "city fathers."

Similarly, historical reputations associated with the complex achievements that brought about the formal beginnings of the United States are misunderstood because of careless usages of the phrase "founding fathers." A simple "framers of our constitution" is more appropriate.

February 20, 1958 Thursday

Saying or writing a statement with an intensity shaped by firmly held convictions doesn't necessarily make the statement true and/or good.

February 24, 1958 Monday

When we are urged to be done with words and get on with deeds, we are usually being asked to make ourselves unaware not only of the manners in which deeds result from usages of words but also of the ways in which deeds prepare for *and accompany* all such usages. In fact, to use a word is to perform a deed; and after infancy, no deeds separated from words can occur.

February 27, 1958 Thursday

The poetic idea that beauty and truth are equivalent seems to me an example of nonsense. Human experiences range from the totally ugly to the totally beautiful and form a portion of what we term reality—a portion that is partially comprised of words; and words function in a variety of ways, among them identifying—for the sake of our being able to know truths which, again, can be ugly as well as beautiful—bits of the rest of experience.

March 2, 1958 Sunday

I am very discouraged. I fear that anyone who comes to a mental health practitioner is thereby defined as ill, simply from having sought help, and then is fitted into one of several classifications so vague they would not serve to identify illness or health within the population, if applied apart from someone's presence on the other side of the desk. Furthermore, I am convinced some people develop illnesses simply from exposure to techniques meant to cure them. Perhaps I'm overtired, or perhaps I'm usually not prepared to face how little justified agreement there is in psychiatric approaches, practices.

How much there is to be discovered if my hopes for employing efficacious, scientific techniques are ever to be gratified!

June 21, 1958 Saturday

Already formally summer, although spring seems to have lasted but a few days.

I have been with the hospital and the clinic for a year. I've seen patients arrive, leave, return, and be shuffled off to other hospitals. I now have some working conclusions: A patient frequently departs from the hospital only to re-enter circumstances that had been untenable in the first place. Usually the patient is considered to be seriously in need of fundamental behavioral alterations, while—unfortunately—little or no professional attention is given to changes probably also necessary in the patient's environment. Often someone will be hospitalized in the midst of a crisis which ought to be dealt with immediately in therapy, but which, instead, is drugged practically out of consciousness in order that the person become quiescent enough to be easily managed by the overworked, too small staff. The capacity to acquire health insurance is frequently lost after even a short hospital stay. Opportunities for employment are severely reduced. Upon admission, patients seldom realize the probabilities of either hardship. Patients are, moreover, likely to be thought of and to think of themselves after a stay here as incurable. Once admission has occurred, I do whatever I can to make the hospitalization one of brief duration. The discouraging thing about psychiatric chemotherapy is not the lack of information concerning the effects of the many new drugs, which are powerful, indeed, but is instead the unexamined nature of the ends for which the drugs are used.

September 7, 1958 Sunday

Basic social questions to which psychiatry should be addressing itself are too often overlooked by those within the profession. Surely we must seek to achieve beneficial societal forms based on knowledge; for our very survival continues to hang in balance. There has been nothing yet offered, not in history, nor art, nor medicine, adequately explaining the causes of war. I cannot help but think that those of us engaged in psychiatry and psychology are especially to be faulted for continuing to offer so few viable insights that might reduce the possibility of that horror in the future, or lessen the tensions of the frightful global situations we presently face. Surely answers can be found if the right questions are asked and the proper avenues explored.

Merely to concentrate on methods of making feasible local adjustments, as many therapists do, is an indefensible goal. It makes us the midwives for whatever winds of power blow. The assumption that one way of life is as healthy as another so long as the majority (within a particular set of boundaries) follow it is implicit; a conception of human sanity is thereby necessarily assumed to be an impossible goal, a meaningless goal. Confusion abounds between standards of good and evil and standards of health and ill health; I am only now realizing how frequently I have been mistaking visions of goodness for visions of health.

January 8, 1959 Thursday

I return from a week in Toledo. Although the neighborhood continues on as before, I was surprised at how often I had to be nudged by renewed experience. For instance, I found myself wrongly identifying houses, thinking that people had lived in one who had lived elsewhere. What mistaken memories time brings! This makes me doubt the value of professional approaches that emphasize recitation of the events of childhood.

January 9, 1959 Friday

So many aspects of contemporary life have been of brief duration, their roots having been sunk in 1945. Within the United States, the common way of viewing war of the forties is peculiar. Scarcely any mention of Japan and Italy as former enemies is ever made anymore. Indeed, Germany is rarely mentioned in that light. Instead the conflict is presented as if it involved the defeat of one evil man, Hitler, with no consideration given to the social conditions and the people upon whom his power was based. Mention is often made of the concentration camps, while all the other elements are simply not spoken of. Hitler is presented as if he were born without even the potential for any goodness whatsoever.

April 12, 1959 Sunday

I am attending few movies anymore. They no longer allow a rest. The newer trends of "realism" are wretchedly ill-informed in comparison with the detailed tragedies and joys I encounter daily.

April 15, 1959 Wednesday

Death may be certain—but not taxes!

June 7, 1959 Sunday

Since economic matters will finally soon be completely in my own hands, I had best set down some of my basic professional thoughts.

Psychiatry now is in a similar position to anthropology when it ceased to function as a tool of colonialism and began to become a discipline in its own right, unrelated to the maintenance of wealth and able to focus on all of humanity. Although the adaptation of anthropological techniques to a study of the cultures from which they arose continues to be slow, clearly it is happening. Hopefully psychiatry and anthropology will one day unite to eliminate political divisiveness. I am convinced that widespread improvements in health must be accompanied by changes in patterns of work, patterns of economic distribution, even patterns of love. I am obligated to discover the hypothetical natures of these possible changes and must employ whatever deductive and inductive methods I come to consider appropriate in order to be able to demonstrate the reasons for the necessity of the changes and for the selection of the particular alternatives to be implemented.

August 8, 1960 Monday

I must maintain an awareness of what I do not know, since continual confrontations with suffering may make me reluctant to face my own ignorance.

December 10, 1960 Saturday

The wife of the President-elect has given birth to a son. The Vice President-elect was quoted as clearly saying that the new administration will be structured so as to ensure that when the baby becomes a man there will be no reason for him or for anyone to engage in war to defend "any system."

Certainly a sense of great change is in the air.

I am succeeding in combining private practice with ongoing work at the clinic. I'm making far less money than I could but find this arrangement more gratifying than I expect private practice alone would be and am pleased to be on my own after so many long years. I am allowed what I perceive to be an amazing amount of latitude in technique. I wonder sometimes if I would have gone through with all my training had I known at the start how little of the nature of human behavior is truly understood. Unsolvable.

January 22, 1961 Sunday

The past months have shown me my considerable naiveté. It is not that I have become less hopeful, but rather it is that I cannot hope as easily again. I hesitate to write it, yet the truth is that I have received a series of shocks, resulting not only from patient contact but also from extensive exploration of the community. I have found a common unawareness of the links between one's work and the lives and work of others, a wide-spread lack of encouragement for growth and change, an acceptance of boredom in cycles without end, a dearth of meaningful, lasting personal affinities, a failure to accept political responsibilities, and the ever-present belief that government is an incomprehensible force. To what extent has my loneliness been responsible for what I have perceived, for what I have…seen?

June 18, 1961 Sunday

Unmarried applicants are regarded by employers as poor prospects for several reasons. Lacking obligations, they are more apt to resign when conditions become unpleasant; whereas the married, especially the men, face so many economic entanglements that there often is no alternative but to stay on when the going gets rough or tedious. A single person creates sexual discomfort, too, not so much from availability, but rather more often from the obviousness of the availability, which counters the secrecy of the liaisons occurring fleetingly under the shelter of silence that the appearances of stable marriages allow.

July 9, 1961 Sunday

When I know that some of reported news is composed of falsehoods, it is tempting to pretend that the most difficult-to-accept true statements are untrue. Thus far, I refrain from doing this. Accurate social awareness is, however, fundamental to my work. I wonder if a course in speed-reading would help me. Or would I rather, through those unfamiliar techniques, establish an inappropriately comforting and almost hallucinatory series of internal paragraphs consisting of an unexamined mixture of falsehoods and truths? As I know what I want from such a course, I shall investigate the possibilities and then decide whether any of these might be useful to me.

July 11, 1961 Tuesday

Unwarranted disgust with myself and my profession could lead first to weakened capacities of mine (and of other people) for hope and then to the virtual murder of some patients resultant from the symptomatic attitude that *incurable* is a realistic medical term.

August 13, 1961 Sunday

I've been seeing many male patients in their early fifties afflicted by depressions (often beginning when children leave the home) based on the feeling that they can retain security if they continue on as they are, but that all their chances for rewarding work have gone. I'm attempting to discover what economic reforms might be suggested, be made, where, how, in order not simply to prevent the onslaught of such despair, but also to establish structures that would enable us all to live more productively throughout life. I am seeking in-depth contact with varying sectors of the city, and perhaps this will eventually prove worthwhile for planning of this kind. I am not prepared to accept the notion that people do not want to create life-enhancing opportunities with and for each other.

August 27, 1961 Sunday

Vital to our health is the nature of publicly available symbols in books, movies, and similar forms. Whereas what are called "biographical novels" bring with them confusions about journalism, history, and gossip, what are called "autobiographical novels" bring these three confusions and yet another one: readers who believe the main purpose of fiction is to summon forth attention on its authors. Such readers, some of whom are among my patients, frequently express the commonplace delusion that every person contains a book able at the right moment easily to be slipped into bindings. These people are not only prone to be saying at regular intervals something like, "When I write my book, you'll appreciate what I've been through" but also tend to transform their observations of most anything into apparent statements different enough from what references to actualities would be for it to seem like much of what they are saying is akin to scripts for television series of the sort meant to provide seemingly sophisticated surfaces that yet gloss over (and are silent about) the most notable realities of our lives.

August 29, 1961 Tuesday

Even the weather has been twisted into rarely mentioned weapons: clouds come to be seeded not for agricultural well-being but to cause floods!

September 3, 1961 Sunday

The world of celebrity exists in television and the popular press in ways awfully demeaning not just to ordinary people but also to those who are supposedly being celebrated yet who are actually being presented as if they live in a self-absorbed plane that does not intersect with the rest of human life—as if they all are performers in an endless movie the rest of us are obligated but to watch.

September 10, 1961 Sunday

The daily pauses of dawn and twilight have long been impossible for some of us to experience within the fabrics of cities. Occasionally, however, interlapping strands of the concealing, sheltering fabric itself accidentally combine with pronounced alterations in climate to produce similar transitional pauses. Since these artificial haltings occur irregularly and unpredictably, they are apt to be jarring reminders of metropolitan tensions rather than comforting reassurances of immutable rhythms.

November 6, 1961 Monday

I have been thinking about the natures of integrity and of innocence. It is sometimes said that maturity necessitates the loss of both. I suspect it more likely that adult lives, rather than involving betrayals of youthful idealism, reflect the gradual development of integrity and allow expressions of decency with more care than youth can supply. This is not to deny that the young regularly mature themselves in ways with which adults have nothing directly to do.

November 20, 1961 Monday

Autistic absorption in externalized fantasies has sometimes been mistaken for creativity and even falsely honored as such.

May 12, 1962 Saturday

This nation was settled by those who had made breaks with their pasts, who thought of themselves as purveyors of the new, who had contempt for many aspects of their heritage and an unwillingness to consider any external authority as valid, seeking to trust their own ingenuities in contact with raw experiences. In light of such attitudes, teachers have frequently been viewed as rather irrelevant, token necessities, as social rejects, who would have failed in other pursuits. Often they have been the sole bearers of the best portions of culture; yet their appreciation of other parts of life has sometimes been so minimal that many people have come to regard art, music, and literature as provinces only for the young.

It is common for children of high school age to exhibit talents in one of these realms, often many talents, and then for all development of the skills refining the talents to end when, as adults, people come to view artistic endeavor as economically irrelevant. A proper integration has not been demonstrated for the young either by teachers or by employers. Perhaps it would be possible to merge the worlds of work and school more effectively. Teachers, for instance, might be more respected if they were required to have experiences with the working world apart from their profession. Business and government might also profit from interchanges with school personnel.

So many talents might then not be lost; their continued cultivation could be accomplished, as leisure becomes more broadly accessible.

Shouldn't we be spending a significant quantity of our time bringing forth
a noneconomic flourishing of the many facets of being human which the
schools develop so excellently and which are currently crushed so soon
after graduation?

November 14, 1962 Wednesday

It was quite powerfully constructed and extraordinarily beautiful, but I
regret the setting was not other than a college. The young are apt to regard it
as a depiction of their professors, which I doubt it is intended to be, and
entirely to miss the interweaving of metaphor and historical observation. The
awkwardness so inevitable to the early stage of the literature with which
I'm primarily acquainted had almost turned into a national gimmick, but
perhaps it won't—now that grace has become a component of style.

November 25, 1962 Sunday

Events of last month require new terms. Silence is not a proper alternative. The global terror was of such magnitude that attempts to use ordinary
language to deal with it, no matter what the choice of words, weaken the
moorings of all definition.

November 28, 1962 Wednesday

One of the worst developments in relation to the horribly pessimistic
view humankind is such that only ever more undeployable weaponry will
prevent us from tearing each other apart is that many people have begun
to shape their behaviors in accordance with this view. Ethics and morals
are tossed to the winds along with common sense.

In a comparable vein, lives are being lived as if there will be no future,
as if the consequences for even the most heinous actions will never have
to be faced. Whatever causes present satisfaction is seen as right. The
ephemeral reigns supreme. Debts mount up along with enormous losses
of funds due to widespread gambling.

Meanwhile, the amount of stockpiled weaponry continues to grow as if through a momentum nothing can stop.

December 10, 1962 Monday

Various people have referred to humankind's current state as terminal. One of the most worrisome aspects of movements for offering assisted suicide to people called "terminally ill" is that some people manning nuclear weaponry may adopt this attitude and decide to bring about what they see as a merciful end for us all. If our nature is such only weaponry is keeping us alive, then why not, it might be thought by such people, use the weaponry for global self-destruction. It is far from fanciful to imagine someone thinking this way.

February 8, 1963 Friday

What depths and kinds of loneliness have been presented to me! What many patients learn from me are the rudiments of friendship. How shallow are our expectations for mutual concern! How feeble our development of such concerns! How frequently attitudes of trust are attacked and wither! And how difficult it is to reacquire them! We do not get much help from all of art. Matters of how to be friends, how to care for one another, how to love enduringly are seldom dealt with in our literature. Admonitions unaccompanied by example are meant to suffice. So many serious movies and plays are chronicles of failure. I'm feeling awfully despairing tonight; and in such a mood the best of our culture seems to me a moan of single-hued anguish, offering neither guidance, nor solace.

February 14, 1963 Thursday

Healthy sexuality has components of neither sadism nor masochism. The latter are always diseased (often schizophrenic). Masochistic obesity regularly leads to heart failure, and actions such as the presently fashionable worship of the sun can lead directly and quickly to skin cancer. Smoking, tanning, and overeating also have narcissistic aspects, which is to say they are activities stemming not from too much self-love but from *not enough*.

March 3, 1963 Sunday

I cannot accept the notion that life is *necessarily* absurd; but I waver toward doing so and wish I had more support for my usual, far more optimistic, benchmark attitudes favoring the slowly experimental creation of inherently benevolent social forms able to enhance our creative capacities and our rational powers, while strengthening our tendencies toward generosity.

May 2, 1963 Thursday

Collegiate instruction—in the past attuned primarily to the wealthy— has not sufficiently adjusted to the influx of students from all sectors of the population; hence the protesting outcries for relevance. I expect new practitioners who grew up in the midst of poverty, their medical training having been supported by scholarships, will soon be bringing psychiatric techniques to many people within communities overlooked by most of the rest of us.

August 31, 1963 Saturday

Since science is a way of knowing for human benefit, only so-called tests, not genuine tests, can occur in the development of weapons. How recognition of that fact would change for the better many budgets, particularly those of universities!

September 24, 1963 Tuesday

I cannot help but wonder about earthquakes and volcanoes in relation to what's now called "underground testing of nuclear weaponry."

October 7, 1963 Monday

I have seen enough major behavioral changes made late in life to cause me to doubt the validity and value of theory suggesting that character formation is completed by the age of five. I suspect this probably mistaken idea is another vehicle for the tired, admittedly overworked, therapist, who chooses to aid manifold forces promoting economic oppression and emotional stagnation (it is an easy route) by failing to devise procedures for discovering and implementing new constructive forms which would require the reinforcements of economic sanction and individual acceptance.

October 9, 1963 Wednesday

What follows reminds me of my long failure to appreciate that people with forebears called property a century ago would have unique attitudes toward such things as receipts, titles, and thefts!

I feel like this will be the hardest entry I've written in this journal so far:

In suburban ("white," so-called) areas, some of the children who have suffered and recovered from breakdowns are exposed to bigotries of their parents, siblings, and neighbors every bit as vivid as were those suffered by, say, a portion of the children whose mothers were slaveholders and fathers slaves. I refer to bigotries devoted to the idea that mental illnesses can be neither cured nor otherwise end. Former patients struggle against the force of these attitudes of some of the so-called healthy—attitudes meant to spread delusions (that recoveries can't occur) by actually motivating recurrent attempts (by people who hold these attitudes) to bring about new breakdowns in ex-patients. Such ex-patients struggle on every side against the *seeming* inabilities of others to perceive their newfound (and sometimes arduously won) health; they are struggling against not just genuine and passive inabilities of this sort, but also against semblances of them that, in truth, are active and incredibly vicious attempts to force upon these former patients misconceptions meant to replace newly accurate conceptions of themselves and the rest of reality.

In this regard, family gatherings sometimes become brutal complements to both mail from former patients relatives have regularly left
unopened and phone calls they have not returned (or worse, have ended
with savageries that can be lethal). Apparent cards for holidays can
become, just beneath the surface, violent tools of attack that again can be
fatal to former patients. Moreover, a sort of parody of dancing can occur
whereby these many cruelties are denied by all those perpetuating them,
making it appear, so very wrongly, that former patients are fantasizing
what *truly is* outside themselves. To triumph over this takes every recourse
a no longer sick person has.

Treatably dysfunctional groups, then, are in cases like this uniting to
attack the very people who have sought for (and gotten) help that's a
beginning of what the group itself needs. Not that there aren't sane people in
groups that never encounter in any way, and never should need to
encounter, professionals of my sort.

Lest I am appearing in what I am saying here to be making heroes and
heroines out of patients, I must note that the idea a lot of them can
have—that people, upon learning of former patients' past symptoms, fear
their own incipient breakdowns—is selfish, untrue, simplistic, and malicious
in ways information and mercy can help end.

How destructive and inaccurate is the view that, once a person's termed
"crazy," always the person will be crazy! If I can't help, help can still come
from sources both known and unknown by me.

It is hard on me to find supposedly "sick social withdrawal" by ex-patients
turn out to be shunning by those in some ways close to them, including,
sometimes in complex ways, those doctors who mix up their own lives at
work with their own lives at home by maintaining they are not "the same
people" in both realms. Little phrases can cause much suffering.

Long silences from relatives amount to another unfortunate example of
this sort of shunning....

On a related and more pleasing note: I am finding in some postthera-
peutic situations compassion and constructive honesty developing outside

and, I gather, inside both ex-patients and people with whom they have especially significant relationships.

October 12, 1963 Saturday

We have begun to accustom ourselves to the imagery surrounding us in films, newspapers, magazines, books, and on television by using large portions of these arrangements of symbols in ways previously reserved for verbal phrases or even for single words. The structures of English grammar in the United States are currently interacting with remembered segments selected from the public media, thereby creating internal collages that operate in private thought similarly to sentences. A few words heard months earlier from a friend might, thus, be combined with a portion of televised news from the previous evening and with a snatch of motion picture dialogue in order to form and to evaluate an idea.

Media symbols are also being used as preparations for experiences, which, if they occur, are often perceived in a manner suggested by the previously encountered public forms. Drama on television screens is viewed similarly to rules of behavior on nineteenth-century school chalkboards. In the day of history during which consciousness began to reflect the great rooster cry of moveable type, it is, however, yet morning.

April 24, 1964 Friday

The assassination of the President left me for nearly six months unable to compose thoughts to be placed as entries herein, partly because that event unleashed torrents of emotion in my patients I had to spend most of my time helping them manage in ways that needed to be different for each one of them.

May 7, 1964 Thursday

Affections are often ecstatic at first and then exhibit a kind of cooling-off which results not because of a disappointed discovery that the qualities of another person had been imagined but because much of the ensuing relationship will consist of summoning forth dormant qualities that one had initially intuited within the other person.

June 14, 1964 Sunday

There has developed what is almost a sort of underground group of people bent on saving others from suicidal impulses both caused and heightened by those describing themselves as proponents of assisted suicide.

Some of the suicidal are even being hidden from what are, in effect, their would-be assailants—as if we are living in a place akin to Nazi Germany, with people suffering from depression being those to be eliminated.

August 28, 1964 Friday

I am surprised to report that, despite its awful ending, I found *A Hard Day's Night* to be one of the best films I've seen, a truly joyful experience. I expect that it will be a movie with far-reaching social consequences, a rare thing. The vision is of overriding meaninglessness and is akin to the work of Samuel Beckett, but the approach is one of gleeful acceptance and impudent revelry. It's been a long while since I left a theater surrounded by an audience buoyed up by good feelings!

November 8, 1964 Sunday

Thankfully the President has been reelected. If his manner is abrasively unpleasant, still the office is, I think, in capable hands. How awful it was to contemplate the possibility of a full-scale war in Southeast Asia, which surely the other candidate would have waged!

December 20, 1964 Sunday

I have completed reading *The Deputy*, a condemnation of Pope Pius XII for his silence about—and hence his complicity with—Nazi Germany. Since psychiatrists are often compared to priests, less to ministers (probably because of the more powerful structure of Catholicism), I think it important to set down some observations I have in regard to the use of ethical terms. Certainly they become entangled with notions of health and disease in practical, daily lives and within my profession itself. Freud's superego model is inapplicable to many current actualities. Perhaps detailed notations of observed phenomena will suggest more useful constructs.

Children learn the terms "good" and "bad" in reference to themselves or to others on a spectrum ranging from a pole of self-definition (they are either good or bad because they do certain "things") to a pole of behavioral definition (certain acts are good or bad). Rarely is anyone presented with a simple set of ethical standards, or indeed, even with a definite but complex set. Home, school, peers, other families, work, television, movies—all are apt to offer different judgments for the same behavior. Often there are contradictions between what is verbally advocated and what is nonverbally demonstrated.

By the age of twenty a division of behaviors used contextually in order to fulfill various structural expectations is far more common than an ego mediating between libidinous impulse and superego. As one moves among the contradictory frameworks, as one changes behavior to suit each framework, one is inclined to think of oneself as doing good and/or as good if one is fulfilling the environmental expectations at hand.

Certainly the wars of this century have had a great deal to do with our current ethical state; for during them, while preparing for them, many people learned to do what they had regarded as wrong; and when peace has arrived, they have been expected to resume their former attitudes.

January 31, 1965 Sunday

In effect, the present-day political ideology divides humanity into three species, those of us in the West, those in the East, and those in what is called "The Third World." Does the assumption that the people in "the underdeveloped nations" will soon be wanting what either we or the Soviets or both have, itself foment rebellion and revolution?

February 8, 1965 Monday

What an ugly unwillingness to participate in the beneficial processes and results of global scientific research is being demonstrated by urgings that physicians employ drugs to kill instead of to heal, by pleas for legalization of the murders that are assisted suicides, and even by the hospice movement seeming (wrongly so) to justify sets of decisions that lead to deaths instead of to the continued lives that might have been!

The range of life's possibilities include anyone's last moments resulting (even accidentally and even only internally) in an irreplaceable bit of wisdom, the effects of which might include its recording for the benefit of the rest of us. These moments can also result in gestures capable of resolving an interpersonal conflict, of deepening already close relationships, or simply of bringing to the dying person a long-desired or otherwise satisfying thought no one else will know the decedent had and which no one could have predicted that person would ever have. Last words can be heard, but only the dying know last thoughts.

Instead of disseminating knowledge of means of suicide, we need ideas for lessening pain. And if suffering can't be lessened or ended, we need to help it be borne. Sometimes we even need to use it for research that one day will end it for all of us.

March 7, 1965 Sunday

It is commonly said that scientific investigations often result in similar discoveries that are independently made at roughly the same times. Is this true of art as well? It seems to me that both art and science thrive more in communities of sympathetic minds than in solitude.

March 28, 1965 Sunday

I'm troubled by a phenomenon that has become increasingly common among those who have grown up with television. The proximity of so many disembodied voices and faraway scenes is producing confusion in regard to what a real person is!

Surrounded by an assortment of characters in fictional situations, a percentage of the young not only are expecting their own lives to be like "lives" of characters, but also are reacting *as if* some of the people around them—often strangers—*are* the characters viewed/heard.

In order that pronouns, etc. might be applied solely to people, linguistic terms should be devised that would be used only in relation to fictional characters. Our minds are weighed down by many a *he* and a *she* that refer to imaginary constructs; the manners in which those constructs relate to our experiences would be helpfully clarified by the development of terms appropriate merely for *them*.

September 23, 1965 Thursday

The President is carrying out the foreign policies he campaigned against and has relegated his own campaign promises to sad, duped history. A personality can develop so many defenses that finally there is little left to be defended. So can a nation. I've got to come up with a convincing, justified stand on the Southeast Asian conflict. And soon. My caseload is increasing. Patients are becoming more frantic, more dislocated. Congress has settled on a maximum sentence of five years for burning draft cards.

March 27, 1966 Sunday

I wish that the word *green* could apply only to a category of color, rather than also referring, as it does, to envy, innocence, and immaturity. If visual *green* has any relationships to those emotional qualities, they are relationships I have yet to discover.

September 4, 1966 Sunday

I am worn out. The war is tearing at us all. I am dispersing drugs on as widespread a scale as anyone. That as many of us as possible survive these years is what I tell myself I must be concerned with. I forsake questions pertaining to the quality of survival.

The halfway house has folded due to a denial of federal funds that have been rechanneled toward the Pentagon.

September 26, 1966 Monday

It is commonly said we are apt to become the people we fear we will become. I don't think that's true. Too seldom are the reasonable qualities and the tragedy-preventing capacities of the many varieties of fear appreciated.

January 2, 1967 Monday

I acted in part from twofold jealousy stemming not only from her regard for him, but also from his very youth. I violated my hard-won knowledge that ripening courage often needs external support. Moreover, it is less that I love her than that I expect I eventually could; it is a fondness, it is friendship now. And I betrayed it by letting myself think my reprehensible and degrading offer was well intentioned. That I hid jealousy under the guise of indirect medical advice appalls me. In one tired moment, I hastily chose to abuse *many* of the assumptions upon which I have tried to base my practice and which I have explored in this journal. Societal disease and disintegration partially caused a personal malfunction of my own ethical and psychological integrities! There is no remedy now for the damage I have done. I must take care to try to prevent anything similar from happening again. It can no longer be the simple matter of a series of letters to draft boards I had envisioned sending for so many of them; instead, each person's plight must be dealt with on a highly individual basis.

April 23, 1967 Sunday

Health involves the capacities to predict and to plan. A capacity to care enduringly for others in a manner bringing mutual benefits. A capacity to change both views and life techniques in response to new circumstances and new evidence. A capacity for sustained development of skills productive in work and constructive in leisure.

September 10, 1967 Sunday

It has taken me several weeks to get my papers in order after racial rioting that burned to the ground the building in which I had my office. Part of Boston resembles the bombed-out wreckage I came to know in Europe during my time with the military.

Will this make it clear to the profession that social organization has much to do with the quality of individual health and that drastic alterations in the structures of city life are necessary?

At its nonviolent best, the Civil Rights Movement, it should be widely noted, has been about how all of us can get what we want without wrongly exploiting each other.

September 21, 1967 Thursday

I think weapons (of any kind, including verbal) aimed or potentially aimed at even one person neither preserve nor enhance the capacities of anyone to do anything worthwhile. Progress, I know, occurs *despite* all such weapons.

No aware person could discount the possibilities of combinations of verbal and physical weapons bringing about the end of all our lives.

January 21, 1968 Sunday

During the past year, I have come to know well several attorneys. We often remark on the compatibility of our work and find each other reinforcing. Currently I experience a keener sense of communion with them than with anyone else. Both professions require a sensitivity capable of eliciting truth from within or behind what are initially rather vast networks of confusion and lies. Both involve confrontations with people who are in desperate emotional states, people who have come to us as a necessary last resort. The best attorneys are actively seeking reform in harmony with carefully thought-out conceptions of justice, of equity, just as I am seeking change in accordance with a developing vision of global health.

When we are able to work together on areas of common ground, and there are many, we can be quite effective.

February 18, 1968 Sunday
    "Too much" has become a term of approval.

March 3, 1968 Sunday
    War confusion abounds.
    President Johnson contends access to information necessitates that his judgment alone be trusted; he asks for blind loyalty; due to the Tonkin Gulf Resolution, his powers are probably greater than were Roosevelt's in 1943.
    Any position on this war seemingly can be supported by the assortments of evidence. We are told we are fighting either a small force from South Vietnam or a large force from North Vietnam or a combination of North and South Vietnamese; we are told it is a civil war and conversely that China or the Soviet Union is the real power behind the struggle.
    I hope future historians will recognize that journalism has become useless in the face of so many contradictions.
    Some people are asserting that the plenitude of antiwar protests signifies that the American dream of independent judgments uniting to determine national policy is fitfully at last being realized. I'm not sure that's true. I'm not sure it should be realized. I'm not sure it can be realized.
    I pity the young. It's the worst time to be alive I've ever known.

April 1, 1968 Monday
    A gasp of relief is spreading throughout the city in response to President Johnson's speech last evening indicating he has chosen not to seek another term. His international assumptions have been gleaned from theories of "the nature of man" in vogue two centuries ago. Such simplicity is inexcusable in light of the vast accumulation of anthropological data he might have turned to instead. He has described the war as equivalent to the

American Revolution and in so doing, has ignored linguistic, religious, and organizational differences between ourselves and the people of Southeast Asia. His actions have prevented both further evidence from being found and additional hypotheses about the common nature of humanity from being tested.

April 24, 1968 Wednesday

Rather than thinking of them as symbolic elements of religions, considering figures such as Moses and Mohammed people who actually lived (thus, able to be treated with empathy and to be imitated) tempts very dangerously (and sometimes extremely tragically) some people into deludedly thinking they, too, are more than human.

October 2, 1968 Wednesday

Since remedies and cures can be discovered at any time, *terminal* is a word to use with the word *illness* only after a death and then only hypothetically.

October 6, 1968 Sunday

The idiosyncratic imaginings of a patient may be no more bizarre than conventional religious doctrines that are shared within denominations. Are minds malfunctioning in both cases?

April 20, 1969 Sunday

The tone set and reflected by the Nixon administration has brought attacks upon my practice from some in the profession who cater to wealthy white neighborhoods and focus solely on private adjustments to what I consider partially untenable social structures.

November 1, 1969 Saturday

A fair number of my patients are saying that the recent landing on that traditional symbol of lunacy, the moon, has resulted in a strain of madness that otherwise would never have appeared.

November 23, 1969 Sunday

The massive number of handguns here indicates that many of us have learned to think of our temporary allotments as more valuable than the lives of our fellows.

February 15, 1970 Sunday

Although I am still hopeful that methods of chemotherapy, used for carefully evaluated ends, will eventually justify my medical training, I now suspect I could have done as much as I have, perhaps more, had I opted for a degree in socially related psychology. Side effects of psychoactive drugs after long periods of usage can be quite ghastly.

August 6, 1970 Thursday

Some of my more socially withdrawn colleagues fatuously insist that efforts toward societal reform primarily involve simply Oedipal conflict!

Moreover, *apparently no one* in this entire global/spatial community is pointing out that true consciousness expansion should be the responsibility of teachers and artists, reporters and publishers, instead of the makers and purveyors of drugs!

September 30, 1970 Wednesday

By envisioning power in terms of the configurations usually considered appropriate for white males—many blacks and white women are unintentionally seeking to adopt the same qualities by which they have been oppressed. Hopefully, the demeaning stereotypes of self-definition men have been offered will soon be viewed as inadequate, too, so that all of us can get on with instituting ways of meeting each other with honest, open integrity and decency.

October 18, 1970 Sunday

Many people are so discouraged that they regard money, however attained, as the sole indication of success. Lives dependent on variety of purchases are not empty; but how awful that the pleasures that can be so derived are frequently thought of as the only possible ones!

January 1, 1971 Friday

I often wonder whether a stranger could recognize me from my journal and if someone who knows me well would find surprises within it. I am remembering that articles written by friends have altered my expectations and images of their authors. Certainly the styles of expression I use in communing with myself are different from those I employ in public situations; but I wonder if there is a difference in content, too. Is there sufficient harmony between what I do and what I write? I suppose we all might know each other more satisfyingly were we to display ourselves through various forms of communication.

January 4, 1971 Monday

I've just realized and must remember (especially as politicians have often denied and/or misunderstood this) that writing and talking are forms of action, of doing. So are reading and listening.

June 20, 1971 Sunday

The professional psychiatric tendency to seek transformation of the viewer rather than the viewed can be like putting a gag on a person who stands near a real fire shouting, "Fire!"—instead of our acknowledging the warning and supplying water or a blanket, etc.

July 10, 1971 Saturday

I have returned from a week of meetings in Toronto. The effects of the tensions of the past couple of years on the people in the United States are more obvious to me now in comparison with Canadian life. Our postures are far more rigid than theirs; we have come to move as if we are strung together with wire. Contrasted with ordinary Canadian vibrancy, our eyes appear ridden with anxiety, our faces wan and prematurely lined. So much is similar in Boston and Toronto that the divergencies in manner were immediately obvious.

September 26, 1971 Sunday

A trend has come into being involving a philosophy that seeks to reverse psychiatric definitions, thereby viewing patients as minority islands of sanity in the midst of cataclysmic madness. At times I have been thought to be an advocate of this approach. I am not. In contrast to many practitioners who focus on returning the patient to the state manifested before the onslaught of symptoms, I do, however, treat the struggles I encounter as indications of the need for changes both in the person and in the environment. It is not that I consider the patients saner than others, but that I regard their difficulties as potential tools for achieving more health than they have, thus far, known within and outside of themselves.

November 14, 1971 Sunday

Some people become psychiatric patients because they want to eliminate sorrow. I attempt to demonstrate to them that sorrow is a necessary part of life and that problems arise when the validity of its expression is denied.

December 7, 1971 Tuesday

Bit by bit, I have come to have what can only be called a religious faith that is gratifyingly reverential, however unable I find it to be either described or expressed by words.

March 22, 1972 Wednesday

A patient can be a representative of a malfunctioning entity. There are many variations of this theme. A family in crisis may collectively need or allow one person to express their common dilemma. A firm in conflict may attain a measure of stability by throwing one employee overboard into the lifeboat of my office. It is sometimes difficult to know where to draw the limits of my concerns, especially when large institutions are involved. On the other hand, I am certain that groups do not necessarily have equilibriums of sickness and health—certain, I mean, that when one person becomes healthy, another need neither appear nor become sick.

June 11, 1972 Sunday

Too rarely are depressive states considered in relation to the circumstances by which a person has been affected. The depression may be justified; and depression, moreover, shifts easily into being a highly constructive, gently liberating force for needed changes in oneself and one's environment.

December 10, 1972 Sunday

As a result (one of the many results) of Mao-Tse-Tung's presence with Richard Nixon in the same room (surely among the most incredible events of these times), discussions of medical techniques presently used in China are at last occurring in the United States. Many surgeons here had been as unaware of processes of acupuncture as had been the rest of us. The American Medical Association is to be faulted for its antiquated approach to dissemination of knowledge of methods different from those it endorses. In European medical journals there have for years been considerations of Chinese procedures.

Science should be an international effort, could be, probably will be; but at present it is not. We are all the losers.

March 11, 1973 Sunday

And so this near ten years of war is apparently ending. Many of us in the United States have learned to distrust the words of anyone in government. How quickly journalistic modes are transformed! Just half a year ago the wife of the democratic presidential nominee was nearly laughed off an interview stage when she suggested that the Watergate break-in was symptomatic of the Nixon Administration. Martha Mitchell, once a figure of farce, is now portrayed as a tragic prophetess, as having actually been the political prisoner of her Attorney General husband she claimed she was last summer. Meanwhile, a stunning document produced by *The New York Times* cites the violation of international codes by various Washington officials and suggests that many of them were/are war criminals.

March 25, 1973 Sunday

Effective mechanisms for the global distribution of food must be devised. The same skills presently allowing the continued production and distribution of unnecessary products and the development and maintenance of weaponry, if directed toward wiser and more humane goals, could bring about global well-being. The termination of humanity has become easier for us to contemplate than a modest state of peace.

September 24, 1973 Monday

Societal events do not occur in ten-year cycles. The journalistic penchant for reducing a decade to a few catch phrases is utterly unwarranted, blinds us to realities by comforting us with inaccuracy, and destroys any sense of the vitality that had been within the selected events it improperly appears to be analyzing. Generally it ignores all life outside the United States.

October 21, 1973 Sunday

Habitually used to distrusting any statement of the President, I could only wonder if he had hallucinated a crisis of energy. Figures estimating the future availability of raw materials, however, may justify his terminology. Much that is good will eventually come out of the necessity for more austere approaches to being alive. Perhaps soon our places of work will be conveniently closer to our homes, so that we can breathe safely again in our cities. A return to walking can only increase our health.

November 20, 1973 Tuesday

I was counting on attending a lecture by Leonard Bernstein at Harvard this evening, but the worldwide alert of our military aircraft has thrown me into a depression not even music could get me out of. The resignation of the Vice President and the continued investigation of the President and his staff are minimally important in comparison with what we really need: a thorough examination of these many years of war and racism—an examination that would indict and, thus, potentially improve many of us. We require a fundamental social overhaul and are getting minor surgery.

December 2, 1973 Sunday

Horrible as both local police forces and federal surveillance agencies can sometimes be (they are, after all, paramilitary, which means they at times bring to civilian lives some of the most ghastly characteristics of war), neighborhood civic groups meant peacefully to fight crime can be as awful, particularly when, with the support of their leaders, they descend into being linkages for spreading gossip and savage rumors throughout whole cities.

December 7, 1973 Friday

Already it is difficult to remember that references to China were largely taboo within the United States for most of the past twenty-five years. Attitudes enforcing this aspect of the unspoken are rapidly disappearing. In fact, we are beginning to speak of the Chinese so facilely that it appears there had never been a wall of silence.

December 10, 1973 Monday

Teachers and textbooks too often neglect to mention that the living people being studied—in whatever field—frequently are unaware of each other's work in progress and may, indeed, be entirely unacquainted with one another.

December 16, 1973 Sunday

Have I waited too long?

Certainly I've been involved in an intentional putting-off. I feel age weighing upon me, and I am no longer young.

I needed these many years to grapple with questions that have plagued me.

It has been a long, necessary process of determining and creating my own nature.

I am ready now.

But will someone else be?

December 25, 1973 Tuesday

Instead of saying, "I am amazed," it has become common for one to say, "I don't believe it."

December 30, 1973 Sunday

The less stress we make for each other, the better off we all are.

February 2, 1974 Saturday

Assisted suicides are *especially* dangerous with *omnicide* said to be possible. For people in life-threatening states due either to accidents, illnesses, and/or victimizations, one thing that exists, instead of suicide, is the chance to cooperate with scientifically ethical researchers of their malady at whatever level of its development—researchers, who *may* maintain and increase the healths of *all of us*, including those on whom the research is performed, by means of newly discovered knowledge. Knowledge of this chance must be brought to those participating in some kinds of death-watches (both brief and prolonged)—deathwatches that are not just highly irrational, however socially approved, but wasteful of some of our best energies. Trying to find that which is ecologically beneficial by using methods that are at least civil—that's what research can and should be. And *truly is* for some people. Fortunately.

February 4, 1974 Monday
Only the bombed dead knew what they suffered in all those sudden and brief last moments amid…many wars.

November 5, 1974 Tuesday
Although Oliver Wendell Holmes, Jr. may have been wrong in objecting to pacifism, he was correct about the wrongness of falsely yelling "fire" in crowded theaters, including, as the life of Vivien Leigh may have made apparent, both on stages and through screens, as well as via any other media.

November 6, 1974 Wednesday
Two people are enough to make a war. Sometimes even one person is enough, unfortunately.

February 23, 1975 Sunday
Requirements on my time have made me decide this will be my last entry, at least for awhile, of what began to be externalized nearly thirty years ago! Transcribing from audio recordings is not something I've wanted to take the time to do since making first steps toward doing so in 1966. Those pages were discarded.

I'll let these entries, then, be reminders of…how time flies. From now on, I'll be recording these only for…ears. Probably.

3 Soul-searchings

1

I had no choice but to lie, thought Mrs. Tane, as she replaced the telephone receiver and stared at the mail she had just finished assuring her husband had not yet been delivered.

Every weekday morning Mr. Tane would phone her at precisely ten o'clock; and they would speak for a few minutes about household concerns—what groceries he should purchase, whether the plumber or the electrician or the gardener had arrived, whether the air conditioning or the heating was working properly, when to plan on having dinner. Seldom did the telephone ring at any other time during the day. If it did, she could depend on the call being from a teenager associated with one of several charitable organizations that regularly collected discards, or from a campaign worker seeking support for a local candidate, or from a solicitor offering national magazine subscriptions at a discount; and she long ago had devised conversational routines that reliably enabled her always to agree to place something in the driveway for each of the charities, always to insist that politics was a private matter, and always to ask the solicitors, after listening to them recite their standard speeches, if they knew of any groups willing to accept the magazines accumulating in her basement.

Letters obligating replies from Mrs. Tane had, however, been even less
frequent through the twenty-three years of her married life than telephone
calls; and she had been looking forward to learning how to deal with
them, when two months earlier at the Denver airport on the hot, humid
morning of the day he had left Colorado in order to begin his freshman
year at Yale, her son, Jack—the Tanes' only child, had offhandedly informed
her of his decision that the first and last pages of all his letters home would
be written for both parents, but that the intervening pages would contain
information potentially annoying to his father and would, therefore, be
composed for her certainly initial and possibly sole perusal. Without time
for discussion, she reluctantly had promised to decide how much of each
letter to give her husband and to inform Jack of her decisions.

As she studied the New Haven postmark on the unopened envelope in
front of her, her throat constricted; and she got up from her kitchen chair,
went to the recreation room stereo, put the soundtrack recording from
Raintree County on the spindle, raised the volume, and returned to the
kitchen. There she lowered an outside shade by adjusting a handle adjacent
to a window above a spacious sink.

Raintree County, a rambling epic seemingly set in the mid-nineteenth
century, had been her favorite motion picture since its first release in 1957.
She had followed its path from a Denver theater to a network television
showing to a late evening local airing to an afternoon version to Saturday
morning fragments; and every week, already a virtual part of a market for
the video cassette and digital-video disk she yet had no idea would ever be
available, she would check the newspaper entertainment listings for yet
another video rerun. Whenever she watched the film, she became so
absorbed in the mysteries of a devastating fire on a plantation of the
United States that she could never remember afterwards if the story had
contained a definite explanation of the title. She was uncertain whether
there actually were raintrees, knew only that golden leaves had somehow
been involved in the trials and yearnings of the characters, and often
wondered, especially when listening to the music that had accompanied

the film, if an aspen seed had at some point in the distant past miraculously found its way from the Colorado Territory to the foreign soil of
Indiana, sprouted, and subsequently been woven into legend.

Confident she would not be hearing from her husband again until
dinnertime, Mrs. Tane considered donning a suit, driving to a restaurant,
and taking the letter with her. Having fixed enough meals over the past
quarter-century to have lost much of the capacity to enjoy her own preparations, someone else's cooking was more important to her than it was
possible for her to convey to her family; and the last two months had
allowed her at last secretly to venture out of the house for occasional
lunches. Recalling, however, that she once again would have to take the
hour's trip to Denver, since she felt it would not be practicable to be seen
eating alone at the one restaurant in town, and apprehending that she
might need the travel time for deciding what course to follow with the
apparent majority of her son's words, she looked again at the thick envelope
and opened it, thinking, I must see about getting a library card soon.

November 2, 1962

Dear Mother and Dad,

Sorry it took me two months to manage to write. I'm glad you
are well. I heard on the radio about your blizzard and hope this
letter won't be delayed by highway problems.

Thank you for all of your questions. I'll try to answer as many
as I can. They are helpful to me in putting together the disorders
of school.

Yes, I do wonder if I made the right decision. I did not realize
how confused I would be by the entirely unfamiliar campus. A
lot of the problems would have been the same at the University
of Colorado, but at least I knew my way around Boulder and
also could have gotten to the country easily, especially for skiing.

I apologize again for changing my mind and leaving my car with you, but I was more scared of driving two thousand miles by myself than I'd expected to be. No, I don't need anything much from the stuff I'd intended to bring in it; but I would really appreciate my skis, so please send them by whatever means is convenient and let me know when and how to expect them.

One of the things that's going on as I think about writing you is that my mind can slip and let me ease up on worrying about grammar like I've had to do while writing course papers. Even exams. I have had three of them so far, and there isn't time for me to put in what I want to like I usually can with a paper. Outlines aren't acceptable. Even if they were I couldn't make one in only a few minutes without crossing out a lot.

Oh, well, I am passing, but just barely. Quite a change. One I may have to get used to. It feels strange to be writing instead of hearing you answer over dinner. Please, though, let me know if I'm not getting through on anything. Also, can you read my handwriting okay?

The first page ended here, and Mrs. Tane turned quickly to the last one:

Almost always when I say I'm from Colorado, I get asked about agriculture; people are amazed when I tell them I've not been living on a farm. The West looks newer to me now; I've started to realize how much longer New England has been inhabited and how different from home the communities are here due to the depth of their roots.

There are buildings on the campus that were put up a hundred years before anything was in Colorado except tents. Writing of buildings, you know my long-standing difficulties with maps. After two weeks of following a fifteen-minute route I'd marked out to one of my classes, I discovered (by looking up from my map) that the building is right behind the one I live in, so that if I go out another door I can get to the class in a couple of seconds.

I didn't think at all about how I'd get laundry done. Some of the scholarship students take care of the bedding changes and cleaning my room, but I've got to do everything else. There are washers and dryers in the basement; but, Mother, could you please send me some instructions about what kind of soap to use and how to separate my things, whatever else I should know? Then I'll take shirts to the cleaners for ironing. It sure is more work than I knew, and I'd appreciate any tips to make it easier.

I must leave off and get busy studying.

Your son,
Jack

PS I got my haircut differently today and am parting it on the other side.

This would do: Mr. Tane would be amused and would make arrangements from work to have the skis shipped to New Haven; no mediation between her husband and son would be necessary. With the rest of the day to determine how to handle the inside portion of the letter, Mrs. Tane poured a glass of milk, fixed two pieces of buttered toast, and ate, while continuing to read:

I've got a list of things I want to let you know about and am going to try to describe what's been going on outside and inside myself.

First off I can tell you that you must get prepared for shiftings in how I am, since course work has already turned some of my ideas around and caused me to think about issues I hadn't suspected existed. Like take the last paragraph where it says "inside and outside myself." My philosophy course has upset my whole sense about what is real. Since my awareness of experiences takes place inside me, how can I know what exists outside?

You ask me to describe Connecticut, but I think I'd better put that off until I've seen more. I can say this much, though: people move very differently than they do at home, tenser here, sort of, tighter; it's as if the space I'm used to walking in has to shrink because there are so many more people put together in what for me are such small areas. Even Denver from here seems as if it has more room. I notice myself having to I don't know what exactly, modify, I guess, my sense of what is mine, around me, sort of, even though it isn't mine.

I'm glad I left the car because streets are laid out way more complicatedly than I'm used to. I really don't have cause to leave the campus area especially often, anyway. The altitude is also affecting these changes in my movements, since my breathing reflexes are altering due to more oxygen at this level. The air is very polluted, although it's not as awful as in Denver. Even so, my eyes are often red and I've had to get used to feeling like I have a continual, minor cold.

No, I haven't been to New York City yet. But I did get to Boston, and I want to explain what happened there, because nothing has ever affected me so much. I'm starting to shake right now just thinking about what we all went through ten days ago.

Early the morning after the President's speech I was sitting alone on the campus feeling pretty bad. I couldn't understand what was happening, still can't really, although I'm glad the crisis is apparently over, so that we can rest easier and work better, maybe. I never really thought about politics much before; I guess *politics* is the right word. Although I knew about all the weaponry that has been under construction since I was born, it didn't seem real until that morning when I had to sit there and—I am scarcely able to write this and the truth is it makes me feel ashamed to be human to do so—but—sit there and think about the possible end of the earth. No people have had to face anything so dreadful. There's no help I can find in history; no examples have been set; our actions are of a new kind.

It seems to me I am surrounded by the greatest madness or the worst evil or both that has ever been. It's not like facing an earlier war when I would've had to consider the possibility of just my own death. That I'm part of all this is—I don't know—not manageable, I guess.

I'm sure you'll disagree with what follows, but I don't think what's called "the Free World" can be worth what we're doing. Nothing could be. No way of life could be good and necessary enough to require protection with such savage possibilities. I find myself unable to grasp what this "vast struggle" is about.

People need food and shelter so they can spend time with all the activities that can result in a humane civilization of which everyone on earth can partake. I don't see why all sides can't understand that. There's nothing I can do except go on and continue to feel helpless for seven more years. With a law degree, perhaps I can better this situation somehow. Everything indicates that our destructive capacities are going to get greater, although I do not see how life can get worse than it was ten days ago unless those weapons are used. Such times are beyond all reason and decency.

I know you'll think my attitude is a result of the Yale influences, but you're wrong as I'm sure I would have felt the same at Boulder. I feel like we're victims of our own government.

Anyway—a boy (am I supposed to call myself "a young man" now?) who is in one of my classes and who is from a suburb of Boston asked me that morning if I wanted to take off and go to his place until the missile crisis got resolved. His name is C. J.

Rongo. He pronounces the initials as if they are his first name and in such a way that one realizes one shouldn't ask what they stand for. His father is dead. He and his mother have an apartment. It's weird to say, but I never thought of people as living in apartments before. I've known they do, of course. But with Dad doing the contracting for so much of the neighborhood, all I've ever experienced are people who live in houses. This is something that's happening often here. Encountering things I haven't completely known have existed because I haven't been in the presence of them before. The bus trip was about four hours long. I had my first clams. From Boston we took a couple of subways and buses out to Walden Pond where we spent the rest of the afternoon. We didn't really talk much. The time was so tense, but we figured that if the world was going to blow up, we might as well be at Walden Pond trying to figure out why.

Sitting there waiting to become a possible statistic on a world-wide casualty list, knowing that the Cuban blockade was in effect with Soviet ships heading toward it, gave me awful stomach wrenchings I'm still having most every day.

I haven't even had much of a chance to live yet, and every second might be our last one.

Having read the entire letter, Mrs. Tane put it on the kitchen table, went again to the phonograph, turned over the recording, and manipulated the controls so that the speakers in her bedroom would function. Breathing with difficulty and sweating, she then walked along the hallway to her room, entered it, lay down on her bed, gripped a cotton coverlet about her chin, and proceeded, as occasionally she recently had been allowing herself to do, to marvel at the unfairness that seemed to be coiled within the core of her life, marvel at the voluted fabric of processes whereby her son's eyes, which had gazed first at her, his sounds, which she had comforted and transformed into a sharable consciousness, his fingers, which had grappled at her breasts—marvel that all these elements and many other comparable ones had come to be united in a body that had grown more than a foot beyond her own height and expressed a personality necessarily unaware of nearly everything she had done to create it.

When the music ended, she sorted the lines of her face into an expression of polite interest she had habitually worn for the times of discussing Jack's schoolwork with him. Trying to frame a response to his letter, she pondered what he had written about his philosophy course. Imagining him referring to his own inside while sitting in a college dormitory, she began to remember the months before his birth; and her fingers stabbed the air with a forgotten potential for harshness.

"How dare he!" she said aloud.

After brushing with sullen strokes her auburn curls, she walked back down the hallway to the recreation room and, wondering whether to suggest the purchase of an additional mechanism that would automatically turn off the phonograph, picked up a dustcloth from where she had placed it when the mail had arrived. Languorously she drifted into the parlor.

Feeling renewed relief at what she knew would be Mr. Tane's reaction to the abridged letter, she paused and smiled at an upright piano her paternal grandparents had carted across the prairie in a covered wagon. The girl she had been had played the heirloom instrument well and frequently in the Denver home of her parents. She had learned from its keys how much work could be necessary to produce the appearances of ease and grace, how much effort had to be disguised in order to inspire an air of courtliness in others; and it had continually reminded her, though she had seldom played it for more than twenty years, that a properly functioning household must appear to have maintained itself, that hints of weariness, of carelessness, or of struggle must not be discernible.

During the first months of her marriage, while she had created an atmosphere of impending success and her husband had acquired contacts within the construction industry throughout a three-county area, the piano had been not only a stolid monument to genteel ghosts, but also a beckoning guidepost to the future. It had been the most prominent possession in their rented farmhouse when in 1948 Mr. Tane had learned of the scheduled incorporation of a new town near Denver, a town that was to be composed primarily of homes and that would, thus, be dependent upon nearby larger communities for the majority of its goods and services. Inspired, eager, and resolutely determined to more than match at last the substantial wealth his wife's father had accumulated manufacturing and distributing formal clothing, Mr. Tane had not waited to evaluate the opportunity, but instead had seized it immediately, established himself as the sole contractor for the novel, self-governing community, and moved his family into one of the first houses that subsequently had been constructed there—a house he had intended to use as a model and a stimulant for the developmental processes he would oversee.

Still smiling, Mrs. Tane opened the piano bench and slowly leafed through the music it contained, humming portions of songs she had learned in her early twenties: *Swinging Along with Lindy, White House Is the Light House of the World, You'll Be Welcome as the Flowers in Maytime.* She had often given impromptu concerts for her parents in the midst of evenings that also had included reading aloud, card games, and elegantly listless conversations. Usually well-dressed as a girl, she had been more luxuriously attired during those evenings at home than during her hours at school; and she habitually still changed her clothing before the late afternoon return of her husband. Much of the day she was unaccustomed to being seen by anyone, and her clothes for those solitary hours included some of the youthful dresses she knew Mr. Tane assumed had long ago been discarded.

Intent on testing her coordinations, she sat down on the piano bench, and with one finger picked out the melody to *Till We Meet Again*, a song her parents had frequently requested. Attempting to accompany herself by adding scattered chords to her series of single notes, she sang:

"There's a song in the land of the lily—
Each sweetheart has heard with a sigh
Over high garden walls
This sweet echo falls
So wait
And pray each night for me."

In her childhood years she had thought the florid illustrations on the covers of her mother's sheet music to be quaintly drawn; but now the faces and clothes depicted on her own music blended in smoothly with the others, so accustomed had she become to the broken lines, the obliquities, and the complex juxtapositions that characterized images in the current magazines and newspapers, both of which appeared in daily abundance on her front doorstep.

Doubting that she would have enough confidence ever to play again, even with the renewed practice she had been counting on, telling herself with sadness that those who had found in her their single source of music were gone and that one now could easily listen again and again to sounds produced with a skill surpassing any she could ever have expected to acquire, she lowered the keyboard shield, walked to the kitchen, picked up her son's letter, and reread it.

2

Although he had slept less than an hour, Jack opened his eyes. Finding himself lying fully dressed on a bare mattress, he relaxed his fists and searched unsuccessfully for the familiar trappings of his Colorado home. Startled, disoriented, he quickly sat up, gnashing the bedsprings. Gradually realizing where he was, he rose and, shivering, paced through the early morning darkness of his musty room.

'Too soon for breakfast, but I can't study now. Got to get outside. Got to get air.'

Skittishly he slid his arms into a blue, waterproof parka, stole through the door, and stood for a moment by the ivy-covered front entrance to his dormitory. His socks felt wet and greasy; and he noticed in the shrouded sunlight that his thick-soled, mountaineering boots were loose. After tightening and knotting the laces, he sank his hands into his rear pants pockets and began to stroll glumly along an involuted, cobblestone path.

'The difference between the air of home and here is like I'm learning to dive when all I've ever done is wade. Yeah, but my classes are making me wonder if anywhere there's ever been water!'

Amidst the secluded ambiance of a residential college campus, it is common for a student to experience the disquieting sensation of being hedged within a capriciously administered limbo wherein numerous, hitherto taken-for-granted rights and responsibilities appear either to have been nebulously redefined or to have mysteriously disappeared. The salient characteristic of a university environment, moreover, is apt to be a precarious, fastidiously cultivated indeterminacy, which serves to encourage the harmonious intermingling of numerous, highly varied, specialized approaches to departmentalized spectrums of scholarship. Thus, it was not unusual for Jack, having lived in New Haven but six weeks, already to be observing, as he had been doing for the past two days, that his customary decision-making processes were steadily being tempered by the requisite uncertainties of a skepticism that threatened to become routine.

Endeavoring to defeat a lingering fatigue by clumsily shaking his head from side to side, he turned onto a dirt path that led to a newly constructed rare books library building. Upon reaching what he had been informed was an in-process sculptural garden, he stopped, sat down on one of the enclosing walls, and pondered what for weeks had continued to look to him like the foundation for a large house incomprehensibly enclosing huge chunks of haphazardly positioned, unpolished stone.

'I will not ever call that "sculpture." Yes, I will. Maybe. If I can understand. But I do not know what it is meant for. I do not know how to ask without being laughed at.

'The walls of that library, they say, are marble so thin, a quarter inch, they let in sunlight as if the whole building were made of translucent glass.... I wonder whether something from electric lights inside comes out here in the same way. And what happens to all the shadows?

'Someday I'll go in there and see.

'See through the sunlight.

'Through the marble.'

A long, carefully trained, sandy lock, its wave belying the time it had taken for him to achieve its casual effect, swept over Jack's forehead. His face was pudgy; his cheekbones, elongated; his eyebrows, black and heavy. His skin was smooth, tanned, and freckle-browned.

U-2 planes flying where we said they weren't, Jack thought. 'Reactors built where they said they wouldn't have any. Summit conferences. Missile gaps. Racing to the moon. Self-evident. Materialism. Bases in Cuba. Bases in Turkey. Stars and sickles. Pumpkin papers and points of order. Espionage and diplomats. Peace Corps and quarantines. Ninety ships. "We will bury you." Better dead than red. Red than dead. "Let the word go forth." Air strikes and blockades.

'Ninety ships.

'"Bear any burden."

'Protect the ideas, yeah, but the ideas you're born into mostly make you what you are.

'So why can't they be ideas that don't need to have mushroom clouds ahead of them?

'Before, they could not face what they were doing.

'This will show them.

'If we get through it, all over the earth, they will start to dismantle the weapons. They'll have to. There's no other way we can go on.'

Finally convinced that his shadow was going to fail to indicate his presence behind Jack, C. J., after several minutes of having stood in motionless silence, quietly, but distinctly, said, "Not fair."

Immediately identifying a Boston accent, Jack looked over his shoulder, examined C. J.'s bridled, angular form, and said, "I don't know if I heard you right."

Frowning, C. J. put a finger in his mouth, glanced upward, waited half a minute, pointed to the sky, and said, "Heavy wind later."

"Is that what you meant at first? The weather?"

"They going to end us?"

"I don't know. Maybe. Which side?"

"Not you and me," C. J. replied, shrugging and sitting down on the wall. His hair was as short as it had been most of his life; but he had grown a scraggly beard he had learned to stroke repeatedly with both hands, intending thereby to disguise the awkwardness of his speech and his recurrent, long silences. "Talk more. You? Usually."

"I don't know. I was thinking. You're right. I guess I do talk quite a bit. How'd you know that?"

"Section. History."

"That's a good course. It seems to be, anyway. I'm sorry. I can't remember you. What's your name?"

"C. J. Rongo...Do you think the world will end today?"

"Don't think so."

"Wasn't asking you."

"Who were you asking?"

"Not."

"But you asked."

"The air."

"Air doesn't hear English."

"God."

"I don't know if God cares much about English," Jack said musingly. "Sometimes it seems like people who use it don't pay much attention to it, so why should God?"

"…Winds answer," said C. J., smiling.

"What'd you say?"

"Didn't."

"My name is…I mean, I'm Jack Tane."

"Know that."

"You know everyone's name in that section already?"

"Probably."

"I've got to quit talking so much. I must be missing a lot that's right in front of me."

"No!" said C. J., curling his thin shoulders forward and kicking the wall with his dangling heels.

"I guess I think out loud. I don't know what I'm going to say very often. Sometimes it's almost like hearing someone else. But if my mouth is open, there's no way I can quit talking and decide where I mean to get to. So I just go on…And after while I get there."

"You talk fine," said C. J. He scraped his two front teeth back and forth across his lower lip.

"It's so different here from where I grew up," Jack said quietly. "Colorado."

"I been there."

"I live close to Denver. Lived."

"More up than me."

"North?"

"Higher, too."

"When was that?"

"Last year sometime. I don't know. Winter."

"What were you doing?"

"Looking."

"You traveled for a year after high school or prep school or whatever?"

"Some…Let's go to Boston."

"When?"

"Now."

"I don't have a car. Besides it's Tuesday."

"Missiles."

"Yeah, you're right," Jack said slowly. "I'd forgotten…It's not going to be an ordinary day…The blockade was mostly all I could think about alone…but…you came over…and I forgot."

"Bus."

"I hardly slept at all."

"Sleep on the bus."

"What would we do in Boston?"

"My mother's there."

"How long could we stay?"

"Tonight."

"What did you say your name is?"

"C. J."

"All right, yes," said Jack decisively. "Let's go."

"Station. Seven-fifteen."

"I don't know where it is."

"Here. Fifteen minutes."

"When will we get to Boston?"

"End of morning."

"Here, then, fifteen minutes," said Jack, jumping to the ground. Rummaging in his pockets for a ballpoint pen and trying to remember how much was left of his allowance, he hurried back along the path to his dormitory.

C. J., meanwhile, scrambled off the wall and in a series of rigidly defined, darting movements, sprinted a direct line across the dry, crumpled grass.

Knowing how unending would come to seem the snow that soon would be arriving, he had for the past month intentionally left the many sidewalks and the paths of the campus unused.

3

"High Street," said Jack, gathering a sweater and a book together under one arm and following C. J. into the bus terminal. "This's the street the Yale Library's on. You'd think they'd change names when they go through the campus. Everything else gets so different. I don't know where I am half the time. I haven't had a chance to see much of New Haven. Except once I hiked over to the harbor. I couldn't exactly understand where I was supposed to be, but no one stopped me. It was late; and I went back into town along the railroad tracks, at least I hoped it was back, crossing through so many barriers to where the track divides, before I could find Elm or that avenue, whatever it is, where Elm is called something else. I can't get used yet to one street becoming another without even a turnoff."

Nodding, C. J. took a wadded ten-dollar bill from a rear pocket of his denims, handed it to Jack, brusquely said, "Round trip," then bent over two newspaper vending machines and scanned the front pages through the glass. The headlines were the largest he had ever seen.

"We've got almost half an hour," said Jack, joining C. J. and giving him a ticket. "I'm going to get some breakfast. You want anything?"

"No," C. J. replied, biting his lower lip and slinking into a waiting room seat equipped with a small, coin-operated television screen. As he watched Jack amble to the station coffee shop, he stretched out his legs on a backpack he had brought with him, crooked his shoulders forward, and buckled his hands about his neck:

'Will-uh-wish-uh-will-uh-don't. Splatter springs and the dorey. Send them off. They explode in the air, but the falling moves faster than the sound. Or is it the changing that falls?...If there's anyplace safe to go, it must be far; and no one would tell us where, because most of us would have gone to it by now. Bombs get bigger and bigger, and people do nothing at all. So that if the ending isn't today, it will be soon; and it's no good to ask why, because they don't know and wouldn't tell the truth, anyway. The most we ever get is that every few years there's a more powerful one, but they never say why unless it's to stop the others from making them. Except what does it matter? It was enough the beginning. So what that Russia got them? Because it was already over. Only question was when. Accident could do it, too...

'Maybe there's a place, a cave, maybe, deep, away, or under a sea, where they'll get off to. Kennedy and Khruschev in the same one even. He might have made the speech from there last night. Had a double in the White House. Sent out tapes to make it seem like they aren't in hiding. So after the fire has burned out and the ashes have settled and the clouds gone away and the sun can be seen again, a few of them could start it all over. Maybe it happened like that lots of years ago. Maybe more than once.'

Yawning and scowling, he unbuttoned his jacket, more durable than the ever larger sizes of evanescence that had accompanied his boyhood growth. Then leisurely he ran a hand through his hair, downturned his eyes, leaned back, and fixed his gaze on the knees of his faded and wrinkled trousers.

4

"I remember," said Jack, taking a seat next to C. J., who was fiddling with the dials adjacent to the vacant screen in front of him, "when I was six, or maybe seven, I'm not sure which, but then...They let us off from school, so we could see the test, it was in the morning, before hardly anything was videotaped, hydrogen, I think it was, from Nevada, or maybe before hydrogen, I can't remember what they said it was, but there was no sound, only the gray flat of the land, desert, and the white, with a little hill behind it, all white, the sky, and the cloud rising up, gray, turning black, and the announcer shouting, 'Mushroom.' The camera rose, too, focusing on the top of the cloud, spreading out, and in school later, we all, in the auditorium, they told us we wouldn't have to worry again. Because the test had shown everyone how strong we were."

"I watched," C. J. said. "Here it was on in the afternoon."

"Once, third grade, I think, they interrupted a program and said that Stalin had died. I didn't know who he had been; but it was almost like the devil had given up or something, the way they said his name; and I thought they'd been somehow the same, he and the devil, like on the radio if they'd had a funeral for an imaginary character in a series, Baby Snooks, the last program, only it'd been who'd played the part had died."

"I listened...."

"And then, after that actress was dead, I couldn't remember anymore what the stories had been," Jack continued. "Just that I'd liked them. Baby Snooks, I mean. After awhile I got to expect the same programs being on television that had been on radio. I'd get excited every time to see if the people'd look like their voices, and they never would, so I'd blame them at first, but pretty soon I'd decide it had been me who had been wrong about the way I'd been imagining them, and later on I'd forget I'd not always seen them. Every time they got bodies, it was as different as if they'd died..."

Gliding the tops of his thumbs down his cheeks, C. J., though unmistakably having been listening to Jack, abruptly and urgently said, "Is. A question. A statement?"

"What'd you...? Would you repeat that?"

"Can a question be a statement?"

"That's at least two separate things you want to know," said Jack. He thrust his head forward so that his lock would quickly rise and idly fall back to its assigned place. "Give me awhile to think."

"What you think, tell me," said C. J. He clasped the television set, pulled himself up out of the chair, strapped his backpack over his shoulders, walked to the newspaper machine, put in a coin, and opened one of the doors. Holding a front page against his chin, so that his trunk and limbs were aligned with a huge picture of President Kennedy's face, he said loudly, "I can do for the it that's the country without anybody inside left alive to ask."

Laughing scornfully, he folded the newspaper in half and tossed it onto the arm of the chair he had been sitting in.

"Let's go," he said.

"Yeah, it's time," Jack replied. Wearily he stumbled to his feet. "Why'd you do that?" he asked, as he trailed C. J. to the embarkation platform. "Leave the newspaper there, I mean."

"Ones for to get along without money," C. J. replied, thinking, 'Too soon for a kite. He has to be ready. I'll show him the winds today.'

5

An ebony sky above Boston rolled out from a narrow, central strip of bronze like a fat giant's belly oozing from above and beneath a navel-lined belt. The city sidewalks were awash with people streaming away from offices and into restaurants. The cramped crowds were larger than any Jack had thought possible; and his anticipations were clashing so severely with what he was seeing that, as he struggled to achieve a reconciliation, his stomach contracted like an accordion, impelling him to apprehend with chagrin that he had vaguely expected to have been transported to the mid-nineteenth century where top hats would be gallantly lifted to reveal monocled eyes staring sedately at demure, ruffled parasols carried above hooped skirts and lace by white-gloved hands, where hansom cabs would be drawn by horses over red-brick roadways or tied to hitching posts outside inns equipped with sawdust floors, pewter teapots, and perpetually polite conversations. Being familiar only with thoroughfares laid out perpendicularly to each other in grids, he could acquire no sense of direction, as he and C. J. wove past a tangle of boulevards and avenues to Tremont Street where traffic thinned and drivers honked their ways to major arteries rather than to parking spaces.

"Seafood?" C. J. asked, prepossessively casting an upturned hand toward the sidewalk entrance of an unimposing cafe.

"I haven't ever had any," Jack said. He gripped the cafe door unsteadily. "I'll try some, though. What's good?"

"Everything," said C. J. Grinning, he sidled to an order window and snapped his fingers twice at a harried crone who from the kitchen beamed with crimson-faced majesty; her neck had been bent forward so many years that the curve of her back seemed higher than her shoulders.

Habitually reading through an overhead menu in order to locate the prices of tacos, burritos, enchiladas and tostadas, Jack winced in recognition of his chronic failure at geographical adjustment. "I'm staying with you tonight, so I'll pay for this," he said, edging past C. J. to the cash register counter.

"The couch's comfortable," said C. J.

6

"This is Boston Common? Really?"

"It's just a park."

"Yeah, but it's Boston Common."

"So what?"

"I don't know. I guess it's that...I don't know, but it feels for me like how it must be to land in Paris and see the Eiffel Tower."

"We can eat here."

"What'd you get?"

"Clams. Frappes."

"What's a frappe, then?"

"Milk shake."

"But milk shakes were on the menu."

"No ice cream."

"Milk shakes here just have milk and syrup?"

"Usually."

"Is that only in Boston?"

"Lots of other places."

"Nowhere I've been."

"East Coast, mostly," said C. J. "Want to sit on the ground?—or on a bench?"

"Ground."

"It's California, too. Frappes."

"Funny how things like that get to hinge on state lines."

"Yeah," agreed C. J., upturning his eyes and kneeling. "Dinners depend on maps..."

"There's so many things I know about that have happened in the Common," Jack, now thoroughly alert, explained with a trace of defensive pride, as he watched C. J. arrange on the grass between them a pint carton of fried clams, a bowl of tartar sauce, two-dozen steamed littleneck clams, a dozen freshly opened, chilled cherrystone clams, a mug of melted butter, and two plastic-covered paper cups. "So many famous people. I've read about them walking here, what they've said, it's that they've always moved in my head before; and now I'm here, so I can almost see them, where they were."

"Once," said C. J., dipping a clam into the melted butter, "I saw a billboard sign being put up." He pointed to a spot on Boylston Street dozens of stories above the Colonial Theater. "Way up there. They were painting it."

"You mean the words," said Jack. Warily he bit into a fried clam he had chosen because it resembled a shoestring potato.

"The picture they were painting, too."

"I always thought they pasted them on."

"So did I. They painted that one, though."

"What was it advertising?"

"Some movie," C. J. replied, adding, "Don't eat those if you want to buy a sandwich or…"

"No, I'm fine," Jack interrupted, smiling wanly, as he piled tartar sauce on a cherrystone clam. "I've got to get used to them, is all."

"Want to go anywhere this afternoon?"

"Yeah, sort of."

"The ocean?"

"No, I…I was wondering…I was wondering if you know how to get to Walden Pond."

"Far," C. J. answered. He made a shoulder to shoulder arc with his chin.

"I've always wanted to see it. Do you think we'd have enough time to spend a couple of hours there? The truth is, I don't know if I'll be back here soon, ever, I mean. The way school is going, the way I'm going, I guess I should say, I feel like I maybe might get expelled next January. I really do. So that's why I'd like to go there, if we could. Then I'll be sure I've been."

Experimentally C. J. dipped a fried clam into the melted butter instead of the tartar sauce and eyed the mug patiently as part of the crusted coating broke away from the clam's stomach, floated, bobbed, and sank. "Like I always wanted to go to the Grand Canyon," he said. "Yes. To Walden Pond!"

7

After debarking from a bus on a sumac-bordered highway, the two of them walked such a long while that Jack started to wonder whether C. J., half a step ahead of him, knew where he was going; but he followed complacently, amazed there was so much open country only a few miles from the city, for the view from his flight had caused him to conceive of the East Coast as an immense expanse of unrelieved population. When at last they were directed off the highway by a small wooden sign, he felt a surge of excitement course upward from his stomach; and when he was able to see the pond itself, he grew ecstatic. Having feared that the legendary sanctuary had been transformed into a heavily commercialized tourist vulgarity, he was relieved and inspirited to find the rustic terrain as tranquil as he had envisioned it while reading Thoreau.

Maniacally he ran to the water, pitching his sweater and book behind him, while C. J. took off his backpack and, openmouthed, peered at the sky. Liberated, unspeaking, they both soon began to race along the gently sloped shore, leaping over rocks and tiny inlets and finally flinging themselves headlong, breathless, onto a patch of purslane and white mulberry.

"I keep remembering the smell of burning leaves…" said Jack, as soon as he could breathe normally. "That was always my favorite part of fall, but we got an ordinance last year outlawing fires inside the town limits."

Without replying, C. J. stood, chased a toad into a snarled nest of cattails, straddled a log, and immediately began to skip stones over the even, luminous surface of the gelid pond, moving his lips as, restive and withdrawn, he silently counted the intersecting ripples momentarily defining the multiarched paths of his tosses.

Wandering off alone, Jack traced his way back to his and C. J.'s things, collected together a quiltlike pile of dead weeds, and lay down upon it. Suddenly aware of the late afternoon chill, he sat up, groped into his sweater, shaded his eyes with one hand, put his other hand funnel-like to his mouth, and called out to C. J., "We're still here"

"So what?" C. J. shouted back.

"I've got to tell you something," Jack hollered.

Waving as if he were flagging down a train, C. J. whistled, and, barefoot, his tennis shoes hanging over his shoulders, his socks gloving his hands, dawdled back around the water.

"I get what you were wanting to know," said Jack. "I think I can answer it partly now."

"Partly's better'n what I've got," said C. J. "Go ahead."

"There's more to say than I'm sure of…It's that a question can imply…I mean, it depends on what you're doing when you ask. Or who you're with. Something can seem like it's a question, but what's really going on is that more than one thing is involved. Like someone could ask, 'Do you think it will rain?' But what they're driving at might be, 'I'm laying the groundwork for telling you something later on.' And something might be said like a question but really be kind of an assault. Draft boards and people at military recruitment offices must talk like that a lot of times. Even some examining boards for doctorates and groups that give medical certifications probably do…. You learn those things without looking at them much. I did, anyway. They all work on kind of an agreement that something different is meant from what's being said. Questions…they have to be answered as if they're just questions, and whatever is being told has to be got to sort of roundabout. Whatever is being stated. Do you see what I mean?"

"Yes, but…I wish it all could be clear. Or nothing. Saying what's said without having said something else…. Some lectures, like, I don't think the words fit anything, except into themselves."

"Yeah, that's how it gets to seem. I've been assuming it must be me, though. School feels pointless lots of times. I cannot, them standing up there, today, lecturing, it's even worse, them, than other people, going on like normal. Because they're supposed to…"

"Understand," said C. J. As he completed Jack's thought, he circled his hands inclusively on a line parallel to the reddening horizon.

"Yes," said Jack, "and *fix things* ." He sighed, rubbed his stomach, and cautiously asked, "Where…Where is your father?"

Holding out his left arm, C. J. straightened his elbow, tilted his palm toward the earth, and then slowly touched three fingers of his right hand to his chest.

Having instantly grasped C. J. had mimed that during his third year his father had died, Jack said, "We've got to find better ways of being adults than they did."

"If we have any time," C. J. added. Abstractedly he flung a handful of pebbles into the pond.

Then he pointed both his forefingers at the sky.

8

Black clouds were layered upon each other in contiguous, steplike rows. On the plains to the east they would have been accompanied by marrow-smiting cold wind, an icy rain, or hail; but in the mountain valley they trapped a dense, stale warmth within a peaked cup about the town.

Having been unaware, prior to reading her son's letter, of most of the publicly available details pertaining to the Cuban missile crisis, Mrs. Tane had spent the afternoon in her husband's room, leafing through his weekly news magazines for an explanation. When she heard a car in the driveway, she had not made a decision; but as the automatic garage door opened, she placed the abridged letter on the bed, carried the remaining pages along the hall to her room, and deposited them within a bureau drawer she had emptied in September with just such an eventuality in mind.

I must remember not to mention to clients the influence of Chinese art on Frank Lloyd Wright, thought Mr. Tane, while rolling up the window next to the driver's seat of his car.

4
Solvencies

1

'"Dad, please, there's no reason to be going to all this trouble." If I could say that so he'd understand. But no matter how I'd put it, he'd shake his head and smile and look past me like he hasn't listened at all. He has said, "Mr. Rongo lives in Boston, I believe" fifteen times in the past three days, even though I've kept on telling him, "Please don't call him Mr. Rongo, call him C. J., and he's lived in Arlington, which is not Boston!" He'll blink and five minutes later he'll say, "I believe Mr. Rongo has always lived in Boston."'

Wearing a yellow tee shirt and blue jeans, Jack lay on his bed in his room at home, his arms folded tightly across his chest, a pillow under his thighs. Moccasins dangled from his ankles, and his feet were anchored against the wall.

'Out of here as early as we can tomorrow. Up for breakfast before they are, even if C. J. is late today. They'll hold off dinner, no matter what.... I could see that smile Father hides behind starting to build three days ago. Like he is at work. He charms them, all of them, that domineering air of his wrapped up in friendliness, so nobody can ever not be taken in. Humiliates them is what he does.'

Kicking his moccasins to the floor, he padded to a bureau built into one of the walls, flung open a drawer, took out a pair of white socks, examined his hair in a three-faced mirror, then spat on his hand, and rubbed a cowlick, as he flicked off the air conditioner and rolled open an adjoining window framed with aluminum.

"Jack?" Mrs. Tane's voice echoed from the kitchen.

"Yes, Mother."

"Did you turn off your air conditioner?"

"Yes."

"Why?"

"I want some fresh air."

"Why don't you go outside?"

"It's too hot."

"You know opening the window upsets the ventilation in the rest of the house."

"No, it doesn't."

"Yes, it does, Jack. Most everything else has to work that much harder."

"Dad says it's all right. For awhile."

"Keep your door closed, then."

"I wasn't going to open it, Mother."

"And turn the air conditioner on when you leave there."

"Yes, Mother."

"Don't forget, Jack."

'I should've stayed in New Haven. They treat me like I'd never been gone. Like I haven't changed. It feels like I've got to start the whole freshman year over again. I should've gone to New York. Up to Boston. I should've taken a job in a resort on Cape Cod. I could've learned to sail. Gotten some experiences instead of dissolving into this place.'

Morosely he chose a phonograph recording from a collection of several hundred and started his portable turntable, which was lodged temporarily on a desk spacious enough to have served an architectural draftsman. The largest section of the desk top could be raised and lowered and positioned at any angle. Usually it was covered with books left open with such negligent regularity that many of their spines had been broken; but Jack had returned from Denver two days earlier to discover indignantly that his mother had cleaned and rearranged everything in his room.

'It's like they own me sometimes, like I've got to be whatever it is they want, no matter what I am. They couldn't stop me if I told them from there I was going to stay the summer. Maybe it'd be better to sign up in June for classes and say I couldn't fit them into my semester schedule. But I want to get away from school, too. Couldn't do the same thing all year. Not before I have to.'

He lifted the arm of the phonograph off the record and scrupulously set the needle on a division between songs.

'There I wouldn't even want to listen to this. Six years ago this song is from. They've got me falling back into it like I was fourteen, like last year didn't happen.'

"Jack," Mrs. Tane said from the hallway.

"Yes, Mother?"

"May I come in, Jack?"

"Yes, Mother."

Smiling guardedly, Mrs. Tane swept into the room, closing the door behind her. She wore a new, red and pink housedress, elaborately swirled with peony-shaped designs. Lightly starched, white half-sleeves ended just about her elbows. Her auburn curls had been freshly set that morning; and her plump, waxen face was lightly powdered.

"You look nice, Mother."

"Don't you want to change your clothes, Jack?"

"I wish you'd say what you mean, Mother. 'Change your clothes' or 'Do you need to change your clothes?' Then at least I'd get a chance to give my view. But you always start out with, 'Don't you...' when it's obvious I don't because I haven't—what you mean is that you want me to."

"I don't ever tell you what to do, Jack."

"Yes, you do, Mother. But you make it sound like you don't. I've already said I'd rather not have this show you're both putting on, like a prince was showing up."

"Don't be hard on your father, Jack."

"I'm not hard on him. But I wish I could be heard."

"You don't see how much this means to him. I wish you'd try to, just a little bit. This time right now is what he's been working for all his life. You at Yale. The house nearly his. He's finally beginning to get what he'd planned on. He's so happy about your friend visiting. It means so much to him. It's not often others get to enjoy the house, really appreciate it, you know."

"Yes, Mother."

"You're used to meeting people from all over the country, but your father isn't. He never had the chances to travel you've had. It means more to him than you suspect having someone from Boston visit us here."

"C. J. is not from Boston, Mother. He's from Arlington. They're two different communities."

"What matters is that he's from somewhere we've never had contact with. He's part of a world your father is proud to see you join."

"C. J. is just my friend, Mother. Not that a prince couldn't be, but…"

"Of course, Jack. And I'm pleased for you. But let your father have his time. It's only for tonight and the two mornings. That's not too much to ask, is it?"

"I'm going to try, Mother. I really don't know what more I can say."

"Don't you want to change your clothes, then?"

"C. J.'s been traveling for two weeks. He's not going to arrive in a tuxedo! Besides, people shouldn't ever have to wear anything except what's comfortable."

"I wish you wouldn't do that," said Mrs. Tane, more with a trace of longing than with irritation. "I wish it. You didn't used to take that tone with me."

"I'm sorry, Mother. But I've said the same things so many times that I don't know how to keep on saying them without getting angry."

"What I ask," Mrs. Tane said, opening the door, "is that you only try to understand something of what this means for your father and that you make an effort to help him enjoy it."

"Yes, Mother, all right. You look nice. I mean it."

Alone again, Jack slid a guitar out from under his bed, clumsily strummed an E-flat minor chord without bothering to tune the strings, and absentmindedly wrote his name in a layer of dust that had collected between the rosette and the bridge.

'I wish we could get out of here tonight. I've got to talk to him first and tell him to just sit through this. Awake by five so we can be gone by seven. They won't be up until six-thirty. I don't want the day ruined by another stilted meal, even if she is counting on a big breakfast for all of us. Grandpa will be up by the time it'd take to get there. Set the guest room alarm clock. Set it now.'

"Jack," Mrs. Tane called out at the sound of her son's footsteps in the hall. "Did you close your window?"

"Not yet, Mother."

"Won't you do that, please?"

"Yes, Mother."

"And turn on the air conditioner."

"Yes, Mother. I'm sorry. I forgot."

2

Seeming more to be reflecting light than radiating it, the sun hung flat as a late afternoon, full moon. Although it was not quite five o'clock, streaks of purple and orange shingled the western sky. Suspended in the east over the plains were several dozen, argent, rhomboidal clouds; similar in size, iceberglike, they resembled elements of a mobile in the process of being wired together.

Grateful he had forgotten the change from central to mountain time and, thus, was two hours late rather than three, C. J., clean-shaven, shambled along a pebble-strewn road in front of the Tane house, which he had easily recognized from Jack's description. It was perched on the summit of a lawn that inclined a quarter of a mile to a white rail fence, beside which he stopped to adjust his backpack. He wore a blue, cotton sweatshirt, cut off at the shoulders; and strands of thread straggled over his inflamed arms.

Wiping a hand through his sweaty hair, he stared up the manicured hill and with his mouth wide open, whistled through his teeth.

'Shouldn't have come. Should have met him somewhere else.'

In constructing the showpiece exterior of his family home, Mr. Tane had employed three materials: irregular, yellow bricks ascended from the ground to the window frames; on top of these, was a band of orange sandstone; a section of dark, unfinished redwood stretched above this to the roof and melted into a patio, which extended over a four-car garage and had been designed to resemble the hull of a ship. Boulders of both types of rock were scattered about the yard and were combined near the house into a lichen-covered ledge, which supported a blooming desert garden of coral cacti, firecrowns, and golden stars.

Now wearing a red and white striped, short-sleeved sport shirt and black corduroys, Jack loped down the winding driveway to its intersection with the road.

"Hi, Jack."

"Hi, C. J."

"Thistles," said C. J., shaking Jack's hand.

"What?"

"Thistles. From Denver to here. My legs are all scratched. I can't get out the thorns."

"Oh, yeah, those sort of bluish flowers…Now that I think about it, they are all over the place. I hadn't really noticed them…What'd you do with your beard?"

"Itched it off," replied C. J. offhandedly, adding, "Maybe we should leave now, do you think?"

"Yeah, I know. But there's no way we could. There really isn't. Mom and Dad wouldn't forgive me. It's like you're the circus for them. Just sit through it, and let them imagine their show. We can be gone early tomorrow…. Want me to take your pack?"

Nodding, C. J. loosened the pack straps, and it began to fall, but Jack caught it before it hit the ground and held it while C. J. slipped free.

"Not as heavy as I expected," Jack said.

"Gets heavier."

"I suppose it does. Where'd you start from today?"

"Sterling. Trooper picked me up and made me take a bus."

"All the way to Denver?"

"Had to. Wouldn't let me hitch."

"Did he fine you?"

"Almost."

"How'd you get here from Denver?"

"Local bus. A ride. Walked."

"You ought to've called. This is the hottest day of the year so far. It's over a hundred."

"Yeah, I…I need to get a shower," said C. J., as they mounted the driveway.

"Dad'll want to meet you right away. But a couple of minutes later you can. Take a bath if you want."

"Here…" C. J. faltered, "…is more than I thought."

"It's all recent," said Jack, referring to the town. "There's not more than a couple of buildings older than twenty years..."

Arranging his face into an expression that was both polite and non-committal, C. J. started to turn onto a stone path that spiraled to the front door; but Jack grasped his shoulder, led him into the garage, and, proudly fondling a rear fender of a blue 1959 Ford Thunderbird, said, "I had the carburetor adjusted for the mountains. I don't think it'll be any problem tomorrow. It stalled at the Continental Divide once, but we won't be getting up that high." He unlocked the trunk of his car, lifted the lid, stepped back, and, flushed, elated, angled a hand down toward six, foot-long, cloth and bamboo cylinders that had been lashed onto three crosspieces and bridled twice to a central, wooden staff. "I found it at a store in Aspen," he said, grinning at C. J., who, paling after a glance into the trunk, was inching backwards away from the car. "I think I put it together right. It's a lantern kite. The instructions were in two languages. It took me all an afternoon to assemble it. I can drive it east for you in September. It came from Japan. Welcome to Colorado!"

"China."

"In English it says from Japan."

"China," C. J. repeated. "For festivals. Six candles go inside."

"Well, anyway, you can fly it tomorrow, if you want."

"No," said C. J., stiffening. "It's only for special days. It has to be released in flight and not touched again."

"That's what they do in China?"

"Anyone. Anywhere," said C. J., deeply in earnest.

"I didn't know you took customs like that so seriously, C. J.," said Jack, slamming the trunk lid. "But what about the flames?"

"...There is more than the wind..."

"It's all right I bought it, isn't it?"

Making no reply, C. J. narrowed his eyelids and raised the corners of his lips enigmatically.

As they proceeded up the stone path, Jack, having grown accustomed to C. J.'s frequent silences, said, "The door from the garage leads to the kitchen. Mother is busy with dinner and all, so you'd best meet my Dad first. I guess that's how he would want it. I mean, does want it. The key's in my pocket. Ring the bell, would you?"

Awkwardly bending toward a waist-high, lighted button, C. J. pressed it twice; and at the immediate sound of a buzzer, Jack pushed the door open with his hip.

"Automatic lock," he said.

From somewhere C. J. heard a clamant ticking, and the sudden change in temperature made him shiver. Instinctively guided by somber, interior lines and spaces, he pulled back his shoulders, squeezed his legs together, and cradled his hands into an attitude of formal prayer. From an anteway where they stood, he surveyed the room to his left through a wall of tiered metal and glass shelves. The carpet appeared to be made of white fur, and a Navajo rug was framed above a grandfather clock on the far side of the room.

"What's the...?" he started to ask; but Jack nudged him forward.

The wall to their right was sheathed by separately fired, ceramic tiles, the multicolored components of an abstract mosaic depicting a Southwest American landscape. Ahead of them—cut to the ceiling—was a doorway within which had been affixed an antelope head, balanced sideways, so that its antlers projected both into the anteway and the adjoining room. Stepping under it, they faced a wall of glass displaying an extensive mountain view that had been entirely invisible from the roadway. Everything in the room—furniture, wall hangings, even the inlaid floor—seemed to be composed of unvarnished cane.

Until he was shaking a hand, C. J., dazzled, was unaware that Jack had made an introduction. Mr. Tane had leaned forward by then, had stepped back, and disconcertingly was rising to his full height of six feet four inches, as C. J., trying unsuccessfully to prevent his voice from quavering, said, "I'm glad to meet you, sir."

"We're privileged you're able to visit us," said Mr. Tane. His rugged frame intentionally was held in check by his polished attire. "The country here must be quite a surprise to you." Across the vest of his staid, blue suit was fastened a delicate, gold chain from which hung an antique watch. Two peaks of a handkerchief crept out from the breast pocket of his coat. The gleam of his formal white shirt was offset by a silver-flecked, crimson necktie. His reddish-brown hair was parted on his left side and combed with genial informality. He blinked often and habitually darted his eyes in a succession of focuses meant to ensure that the attention of anyone with whom he might be speaking would be diverted from his face. Having learned as a boy that his height could be startling, he customarily displayed it to strangers as gradually as possible. He prided himself on his hardiness, his muscular potential. On his next birthday, he would be sixty years old. "Jack tells me you've always lived in Massachusetts."

"Except last year," C. J. stuttered.

"Of course college is not truly a time of residence," said Mr. Tane. "We're quite honored that you should stop with us. Pleased and honored. Delighted." His sinewy torso intimated that his voice would be resonant and sonorous; but it was, instead, nasal and muffled. "You must be tired. Would you care to sit down before dinner? What about a glass of ice water? Or some fresh lemonade that's waiting?"

"I'd better take him up the hall and show him the guest room, Dad. I think he wants to shower."

"Yes, naturally. I should have guessed. There are towels provided, Jack?"

"I saw to all of that."

"Please, Mr. Rongo, please put aside what you'd like to have washed this evening; and it will be dry in the morning, if not before. Clothing is difficult to maintain in traveling, I know."

"Come on, C. J.," Jack said, hoisting the backpack to his shoulders. "I'll show you your room. Lemonade sounds good, Dad. Why don't you pour some?"

"I believe I heard your mother say dinner will be ready in about an hour," Mr. Tane said.

"Yes, Dad. Go ahead and have some lemonade." He guided C. J. into and along the hallway, twisted an elbow toward a bathroom, and dropped the pack outside the room next to it. "In here," he said. "Towels are on the bureau. If you set what you want washed outside the door, Mother'll take care of it. Can you find your way back to the recreation room?"

"Where we were?"

"Yes."

"Sure."

"I'll meet you there with Dad, then, whenever. You do want lemonade, don't you?"

"I don't know."

"It may be a long night. Kind of trying for you. For everyone. I mean it."

"Lemonade makes me sick sometimes."

"Whatever you want. Decide later," Jack said. He lounged down the hall, turned around, grinned, and as C. J. was entering the guest room, added, "I'm glad you're here...Don't let my folks make you nervous."

Taking a deep breath, C. J. sat on the edge of the bed, exhaled, closed his eyes, pulled his pack beneath him with his feet, opened it, and drew out a plastic bag containing a change of clothes he had carried unworn from home. Regarding his shaving kit disdainfully, he ran a hand over his cheeks.

'Didn't think. Should've brought black shoes. Would've been too heavy. They probably won't notice...Even if he could get me on as an apprentice, he wouldn't do it. Because that's not what he wants for Jack. Can't mention it. Should've known. Shouldn't have come. He likely works with people higher up than would be handling apprenticeships, anyway.'

Plastic bag in hand, he eased off his dusty shoes, grabbed the washcloth and towel, went into the bathroom, and locked the door. As soon as he had regulated the water of the shower to a sprinkle, he took a mouthful of it and stuck his arms into the cold stream, which immediately splashed onto the floor the beginnings of a soot brown puddle.

'I don't see how I got so red with the tan I had, but maybe being closer to the sun did it…The water tastes sweet like rain…I've got to remember to write a postcard for Mother…Hope they're clean enough. So what? She's seen theirs plenty of times. If I don't put them out, she'll think I don't wear any. At least they're not the ones with the hole.'

After making a pile of his dirty clothes, he wrapped the towel around his waist, opened the door, tossed the pile into the hallway, closed the door, opened it again, took up the clothes, folded them, set them carefully on the hall carpet, bent down to them yet again, separated the pants from his other things, and closed the door, locking it.

'I should tell her about the thorns. They might catch into everything else. So what? She must be used to them.

'Maybe the shower will stop it bleeding…I'm taking too much time…Water all over.…I'll tell him I wasn't used to a glass door.

'And if they ask me what, I'll say "aeronautical engineering." Probably expect everybody to have it all figured out like Jack does. Chart it down.

'If they could tell me who to talk to without mentioning them.

'No.'

Fumbling, he turned on the warm water, stepped into the shower, closed the glass door, and with his head arched back as far as he could manage, stood facing the flow.

'I bet neither one of them has seen a hot that comes out cold in their lives.…

'Shafts of light by the Platte River, golden ties without clouds, from the sun almost to the edge of the plain. If I'd caught a steady wind at the right angle, the string might have lined up with the shafts like the kite and the sun were part of a train heading for the eye of heaven.…

'I should have found out if they make sterling silver there. But that cop didn't want anything but me gone. People who've always been in one spot, sometimes they don't think there's anywhere else in the world, because all they ever see is what they've always known. Something different comes by, and they get rid of it so fast they don't even have to remember it was ever there.'

3

Dressed in brown corduroys, a matching flannel shirt, fiery agate cuff links, and a black knitted vest, C. J. sauntered through the hall, not realizing he had gone the wrong direction until he reached the kitchen doorway. Clearly wanting to pretend not to have seen him, Mrs. Tane spun quickly toward the door opening into the garage; and quietly C. J. retraced his steps, noting as he passed the guest room that his clothes had been removed.

"Ah," said Mr. Tane. "Here he is, Jack. Please find a place to sit, Mr. Rongo. Anywhere that looks comfortable to you is fine. Make yourself at home, as they say, and we say. Would you like something to drink?"

"Water, sir."

"You're perfectly welcome to something else. No need to be shy. Water, you're sure, is all you'd like?"

"It tastes good, sir. Especially."

"Yes, of course. I hadn't thought how different it would be from what you're used to…My, I wish you'd been here when we first built the house. We had our own pump then. But…we have the town about us now."

"I saw a water tower, sir."

"Grandpa says the streams are so polluted they make trout taste like rubber boots," said Jack, "and that the Arkansas River lately is like a corpse compared to twenty-five years ago."

"Your grandfather forgets how much more plentiful are the conveniences of our lives than they were in the time of his youth. Besides," Mr. Tane winked, "I expect he's said those things to keep the fishing more to himself."

"Dad says Grandpa ties flies that'll look good to the people he sells them to but that fish won't touch."

"Do you fish, Mr. Rongo?"

"I used to, sometimes."

"He fished on the ocean, Dad. With a kite. It can get way beyond a cast."

"Rather like a bobber," said Mr. Tane.

"Not like a bobber, Dad, it…"

"No," interrupted C. J., "it *is* like a bobber. I see."

"What kind of fish do you catch, Mr. Rongo? Usually, I mean."

"Flounder mostly," replied C. J., tentatively crossing his legs and gripping his glass of water close to his chest.

"They're what we call 'sole,' Dad."

"Jack has told us his introduction to clams came about at your hands, Mr. Rongo. That was most considerate of you."

"I think I'll see about dinner, Dad," said Jack, getting up, flicking on a light switch, and smiling at C. J.

"That's a good idea, son," said Mr. Tane, as he settled back into an armchair that faced away from the wall of glass. "Be careful not to hurry your mother, though."

While C. J. self-consciously gazed out the window at the flattened sun disappearing behind the mountains, Mr. Tane blinked, rubbed his lips together through more than a minute of silence, and then said, "Your father, I believe, was in the war."

"He was."

"I wonder, perhaps I shouldn't, but I wonder what he would think were he yet with us."

"Sir?" said C. J., ready, since Jack had read portions of Mr. Tane's letters aloud to him the previous spring, for what he heard next:

"It's terribly hard, terribly hard on such men, to find all they fought for, sacrificed for, being so consistently worn away by those who shamelessly stooped to the false counting of ballots in the city of Chicago. An outcry is building, that is certainly true, we can all take faith from that, building so steadily that a year from now, well…Such damage there will be to undo by then I near refrain from considering. But you must be familiar with that, being from Massachusetts."

"The President's not like he was, sir. Away."

"To appoint a man who had never tried a case in a courtroom into the office of the Attorney General of the United States, and for that man to be his own brother! I should think the followers in the traditions of Jefferson and Hamilton and Gallatin would all enlist themselves in our behalf."

"Perhaps they have, sir."

"That we should continue to allow the Soviets to strangle a once civilized island by means of a foul, illiterate, bearded, puppet peasant makes me hesitant at times to hold up my head. Truly. I dare say, our patience has been tried, Mr. Rongo, over these near three years. Sorely tried. And I can tell you this: a new frontier cannot be won with a faithlessness to the foundations. I'm grateful I'm still living within the old frontier, and I look forward to the election of a man with courage and good sense enough to have embraced its heart."

"I'll turn twenty-one next year, sir; but I'll just miss being able to vote," C. J. lied, quickly subtracting several months from his actual age.

"Jack has been somewhat vague in regard to your future plans, Mr. Rongo. What, if I may ask, is your current field of study?"

"Aeronautical engineering."

"An excellent choice. Excellent. The defense industries will offer you an ample selection of jobs, I am sure."

"Private research, sir."

"I see. Of what sort?"

"Related to housing."

"Housing?"

"Yes, sir. Constructing communities in space, sir."

"I'm afraid I still don't quite get your meaning."

"With the population increasing like it is, sir," said C. J. quietly, "at the rate it is..." Hearing a sound in the hall and hoping to be spared the necessity of improvising elaborations of ideas that were occurring to him for the first time at that moment, he turned toward the doorway, anticipating Jack's return but finding, instead, framed within the briared arch, Mrs. Tane, her head bowed, her fingers rapidly tracing the outlines of her hair.

"Excuse me, you two, for interrupting," she said, "though I expect you'll be pleased to know you may come to table now."

As she spoke, C. J. suddenly noticed that light from a series of fluorescent wall panels made the recreation room appear to be completely without shadows. Fidgeting, he stood and attempted a smile.

"What good news," said Mr. Tane. "Mr. Rongo, I don't believe you've met my wife, Jack's mother."

"I…"

"My how nicely you're dressed!" said Mrs. Tane quickly. "Goodness, that certainly is a worthy accomplishment for one so far from home. I hope Jack does as well when he is East. It's so nice to meet you. I can't tell you how nice. Welcome to Colorado."

"I brought you something from my mother," C. J. said, taking a small package from his shirt pocket and handing it to Mrs. Tane. "It was meant to have a name card. I lost it on the way. But…"

"Why, what a surprise. What a *nice* surprise. How thoughtful. I can't imagine what it is," Mrs. Tane said. She had continued to look directly at the floor and had spoken briskly with traces of rehearsal filtering her tones.

"Well," said her husband, chuckling, "I'm sure we're all eager to attend to your doings. Isn't that right, Mr. Rongo?"

4

The Tanes' dining room had been designed to promote an intimacy dependent upon isolation. There were no windows; and paper, its rose background highlighting an exceedingly simple pattern of interlocking gray rectangles, covered the walls. Six linear chairs, precisely aligned about an oak table, seemed to have been carved from solid pieces of wood; all of them, with one exception, were without arms.

Upon entering the room, Mr. Tane scowled at Jack, who at each setting at the table was dispensing small plates between cups of pineapple sherbet and glasses of water, and said, "You needn't do that, son."

"It's all right, Dad. Don't worry. I won't break anything."

"Please do be seated where you'd like," said Mrs. Tane, fluttering.

"You might as well be across from me, C. J.," Jack said. He pointed to a chair at the center of one of the long sides of the rectangular table.

Issuing an obliging and subservient nod, Mrs. Tane sat down at the table end closest to the kitchen doorway and smiled effusively, while her husband pushed her chair forward, pulled shut a sliding door connecting the dining room to the anteway, and seated himself in the chair with arms.

"I think it would be appropriate for us to share in a few moments of silent prayer," said Mr. Tane.

"With special thanks for the arrival of our guest," added his wife.

Quickly breaking the momentary silence, Jack asked, "Do you mind if I switch up the lights? You always have it dark as funeral homes in here."

"Goodness, son, you make it sound as if I were poisoning you," said Mrs. Tane, as C. J. fingered his glass of water and pushed his chair closer to the table.

"I don't know where you got that from, Mother. That's not what I said at all."

"Please, Jack, sharpen the light, if it makes you more content," said Mr. Tane. He took a spoonful of pineapple sherbet and, glancing at his wife, added, "Perhaps now would be a good time for the lemonade."

"What would you like to drink?" Mrs. Tane asked C. J. "Lemonade?"

"Water's enough, ma'am."

"Yes, Mr. Rongo seems to be quite fond of our water. Rather unlike that to which he's accustomed," Mr. Tane said, giving his glass to Jack, who passed it to Mrs. Tane.

"There is plenty of lemonade, if you'd like some," said Mrs. Tane to C. J.

"Thank you. I'm fine."

"Mother," said Jack. "I give up...What do we have here, tell me, that I brought in so inconspicuously?"

"I'm afraid I didn't make it myself.... It's salmon loaf. It looked so good I couldn't resist," replied Mrs. Tane, not mentioning she had meant for the loaf to be served after the sherbet. "Pacific salmon…" she added, as she returned to her husband his glass she had filled with lemonade from one of three pitchers at her side.

Intending that his example provide whatever instructions about usages of utensils might prove necessary, Mr. Tane selected from a setting of seven pieces of silverware the smallest knife and fork and held them poised over his plate. "Mr. Rongo, is the section of roadway crossing into Nebraska completed yet?"

"Not really, sir. Highways seem to be the sorts of things that aren't finished until they're no longer used."

"It soon shall be used more, I'm sure. The network of national highway with which we shall be blest is one of the great achievements of the past decade, minor though it was in comparison with the General's other accomplishments."

"I wonder," said Mrs. Tane, as if her husband and C. J. had not just spoken, "if the salmon will ever take leave for the Atlantic."

"Is there any Hawaiian punch?" asked Jack, seemingly oblivious to the words of both his parents. Instantly, Mrs. Tane lifted another of the pitchers beside her.

His knife and fork clutched in one hand, C. J. timidly raised his eyes, glanced at Mr. Tane, and asked, "Is it all right, sir, with the land?"

"He means," Jack interpreted, "are the highways going to be good for the environment, Dad?"

'For the *rest* of the environment,' thought Mrs. Tane, deciding to leave Jack uncorrected.

"Of course, Jack," said Mr. Tane. "I was deciding how to answer. That will depend upon a great many local decisions, I should say. The framework is certainly one I feel Sullivan himself would have applauded." Having intended to refrain from mentioning his longtime hero, Louis Sullivan, an architect and social philosopher, so deeply had he been hoping that C. J. might be drawn into a miraculous citing of the name, Mr. Tane frowned slightly and busied himself with spooning hollandaise sauce onto his plate.

Warily observing that Jack had cut his loaf into small bits and was spreading them one by one with sauce, C. J. understood that he was probably expected to comment and said quickly, "Or Emerson, sir."

"Precisely," said Mr. Tane. He put down his fork and wiped his mouth with a napkin. "Sullivan was very much taken with Emerson's work. The manner in which their lives overlapped is of major importance."

"I agree, sir," bluffed C. J., who was thoroughly unfamiliar with Sullivan's philosophy detailing rudiments of organic, functional design and had mentioned Ralph Waldo Emerson by chance.

"Yeah, but the truth is Sullivan was a lot more influenced by Thoreau than by Emerson," said Jack, shaking his glass back and forth so that the ice cubes clinked against each other noisily.

"Emerson and Thoreau were quite similar," said Mr. Tane.

"No, they weren't," replied Jack. "They were the two poles of Concord."

Recognizing the initial phrases of a long-standing argument, Mrs. Tane stood and diplomatically made ready to depart for the kitchen. "Please, all, excuse me for a moment," she said. "Take your time. No need to hurry…"

"I think I'll change my mind," said C. J., lifting his now empty glass as soon as Mrs. Tane had left the room and handing it to Jack.

"Ah, now that's what I need to hear," replied Mr. Tane. "There's nothing likelier than a good liquid refreshment to bring out the tastes of a meal and aid the digestion. Nothing at all…How many years of schooling do you plan on, Mr. Rongo? Graduate school, I assume. A doctorate probably?"

"I'd thought of the Peace Corps, sir," answered C. J. Experimentally he sipped the lemonade Jack had poured. "After graduation."

"I must confess it saddens me to hear that. An interruption of that nature would surely be an unfortunate and needless loss of time, likely to bring no advancements, and apt to set one back in the stream of competition. I do hate to see the energies of the young misplaced."

"The Peace Corps isn't only for the young, Dad."

"No successfully employed person would consider such career suspensions warranted, Jack. I favor all efforts to bring the opportunities of our way of life, of freedom, the advantages we enjoy, to the rest of the world, as speedily as possible, since they are the God-given rights of everyone, not merely ourselves; but this must be accomplished by those professionally trained in the mechanisms of law and in the appropriate use of force."

"I thought the Peace Corps would be a good alternative to the draft, sir. I don't know that it's fair, my not being subject to it."

"I don't see why you should feel that," Mr. Tane said. "No reason to. Educational deferments are justified because your work is going to be important to the rest of us. You and Jack, after all, are far more qualified than many, many people your age, who are destined for other paths; and you must be careful not to misuse or waste your talents."

"Why 'destined,' Dad? Lots of people just don't get a chance."

"That's nonsense, son. Nonsense. Opportunity is open to all in this nation; that is why we are the hope of the world."

"I don't see any black people in town, Dad, or working at the plant."

"Anyone is welcome to apply for a position at the plant, more than welcome, as they are anywhere. Being hired is simply a matter of appropriate qualifications."

"But the point is they can't get those qualifications because of what they were born into."

"I come in contact with such people at times in my work, Jack; and it's obvious to me, as I'm sure it would be to you if you had similar contact, that many of our fellow citizens are lacking in the qualities of perseverance and intelligence that would allow them to gain what others are more entitled to by reason of endowment. It is perhaps difficult to accept the high quality of your own abilities, son; but a humility based on ignorance, however well-intentioned, can only work against your best interests."

Deferentially, but cordially, Mrs. Tane then wheeled a cart piled high with food into the room and pushed it to Mr. Tane's end of the table. "Jack," she said, while distributing bowls of vegetables, potatoes, and rolls about the table, "will you kindly see to the salads?"

"Of course, Mother," answered Jack, standing quickly and moving to the cart.

"I've found my cart a most convenient device," Mrs. Tane said to C. J., as she reseated herself and Jack transferred plates of salad from the cart to each of the four place settings. "I hope you'll excuse the untidiness."

"It reminds me of shopping when I was little," C. J. replied. "My mother and I used a red wagon."

"Help yourself to a roll while we're waiting...Yes, Jack went shopping with me at that age, too. I'd forgotten. Naturally we took the car then. Into the city. It's much easier now with the community center so near...I'm sure you're aware we're quite satisfied with the way our town has grown."

"Perhaps," said Mr. Tane, as Jack reseated himself, "Jack has told you we have written the ordinances in such a way so as to guarantee there never being more of a business district than we presently have."

"Yes, he has, sir," replied C. J. "...It's more quiet here. Than anywhere I have known."

"I suppose it is," said Mrs. Tane. "I get so used to that, my, I forget...I expect we're more fortunate than we know. All of us. All of us..."

"I was wondering," said Mr. Tane, pointing a finger toward a platter Mrs. Tane had left on the cart and unceasingly darting his eyes about the room, "when that pheasant was going to make its appearance. What a splendid choice for this evening!"

"Is that the one you shot last fall, Dad?" Jack asked. "The one you wrote me about?"

"It most certainly is," said Mrs. Tane, though she had purchased it the day before at a specialty butcher shop in the luxurious Cherry Creek section of Denver and had secretly disposed of the buckshot-ridden carcass her husband had presented her. "I hope you like pheasant," she continued, addressing C. J. and warmly adding, "I thought it fitting you see how thoroughly Jack's father provides for us."

"I haven't ever had it before," said C. J.

"Well, then, we can reverse the introduction of clams, in a manner of speaking. How appropriate!" said Mr. Tane. "Jack has never displayed a taste for hunting, Mr. Rongo. I imagine that's just as well. The opportunities become fewer and fewer every year, I'm afraid."

"Mother, I hope you got all the buckshot out this time," said Jack, as his father took up a carving knife.

"You embarrass me, son…I think you'll be pleased…"

"Mexican cheese," Jack quickly clarified, noticing that C. J. had shifted his salad bowl to the edge of the table and was picking through it exploratorially with one of his forks. "It's really common here, but I haven't seen it in the East. Probably there, somewhere. Everything else is. And mushrooms. Are those from Grandpa?"

"He brought them down the day before yesterday," Mrs. Tane said. "He'd gathered them early that morning." She waved her left hand toward C. J. and appended, "Jack must have told you that his grandfather, Mr. Tane's father, lives nearby."

"I'm counting on meeting him tomorrow, Mrs. Tane."

"I didn't know you were going up there, Jack," said Mr. Tane, in the midst of passing the plates he had served. "Why do you want to do that?"

"I haven't been around him much this summer. Anyway, I figured C. J. ought to see some of the land higher than here."

"And I suppose those on the East would have, would have lost, that…"

"Bent, Dad."

"Yes, 'bent' will do…as a way of referring to my father's manner of living," said Mr. Tane, frowning again and laying aside the carving knife. "…You must all forgive me for failing to ask your preferences in meat; but the wants of the two of you I am familiar with; and I expect, Mr. Rongo, you will find pheasant so unlike any other fowl you will be grateful for the loss of the need to choose."

"Thank you, sir," said C. J. "…May I have some gravy, please?"

Cringing, Jack hurriedly said, "There's sour cream. Are you sure you don't want that?"

"No, I mean, yes, the gravy, please."

"Jack has attempted," Mrs. Tane said, transforming her previous geniality into haughty tones, "to introduce us to the use of sour cream, which he maintains is a staple at Yale. Unsuccessfully attempted, I am afraid. The two of us long ago learned to consider it improper for human consumption."

With an acutely dignified air, she moved a gravy boat from beside her place setting to a spot immediately in front of C. J. At the sight of the gravy boat, C. J. blanched; nonetheless, he ladled a tablespoon of liquid over his baked potato then circumspectly pushed aside the bowl within which lumps of flour floated in juice so crudely mixed with milk that the resultant concoction resembled both liquid halvah and drying saltwater taffy. Jack was accustomed to his mother's gravy and always refused it; Mr. Tane, too, found it distasteful, but long ago had praised it with such vigor that his wife thought of it as one of her specialties most apt to please him.

"I wonder if you had a chance to visit Pella on your trip," Mrs. Tane cheerfully asked.

"It's in Iowa," Jack said.

"I don't remember so, Mrs. Tane."

"I have always longed to attend the festival there," she said.

"We forget," said Mr. Tane, "that our local understandings may be mysterious to others...My wife is referring to a tulip festival held yearly in Pella."

"You should go next time, Dad. There's lots of things I wish you'd take up now that I'm not around."

"Ah, but Jack, you mustn't consign me to inactivity yet!"

"It must be beautiful," said Mrs. Tane. "Tulips are so much more colorful than roses. Each New Year's Day I wonder why the rose parade of Pasadena provokes such attention. My goodness, those who use our eyes for us should look about more than they do. I wish we could all go."

"Did you get the wishbone?" C. J. asked. "I thought maybe you had got the wishbone," he continued, as Mrs. Tane peered inquiringly at Jack, "and were wishing for tulips."

"The breaking of the wishbone is, I believe, a custom associated with other poultry," said Mr. Tane, tactfully sighing. "My, I remember when a trip to Iowa would have taken three days and been uncertain even then. How many changes we have known!" His mouth, thus far, had been a tense, pale line of tightly inturned flesh; but for a moment he relaxed; and the color his lips added to his face made him appear older.

Holding his almost empty glass of lemonade against his chin and sur-reptitiously loosening his belt, C. J., more offhandedly than abruptly, said—as if he were attempting to bring together somehow all the varied threads of the dinner table conversation, "Legal and moral. What's the difference. Between. Responsibility?"

"What are you thinking of?" Jack asked encouragingly, sitting back in his chair.

"So many ways laws can make good?"

"Who?" Jack asked patiently. "Who do you mean?"

"The other countries. Where the 'advistors,' I mean advisors are. Where some people want to send troops."

"I'm still not…" said Jack.

"We face a serious threat in that part of the world," interjected Mr. Tane. "As Secretary Dulles phrased it, the nations there can be undermined and fall, one by one, like a house of cards."

"People aren't cards," C. J. said uncertainly.

"It's a metaphor," said Jack. "Not a mathematical equation. It shows what one thing is by talking about another."

"Why not talk about the way the one thing is?"

"There are far too many complications and technicalities," said Mr. Tane. "An appropriate metaphor preserves the essence of another situation and allows proper evaluations of diverse elements."

"…I wonder, though…this is going back a little," Jack said slowly, "but I wonder if it's really right, accurate, I mean, to use the word *laws* in reference to how they live. Those people there."

"More how the people who used to live here," C. J. said.

"Yeah, I suppose so. Maybe *customs* would be better than *laws*."

Mr. Tane grazed his lips with his napkin, cleared his throat, and said, "You both are manifesting what sounds to me like an inverted form of racism, I must say, if you are suggesting that people of another color, in this case yellow, are incapable of rational, progressive development. Which is precisely what you were accusing me of earlier, Jack."

"No!" exclaimed C. J. "It's, if there have to be people sent to bring good ways, I'd rather the Peace Corps than the troops."

"But wasn't it about law we started talking?" Jack asked. "What are the parameters of this conversation, anyway?"

"I don't know how to get unconfused..." C. J. said with a glint in his eyes, "except by saying confusion..."

"...We ought to have a vision," Mrs. Tane quietly and solemnly said, "an unclouded vision. To give to the young."

"The obscurity has come in recent years," her husband countered. "It has not been we who are responsible for it."

"Dominoes," said Mrs. Tane. "It was dominoes."

"That's right," agreed Jack. "It was. Dominoes. It wasn't a house of cards."

Lowering his eyes, C. J. grasped his glass of water and held it through a second, brief, motionless and soundless pause at the table.

"Well?" Jack asked, once again breaking the silence, this time with discordant tones unmistakably indicating a gloating over his father's error, though it had also been his own, "What do you think of pheasant, C. J.?"

"Garfish tastes more like the sea than flounder does, too," C. J. replied.

"I wonder that sometimes," said Jack. "It *does* taste more like the woods, sort of. Pheasant. Than chicken. Is that because of the kinds of food they eat, or how they breed, or what?"

"Methods of domestication and mass production," Mr. Tane intoned, "have brought with them a certain dilution of taste, the virtues of variety and ease of purchase notwithstanding."

"Yes, but why, Dad? Even the chickens we used to have when I was little tasted different from now...Every Sunday for a long time," he explained to C. J., "we'd buy a live chicken…and hack off its head with an axe. You should see them. The body runs around flapping its wings, and the head lies there trying to cackle. It's hard to even know whether or not they're dead."

"The protections that have increased our life-spans have brought with them substantial losses," said Mr. Tane.

"That's just another way of putting what I said at first, Dad. That doesn't explain anything. If you don't know any more that I do, I wish you'd say so."

Fixedly angling his head so that he was able both to glare warningly at Jack and to smile at Mr. Tane, C. J. said, "I appreciate your pheasant, sir."

"I'm delighted you're satisfied," Mr. Tane replied. "…You know, I was thinking just now, my, I was thinking of your intent to combine knowledge of flight with community construction, Mr. Rongo. What amazing opportunities that brings to mind! I haven't myself yet been presented at work with any comparable zoning dilemmas. There was some talk at the beginning here of an airport, but Denver remains a happy solution."

"Not for the people who live near the Denver airport," Jack said, joining his mother in clearing the table. "With the flight patterns the way they are. According to what I keep reading about the sound. Sometimes I almost want to take out an ad apologizing for having flown…"

"Is there anything I…?" C. J. began to ask, wondering whether he might help with the removal of the dishes.

"Nonsense, nonsense. Sit still," Mr. Tane interrupted. "That's a matter of concern for Denver county, Jack. It's one of the issues you might well enjoy working with when you acquire your degree."

"How can it be the county, though, when so many other people use a facility like that? All the nonresidents, I mean."

"A matter of statutory concern, son. Certainly there are out-of-state factors worthy of consideration."

"It's, I don't know, the whole thing of boundaries is something I can't understand very well yet," Jack said. "Cars must've had a lot to do with the boundaries we have now. But with planes and computers, why shouldn't we change again? Change quite a bit. I can fly home from New

Haven as fast as most people can drive to work, or close to as fast, so why shouldn't it become like Mexico and the United States and Canada would be sort of what counties are now?"

"Such notions are entertaining, Jack; yet we should face facts, too. You must keep in mind the wall in Berlin, for example."

"Yes, Dad, but next you'll bring up North Korea and South Korea and everything else about the Cold War; and it's, I don't know, after awhile, it's that the whole idea of boundaries starts seeming in the way of progress."

"On the contrary," said Mr. Tane, "boundaries are what allow us to measure progress. The view from an airplane ignores the variety of our communities. The Dutch heritage of Pella, for instance. Maintenance of such variety is vital in preserving the quality of life we enjoy."

"Yeah, but on a larger scale, the preservation of differences is detrimental. It seems like that to me, anyhow. There are other kinds of walls, besides the wall in Berlin, that separate us from each other in ways that don't bring any kind of advantages. To say the least…. There's only one human truth, after all."

"Patterns of life," said Mr. Tane, smiling slightly, "occur independently of the pursuit of truth."

"But how can the scale of what's acceptable be determined then?" Jack asked, as he pushed the dish cart toward the kitchen.

"There will be enough time to consider and discuss that question, I am sure, during your professional days," Mr. Tane replied. He turned to C. J. and added as if in confidence, "Jack and I do enjoy our informal debates. Sometimes I may overstate a position, but I'm sure he'll be grateful one day when he encounters those who lack his innocence. Law will have its unfortunate aspects, I'm confident. Every profession does."

"That's too bad, sir," said C. J.

"The best course is always to be ready for disappointments," Mr. Tane continued. "None of our lives are free of them…."

Adopting, as he re-entered the dining room, the servile guise of an aristocratic waiter, Jack announced with mock ceremoniality, "Dessert,

I am directed to inform you, will be served by candlelight, if that's agreeable to all."

"Perhaps," his father said, "we should also have the lighting at its lowest level."

"That's fine with me," Jack replied. Quickly he dimmed a set of translucent wall panels, which, as in the recreation room, seemed to allow no shadows.

"This won't be as good as you're used to, I'm sure," Mrs. Tane said, wheeling in the cart laden with plates and a Boston cream pie. "I see Jack left everyone a dessert fork. Would you care for some herbal tea?"

"Please," C. J. answered.

"I didn't know you drank that," Jack said.

"Sometimes."

"When did you start doing that?"

"Exams."

"I didn't think you drank it last year."

"I like it more now."

"I don't...I'm trying to get used to it, though."

"It's apple flavored," said Mr. Tane. "Made almost entirely of apples, I believe. One of my favorites...."

"Jack," C. J. said firmly.

"Something else?"

"Cinnamon."

"What for?"

"The pie. Like salt."

"Is there any, Mother?"

"In the second cupboard above the stove, third shelf..." replied Mrs. Tane, smiling warmly. "I'm so pleased you mentioned that...."

"It's what we do at home..." C. J. said.

"Did you want to light the candles soon, Mother?" Jack asked, handing C. J. a jar of ground cinnamon.

"Thank you, Jack. I had forgotten. You're more of a help sometimes than you know," replied Mrs. Tane. She withdrew a book of matches from her apron, lit two tall red candles, and placed one on either side of C. J. The wavering flames brought shadows into the house at last, engendering a drowsy contrast to the strict linearity of the room.

"I surely never thought I'd ever be eating Boston cream pie with a resident of Massachusetts," Mr. Tane said.

"Isn't it strange the surprises life can bring?" added his wife, as C. J. leaned forward toward the flames and Jack sprinkled some cinnamon onto his pie.

"I'm so sad, Mr. Rongo," said Mrs. Tane suddenly, her voice low-pitched and subdued. Aware that this was the first time his mother had used C. J.'s surname, Jack stopped eating and jabbed an elbow onto the table. "So sad about your father."

"Yes," C. J. said, exhaling loudly in a near whistle. "I didn't know him, you see."

"What a tragedy for your poor mother. All those years. My."

"Maybe..." said C. J., "Maybe memory is enough...for some people."

"Yes, perhaps so," said Mrs. Tane. "I haven't truly been faced with considering such a prospect. All the same, I can't help but feel so very unhappy for her...."

"Mother," Jack said hurriedly, intentionally changing the subject, "I must tell you you've really outdone yourself tonight. I shouldn't have had any doubts. The pheasant was perfect."

"Well, thank you, son. It's fine to hear you say that."

"The pie was good, too. Everything was...But, why haven't I ever seen these cloth napkins before. They're nice. When did you get them?"

"They were a gift," Mrs. Tane replied, her momentarily sharp-edged tones belying the sentimentality of her words with a bitterness and triumph so thoroughly intermingled that the mixture approached defiance. "A gift for our wedding. From some friends of my parents. They sent them all the way to Denver from their home in Maine. All this way."

"And you've been saving them since then?" Jack asked.

"The Andres, you remember," she said to her husband. Mr. Tane nodded and said gently, "Since September 2, 1939, son. Such gifts, by joining separate moments, bring an unexpected harmony to life. An unexpected peace."

"Peace," said Mrs. Tane. "Yes." Resuming her customary deference, she added, having noted that C. J.'s head was slowly slipping toward his chest, "I think we are all about asleep!"

"Perhaps you should be showing your friend to the guest room," agreed her husband. "It's late. He's had a long trip."

"I can't recall a more pleasing evening," Mrs. Tane said, nudging C. J.'s shoulder, as she blew out the candles. "It's such a treat having you here...."

"Yes, ma'am," said C. J., wearily rising. "I'm...I'm glad I got to meet you both in this way."

Nodding and smiling graciously, saying nothing, Mr. Tane pulled back the sliding door and stood by it, the fingers of his left hand locked almost in a fist, his right hand suspended diagonally above his eyebrows, poised between a salute and a muted wave.

"I'm sorry," C. J. whispered to Jack when they were alone in the anteroom.
"About what?"

"I got water all over the floor."

"Which floor?"

"The bathroom."

"That's no problem. Don't worry about it...Hey, I forgot to let you know I already set the alarm in your room for five. Can you make it up by then, do you think?"

"I feel kind of...." C. J. revolved his hands in fitfully transverse circles. "The lemonade was good, though. It won't.... I hope I didn't...."

"You were fine. Better than I was..."

"There's something I got to tell you."

"C. J., you'd better get some sleep."

"No, I…"

"What, then?"

"I…I had a lantern kite once."

"Yeah, I figured you might've…Did it fly well?"

"I hardly got to find out. It wasn't even up a hundred feet. I lost control. It landed on an old shed in a park we live close to. The candles set the shed on fire."

"So you got in a lot of trouble."

"But I didn't mind the trouble. It was that no one could understand why I was flying the kite."

"I'm glad you told me."

"Thank you for the kite, but…."

"I've still got the receipt for it. I'll just return it to the store. Take it apart and return it. Don't worry about it. There'll be no trouble at all. Don't even think about it.…Listen, though, you'd better get to bed now, C. J."

"I'll be all right."

"I left you one of my robes in the closet. The light switch is on the left by the door, and the lamp next to the window works. I put a new bulb in it."

"I was…"

"What?"

"I was two hours off."

"Nobody even noticed. Don't worry about anything. I'll see you in the morning. I hope the thorns get washed out of your things."

"I'm sorry I was late."

"You weren't any problem at all. I mean it. See you tomorrow."

"G'night."

"G'night."

5

As soon as she was certain she had heard the closings of three bedroom doors, Mrs. Tane, standing alone in the kitchen, stared out a chintz-lined west window at the dark, ascending miles and, though she made no sounds, opened her mouth as if she were moaning. After several moments, she picked up a dishcloth and discovered she had been pressing a fork against her stainless steel sink with such intensity that the ends of all four tines had been bent perpendicularly to the handle.

"Couldn't You have taught us by now how to enjoy each other?" she asked aloud.

6

An image of interlapping rectangles scudded out of C. J.'s consciousness, as he awoke, clasping a rolled and knotted sheet about his neck. His parched throat felt like a numb wad of dried straw. According to his wristwatch, it was almost two-thirty.

The guest bedroom was bright enough for him to be able to discern the outlines of the furniture; and at first he suspected that the moon was full and close; but when he went to the window to search for it, he saw that the light came solely from the legions of stars in the unfiltered sky. Although he could detect no movement outside, he could hear a faint, high-pitch wind. Far away a dog howled twice, unanswered.

Stealthily he put on Jack's robe, opened the bedroom door, and, listening, tiptoed into the bathroom. Debating whether to turn on the light, he decided that even here, it would be unnecessary. After filling a plastic cup three times with water, the dryness in his throat had not been assuaged, but his stomach was full. Very slowly he sipped a fourth cup, rubbed his neck, and groped his way into the front parlor.

Reflections from the white carpet made the room even brighter than the rest of the house. The fibers were so cushioning that as he edged by the piano and approached the grandfather clock, it felt as if he were stepping in and out of slippers. While studying the frontal, clock decorations of suns and moons and personified seasons, he noticed that the hands did not move. Puzzled, he bent down and found that the ticking came from a small alarm clock, which had been positioned sideways under chimes behind a glass door at an angle that made the reading of its time impossible.

Attempting to lull himself into a readiness for more sleep, he sat down on a sofa that faced an east window. A ceiling-length curtain draped across part of the south wall and followed a curve past the margin of the window, making him wonder whether the glass itself had been molded about the corner. The contours of the town extending for more than a mile to the north were distinctly illuminated by the stars. Only a glowing, beaconlike water tower was lit by electricity. To the east the streetlights and neon of Denver were condensed into a static, smoldering fragment that, framed by the window, reminded him of the last ember in a fireplace. Through foothills in the south, a stream of lights traveled a broken line resembling the networked dots and dashes of a Morse code message. Since the flickerings were too unevenly spaced to be from a train, he decided they must be emanating from a chain of trucks.

Using the roof of his mouth and his tongue, he whistled quietly, scanned the room, and feeling wide-awake, got up and cautiously began to explore, lifting and examining vases, pottery, glassware, and articles of ornamental metal. Passing on the west wall numerous dolls and miniature pieces of furniture affixed within an array of shadow boxes, some of which appeared to be tiny, accurate replicas of various rooms in the house, he again stopped by the clock and was checking his earlier assessment of it, when in a mirror to his right he saw a faint reflection of Mrs. Tane, who stood holding a blanket in the anteroom doorway. Instead of turning toward her, he yawned, walked back to the couch, sat down, crossed his legs, and ambiguously inclined his head in the direction of the piano.

"I thought someone must be cold," murmured Mrs. Tane. Her white, cotton nightgown was so full it seemed to be propelling her waxen head and arms to the couch. "Couldn't sleep?" she asked, sitting down beside C. J.

Disregarding his lack of a reply, she dropped the blanket to the floor, grazed her cheeks with her palms, and said, "This is my room…I suppose that's ordinarily true of a parlor and the one who makes a home. Jack and his father rarely come in here, so when I heard someone up I knew it must be you, although I was half afraid another woodchuck had gotten in from the cellar. I thought you might be cold. Whenever strangers move into the neighborhood, or, oh, just visit, they learn our nights are cool; and they're always quite surprised and quite grateful. But that's all we've known, you see, Mr. Tane and I, never an evening where the light and heat of the day haven't gone away together. I thought you probably hadn't been expecting it. During the summer nights we often have the air level turned to fan. My husband says the problems of construction are so dissimilar in other parts of the country that he'd have to start over again in each one. We feel very lucky here, though not because of relief from a distress to which we'd become accustomed, as is so common with newcomers."

"Sometimes at home," C. J. said, his words haltingly linked together by long and awkward pauses, "it was so humid I couldn't sleep until sunrise."

"My, how unevenly blessings are distributed," said Mrs. Tane, manipulating her fingers in the air, as if she were kneading bread or unraveling a skein of yarn.

"I have been reading more," she continued. "Jack writes us so thoughtfully, so regularly. I do appreciate the sacrifice from his work; and his father does, too. I have been reading. Perhaps because there is time now. And also, certainly because I hope I'll be a help to Jack when he opens his law practice. I feel I understand more than I did when he was younger, or am beginning to, although that's shameful for me to admit. But there seemed so often to be one more matter to attend to here in the house. I feel, though, that recently, these past months, I've become more, aware, you see, so that later on I'll be better able to assist Jack. I think I might even find time to take a course myself in one of the programs, if it, if I could, current events, sometimes there's an announcement on television about it. I can't plan on anything yet, but I'd like to be as prepared for helping him as I can manage to be. I have been reading.

"Of course, there's much that any profession separates others from...I do hope, and Jack's father does, too, but naturally, we want the choices to be Jack's, and we'll support whatever he decides. Even so, I hope he settles on the University of Denver Law School. It's located in the heart of the business district of the city, and it seems to us it would be profitable for him to become acquainted with the people in the community where he'll eventually be working. No start could be too early, as his father says." She got up from the couch, walked to the window, pulled the curtain closed, looked back at C. J., and repeated in a whisper that was both fragile and emphatic, "I have been reading more..."

"Do you...play, Mrs. Tane?" C. J. asked hesitantly.

"Play?"

"The piano, I mean."

"No," Mrs. Tane said, bowing her head and advancing toward the hall-way. "No...no, I do not...I do not play..."

"Thank you for offering the blanket," C. J. said, standing, trailing after her along the hallway, and stretching out his right hand.

"Why, of course," she replied, taking his hand. "Excuse me. Excuse me for interrupting."

"Did you open your present?" he asked, withdrawing his hand.

"Sakes, I'd completely forgotten to mention it. What a perfectly beautiful shell! I must be sure to have your address for a note of acknowledgment."

"Not a shell, ma'am. It's a sand dollar. It's from a kind of sea urchin. Whether it's alive or...a skeleton...like this, it's always called a sand dollar."

"Yes, certainly," said Mrs. Tane, drifting past and beyond the guest room doorway. "A sand dollar," she murmured, as C. J. turned into the guest room. "A sand dollar."

With his face buried in a pillow, C. J. fell asleep immediately.

7

"Should I keep the garage door open for you?" Mrs. Tane, her nightgown flapping in the breeze, called out from the patio.

"No, Mother, it's all right. I won't be using it today," Jack shouted, waving broadly and backing his car down the driveway. "Roll up your window, would you?" he said to C. J. "I'm going to turn on the air conditioner. We might as well get used to it. Today is supposed to be as hot as yesterday…. I didn't think we'd ever get out of there! If we'd gotten up later, I'm sure we couldn't have left before the middle of the morning. Dad would've stayed away from work; he's probably glad he didn't have to…. I took the lantern kite out of the trunk and put in some camping stuff, C. J. Taking it back to the store'll be no problem….Watch out at the end of the driveway; it's almost a curb. I'll take it fast. It's easiest that way. Dad says once every six months he's going to have it graded down, but I don't think he ever will…"

"I could hear the wind, right after the alarm went off," C. J. said, his legs crossed, his hands between his knees, and his elbows pressed against his hips. "But I couldn't see it out the window. Because it was blowing level with the ground."

"Yeah, it's almost always like that in the morning here. Some name for it. I can't remember. Grandpa says it divides the dew from the mist," Jack replied. He put on a pair of sunglasses and guided the car onto a two-lane highway. "This road got paved about ten years ago. It used to be brick. Can you imagine? Laying all those bricks by hand?"

"Some political program of Roosevelt's probably."

"I suppose. I hadn't really thought. It was always there. And when it changed, that's how I knew I was growing up. It wasn't television or something like that; it was those bricks being torn out, and the ride getting smooth…. Dad won't use an automatic shift. Whenever I drive his car, I can't relax because you have to switch gears so often. Sometimes you have to go a long way in second, high up. This car is like skiing. He keeps saying he'll make the change, but every two years he buys the same thing; and then he starts in with, 'The next time.' He won't ever say why he doesn't want the automatic. I guess the stick makes him feel like he's in control. The truth is he doesn't know any more about cars than I do. I probably know more than he does, if it ever came down to finding out…. Is the air all right for you now?"

"It's fine," C. J. said. "Inside here." He wore the same clothes he had arrived in, but Mrs. Tane had snipped off the threads that had dangled from his shoulders. "Good dinner," he added.

"Yeah, Dad wasn't as overbearing as he sometimes is…I meant to tell you *I* picked the asparagus."

"Where's the garden?"

"No, not from a garden. It grows wild all through the foothills lower down. We get lots of stuff that way. From Grandpa, too. Well, not lots, but still quite a bit. Mom used to put up things in the fall, can them. She only makes jams now. And sometimes we get wild honey."

"I didn't ever think of vegetables as just growing."

"There wouldn't have been any reason for you to in the city. Maybe these were cultivated originally, and the seeds scattered. I don't know."

"So you wouldn't even have to buy food?"

"No, I suppose not. For a few more years anyway. If you wanted to live pretty simply. Grandpa gets by mostly eating what grows wild. Dad keeps offering to build him a place, but Grandpa'll never move. He's been living alone most of his life in the same cabin except for when Dad was little and my grandmother was alive. He worked in the mines down by Colorado Springs then. I'm sure he won't talk about that today, though. Every time he starts to, he gets just so far and he stands up in the middle of a sentence and leaves his cabin. It was before unions and there was sort of an unorganized strike. The workers wanting more pay and shorter hours and medical benefits, things like that. I read a book about it. The management called in the state troops to fire at their own employees. It was horrible. Just like all bloodbaths are…. Grandpa left real soon after that. I guess it must be at least forty years he's been by himself. All sorts of ordinary kinds of habits he never got used to having. I'm pretty certain he's been getting some money from Dad all the way along, but maybe not, because he does do some guidework for tourists. Not many people know the area as well as he does. He could get quite a bit more work if he wanted to. Vacationers are coming in every year, wanting him to show them around. Company groups especially. But he won't do it. Singles is all he'll take, mostly, and regular people he's known a long time or ones they recommend." Facing C. J., he added abruptly, "That was a good idea you had last night about the cinnamon."

"I didn't invent doing it," C. J. said. He straightened his legs and locked his hands together behind his head. "That's how we eat."

"Yeah, but I'm glad you showed us, though. You being here makes the summer more interesting. I should've found a job...All I've been doing is lying around."

"The yard looks good."

"Yeah, it's a lot of work. But *I* don't do it. They hire someone for it. Dad does. Mexicans usually. There's a lot of them up here illegally. None of us says anything about it. At least not until we're done using them. People in this part of Colorado who you might think are from reservations, they're more apt to be Mexicans. You'll see a lot of them in the fields we'll be going by...."

"Next to the Missouri River," C. J. said, glancing at the steering wheel, "I didn't know the fields were going to be bigger, in Nebraska, because just east of there it seemed like the wheat waved on forever without a fence. I'd bought a kite. A small diamond. I was going to swim it. The Missouri. Not swim, be pulled by the kite. Across the current would be so different from on a lake. A farmer convinced me out of it. I had to explain what I was doing on his land. I said I was studying aeronautical engineering. That made it all right with him...So that's what I told your father."

"I wondered what he meant by that about airports."

"But what I couldn't understand, and I wanted to ask him, the farmer, and I didn't, is why there only are spreads of cities and spreads of land. Why isn't it more even? One person makes the food for so many people."

"Patterns of homesteading probably. Power. Politics. Besides, the workers in the factories make the farmer's tools."

"Why not everyone on a piece of land with their own gardens?"

"I hadn't ever thought about it."

"People don't know their own food."

"That'd be an awfully big change. I doubt if it could happen."

"China?"

"China what?"

"More even a spread."

"Nobody's said much about China these part few years. Not anything really," said Jack. "...It's funny, C. J., I don't know if it's related, probably is a little; but back when I said 'Mexican,' I thought when I said it that Mexico is in America. I mean I thought that for the first time right then. They call it 'American history,' but that's not what they're talking about. It's the United States they mean. It should be 'United Statesian history.' 'God Bless America' and all that doesn't mean Canada and Mexico. The way 'America' gets said, the geography gets mixed up wrong with the name."

"Probably came from settlers wanting more before they had it that they didn't get."

"Isn't that strange? It's so common here. Talking about 'America' and meaning the wrong thing. It's easier to see something like that in the West than it would be in the East...I still can't get used to people who came to Yale from prep schools asking me what my nationality is. It ought to be, 'What ancestry are you?' instead of 'What's your nationality?'"

"United Statesian," said C. J. testingly.

"I'm going to ask somebody about it this fall. Some history professor probably...."

Upon leaving the outskirts of the town, they had driven past several insular farmhouses. Most of the land, however, had been unfenced, overgrown, and rocky. Climbing steadily after a sharp hairpin curve, Jack said, "The plant is over on the left."

"What!" exclaimed C. J., as he turned his head and looked past Jack.

Behind a fifteen-foot barbed wire fence, acres of parking space led into a flat, carefully maintained, bluegrass lawn bordering a massive expanse of windowless concrete surrounded on three sides by a range of lofty, tortuously sloped, treeless peaks. The sod appeared to have been laid to the very edges of the mountains, and the parklike green was startling to eyes accustomed to the bland yellows that lined the highway. Black smoke poured from eight towers more than a mile away.

"It's like Saturday morning science fiction on television," said C. J.

"It probably seems like that because it's so out in the open. You wouldn't especially notice any of it, if it was in the middle of Boston."

"There's a railroad track on the south. Has it got its own train?"

"I don't know for sure how that works. There's lot of shipments, though. In and out."

"I can't even tell how many buildings there are. Looks like two dozen."

"Yeah, they're interconnected. Some of them are almost all underground."

"Those must be the trucks I saw last night," C. J. said, pointing to the south section of the parking lot.

"When last night?"

"Late…Do trucks drive this two-lane?"

"There's another special access road."

"What is it they do here?"

"Manufacturing. Engineering parts. I don't know exactly. They just call it 'the plant.' They always have. Most everybody in town works here. Some from Denver, too. Boulder even. The management thinks the city'll stretch all the way out where we live someday, and they wanted to get the land when it was cheap. That's what Dad says. They're still expanding. A lot of money goes through here. It's supposed to be one of the best stock investments you can find."

"Sure is reversing."

"Reversing what?"

"Business before homes."

"It happened that way in the East, too, though. Last century. Like those mill towns where they had to use company script to buy anything. There was space here. There still is. Besides that, the chemicals or the ores or whatever they use are close by."

"But what is it gets done here?"

"Honestly I don't know, C. J. It's complicated. Engineering. I've heard some of the words, but I don't understand them. I'm not even sure they get raw materials from around here; I just figured they must."

"The way it fits into the land it almost looks like the mountains were built, too."

"Yeah, Dad had something to do with that. He tries to get his buildings designed so it's like they grew. That's his whole philosophy. To me, it's almost more like camouflaging must be. I have heard him say, 'To emphasize and preserve and manifest the natural rhythms' about five million times…Hey, there's a cow in the road up there!" Honking, Jack slowed the car and swerved past the cow into the oncoming lane. "Some of these roads wind like corkscrews," he said, turning back into the standard lane. "It's hard to ever pass anyone…I wonder where a cow could have come from."

"This television show I saw once, it said that cows, they used to get barbed wire tied to their heads. For when they ran into wood rail fences. That's how somebody in Iowa thought up making the fences out of the wire."

"I never heard that…" Jack said, smiling and angling off the highway onto a gravel road. "It's about a mile up from here…I was going to tell you, C. J., that what Dad said about hunting, about how I didn't take to it, that's not exactly right. He thinks it is, but it was more that he didn't ever give me the chance. He'd always make like he was sorry I didn't want to come with him, like it was my fault; but it'd be before I'd ever have said anything. When I'd tell him I wanted to go, he'd cut out completely what he'd heard; and after awhile I realized it was important to him, just being alone. That's the only time he ever is alone really, hunting.

But…Grandpa'd take me with him sometimes, summers, or late fall, and I wouldn't get a license. Mother and Dad never knew about that, so if we talk about it with him, be sure not to mention it to my parents. All right?"

"I'm not going to be here tomorrow, anyway."

"I thought you were going to stay over another day."

"Maybe you could come with me."

"I asked them already. They think as long as I'm here I should keep mostly at home. Can't blame them, I guess. They pay out enough money to Yale…Where are you going next? Know yet?"

"Black Hills. Dakotas. Wherever I can get a ride to."

"Ever get tired of camping?"

"Sometimes."

"What do you do then?"

"Rent a room."

"In a hotel?"

"Boardinghouse."

"I didn't know there were any boardinghouses around anymore."

"Small towns. That was the South, though…Is he going to ask me anything?"

"I don't think so. All he usually does is sit and talk about the last rain or a beaver fight he's seen or about his first crystal radio. He hardly ever asks much…. Whatever you want to say will be all right."

"Good," said C. J. Contentedly he rolled down his window and leaned outside, while the car slowed to a stop.

"No parallel parking, and no lawn mower," said Jack, shutting off the ignition. "Watch out for your feet. It's always muddy here. That's why I wore sports shoes."

"I'd be afraid of the snow up this high," said C. J., as he stepped onto the damp ground.

"It falls pretty often, but it doesn't stay very long."

"Is it always this quiet?"

"Except for hunting seasons."

"In the city…" said C. J., "the sounds we know are what we don't listen to."

"Yeah," said Jack. "We have to put up lots of walls there."

In the midst of a cluster of evergreen trees was a clapboard, rectangular cabin, weather-stained gray. The warped, shingled roof was pitched nearly flat; and from one corner a rusty drainpipe creaked in the mild breeze. A cord of firewood rested in a heap against the front wall.

After wrenching open a screen door and glancing inside, Jack turned back, saying to C. J., who stood with his feet wide apart and his hands in his back pockets, "He's gone somewhere. I'm sorry. I was afraid he might do this…I guess we may as well wait a few minutes. Come on in."

Most of the rear wall of the single-room interior was shielded by a red-brick fireplace. Carpentry and gardening tools hung from its copper mantel on which had been randomly deposited a microscope, plates, cups, a tin can filled with silverware, a mortar and pestle, a pepper mill, a kerosene lamp, and a screened metal corn popper.

A braided gray and brown rug covered the entire floor. Three of the corners were piled high with newspapers, maps, books, cans of paint and tar, fishing rods, rifles, nets, and heavy knee-length rubber boots; two axes were stowed within a bucket of sawdust in the fourth corner.

On either side of the entrance were a black wood stove and an enamel sink to which was attached a hand pump. Above the sink were shelves packed with jars of rice, beans, flour, corn, and sections of dried fruits. Next to the stove was an upright oak cabinet, its doors firmly shut. The remainder of the furniture—an overstuffed couch upholstered with leather, a plywood footstool, three cane chairs, and a small table strewn with fishing hooks, lines, plugs, artificial flies, and varied sizes of tweezers— was scattered about the room as if by whim.

"You feeling okay, C. J.?" asked Jack, sitting down on the couch. "You look sort of pale."

"Altitude," C. J. said, sinking into one of the cane chairs.

"Yeah, it can do that. We're almost at the timberline. And you were up late last night. Up early, too…Hey, before I forget, can you see that stone out the back window?" He pointed to a piece of white rock the size of a refrigerator.

"I see it," C. J. replied.

"It's solid marble. From a quarry a couple of hundred miles west. For awhile it was one of the biggest quarries anywhere in the world. The Lincoln Memorial was made from it. There's nothing but chips left now. Grandpa hauled that piece up here before I was born. He says it's going to be his tombstone, and he picks at it with a chisel every so often. He wants to do all the carving on it himself—except for the last number…"

Queasily C. J. coughed and said, "Maybe we'd better go."

"No, I…no, let's wait," said Jack. Sighing, he took off his sunglasses, sat down on the couch, and began to speak casually and ramblingly. It felt to C. J., listening, his legs crossed, his hands held tightly in the vice of his thighs, as if the law of gravity were somehow threatening to disappear.

"When I was about eight…" Jack said. "Yes, eight, because it was second grade. We had a lot of people over for a Christmas dinner. It's the last party I can remember in our house. The town was new then, and things were a lot less formal than they are now. Some of the people brought me presents. We never had relatives around to have over for holidays…I guess you wouldn't have had any either."

"No."

"I didn't understand what I was supposed to do, but my mother told me to be sure to thank everybody. This one package had writing on the box. Under the ribbons and the paper. Printing. It said *Christmas Cards*. I put on a big smile and went over to the people who'd handed me the package and thanked them. They laughed and said I should open the box first. So I did, and inside there was a white shirt."

"Which you wanted even less than Christmas cards."

"Yes, but I kept the smile on and took the shirt out and thanked them again. When I was up here the next day, I told Grandpa what I'd done;

and he pulled off his belt and whipped me. I knew exactly why he had; and I was glad he had, even then. Because no one else would have. And it was the only time he ever did. He did it because of the fake smile I'd put on. In a weird kind of way, it was like he was sort of bracing me against Mother and Dad and the others, too…" After briefly pausing, he added, "Lately it's started to seem like that's what most of my growing-up was, C. J. That smile I didn't mean…."

"In *my* second grade…" C. J. slowly replied, "I was sick. For a long time. Everybody had brought me presents. When I got back. I opened them at lunch. The teacher told the class I had something to say. I didn't know what. So I said, "I got a yoyo and crayons and a softball.' On and on…It wasn't until the next day I figured out the teacher'd meant 'thank you.'"

"Yeah…" Jack said, laughing. "Yeah…presents are…well…like Grandpa, C. J. Christmases, I'd always come up here. For one night. No matter how much snow there was, the evergreen trees in front were decorated with strings of cranberry and popcorn. This couch opens into a bed, only I don't think Grandpa uses it for himself very often. But he'd set it up for me, get out his sleeping bag, and play his guitar. And he'd give me one cup of cocoa with marshmallows. Every year. Just that. It was always my favorite part of vacation." Smiling broadly, he stood, ambled to the cabinet, looked inside, and then said irritably, "Nope, his guitar's gone. He won't be back. I'm sorry. He told me he'd be sure to be here. I guess he's sort of shy—in his own way. Let's go."

"What's he use the microscope for?" C. J. asked, as giddily he lifted himself up from the chair.

"He chloroforms insects and puts them on slides to get ideas for tying flies." Jack opened the screen door. "That's how he spends the winters. Tying flies…He sells them somewhere. Or gives them away. I must've seen hundreds of them…He's got a root cellar out back, and some winters he'll have a big, wooden bucket of sauerkraut stored there he's made himself. And there's a stream he keeps things in, eggs and cheese and fruit. He built a contraption made out of an old stump for holding them in the water. It's like an icebox."

Leisurely Jack put the car into reverse, wound back down the gravel road, turned onto the highway in the direction they had been going earlier, and pressed the accelerator. "It'll be flat now, mostly, until Canon City," he said. "Want to go by way of Denver?"

"Fine," C. J. replied, curling his head between the seat and the door. "I didn't get to see much of it yesterday."

"Would you shut your window?" Jack asked, as he resumed his sunglasses.

"I don't...Could it stay like it is?"

"Sure, I guess so. Why? Do you think it's the air conditioner bothering you?"

"No, I...I'm not ever in a car much. I...like...the feeling of the breeze."

8

"You awake?"

"We there already?"

"It's been almost an hour. We'll be downtown in a minute."

"Didn't know the air was so dirty here."

"It's supposed to be almost as bad as Los Angeles. They say it's because Denver has grown so fast. People get amazed when they find out Mother was born here. Almost everybody is from somewhere else. This whole area is going to get torn down soon for new buildings. Offices and hotels. Banks. It's all planned. Downtown isn't much right now. The one ways came in a few years ago. But you can see driving is nothing like it is in New England. I'm going to have to learn all over again this fall. It'll be good to be able to get out of New Haven, though. Especially for skiing." He angled south off Seventeenth Street onto Broadway, the city's major east/west line of division. "This block is where I'll probably have my office. At first anyway. Those are county buildings on the right. There's more federal employees here than any city except for Washington. I always heard Denver was a good place to practice law in because of that. The statehouse is up ahead. It's supposed to have a layer of gold…"

"Could you stop for a minute?" C. J. interrupted.

"Sure," Jack said. He shifted out of his lane and idled the car at a bus stop. "You feeling sick again?"

"No," said C. J., already out the door. "I want to see something."

Dashing across the street, he circled intently about a stone fountain isolated within an intersection, lay down on the surrounding cement, positioned his body in imitation of a life-sized sculptured human figure that formed the base of the fountain, held the pose for a moment, then scurried back into the car.

"It's a miner," he explained. "With a nugget of gold. He sits there like he's judging whether the city's living up to what he'd hoped for."

"I know what the statue is, C. J. But what were you doing?"

"I always shape myself to those kinds of things."

"Why?"

"To find out better what they mean."

"First time I ever heard of anyone doing that," said Jack, veering to the left. "It's a good idea. It really is."

"I oughta think more about who's around, though. Sorry if I scared you."

"You just surprised me is all."

They were traveling a looped path through the section of Denver within which Jack's mother had spent her youth. Many of the buildings had been constructed during the late nineteenth century in defiance of ornate European structures that had been glimpsed by hordes of visionary peasants and servants, who subsequently had fled to the United States, had struggled past the boundaries of the Mississippi and Missouri Rivers, had forsaken the possibilities of homesteading on the Great Plains, and had at last ceased their wanderings upon wearily sighting the awesomely treacherous peaks of the Rocky Mountains. The uniform facades of the myriad houses in the neighborhood (most of which—due to suburban growth—had recently been converted into apartments) were characterized both by a bold, garish elegance and by an exaggerated, virile adventuresomeness. It was a combination unique in the United States—a combination that initially had embodied the cornerstone attitudes of a frontier mode nourished on vast space, quick wealth, an immense supply of what were said to be raw materials, and expansive, quixotic dreams.

Nearing the southeastern edge of the city, Jack said, "I don't really get in here very often, C. J. It always seems like a big mirage to me, sort of, especially now compared to New Haven. A mirage without a sky."

"What do you do when you do come here?"

"Mostly I just use the library for a few minutes. There isn't much that's modern at the one in town. It pretty much stops with the war. But I haven't even done that this summer. I wanted to finish the rest of Eugene Webber's novels last month. It's been a year since I started reading them all."

"What'd you get from that? All the books of one author?"

"I don't know."

"What do you mean you don't know? Did you really read it?"

"Yeah, but I never expected anybody to ask me what I got out of it. I'm used to people around home just being impressed I made it through all nine of the books. I'll have to think...."

Slanting the corners of his mouth downward in a studied aspect of patient skepticism, C. J. brushed his hand across his forehead, relaxed, lay back, and pillowed his shoulder against the passenger door.

"You going to sleep again?" Jack asked.

"Probably. Anything to see?"

"Not much more than concrete and tar."

"Wake me up if you want."

Within another hour the car sped past an arrow-shaped sign, its faded, golden letters reading Temple Canyon Park; and Jack soon turned off the highway onto a pitted, dirt road.

Dazed, C. J. sat up, eyed his watch, and asked, "How much longer?"

"We're almost there."

"Thought you were going to stop at the state prison first."

"I changed my mind," said Jack. "I'm sure we couldn't get in. Besides, I saw everything I could last month. I've never been so depressed anywhere, C. J. I don't want to see it again until I've got some idea how to handle it all..."

After more than a minute-long pause, his shoulders bent forward, C. J. started to reply in hollow, expressionless tones, decisively pronouncing each of his words as if they were a succession of measured, quarter notes: "Yale sometimes feels to me like a jail...They wrote me in June everybody on scholarships had to come down and meet the people who give them. The man I got assigned to hadn't known anything about who I was until two months past when he'd paid my tuition. I got a letter from him in April. He owns an office machine company. The scholarship is a memorial for his son. I never answered the letter. I didn't know what he wanted from me. It was two weeks ago. He was very fat. There was a purple vein in the center of his forehead. He had a red handkerchief in his coat pocket. He kept taking it out and unfolding it and folding it back up again. And he said 'communist' so many times it seemed like it was his every tenth word. His son's plane was shot down in Korea. All he and his wife got sent them were a few bones. That's what he told me. He wants me to see his son's medals.... Who needs medals?" Craning his neck backward, he pawed the dashboard, stared out the open window at his side, and added, "That's how all the alumni I saw then looked. Fat and rich and blank-eyed. I'm not going to get like that."

"At least nobody's pressuring you into anything," Jack said.

"So what difference does that make?"

"It couldn't have been everyone looked like he did."

"You weren't *there*. It was like they were a roomful of mirrors."

"...The way you describe that man, he reminds me of the principal I had in high school...My senior year...you may not believe it, C. J...."

"I'll believe it. After that afternoon at Yale, I'm ready to believe anything...What happened?"

"Well, there was a ceremony for planting a tree in the schoolyard. The junior high band played, and the pep squad marched. The tree was supposed to be some kind of memorial. That night it got chopped down. The next day rumors went everywhere about who'd done it. Kid after kid got called out of classes to the front office. The last period we all had to go to the auditorium. The principal was up on stage. He usually seemed like he'd just gotten out of a shower, his clothes always in perfect shape, his hair always combed exactly into place. But that day his tie was crooked; and his face was red; and he paced back and forth, talking real loud, not using a microphone. He said whoever'd done it was a communist."

"He actually said that about one of you."

"Yeah, and he meant it, too. He even said anyone who knew who'd chopped the tree down was doing the worst thing possible: protecting a communist."

"They find out who'd done it?"

"No…. But after that I didn't do anything besides wait to get out of there."

"He sounds crazy."

"I think he was. I think a lot of them were in some ways…." Jack said, adding in lighter tones, "C. J., I don't think we can get much higher. The river's close now. You want to camp here?"

"Seems like there won't be anyone else around. That's good."

"Yeah, hardly any tourists ever come here."

"Looks fine to me."

"Watch out for prairie dogs," said Jack, as he parked the car.

"Why's that?"

"A couple of people caught bubonic plague from them near here a few weeks back."

"Bubonic plague was four hundred years ago."

"I thought so, too. But that's what I read in the Denver papers."

Slamming his door, C. J. said, "The Air Force Academy probably puts that story out to make it so nobody'll stumble into their training setups."

"Maybe. I don't know. Look, I'm going to lock up the car. Want to take the sandwiches now?"

"I'm getting hungry already."

The surrounding hundreds of acres of parkland were hilly, though rarely steep. Patches of yellow and gray sand were interspersed with red veins of clay and black boulders studded with blue and green lichens. From the east came the ceaseless roar of the Arkansas River. While Jack and C. J. were heading toward it at an unhurried gait, C. J. picked up a crushed, mud-caked football; and the two boys tossed it between them until they came to a narrow rivulet. Hopping across its shining, clay bed with smooth coordination, Jack waited on the opposite side, as C. J. nervously lifted a leg, hesitated, finally made a clumsy spring, and landed precariously balanced on one foot.

After crossing a gully dense with an undergrowth of amaranthus and sage, they arrived at the brim of a sheer cliff, which proved to be a more than one hundred-foot side of the river chasm. Immediately they both plunged onto the dusty slope and, unhindered by any plant life or irregularities in the subsoil, careened all the way to the water. Sweating and panting, exhilarated, they proceeded upstream along a railroad track, found an aspen tree, stopped beneath it to eat the lunch Mrs. Tane had that morning prepared for them, then rolled up their pant legs and with Jack leading, made a string of cautious hops onto slippery, granite rocks protruding out of the coursing river and forming a jagged path to the opposite shore.

The soil became sandier, as they wended east; and though there were more trees, the midday sun sacrificed all traces of shade. Spying ahead of them, tall as a single-story house, a tapered, red-sandstone column erosion had sculpted away from yielding, interstratified clays, C. J., embarrassed by the lack of outdoor skills he had, thus far, demonstrated, ran to its several-yards-in-diameter base, wrapped his arms about it, and supporting himself on ledges barely six inches wide, climbed to the top. "Come on up," he shouted. "There's some oak trees have taken root here."

"Yeah, but is it any cooler?" Jack asked.

"You can see the river good from here. Come on up!"

"If I didn't know better," said Jack, as he pulled himself onto the brittle, circular summit of the column, "I'd say this was a petrified redwood trunk."

"Maybe it's from whatever the temple was the canyon's named for."

"Not likely. I'm not even sure we're still in the park."

Deciding to leave unmentioned a No Trespassing sign he had seen close to the river shore, C. J. closed his eyes, cradled his head in his arms, rocked his shoulders back and forth, and said, "…The high school I went to, there was a principal was probably about as crazy as yours. Except in a different way. Mine was more a dictator, sort of…This teacher I had once, sociology, she had us do things like go to another suburb, pick out a street corner, stay there awhile, then write about it. That was the best assignment I ever had. And she was mostly the best teacher. The principal, he'd show up outside her class door. Complain we were making too much noise.

Insinuate she didn't know how to handle us. But she was the only one who did. Not in the way the principal had meant, though. She was trying to get at what we wanted for ourselves, instead of making us pretend we were like how all the other teachers thought we should be…She got fired at the end of the first semester."

"I hate it when things like that happen," said Jack. "You get a little bit of hope, and somebody takes it away, and then things are almost worse than if there hadn't been any hope in the first place. I had so many dreams about how college would be. I didn't think of them as hopes exactly, but that's what they were. I didn't expect the kind of competition there is at Yale. Lots of times people are more interested in proving how much they supposedly know than in finding out anything. It should be more cooperative…The way Eugene Webber described school in his books, everyone was always sitting around having these amazing long talks about Dostoevsky and justice and the general theory of relativity…But we don't do that. I wonder why. Every time I've said something in class sections I've gotten good grades for it, but what I've done too much is pull a chunk of a book out of my head and quote it almost. I was hoping to learn how to put all those chunks into some kind of pattern. That's not happening. It's like the books are talking through me instead of me talking. I don't know how to use what I've read or how to relate it all together. The words are collected up in separate drawers inside my mind, and the truth is I'm not really sure how to mean anything from thinking on my own. I kept concentrating on getting away from Colorado; and now that I'm away, I'm not handling all that much of anything very well."

"I wish we could only explore. For the first two years, anyway," C. J. said, interlocking his fingers about his ankles. "How am I supposed to know what I want to take until after I've had time to look at what it might be?"

"It's starting to seem like a diploma mainly depends on keeping what you don't know hidden," Jack replied. "And diplomas are supposed to be pretty much basically what are going to give us how our lives turn out." Absently he added, as he shredded a handful of leaves from the branches of a small tree growing beside him in what was scarcely more than a thin layer of dust, "Funny how little it takes to keep something alive…"

"I wish you'd stop doing that," said C. J. sharply. "You shouldn't do that to plants."

"Why not? They wouldn't last very long up here, anyway."

"So what? Trees feel."

"Who says that?"

"Some people."

"What people?"

"People somewhere."

"How do they know?"

"It's what they believe. Maybe it's right. That was the point of the last history lecture, wasn't it? 'Knowledge is limited by human boundaries.' We can't come up against anything but our own limits."

"Yeah, only what does that have to do with saying a tree has emotions?"

"Maybe knowing about something like that is outside our limits. The maybe of pain is enough."

"…My mother says talking with plants makes them grow better, and that's why she does it. But I don't believe it. I think she's just lonely…."

Taking off his shoes and throwing them over the edge of the stone column, C. J. asked, "Why do you always have to turn what your parents say into something else? Why can't you just hear them?"

"Because just hearing him isn't what Dad wants. It's not what he expects. Whether he knows it or not. And Mother relies on him for so much, it's practically like he's a warden. She has to fit her ways to his. Stay here longer, and you'll see what I mean."

"…The way you talk about your father, it almost makes me glad I didn't have one."

"Yeah, well, you're lucky there's nothing for you to reject. I mean that."

"Nothing to follow either," said C. J. His voice was barely audible; and he was uncertain whether he was going to continue speaking; but at last he quietly said, "My father was from Tennessee. I knew my grandmother was still there. My uncles. I didn't know anything more about them than what town they were in. And that my father had been cut off by them. I didn't know why. I don't know if my mother knows why. I wanted to see them. It was a very small town. Under a thousand. I found them easy. From the phone book. That was a year and a half ago. The first night I was there, I went by my grandmother's house. Late. It was dark in the windows. The next morning I went back. A cop drove up and made me get in his car. I told him my name. He took me to the police station. One of my uncles came. He looked me over and said, "Wouldn't you know it'd be that brother of mine again, riding on one of those buses and counting on turning the whole South upside down?' He asked me how much money I wanted. I said I just was there to see them. He handed the cop fifty dollars. The cop drove me about five miles out of town. Gave me the money. Took out his gun. Twirled it. Told me to stay away from the county. I didn't know where I was. I walked for awhile. When I got to the Tennessee River, I tore up all the money and floated it downstream. I decided if they thought I was one of the people like they'd seen on television, I might as well become one. So I hitched to Montgomery for the sit-ins."

"And you never saw your grandmother?"

"No."

"I wonder what your father did."

"I guess I won't find out."

"That sure is strange, C. J."

"Yeah."

"What happened in Montgomery?"

"I wasn't there for very long."

"Why not?"

"'Cause it seemed after awhile like a lot of people in the civil rights movement, they were trying to get what wasn't worth having. I have most of what they said they want, and I don't think it deserves all the trouble. They were making things too simple…I don't know if ways of living together ever got better. Maybe they just get different."

"If they get different, they have to be better or worse. They can't change and be the same both at once."

"That's how they thought," C. J. replied. "You should be at places like that instead of me." He grappled his legs about the column and skidded down it, saying, "I'd rather forget all that and live in a treehouse!"

"I couldn't hear you. What'd you say?" Jack called out, beginning to wriggle to the ground.

"Nothing," replied C. J., as he pensively tied his shoestrings, adding good-naturedlly, "You take it so much for granted the ones who work this land are Mexicans, some of them could be from anywhere and you'd never notice."

"Yeah," said Jack, standing now beside C. J. "Some of them could be off-season professionally skiing Eskimos trying to set all the words they have for snow straight in their minds, and I'd probably be the last person to find out about it!"

Kicking small stones back and forth to each other, they rambled back west in silence. After they had recrossed the river, Jack suggested they gather a supply of firewood; and by the time they returned to their campsite, each had an armful.

"We ought to build a fire that'll burn long enough to keep the mosquitoes away until we're asleep," Jack said, unlocking the driver's door of his car. "…What're you thinking about so hard, C. J.?"

"I'm working on how to make an octagonal kite out of aluminum foil. For an experiment. An experiment with the sun."

"What kind of experiment?"

"I want to see if I can predict what colors of sunlight'd be reflected. Depending on the time and the weather and on how high the kite flies and on the direction of the wind…."

"It sure is good to hear you talking more, C. J."

"I didn't exactly know I've been."

"…C. J., what do you think about them trying to land on the moon?"

"I don't know…I guess I…I don't know, I guess I…feel afraid for the moon."

9

Twilight was ending, as Mr. Tane shut off the television set and joined his wife on their redwood patio. "Idiocies," he muttered.

"I'm so sorry they didn't stay for breakfast," said Mrs. Tane. Her shoulders were cloaked in a shawl, and a crocheted blanket was wrapped about her legs.

"An early start, perhaps, was wise," Mr. Tane replied. He wore a red, satin necktie over a brown and white check sport shirt; his trousers were gray, loose fitting, and sharply creased.

"Will this…affect us here?" asked Mrs. Tane.

"Doubtless it will at least bring a temporary hold on new employees at the plant."

"It's more than their accent, you know. I'm sure the Attorney General stutters."

"This 'first step,' as the President calls it, has relegated Mr. Chamberlain to a minor chapter in the history of appeasement."

"I had planned on waffles," said Mrs. Tane. "It's been so long since we've had waffles."

"Perhaps for Saturday lunch."

"You're certain it will be only temporary?"

"If he had counseled with any adult in town, as even common sense should have led him to do," replied Mr. Tane. "I dare say he would have been presented with ample refutations of whatever reasoning there can possibly have been behind a nuclear test ban treaty. Next they'll be talking about eliminating the weather manipulation weapons it's taken three decades to perfect."

"I do wish he'd taken his ski sweater."

"And you heard the Peace Corps nonsense last evening."

"Jack told me."

"This present action of his makes me truly doubt the man's sanity…"

"I wonder…" said Mrs. Tane, tracing her fingers over each other in the air, upturning her head, gazing at the Big Dipper and the North Star. "I wonder if…I wonder if Jack…if Jack…knows."

"You wonder if Jack knows what?"

"Why, knows what happens at the plant."

"I am quite confident he does not. None of the children do. None of them could, after all."

"I wonder if he should be told."

"There is no cause to be burdening him with rumor."

"It wouldn't be rumor. Not from us. How can any...?"

"All in good time," interrupted Mr. Tane. "All in good time."

"What if it gets worse, though? What if the limiting of the personnel becomes permanent?"

"There is simply no chance of that occurring. It's foolish to be concerning yourself with the impossible."

"He does have the power to take more such steps, that's sure. What if it should come to closing the plant? There would be no way of our continuing to support Jack's schooling. Don't you think he should know of the possibility, however unlikely it is?"

"Under the worst of conditions we would sacrifice our home for Jack's education."

"He must find out sometime."

"There's no need to worry ourselves about matters over which we have no control," said Mr. Tane firmly. "Ballots will not be miscounted forever, no matter what sort of dynastic pretensions are displayed."

"I can't so much as turn on the television anymore," said Mrs. Tane, "without seeing one of them water-skiing. And if it isn't water-skiing, it's football on the White House lawn."

"Perhaps the waffles for Sunday breakfast."

"I'd planned on huevos rancheros. Jack says there's so little Mexican food out East...."

"Certainly a quiet young man."

"Good to see Jack with someone his own age."

"Yes," said Mr. Tane, "yes, it was."

"...Did you hear it thundering this afternoon?" asked Mrs. Tane.

"Briefly."

"That could mean hail."

"Sleet in the foothills, more likely."

"An early frost, I expect."

"Yes...."

"I wish the weather would stop...changing so. It's...."

"The weather has always been changing."

"But not so quickly as in these last years. I think it must be those satellites."

"Such ill-considered projects drain funds that ought to be used in furthering our efforts for defense. Of course, scientific research has its cotton mice, as does any field."

"'Cotton mice'? Where on earth did you find that expression?"

"It amused me. I overheard one of the staff use it."

"Certainly is accurate sounding. I wonder if Jack's heard it."

"I imagine so. It must be commonly said."

"...Watching the satellites was nice, though, wasn't it? Remember? We used to all sit out here so late some evenings...I wonder if they're still flying about. I wonder if anyone in town would know."

"Best wait and hear it on the news," said Mr. Tane, yawning.

"There's nothing specific we could have told him."

"Nothing."

"I'm sure they'll welcome our air conditioning tomorrow."

"One night of open air should prove to be quite enough."

Lumbering to her feet, Mrs. Tane folded the blanket, placed it in her husband's lap, stepped behind him, and settled her hands on the back of his chair.

"It's past time," she said.

"Yes, it is," he said. "It certainly is. Past time."

"Good night, then."

"Good night."

PART II

5 Sole Dispatch

'Move into a cabbie-porter-janitor-longshoreman diner, they'll shape an off-limits you. Two-a.m.-hands-on-counter-charged-triple thoughts (do care), stay, "welcome," yes. Wide-awake-not-yet-is-sun-up here. Out, go, no. Just as was: they stare-made a me I am not. More than clothes show how I am. Say my name and I'll answer. My passport's in my pocket. Ten-o'clock secretaries out-for-air boss, nap: cover, please (time off) sip (wake up), to go, that they know. We reserve the right to....

'Hypothesis: red, blue, silver, orange, bronze, someone.

'Procedure: Divide the number of seconds between launch at sun sight and first change of color by degree of angle of string the moment after blue. Multiply the quotient by May fifth and walk that many ties along the tracks off Union, then let out as much string as the wind will take. If the next color happens sooner, it will have been caused by the flight-angle increase produced by speed of walking. In that case, measure how many degrees west of due south the track is angling at the where-when of change; and walk that number of ties.

'...Draft should be only for the wind.

'History books are written by the Joint Chiefs of Staff, and they don't tell about...the eternal-flame-winter-hope-almost-gone-sad-sorry eyes, caught pretending that death had been computerized away.

'Frozen Frankenstein's us floating out of natural selection.

'Mammoths in radioactive ice.

'Almost.

'Almost.

'Senselessness of any-second-end called sense for long enough.

'And all it took were a few songs.

'Yeah.

'Yeah.

'Yeah.

'The leaves came back.

'Over to fear.

'Help everyone hear.

'Changes have begun.

'Yeah.'

"Steady. Soon."

'Electric-born, I wax on key. Rusted bombers frozen in ice red with throats-cut-our-blood that too-soon-ago seemed to have drowned almost all the grass in the world.

'Wrong-for-so-long wasn't me; old songs didn't have the right beat...

'The tail is enough. The tide is cast. May 5, 1964. Wind from the southeast. Lengthen the bridge. Won't fly slack...

'I could still beat the sun to DeWitt Street. The silver octagon could still land in New Haven Green. Deepen the bow one more time. Best I can do. As contrastable to reckless as can be managed. Corner of Spring and Union is enough.

'All it took were a few songs.

'Oh, the sun again.

'Daylight. Kite. An even-up.'

"There."

'Time.

'One kite.

'The subject: how time and kites fly.

'Myself, as usual. Myself, healthy.

'Self-evident: I am wanted to say an I who isn't me.

'They cut out my heart, yeah, but does my blood in their mouths give them the right to say "ours" when a Harvey's beat still sings in my throat?'

"Red."

'How around will the earth be when the next color comes? If someone else sees until silver, the string angle will be so acute they can follow it to questions being easy.'

"Blue."

'Seventy-two seconds divided by thirty-seven degrees multiplied by five times five equals forty-eight ties—and what I now will do, is imagine a conversation that I do not want to happen:

"'Do you follow me? Is the railroad yard your office, sir, officer? There's no lightning, so why your rod? Something is up; and I am holding it up. Alexander Graham Bell's equilibrium-perfect visible-speech kites voices-on-wires, Benjamin Franklin's house-key-hair-to-shoulders lost-time-is-never-found-again kites postage-sought. Remember for me. Welcome forward, officer. Welcome ahead. There are precedents. Compare.'"

"Forty-eight."

"'I'm sighting up reflections of natural laws. Isn't your badge supposed to reflect them, too?'"

"Silver."

"'But officer, I checked that, sir, I did, sir: there are no scheduled air-line arrivals or departures for the next two hours, sir.'"

"Orange."

"'I'm honestly not lying, thus far, officer. I have no lair. Even I can tell more truth. And I'll do it. I'll do it for you: glued to the kite is an unpostmarked stamp with a folded corner flapping. If the orange turns to bronze, I say to you now I'm going to let go of the line.

"'Because on the back of the stamp are printed the letters of my name....

"'Supposing you walkie-talkie-ask whether anyone is seeing what's getting ready to fall? What are the odds you'd be a causer of seeing instead of a poller? I guess the best thing this century has let us know is that investigations create evidence, officer. That's constitutional. Wait. The kite'll soon be far enough up so your answerers could not tell who holds the string. Don't spoil the experiment by eliminating the factor of good surprise. This line's in my hands, sir; but you're my public servant; and all humans dwell together in a community, so let the kite be ours for this morning. Without an envelope or a telephone number to my name, I am here. Who owns the reflections?"'

"Bronze. Hypothesis five-sixths safely verified."

'Find it!'

6 Solidary Lines

Applauding enthusiastically, Dr. Colin Tsampa examined the rest of the meager audience. Surprised to discover he was the oldest person in the tiny, chilly auditorium, he kneaded his frayed, button-down shirt collar and looked again at his hand-stenciled, circular program. Crustlike around the edge had been printed: "*How Did the Point(s) Go?* written and directed by common agreement of the cast: In Performance March 3-6, 1965."

The play had begun an hour and a half earlier, when an actor carrying a thin, cardboard box had raced a bicycle down the center aisle to a huge model of a television screen defined by a rectangular scrim curtain, lighted green, and a stage left control panel the size of a door. The cyclist had then ridden to the left of the stage, stopped, and pressed an oversized button; instantly the green light had changed to white, disclosing a simple, living room set. Two actresses and three actors had been seated on a couch and chairs, stage right; another actress had been perched, birdlike, on a stepladder beside a card table, stage left. A film projector had been stage center, and behind it had been a movie screen bordered with window curtains. All of the performers had been costumed in black and white. The props and background flats had been painted in monotonous shades of gray.

Following a brief tableau, the actress on the ladder had stepped down, walked to the left edge of the screen, taken the cardboard box, placed it on the card table, and reseated herself, all the while having paid no attention to the cyclist, who had stood by, unmoving, as if waiting to be paid.

The remaining players had then each delivered a portion of one of five speeches, thereby portraying a physicist considering the implications of the Heisenberg Uncertainty Principle, a high school teacher commenting on the results of an essay assignment titled *Religious Beliefs and Homesteading Trends*, a gossip columnist volunteering intimate descriptions of unnamed celebrities, a philosopher discussing possible criteria for an appraisal of trans-historical and cross-cultural value systems, and a telephone installer chronicling the encounters of one day's work.

As each performer had spoken, the other four, stage right, had reacted with semblances of inappropriately timed smiles, frowns, and occasional applause. At the end of every segment, the actress on the ladder had asked, "How did the deposition go?" Her words had been more than repeated, however; she had varied her intonations and facial gestures in order to suggest five characters—an impartial judge, a testifying witness, the ambitious wife of an attorney, a harried secretary, and a bored reporter in search of topical scandal. After her fifth phrasing, the cyclist had started the projector, which had produced on the windowlike screen an image of one of the five-member group of performers again asking, though in spiritless recorded tones empty of meaning, "How did the deposition go?" At the same time, the actor who had been photographed had risen, walked to the table, opened the box, taken out a slice of bread, eaten it, left some small change, and returned to a seated position.

As soon as the film had ended, the recitations had continued as before; but the performers had each taken up the theme of one of the four other speeches. The question had been asked five more times by the solitary actress; and with but five words she had convincingly managed to portray a pedantic historian, a nerve-wracked defendant, an election-minded prosecutor, a naive law student, and a seasoned convict. Again the cyclist had run film of a performer, who simultaneously had walked to the table, eaten a slice of bread, left some coins, and resumed a seat.

By the time each of the five speakers had taken a turn with a section of each speech, had been screened, had eaten, and had deposited change, the actress on the ladder had created twenty-five miniature portraits. At that point the deliveryman had taken all of the money and ridden back up the aisle; the stage, meanwhile, had turned so red that the television set had appeared to have exploded. The questioning actress had then gotten up, transferred the empty bread box to the stool, and, framed in front of the screen by a white spotlight, had once more asked, "How did the deposition go?" pronouncing the last word with her voice pitched at its lowest tone, thus implying, within the context of the play, that a terrifying, nearly total dissolution of all viable, conventional forms of civilization had just occurred. The last and final question had also been asked not as if expecting an answer nor to indicate yet another character but as if to offer the future a bridge of very profound longing for the continuation of the human community—a bridge of resilient hope arising amid desolation.

The energetic ingenuousness of the production had intrigued and touched Dr. Tsampa; but solitarily free as he was from having any psychic numbing, he could detect only confusion and boredom in the rapidly departing audience. Disappointed, he took a scarf from his coat pocket, wound it about his shaven chin, rolled the program into a cone, tucked it under his jacket, straightened his necktie, stood, and fumbled into a heavy, wool topcoat.

Several years earlier, when he had last been to the same room (which was located within an abandoned church midway between the campuses of Harvard and Massachusetts Institute of Technology), it had functioned as a concert hall featuring folksingers, some of whom had since acquired extensive national reputations; and he knew that other portions of the building were leased to a variety of social action groups. Unfolding and separating a stocking cap, earmuffs, and gloves, he trudged up the aisle toward the exit and resolved sometime to investigate the offices and inquire whether his services might be useful. The organizations seemed always to last no longer than six months; and he guessed that they were largely composed of college students, well-intentioned, but uncertain how to pursue sustained efforts, people easily thwarted and defeated, only to be replaced by other groups of similar composition. His age and experience, he reasoned, might bring a necessary, mature support to the continually floundering ventures.

Almost at the exit, he turned around and headed back down the aisle, mounted the steps the cyclist had used, opened the control-panel door of the set, and entered an improvised dressing area, where the performers were huddled beneath a single light bulb suspended from the ceiling in a netted, wire frame. Webs of shadows enveloped dozens of moths that were swarming over the musty, backstage, brick walls.

Shyly Dr. Tsampa lingered by the partially open door and looked about for the actress who had played the questioner. Finally he realized he had failed to recognize her twice because in the play she had worn a brunette wig. Her real hair was coal black and much longer; it flowed all the way to her waist. She seemed thinner than she had on stage; her pallid face retained not a trace of any of her characterizations; and her brown, saucer eyes gleamed with an impishness that was almost sardonic. As she spoke with one of the actors, her hands shaped a continuous, fluid counterpart to her voice. Dr. Tsampa moved closer and overheard the actor say, "People are used to situation comedies. You can't expect them to appreciate new conventions the first time around."

"I know, but I get so impatient," the actress said. "All we're doing is losing them again and again. Maybe it's our fault."

"We can't play down," the actor replied. "We've got to keep asking them to grow to our level."

"It's difficult enough having hope deferred everywhere else in life," said the actress. "I wasn't ready for that here, too."

"Building an audience can be like irrigating a desert with a watering can," the actor said. "Don't let it bother you."

Resignedly the actress linked her fingers together, stretched her hands palms-outward, and extended her arms downward, cracking her knuckles.

"Miss Tetrao?"

"Yes?" she answered, startled at the unfamiliar, rasping voice.

"Pardon me if I frightened you. I wanted to tell you I admired your work very much."

"Oh," she said, "How...nice."

"Some moments were as powerful as any I've experienced in a theater."

"It seemed to have fallen awfully flat tonight."

"Quite truly, I felt during the final seconds that I was in the presence of something nearly akin to a persuasive representation of the birth of human consciousness. I'm not exaggerating, Miss Tetrao."

"Perhaps it's we who were overambitious," the actress said, pleased by Dr. Tsampa's harmony of intellect and feelings and immediately identifying in him what she considered a clumsiness often accompanying habitual sincerity. "That's pretty much what we meant, though. Rather, I'd say, an overlapping rebirth—the loss of accustomed patterns and the force that's inducing the development of untried ways of surviving without any sense yet of thoroughly ultimate forms."

"That was all quite evident in your delivery. I can't compliment you enough. Your evocations were superb. Sometimes simple but never simplistic."

"I'm grateful to hear that. We don't get much direct feedback, you see."

She smiled, curling her upper lip, dimpling, and revealing her front teeth, held out her right hand to Dr. Tsampa, and tossed her head so that her hair audibly rippled about her shoulders. "I'm Leah Tetrao," she said, her voice mellow and assured. "I suppose those who strive for artistic communication shouldn't shrink back from the possibility that it may have occurred."

"I'm Colin Tsampa," he said, taking her hand. His manner was serious, but not pedantic, genial, but not lighthearted. He stood, as he ordinarily did, with his shoulders slanted forward, as if ready to catch someone about to fall.

"What a peculiar surname!" she said. "Excuse me, perhaps I shouldn't have said that."

"I'm quite used to its being commented on, Miss Tetrao. Family tradition has it that it's the result of a nineteenth-century spelling error on Ellis Island."

"The immigrant's error? Or the clerk's?" Leah asked, laughing.

"The clerk's."

"So be it then, Mr. Tsampa. Error or not, I'm pleased to meet you."

"I should've said, too, it's Doctor, Miss Tetrao."

"Ah, a professor," she said with apparent disappointment. "Where do you teach?"

"No," he said, "I'm a Doctor of Medicine. Please, though, call me Colin."

Her dark, intelligent, round eyes relaxed; and she laughed again, saying, "All right, Colin. Thank you."

"Are you a student?" Dr. Tsampa asked. His voice was relentlessly probing without being overbearing.

"I'm rather more enrolled than a student," she said.

"At what college?"

"Boston University. The School of Fine and Applied Arts. It's my second year there."

"I wonder, I know it's late, and that you probably have classes tomorrow," Dr. Tsampa said, "but I'd certainly like to talk with you about the play. Would you care to have supper with me? We'd have to walk, I'm afraid."

"That's no problem. I was planning to walk to Harvard Square anyway. I'm meeting someone, but I could walk along the river with you. I'd like that."

"Good," he said, although disappointment momentarily clouded his face.

"Company would be nice," said Leah. She draped a shawl around her hair, put on a red cloth coat, wrapped her head in a beige silk scarf, and slung a purse over her left shoulder and a green book bag over her right. "I hope this doesn't offend you," she said, "but do you mind if I look at your identification? I don't mean to..."

"Of course," he said. "I haven't ever...I mean, I wanted to..." He held out his open wallet before her.

"A psychiatrist? You're a psychiatrist?"

"Yes," he answered.

"I hadn't thought of psychiatrists as ever being anywhere but in offices next to couches."

"With notebooks in both hands, I assume."

"You seem too young."

"I've had my own practice in Boston for the past five years."

"Well, I'm a bit...I'm...Are you intent upon studying me, then?" she asked with playful defensiveness.

"Searching for solutions to problems of human behavior is something I'm always doing, Miss Tetrao. That's my major occupational hazard."

"It's honest of you to say so. I'm impressed. I hope I didn't insult you. I was just a bit taken aback."

"Your reaction isn't an uncommon one."

"I suppose not...You must be quite used to having to draw lots of lines between friendships and therapy."

"Yes," Dr. Tsampa said, his left hand pulling at the fingers of his right glove. Wisps of his inattentively combed, curly, brown hair strayed over his ears. "...I've had to learn not to let myself be unduly depended upon in nonprofessional relationships at the same time that I've had to learn to keep sacred the privacies of my patients."

"So you're never really able to share your work," Leah said decisively. "I hope I'm not being too blunt."

"I seek advice and offer observations in a general way, but even my journal has few specific references."

"You keep a journal? How admirable! I've started five diaries in the past two years," Leah said, shrugging her right shoulder in self-amusement.

"Thoughts do look quite different when they're outside oneself," Dr. Tsampa said. "I often wonder if someone could recognize me from my journal."

"That kind of consistency is important, though, don't you think? I mean, for instance, in acting, I want what I act and how I act it to be in harmony with the rest of my life."

"Consistency is very important, Miss Tetrao. Difficult to achieve; but possible, nonetheless."

"You're encouraging to talk with, Colin," Leah said, adding quickly, "I suppose we should be going. If we walk along Memorial Drive, it'll take at least half an hour. I said I'd be there by ten-fifteen. I hope it's no trouble for you taking that route. The river is starting to thaw, and I love hearing the echoes of the ice breaking...Do you mind going that way?"

"No, not at all. I'd prefer it, in fact."

While conversing with Dr. Tsampa, Leah's face had become more animated than it been when earlier he had identified her, her bearing more authoritative; and as she raised her hand, the rest of the performers regarded her with genuinely respectful silence. "Good night," she said in mock regal tones. "Would someone see if they can get the moths to live elsewhere?"

"Touching those moths is bad luck, Leah," said the actor who had played the cyclist.

"You and your whimsical superstitions, sheeplike Zach. Where do you pick them up?"

"Your philosophy doesn't dream, Leah," said the actor.

"And yours is all dream. It's not a philosophy yet!" Leah replied, her eyes satisfied and good-natured. She slipped her hands into elbow-length, brown, leather gloves, tied the belt of her coat, and pointed toward the rear of the stage. "Come on," she said to Dr. Tsampa. "There's an exit back here." As they approached the door, she called out, "Good night again, everyone." And together they stepped into the black, windless cold.

"I've learned the phases of the moon so many times," Leah said, attempting to clothe her words in the lineaments of a sophistication that would be adjudged more luminously sanguine than brazen. "I can always understand them with diagrams and charts; but whenever I try to apply them to the moon itself, I get baffled. It looks silver to me now. Does it to you?"

"Yes," replied Dr. Tsampa, turning up the collar of his coat. "Yes, it does."

"I don't know that I'm correct, but I think contemporary theory has it that astronomical motion can be calculated relative to any object that's assumed to be stationary. And since everything is moving, any pattern depends on what is agreed upon as a hypothetical fixed point for the sake of calculations. So it's no longer strictly proper to say that the earth moves about the sun. Am I right about that?"

"I'm not really sure. I assume there are a limited number of fixed points," Dr. Tsampa replied. His chapped, ruddy lips slued in a progression of contortions, as if he were plucking words from a turbulent snarl of thought; his strides were so long that Leah had to force herself beyond her normal gait in order to keep pace with him.

"I was the same way with tides," she said. "I'd learn the rhythms and the hours, and it would all seem coherent until I was at the beach. Then I'd forget everything."

"You grew up by the ocean, Miss Tetrao?"

"Close to it. West Los Angeles."

"Adjusting to Boston cold must be painful at times."

"It's not the cold so much as it is the absence of sky all winter. I get to feeling rather trapped."

"I had considered practicing in California, but I decided that I'd probably prefer the contrasts of the seasons here…"

"Oh, there are seasons in Los Angeles," Leah said. "You've been taken in by the propaganda. It can get quite cold there. People were so intent on finding the promised land in California that they do quite a bit of ignoring, I'm afraid. There are lots of discouraging surprises for newcomers. But…they learn to forget and disregard and after awhile they're quite convinced they've found whatever it was they'd thought they'd wanted. Los Angeles is fairly crazy overall. I'm glad to be gone. I won't go back. Where are you from, Colin?"

"Toledo, originally. My family has been involved with shipbuilding there."

"Shipbuilding?" Leah asked. "In Ohio?"

"It's the main industry of Toledo. Being on Lake Erie."

"Oh, yes, of course. I tend to forget about the Great Lakes. There's so much I don't know about that's between the coasts. I fly past it all in a few hours and look down at the geometric shapes of the fields and think of that as all there is. With Chicago as sort of a link between the two halves of culture. I need to do more exploring than I've been able to so far."

"Tell me more about Los Angeles, Miss Tetrao," said Dr. Tsampa, glancing at Leah's upturned, aquiline chin. "I've only spent less than a week there."

"I expect the reality is worse than your impressions," Leah said. "You wouldn't have any difficulty finding a practice in L.A., Colin. Frustrated, angry rejects from everywhere show up there with illusions that don't very often relate to any sort of truth. I think it must be the most difficult place on earth to learn to trust anyone."

"That's quite an awful indictment."

"Yes, but, you see, there's so much outsiders usually don't know about. The high percentage of illegal Mexican immigrants, for instance. There's nothing but Spanish spoken in whole areas of the city, and there's sort of a quicksand economy. Ritualized blackmail. False identification documents. Companies without minimum wage. Payoffs to immigration authorities. You should hear my father on that subject; he's an insurance adjuster now. Apart from all that, the black and white populations are almost completely separated. There's so much dissatisfaction and uneasiness in the ghetto, I don't think it can help but explode soon. There's fear all over the city. Trend wealth, reliable patterns of economic corruption…And then, too, movie and television production there has always resulted to some degree from desperate people intertwining their hallucinations. I suppose you know that."

"I suspect I do."

"The people in those industries are so used to rejection that it's probably the rudest professional group there is. I mean it. I grew up around it. When power gets into hands that discontented, actors and producers use it to send back to the places they had probably been thrown out of, movies and television programs that have often been motivated mainly by little more than a desire for revenge. That's the truth! I've been watching it happen all my life. It's a delusion that the trappings of movies and television have to do with art, and the national magazines spread the delusion like a plague virus…Go to a random street corner in Los Angeles; and you'll likely see half a dozen people who've made themselves up to look like copies of one of the newest stars, ready to swear they're the person they're pretending to be. It's pathetic and infuriating, and it's been going on for decades."

"I'm unaccustomed to hearing Los Angeles described as so dismal a community."

"I'll bet you've only heard about the sunlight."

"That's fairly correct."

"And, of course, the air?"

"Yes, the air…"

"I haven't much charity left for L.A., Colin. It's people pretending to be people pretending to be people. Decency and sanity get lost in the lies. From the beginning, that part of the country was the dead end of migration. When there was no more land for the new arrivals, they began to fabricate castles out of nothing; and they've been reinforcing each other's fantasies ever since. That's my human-lemming theory. Although I honestly must say I sometimes wonder whether it's mistaken sorts of human observations that make lemmings behave in some ways they might not if we'd change how we encounter them…The same for guppies…Whatever, if by chance in living in California, one has been able to develop normal rational capacities, one comes to regard movies and television as the bonds that hold together demeaning social networks all over the earth. I'm quite certain whatever I do will be in opposition to a lot of what emanates from Beverly Hills and Malibu, even if I don't intentionally mean it to be."

"I must admit," Dr. Tsampa said, "I was seemingly addicted to movies in my boyhood."

"We can scarcely breathe any air; species after species is dying out; the waters are filthy and radioactive. And some of us turn to precooked dreams for a quarter of the waking day. It's suicidal!"

They had walked a direct path through a middle-income, residential section of the town of Cambridge and had arrived at Memorial Drive, a primary route connecting Boston and its suburbs.

"Let's go over to the trail by the river," Leah said with sudden alacrity. "Do you mind? It may be muddy."

"I don't mind at all. I haven't been on that trail for years. I used to run there when I first started my practice."

As they crossed the street, Leah gripped Dr. Tsampa's arm; but she unobtrusively released it the moment they began to walk along the bank of the river.

"Feeling such antagonism toward Los Angeles, Miss Tetrao, what do you plan on doing with acting in later years?" Dr. Tsampa asked. "Anything?"

"Only the stage. If that. What I mean by acting doesn't have to do with cameras. Movies rely on illusions of acting that stem entirely from processes of editing. There are almost no real performances in film or on television, in spite of awards and critics, Colin. Even the styles a couple of people seem to have result from editing that year after year stresses the same set of traits in them. Acting can occur only with an audience present and only on the stage...I'm using the theater mainly as an antidote to that whole milieu I grew up with. I mean right now that's what I'm doing. I'm not sure I'll go on with it. There are so very few plays that are the least bit life-enhancing."

"Was everyone in the cast tonight from Boston University?"

"Oh, no, they're not even all students. It's a patchwork. The cyclist has studied in New York some. About half of us are dropouts from the Charles Street Playhouse...We wanted a...a more encompassingly human form of theater than what we'd known, Colin. That's how we put it—for ourselves, anyway. We're trying to blend conventions from different eras and other countries. We're experimenting...Instead of creating conventional characters, we're aiming for something more universal, something like an arrangement of musical themes that will have a unified structure and make valid comments, too."

The frozen Charles River had collected the lights of the city and was diffusing them so thoroughly that it was frequently impossible to tell what was being reflected. Although there was still no wind, the chill was more biting than on the sheltered sidewalks. Smoke-ridden clouds hid the majority of the stars.

"Tell me something about the composition techniques you all were involved in," Dr. Tsampa said. "That is if it's appropriate for a member of the audience to be informed of them."

"I'll have to think a bit. I didn't expect to be questioned."

"Can you remember the genesis of the production?"

"The best of it," Leah replied. "Awhile back—I guess it was roughly six months ago—anyway, we were reading aloud some nineteenth-century English translations of anthropological interviews with people in tribes of the Great Plains—people who had been through pretty total losses of faith in basic rituals because of contact with other tribes. And with the pioneers. We started seeing parallels between all that and current disciplines and professions that have evolved like separate tribes, having their own coherency but not having much relation to other fields. We wanted to let the resemblances suggest how close we might be to a kind of cataclysm, I imagine that's the right word—a cataclysm that would be a lot more devastating than what the people of the Plains suffered."

"I'm curious to know if you improvised the play. Or parts of it, perhaps."

"No," answered Leah, loosening her scarf. "Oh, we did some improvisation at first. But after we had decided what the basic structures were going to be, everyone wrote their own speeches. All the lines were tentative at first. Like the lines of coloring books we could crayon through whenever we wanted....We did lots of cutting and editing. And voting. Until we all agreed on every bit of it. I suppose it was rather like an old-fashioned quilting bee. The way we went over lines, it was as if we were kites soaring away with the tales of our parts. There was so much cooperation we're probably spoiled for any other kind of rehearsal procedures..."

"The ending struck me as inherently religious," said Dr. Tsampa, earnest and persistent. "Perhaps I was wrong. Is that how you regarded it?"

"No. At least not in any doctrinaire way. My pet theory is that the theater has lost a sense of what to celebrate. The same thing happened with painting and sculpture when the moorings of the church fell aside. Art should be more tied to science than to religion; we should have reverence for the predictable. Mysticism disguises artifice; and that shouldn't happen. Illusion must remain clearly illusion in order for a work of art to offer any insightful comments. Characters should always be clearly distinct from references to human beings. Of course, it may be too late for any insights to matter…It was more than that we cooperated to convey postures of noncooperation, Colin; but…"

"I marvel at your courage. It was obvious in your work."

"I'm relieved you don't find me wrongly pretentious," Leah said.

"On the contrary, it's rare to hear such forthright intelligence from someone so young."

"Rare for you, perhaps; but, you see, people my age had to mature too quickly in some respects. We've been facing death since we were born, after all. Most of us, or at least a lot of us by now, have pretty strong defenses built up against the generations that thought of war and every-thing associated with it as heroic and admirable. We're dodging about blindfolded trying to stumble onto some means of surviving peacefully with hardly any help from the past. I suppose that's why some of our faculties have developed rather lopsidedly."

"I'm used to patients learning to devise new avenues for themselves, Miss Tetrao, often risky and strenuous ones. I can give encouragement for such explorations when no one else will. That's one of the chief values of my practice…"

"Colin…" Leah said impishly, "I cannot keep up with your feet for another minute! My legs are turning into inner tubes. You've really got to slow down, or else you've got to walk backwards!"

"I'm sorry. I didn't realize," apologized Dr. Tsampa, amused and intrigued by Leah's seesaw swings from frivolity to impassioned harangue.

"You're the fastest walker I've ever known," Leah said. "You've earned the right to call me by my first name."

"I'm honored," said Dr. Tsampa with lonely gallantry. "It's been a truly invigorating night, Leah. Even the circular programs were refreshing."

"Oh, the person I'm having dinner with gave me the idea for those. He goes to Yale. He's changed his major so many times he had to take a summer school course at Harvard. That's how we met. I was there last summer, too, getting a language requirement out of the way…Now why did I tell you that?"

"Perhaps I took improper advantage of my stance as a professional listener. I try not to do that, but I frequently fail."

"…I've been wondering," said Leah, her lips curling into an ironic smile, "when you're going to get around to probing the subconscious motivations of the play, Doctor."

"I'm not going to," said Dr. Tsampa, gravely raising his voice. "Not at all."

"You mean I'm not going to be hearing about our…our what? Our lurking infantilisms?"

"What I liked about the work," Dr. Tsampa said patiently, "was that it had plainly been rigorously thought out. I'm used to being asked to find merit in what seem to me to be merely shoddy creations. I'm certain that some elements of my profession are partially responsible for that. The theoretical notion of the subconscious has won far too much injudicious acceptance; it's been applied terribly inappropriately, especially in reference to processes of creating art. As a result, our talents for communication have been assaulted by meaningless constructs. Nonsense has been dealt with as if it were wisdom."

"I've never heard anyone say that before. You unquestionably can be vehement, Colin."

"I have to be at times. I'm something of a heretic in regard to a few professional traditions."

"I'd gathered that. I…What does your approach involve, then? Can you tell me? Some of it?

"I can give you a general idea, I think…My practice emphasizes reasoning and community responsibilities. I do what I can to help patients strengthen their capacities to plan and to evaluate. I assist them in acquiring the courage to behave in accordance with the life-enhancing standards they originate or discover."

"Excuse me for asking, if you should, I mean, but it seems to me your work must be terribly depressing, Colin. What led you to take it up in the first place?"

"I haven't thought about that in a long time…"

"Perhaps I shouldn't have asked."

"No, I…I was seventeen in 1945, Leah. I wanted…to find ways to prevent war from happening again."

"That sounds admirable enough. I…Don't you wonder, though, if your practice doesn't just…What?…Prop up repressive social forces? I hope you don't mind my being so frank."

"No," replied Dr. Tsampa. "I don't mind at all. I asked myself similar questions enough times years ago. But my procedures have been modified a great deal since then."

"But what's it like? What does it feel like? What you do. Can you give me a sense of it at all?"

"Well, I…I'm constantly experimenting with techniques, Leah, just as you are. A small amount of my time is spent counseling individually, using what are, I hope, befitting considerations of patient incomes. Primarily I work with organizations: Schools. Churches. Factories. Law firms. From all those structures I bring together therapy sessions consisting of people who might not otherwise meet because of the nature of their economic situations and the distances between their neighborhoods. Such diversity allows us to examine the interrelationships we have with many of our institutional frameworks; and those examinations, in turn, help us to change the institutions, if necessary, as well as ourselves. My work is both remedial and preventive."

"I'm afraid I must have insulted you at first," said Leah. "But I really have never thought of a psychiatrist as being anything but wealthy and in a comfortable, secluded office all day."

"My practice is somewhat unique," Dr. Tsampa said. "Although perhaps most of us assume that about the manners in which we earn our livings." He picked up a small stick and threw it onto the icy surface of the river.

"Hear the creakings of the ice?" Leah asked.

"I think they're coming all the way from the harbor," Dr. Tsampa answered.

"Colin...the little bit I said awhile back about science—do you agree with me on that? I sometimes get carried away by my own theories, I'm sorry to say."

"Well, I...I'm sympathetic to your favoring the demonstrations of science over the revelations of religion, Leah," Dr. Tsampa replied. "But less prediction is, thus far, possible than you may realize. Since so little is presently known in the field with which I'm most familiar, I often suspect it might be wise for *all* psychological and psychiatric endeavors to be categorized as research. Doubt, I must confess, is endemic to my profession."

"I suppose your doubts are similar to the ones I've been having about art. It's so difficult to know whether any of it is really helping anyone."

"Yes, but the consequences of our efforts can be surprising, though. We've got to remember that. A small action can have effects years after it has occurred and thousands of miles away. Do we help? Always? Often? Sometimes? Never? That's a research project too complex ever to get off the ground...Then, too, time modifies processes of evaluation. Just a few years ago, an abrupt change in attitude was apt to have been viewed as symptomatic of illness, especially if it was accompanied by conflict at work or in the family. But now the very same sorts of personality transitions are likely to be thought of as healthy, or at least potentially so. The possibilities of growth are being emphasized more than static routines of behavior. That's a hopeful sign...."

Clasping her gloved hands together and turning her eyes toward the sky, Leah raised her voice and intensified her tones, saying, "I keep feeling a need to fight against definitions of myself. Do you know what I mean? It doesn't matter whether the definitions are from me or from someone else. I want to identify with what's purely human. If we're going to survive, I don't see how we can speak of any victories except for those that would include all people. We've got to eliminate nationalisms and every other destructive social barrier. We've got to redefine our needs and limits accurately and comprehensively so that our best selves can mature and can prevail. I keep hearing that art should be like a mirror, but I think it should be more like a window that lets in whatever enlightenment we can find. I know I sound as if my feet are flying in the wind sometimes; but a lot of my thinking has come together only recently. Or so it seems to me. I rarely get an opportunity to discuss any of it with someone. I tend to grate on people's nerves, I'm afraid."

"You've offered me some new ideas, Leah. You certainly don't grate on my nerves. And I agree we're surrounded by political myths that are divisive and demeaning. We're seldom encouraged to build fortifications against the enemies we all share. Hunger. And cold. And disease. Political terms often sound even more nonsensical to me than a good many psychiatric ones. Both vocabularies can deny our common humanity…But, still, I'm hopeful that enough behavioral discoveries will be made in time for a global civilization to be possible. I mean a way of living based on knowledge and values that will be widely understood and accepted, Leah. If it's meaningful to think of sanity apart from conforming adjustment to whatever situation a person happens to be in, the goal of successful global government must be a basic one for all professions dealing with human health. The United Nations Charter is a decent beginning, I think. I've had some good conversations with people at the law school who are working on proposals for revisions."

"Oh, tell them about the theater, would you, Colin, if it's convenient, I mean? That's the audience we need."

"I'm always happy to be a catalyst for those kinds of linkages."

Having angled away from a footbridge which joined sprawling dormi-
tories and ivy-covered brick classroom buildings, they recrossed Memorial
Drive without waiting for a red stoplight to change and walked north on
Boylston Street.

"There's talk," Dr. Tsampa said, "of constructing the Kennedy Library
in this block. I wonder if the tourist invasion might not be a good thing
for Cambridge."

Cupping her hands over her ears, Leah said quickly, "The only virtue
I've found in Massachusetts winters is the sound of breaking ice...Colin,
I'm so glad to have met you. It's been a kind of experiment. It's such a
temptation to let expression end with a performance."

"I feel something of that nature when I'm writing in my journal. I want
all the other aspects of my life to have as much constructive honesty."

"It's easy, isn't it, to have a sense of being who one is, so long as there's
no one around to test it all out with?"

"Unfortunately, I'm certain that's quite true."

A solitary car aimlessly was circling the concrete island of Harvard
Square. The cobbled pathways and student community shop fronts were
deserted. Next to the subway entrance a newspaper kiosk attendant was
rattling locks and chains and slamming his doors; neon signs radiated
discordant, multicolored patches of light onto the fence and the graveyard
across the street.

"Well," said Leah, "thank you for coming along with me. I'm glad to
know there really are stage-door Johnnies, Colin!"

"Perhaps we could have dinner another time."

"I'm in the book."

"So am I," said Dr. Tsampa. "Call me whenever you'd like."

"Are you taking the subway from here?"

"No, I'm planning on walking home."

"Where do you live, though?"

"Near the Museum of Fine Arts...."

"But that's at least ten miles away."

"I don't ever need much sleep. I'll be fine, Leah."

"You're sure you know what you're getting into?"

"I'm sure," answered Dr. Tsampa, turning and beginning to walk again.

"Be careful, then," Leah said, waving. "I'd forgotten how fast you moved."

In his stocking cap, as he scudded east on the sidewalk of Massachusetts Avenue, Dr. Tsampa resembled a disheveled gnome. "Good night," he called back.

After untying her scarf and freeing her hands from her gloves, Leah undid the top button of her coat, lifted her shawl, brushed a handful of her hair forward over her right shoulder, then walked a half-block to a restaurant, where she paused and circumspectly looked through its plate glass window.

Few tables were occupied, and she easily located C. J. hunched in a rear corner booth. His hair, uncut for six months, tumbled from all sides of his head in strawlike shocks. Instead of rounding his frame, the ten pounds he had gained in the past year had increased his angularity. He wore a sheepskin vest and a partially unbuttoned, blue work shirt; his sleeves were rolled to his elbows. One blue-jeaned leg sticking straight out level with the top of the table was supported by a chair arm; his other leg was folded beneath him. While tapping the wall next to him alternately with the heel and toe of his outstretched foot, he periodically nudged with a shoulder his green corduroy parka so that it swung like a metronome from a coat rack behind him.

The restaurant belonged to one of several chains that blandly had girded the nation within the previous fifteen years. Whatever the community or the season, the menus remained the same. No alterations in either cooking or service were ever discernible. Whatever the aromas of the food, faint scents of cleaning fluids and disinfectants were always present. Through openings in the rear walls, cooks passed to counters food that often subsequently sat for minutes illuminated and kept warm by glaring orange lights. Though of a less intense hue, the rest of the interior lightings were also always orange.

The architectural designs of all these franchise establishments seldom utilized natural substances but hinted at them, instead, by employing manifold, inexpensive components which, rather than drawing attention to their own structural qualities, functioned as symbolic references to construction materials of other eras. Thus, appended to the ceiling above C. J. were four, black metallic chandeliers equipped with plastic, mock candlesticks and flame-shaped light bulbs. Styrofoam columns, painted brown to resemble wooden beams, were glued into the corners of the room and were draped with artificial leaves and flowers. Three of the walls were decorated with yellow vinyl, patterned to suggest unvarnished, pine paneling; on the fourth wall were red-plastic strips meant to imitate inlaid bricks. The floor was covered with linoleum pressed and dyed into a simulation of a parquet mosaic. Two faded, posterlike reproductions of painted seascapes hung on a side wall; on the opposite wall had been nailed life-sized green and orange plywood plants. Each heat-resistant, white Formica table was provided with a lighted candle enclosed in an aluminum frame that had been spray-painted into an implication of antique bronze.

As yet unseen by C. J., Leah studied the splintered interplay of external and internal reflections and fragmented shadows on the windowpane. When she noticed that a plump, elderly, white-uniformed waitress with a face dappled like peach ice cream was staring at her from behind the cash register, she knocked on the glass until C. J. looked up and grinned. As he lifted his left hand, palm outward, she swung open the door, stepped blithely past the waitress to the corner table, and, turning her upper lip into a half-smile, sat down across from C. J.

"John Lennon might be knighted in June," C. J. said.

"Wonder what he'd do with that," Leah replied, taking off her coat.

"Sing," said C. J. with whimsical seriousness.

"It's gotten so I check almost every day to see if they've recorded a new album," Leah said. Depositing her book bag and purse on a wall side of the table, she eased away from her shawl; and it slid onto the back of her chair. "I wonder if that's neurotic."

"No!" C. J. kicked the floor. "Neurotic not to."

"Yes, you're right," Leah said, aligning her shoulders and arms so that the shape of the clothing about her breasts would be hidden from patrons at any of the other tables and lodging the little finger of her left hand against her lower lip. "It's hot in here," she added.

"It always is," C. J. said. He pressed his legs together and rested his right hand on his knees; his left hand played with the tufts of hair bristling out over his collar.

"It's going so fast, all of it," Leah said. "Sometimes I want to keep what I can't. Standing at the window, looking at the reflections, I wanted to be able to carry them away. I mean it. Carry them away. But it doesn't ever work, holding on. I don't like dried flowers… It seems all we ever get are the few seconds when everything is right, then nothing is left but memory and hope. And after awhile the memories get blurred. It's going so fast…"

"I was hiking in a gully around home tonight," C. J. said. He crossed his forearms and clasped his elbows to his chest. "There were cattails. Frozen like chocolate ice cream. Most of the milkweed pods haven't opened. The frost must've come too early last fall. I was near the tracks. A train came through real slow. I jumped between two boxcars and pulled myself up onto one of the roofs. It smelled like rot, and there was a pool of oil. But it was nice, lying there. In the center of the sounds. The train sped up, though; and I barely made it off. See?" He showed her the scratched underside of his right arm. "Then I hitched a ride to Fresh Pond and walked some. The houses there are close together, but still with more room than I've ever lived in. It seemed like it was all a museum or an exhibit. Nobody was around. You go for blocks and you never see anyone, and finally you think, 'What do they have the houses for? Just to hide away from everyone else in?' The yards especially. You never see anyone using them. Food could be growing there. That almost never happens. Like a museum. Just as easy to believe people are on the other side of the walls as that they're not. I saw a man at a bus stop, and I asked him if he thought the ones who lived in the neighborhood left tracks, trying to be funny about it, I mean, but serious, too, in a way. Do they leave tracks? How're you supposed to know people are even there?...I wish I could get over starting in talking like somebody else knows what I've been thinking about. That man didn't have any idea what I was getting at."

"He probably just didn't want to tell you he understood you," Leah said. She scanned a plastic menu that, too, was predominantly orange; an embossed hamburger overlapped a banana split on the cover.

"Those aren't communities, not real ones," C. J. said.

"California's worse," Leah replied, noting that deep, black lines engulfed C. J.'s eyes and that he hadn't shaved. "At least people stay in the same places longer here, even if you can't locate them."

"But couldn't they stay, and be around, too?" C. J. asked. He bent toward the floor and untied his shoestrings, as a grim-visaged, muscular waitress appeared at the table.

"I'd like a chef's salad," said Leah. "Oil and vinegar...Do you want anything, C. J.?"

"More tea. More herbal tea."

"Did you have something to eat already?"

"I thought I'd be hungry, but I'm not. Thought I'd be tired, too; but I guess I'll take the bus back tonight. I shouldn't miss another week. Except I might not go to classes, even if I'm on the campus.... Maybe I'll get something to eat at the depot."

"My salad'll probably get here in an Italian dressing," Leah said, eyeing the departing waitress with a mixture of disdain and empathy. "We should find someplace else to eat one of these times."

Preoccupiedly glaring at the tabletop, C. J. moiled a terse nod and then said, "It all seems so much like a dream. They live like their property regulations are engraved in marble and have always been here and are going to last forever. The whole thing about owning seems like a big fiction to me. The whole thing. I wish we could all just use what there is, just use it all, take turns at it, nobody owning anything."

"I've given up on wishes, C. J.," Leah said, glancing at the ceiling. "Next, I'll be calling myself an adult."

"Wait'll you graduate."

"If I ever do."

"You will."

"I don't want to think about it…Tell me about your song. How's it coming? Made any progress?"

"There isn't much of a melody yet. Not a complete one, anyway." Absently he put out with a sigh the flame of the candle in front of him.

"Still about live and recorded?"

"It's more on echoes now. Getting…getting disappointed they don't repeat the first sound. Repeat *exactly*, I mean…"

"Makes me think, we started discussing *Moby Dick* today in my Western Civilization section. I got called on, and all I'd read was the first line. So I improvised about the Bible and wandering, and it sounded like I knew what I was talking about. Awful as it was, it probably sounded better than if I'd done the assignment—because then I would've been thinking too hard to be able to talk smoothly."

"I read part of that book," C. J. said. "It made me angry because it kept treating the ocean and animals like they're human. I finally stopped on 'malicious waves.' I got an A- on the exam, though. For writing about the ocean and how it isn't like a person…. I don't think I can go on anymore majoring in Comparative Literature."

"Oh, no," Leah replied, taking a deep breath.

"All the talk about 'the absurd,'" C. J. continued, "is driving me crazy. It'd be different if I knew the professors mean what they lecture about; but they're just putting words together that don't really matter to how lives get lived. Teachers collect their paychecks and go to grocery stores and make house payments; and they don't talk about 'the absurd' then…Most books you shouldn't read in school. Studying them isn't right. You should read them because you want to. Or need to, even."

"Any ideas yet about what you might change your major to this time?"

"I don't know. Anthropology probably."

"That would make your fourth one, wouldn't it?"

"Fifth. Philosophy. Physics. Biology. Comparative Literature. Anthropology. I can't see much virtue in staying with something just for the sake of staying with it."

"Why not music?"

"I don't want to take courses in what I care about."

"Two years ago I would not have known what you meant. I do now. The college educations we'd hoped for turned out to have been imagined..."

"I'd like the traveling. The digs. I'd go back to physics if I didn't know that most any job I could get'd be related to the war. I've got to keep on with something if I'm going to graduate, that's for sure. Whatever good a diploma is going to do. Anthropology seems like the one thing that might help right now. Practically. If anybody in Washington would listen." Searching Leah's face and relaxing his own, he poured two glasses of water from a pitcher at his side and asked how the performance had gone.

"Better tonight," Leah replied. "I'm very glad you weren't there, though, C. J. I couldn't have handled that. I don't think anyone in the audience knew how much work we had to do. I suppose they shouldn't know. I'm already thinking about what can come after this and if it'll be worth it." She spoke more eagerly and more casually than she had earlier with Dr. Tsampa; and she continually used her hands to mold an accompaniment that both illustrated and guided her words. "I think I may get out of the theater department altogether. And out of the theater."

"You, too. Into what?"

"Painting, maybe. At least I could learn techniques. How to use tools. That much might make school worth it. Even if by a miracle we could keep the theater going, I'm not sure I could get enough from it. There's so little that's worth acting in. I hate to give up, though. Painting would

be as hard, but I'd have only myself to worry about counting on."
Pointing to the opening into the kitchen, she added, "I bet that's my
salad in the window."

"I'll get it for you."

"No, wait. You might hurt the waitress's feelings."

"How long has it been there?"

"A couple of minutes."

"It could sit there forever, you know."

"There she goes. She'll probably pick it up now."

"It'll be a long now," said C. J., stretching and yawning broadly.

"Can you sleep on the bus, C. J.? I hope so."

"If I need to."

"Maybe you should go on the train."

"No, I...the bus'll be good enough. So long as I don't get next to a
grandmother with a scrapbook...."

"Crackers?" the waitress asked in the midst of delivering herbal tea and
a large bowl of lettuce topped by half a hard-boiled egg and thin slices of
ham and cheese.

"Not tonight," Leah answered. "Thank you."

As Leah began to eat, C. J., pensive and withdrawn, steadied his hands
against his chin, anchored his elbows on the table, and said, "I'm thinking
about the Peace Corps again. Nepal, maybe. Thailand. Suppose I did that,
though? If the war keeps on, I'd get drafted afterwards. That'd be four
years. I might even get drafted out of the Peace Corps. There's no telling
how deferments are going to be. There's no telling anything. First you hear
it's the Russians behind it, then the Chinese, then the North Vietnamese,
then the Viet Cong, then that the Viet Cong are the North Vietnamese
are the Chinese. The other side, whatever that is, says it's all the fault of
the Saigon government, some president there or general-in-charge gets
murdered, and the rumor is the CIA was behind it, more Buddhists set
themselves on fire, those are supposed to be some of the people we're

protecting, except they hate the Catholics, and the Catholics there hate us. Nobody will talk about it at school. How can you be sure what you're saying? There isn't any real evidence. After what Johnson got elected on and what he's doing now, you can't take a word of his for true."

"But, C. J....do you ever think about becoming a conscientious objector?"

"Yeah, I sent for an application. Only you have to tell the draft board you believe in God. What right have they got to know? Something like that deserves privacy."

"I think the rule requiring you to have a religion or whatever is going to court soon, though."

"So what? The case won't get decided for years. Probably not until this war's over. They'll find me before then...The closer I get to it all, I mean the whole thing, not just the war, I mean the way they have it: owning a house I don't have time to use, going to a job that doesn't make sense, driving another car so that pretty soon we won't even be able to see the moon, saying it's a free country but knowing what you can do depends on what color you are, getting a raise in salary that only meets higher prices so I end up able to buy less than I could in the first place...the closer I get, the crazier it looks, all of it; and the less I want it. But I don't see anything else instead. A year ago, it seemed like so much would change; now they're stopping the changes every way they can. I wish I could get away somehow. I don't know to where, though. It's not like I feel I have to give up the ideals of youth and all that stuff, it's that there's nothing I want to fit into. Nothing like the way law practice is for Jack, anyway."

"How's Jack been?" Leah asked, nibbling the remains of her salad.

"All he talks about is the Wagner Act," C. J. said. He swallowed a mouthful of tea.

"The Wagner Act? What's that?"

"The thirties. Unions. He's doing a long paper on it. He's trying to work out how there could be an international union of students. I hear him say 'options' twenty times a day. He thinks if we could all get organized that professors would be more careful about what they teach...More *how* they teach than *what*, I guess...There's going to be a march in Washington next month like the one Martin Luther King was at a couple of years ago. This one is against the war. Jack's doing quite a bit of organizing work for that, but still he doesn't talk about Vietnam; I mean, we don't. I guess it just comes down to whether you want any kind of war or not and if you're going to trust the politicians without being able to make any sense of what they're doing. Some of the guys I grew up with, they've already been drafted, and that makes me feel kind of guilty, well, not really, but something *like* guilty...college deferment, I mean. It'd be different if I had any idea why I'm in school, but I just don't want the government to get me, and it's getting them, people I knew, and there's nothing I can do about it, so maybe I should have it over with and let myself be drafted, too."

"Are you going on the march?"

"I don't know. I can't see how it'll do much. The politicians, they're not listening to anybody..."

"I wish," Leah said sharply, "they were drafting women."

"Really?" C. J.'s eyes widened.

"Well, as long as you're exposed to it, I should be, too. This way neither of us can understand what the other one's going through. The whole military hero thing wouldn't allow it, though. There's no worse men than ones who are in the military. I mean that. Pretending to put women on pedestals, protecting us supposedly; and we're supposed to forget what they are, what they do...The best thing about the ones I've met is that they're potential pacifists. Anytime I see a uniform, I go the other way..."

"It seemed like all that was going out, Leah. A year ago, it seemed like none of it could last longer than a few months...Now it looks like it could come back. Get even commoner than it was before, maybe...That stuck-out jaw kind of thing..."

"The movies aren't going to be helping any, that's for sure. Even books probably won't be doing much good...I'm so sick of reading lately, all those male authors describing women for hundreds of years. At least there are *some* characters in literature that are slightly decent models for you.

Slightly accurate. But for us there's scarcely anything. All of it from a male standpoint. Nearly all of it. As if the only thing we could possibly ever care about is how to complement men..."

"Yeah, I...I remember..." said C. J., shading his eyes with both hands, his elbows pressed rigidly together, "how in high school, some girls, they'd be smart. You'd know they were. But they'd pretend not to be. Hoping they'd get more dates. And they did, too. Because nobody knew how to be...I don't know, equal...I guess. More: who they were. Teachers hardly ever helped. They were pretending, too."

Breathing heavily, Leah made a fist with her left hand, slammed it on the table, and said ardently, "The people who should be offering us insights are putting up hurdles that make it harder for us to become what we could!"

Without a pause, his tones, however, deeper and quieter than usual, C. J. said, "Leah, do you...Jack thinks I'm talking looser now...Do you think that?"

"You're talking more," Leah replied, taking a sip of water. "I don't know if looser is the right word. Did he mean it as good or bad?"

"As good," C. J. answered, his voice becoming even more quiet. "I've been trying to let words out not sure what they're going to be. I used always to think I should know exactly what I wanted to say, even though it wouldn't often get said the way I'd wanted it. But things have been so confusing these past couple of months, nobody seems to have any clear ideas of what's going on, so I figured I'd try talking like how my mind's working, just let go. I guess that's what he meant by looser. But it's still not what I want. It's too easy to say things for them sounding right and not because I mean them. I get this sense, though, lately, that I'm doing it better than I ever did. Talking. Tonight I...I feel...freer...than I ever have before."

"I'd pretty much seen that. Your glint's stayed a lot longer than it usually does."

"I'm not sure what you mean."

"Sometimes your eyes clear up, and they get a glint in them. It doesn't happen very often, but when it does, you're more comfortable than you ordinarily are, even if what you're talking about isn't comfortable. Or settled. It's more settled I mean than comfortable."

C. J. spread his legs past both sides of the table, lowered his eyes, and for the first time that evening ran his right hand through the full length of his hair. "You know what?" he asked.

"Unlikely, but maybe," Leah replied, pushing aside her salad bowl and again lodging a finger on her lower lip. "What?"

"All I really want to do is fly kites."

"...Then fly kites."

"But how? People won't let me."

"When they won't, leave. Why should you do anything else? Kites are a probably for you...."

"It's not as if I want to get out of the necessary things. Finding food and keeping warm. But it doesn't have to be anywhere near as complicated as it is. Anybody could see that if they'd look."

"I know it. You don't have to convince me."

"Leah, the only encouragement I ever get," said C. J., his back curved forward, "is from you and Jack...I mean it."

"Well, that's what we should do for each other. No one can figure out how to get along alone."

"Yeah, but I don't...I don't...It's hard enough thinking about taking care of myself. Taking care of anyone else, too...I don't really want to is the truth. I guess that comes from knowing what working and raising me did to my mother. She never had any energy left to fight a lot of the unfairnesses she hated. Especially at the beginning. All she could do was accept them."

"Look, C. J., don't think I agree with the idea that males have to be breadwinners. That's like the military hero image. Those stereotypes degrade everybody. We should go our own paths together; that's the only way we can grow. Lots of women are crippled by men who insist we shouldn't support ourselves…"

"I'm glad at least that about…kites…didn't seem crazy to you…. Flying kites is really all I want. I was scared to say it."

"I think it's rare and wonderful and that it makes perfect sense. Human beings can't ever expect to create much beauty. We should appreciate what's around us. Like you do. Like you do with kites. There could be so much more grace if we'd take the time to let there be. What's *crazy* is the way people have gotten themselves totally numbed to all the mechanisms of war."

Exhaling a whistled sigh of relief, C. J. closed his eyes; and when he opened them a few moments later, Leah said with carefully measured abruptness, "C. J.…my parents are splitting up."

"You mean a divorce?"

"It's a separation. I don't know what that is exactly. Do you?"

"No."

"I don't think anything formal has been done. I hardly ever hear from either one of them; but Dad wrote me they'd both decided it would be better if he'd move out, at least for awhile, and that he'd leased an apartment in a suburb near home. It was a short letter. I should call Mother, but I haven't had the nerve to yet."

"Have you got any idea what happened?"

"Not really, no. Mother's been seeing someone else, a man, for a couple of years. Longer than that probably. I met him last December. He's nine years younger than she is. They seemed very casual about it, all three of them; but maybe it got more complicated. Dad's in some kind of encounter group that seems to pretty much have taken over his life after work. He's been thinking about going back to school and becoming a reporter." Softly she added, "Sometimes late at night I've started pretending I was adopted. I really have. I call my father 'the husband of possibly my mother.' I'm trying to think out how to handle an actual breakup, if it happens, C. J., and that's as far as I've

gotten. I haven't felt especially close to them for these past two years, but
still…they're what I've known."

"I wish I could help."

"Maybe you can think of something."

"Yeah, I'll try to."

Having finished her salad, Leah reached for a paper napkin, hesitated,
wiped her lips, then slowly asked, "C. J.…do you ever feel like you're
almost two different people? Not so much from changing, I mean, but
because of what facets of yourself people will see, or draw out, what they'll
let you know about yourself or let you show them."

"I guess I don't feel that…More, I wonder if I'm *anything at all*. I'm so
used to people not recognizing what I've been sure is there, I'm not sure
it's there anymore."

"Maybe it takes a long time for someone to find all the facets in
someone else."

"Or maybe one person can't find them all."

"I need more integration inside myself," Leah said conclusively. "A lot
more. That much I'm sure of!"

"There was one morning," C. J. said slowly, "last spring in New Haven.
I flew a kite made of aluminum foil at dawn as an experiment. To see if I
could predict what colors'd be reflected as the kite went higher and higher.
It was the sort of thing, like most experiments are, that's supposed to end
with facts that'd be true for anyone to know. Facts that'd have to be found
by *someone* first, though. By a *somebody* even.

"That time in my life," he quietly continued, "I felt even more like no
one than I do now. So much so, I couldn't even let anybody know that day
what I was going to do. But there was one thing about that…that experiment, though, that was different. I'd put my name on that kite. On the
back of a stamp that was glued to the aluminum foil. Thinking of Franklin
and Marconi and all. Thinking that, when I'd learned what I'd wanted to
about color, if I let the kite go, sometime it'd be found. Then after awhile
I'd be found, from my name on that stamp; and I could explain what the

experiment had been and that'd give me a sense of myself in someone else's eyes that'd be enough to make me into *someone*."

"What happened?" Leah asked. "What happened to the kite?"

"After I let go of the string, that kite just kept on rising. After awhile it was like a small pinpoint of white light. Way too tiny for anyone else to notice. Even I could hardly see it. Then I couldn't see it anymore at all. It felt almost as if the sun had disappeared. Burnt out. It felt like it's seeming to turn into nothing made me even more clearly nobody than I'd been before...."

"I think," Leah said quite carefully, "a person has to be someone in his or her own eyes first before being so to anyone else. It's integrity we're talking about really. A unified sense of self. Other people, though, can recognize when a struggle is going on to get that integrity and can do a lot to help out."

Nodding in agreement but simultaneously appearing to withdraw into himself, C. J. suddenly ventured in a light, almost bantering, tone, "Leah, this may sound kind of strange, but..."

"Go ahead, C. J.," Leah replied, acquiescing to what was clearly going to be an abrupt change of both subject and mood. "You should know by now I'm usually ready for anything from you."

"Jack decided his least favorite word is *impossible*, because it implies too much certainty of a limit. He asked me what my least favorite word is; and I said *dumb*, because it usually causes what it seems to name. What's yours? Can you think of it?"

"Oh," said Leah, shoving her chair backward several inches, "*belief*, maybe, because it means that somebody has stopped wanting to find out...No, calling a person a *stranger* is worse. It's such an excluding word...without being obvious about it. It really almost suggests that some people aren't people. As if all of us aren't the same in lots of ways, whether we know each other or not. As if all of us aren't...good and bad." She searched for C. J.'s eyes with her own, found them, and added, " There are no good guys; and no bad guys. There are only people."

"Is it all right if I tell Jack which word you picked?" C. J. asked, slowly turning his eyes toward the ceiling.

"I don't know what good it'll do, but sure, C. J. Wish him luck with the union idea."

"Yeah, I will."

"And the march. I hope it does something. I really do. Maybe I'll go. When is it?"

"Around the fifteenth of April. I don't know the exact day."

"Someone at school should know."

"People are coming from all over. The West even." He stretched his arms above his head and yawned.

"Are you sure you're going to New Haven tonight?" Leah asked.

"Yeah, I...I'd better."

"I suppose I should be getting home, then."

"I guess I'll stay in here for awhile. The bus doesn't leave until one..."

"C. J.," said Leah wistfully, as she wound her scarf about her head, "I still can't get used to a place like this not being filled with brooding painters and sulking writers and intense discussions. Right in the middle of Harvard Square and the only ones ever here besides us are some red-eyed graduate students!"

"I'm starting to think the most creative people never went to college and don't hang around them."

"Maybe we got caught up by the wrong myths. Me more than you," Leah said. She secured her book bag about her shoulder, withdrew a coin from her purse, and put it on the table.

"I hope the rest of the performances go all right," C. J. said. He moved his eyes toward each other, as if he were trying to focus on the end of his nose. "Tell me if you want me to get a ticket. Call Collect the night before, and I won't accept, but I'll know, and I'll be there."

"I'll remember," Leah said, buttoning her coat. "C. J., we can't ever see the tips of our own noses," she added, watching him slowly smile and lift his eyes toward her. "Only each other's. That's a natural law." Then, as if it were an afterthought, she said, "You know what you told me about some scientists not thinking of the sun as the center of the universe anymore…about calculating astronomical motions?"

"Assumed fixed points, you mean?" C. J. replied.

"Yes," Leah answered. She picked up her check. "I've been wondering whether you know if there are a limited number of fixed points?"

"That's the hypothesis. Only I don't think anybody's figured out what the limit is."

"That makes sense."

"A little," C. J. said. "Enough." Drowsily he grasped his water glass, slipped one of the restaurant forks into a pants pocket, and with downcast eyes waved to the waitress for more herbal tea.

"I mean it, C. J. Kites are a probably for you."

"'A probably'…yeah, I…Yeah, probably."

7
Solicitude and the Rain

Although the two desks, the wooden chairs, the bookcase, and the couch had been in virtually the same positions for more than a year, the faded, green walls emphasized an overall atmosphere of unavoidable transiency. An assortment of notebooks, a portable radio, a calendar, some loose pieces of typing paper, and a tray heaped with pencils and erasers were amassed on C. J.'s desk. Most of the bookcase was filled with Jack's volumes of history and political theory; on the lowest shelf were two anthropology textbooks. Amidst thumb-worn stacks of yellow legal pads on Jack's desk were a dictionary, a typewriter, and a boxed collection of ballpoint pens.

Propped against the hearth screen of a colonial fireplace were three kites, a large roll of tissue paper, and a supply of smoothly sanded sticks. A ball of string and a pile of cloths, an array of mussel shells C. J. had accumulated on the Atlantic coast, a fossilized fern Jack had found in the mountains of Colorado, and a jar of fresh chestnuts were on the mantel, along with a desk calendar correctly turned to November, 1965. A bathroom and two small rooms, each containing a cot and a mirrored bureau, adjoined the central room; dirty clothes were strewn beneath both unmade beds.

Confident he would be alone until much later in the evening, Jack shut off the lights in the dormitory suite, locked the entrance door, pulled down all the window shades, closed and locked his bedroom door, and groped for a small lamp on his bureau.

As an outgrowth of enrolling in a comparative religions course the previous term, he had recently acquired a collection of books dealing with many varieties of mysticism that had been synthesized without regard for logic and evidence. While on weekend excursions to Manhattan, he had wandered into secondhand stores and had purchased the assortment of tattered pamphlets and tomes, all of which he kept locked in a bureau drawer. When he knew he could count on not being interrupted, even by C. J., he often perused the hidden material in order to release himself both from strains of absorbing the body of sociological and historical treatises his formal studies required him to read and from the burdens of his political, antiwar involvements, which in the past three months had consumed a larger portion of his time than schoolwork.

He also hoped that by examining in solitude the religious publications he might sharpen his analytical capacities more effectively than by spending additional time with course assignments; for he felt that he had been unable adequately to organize the ideas contained within the many lectures he had heard and in the enormous quantity of attendant readings he had completed, was certain that his ability to engage in serious, constructive thought had been neither strengthened nor refined by any of the teaching methods to which he had been exposed at Yale, and was dismayed that he had expended his more than three years there primarily employed in unreflective memorization.

Though his intellectual posturings seemed to him unstable and the praise he received for them unwarranted, rarely were either his written or spoken statements challenged by anyone. His grades were consistently high, and his occasional protests to C. J. were skeptically treated as the products of modesty. He did not know how to seek help, and his conscience offered him the only testimony that he needed any.

Against the wishes of his parents, he had applied for admission to Harvard Law School; but he suspected that his learning techniques, were he to be accepted, would at last be officially scorned in Cambridge the following fall, just as he had come to feel they would be at any other law school. Appreciating how insubstantial was his knowledge of what law practice would eventually entail, he had yet been so adamant about his early choice of a career that he was unable to conceive any means of sharing with someone other than C. J. his uncertainties and doubts in regard to both his talents and the nature of his future work.

He was, moreover, baffled that legal authorities were bringing little clarity to the fundamental dilemmas of the Southeast Asian war and was saddened and disheartened to have learned that entrenched throughout the United States were many sanctioned textures of political, educational, and occupational alignments patently inimical to strivings for the racial equality that presumably was guaranteed by the official, elaborately defended, national ideology.

Occasionally he would find himself wondering how much of human law actually augments justice. When his concepts of justice subsequently would become confused and elusive, he would decide it was time to exercise his analytic skills and would turn to his locked drawer, where indiscriminately selected volumes elaborating Christian traditions, Navajo rites, Judaic history, and the Tao were intermingled with tracts on astrology, transmigration of souls, astral projection, the principles of Madame Blavatsky, and ancient Greek mythologies.

Any spiritual techniques or incorporeal drills described and recommended within the books, Jack practiced assiduously; and in a note pad labeled *To Consider Accepting*, he regularly copied the theological paragraphs that appealed to him most. During the transitory periods he knew himself to be especially worn out by college routines or by the news reports of the day, he gathered together what he had judged to be the most bizarre portions of his cache and poured over them; believing that no one with whom he was acquainted would condescend to discuss such rhapsodized visions and fantastical conceptions, he allowed himself at these unusually weary moments to forsake his dogged attempts at rational arrangement and to be soothed into reveries that assuaged his fatigue. Thus, at times, he approached his concealed preserve with a double-edged motivation; he sought to develop efficient habits of thought and simultaneously to abandon any criteria for truth ruling the rest of his experience.

Having turned on the light, he unlocked the drawer, sat upon the floor, performed a yogic, arrhythmical breathing exercise, recited a Hindu mantra, took up a biographical reference volume detailing the lives of Catholic saints, leafed through the pages indexed under the month of November, consulted two horoscope books, and scrawled an entry on an ornate chart which utilized interwoven, dotted lines to connect numerous dates and hours. Lying down on his cot, he proceeded to read first a pamphlet meant to explicate the Biblical Book of Revelation of St. John the Devine and then a chapter of a monograph that classified according to topic the sayings of Confucius. Next he shut off the light, drained his mind of thought, and hummed a succession of early Christian melodies and Far Eastern chants he had memorized by listening to recordings via earphones at the Yale undergraduate library. After several minutes of silent meditation, he switched on the light and put the religious material back in the drawer.

As he turned the lock, a wave of uneasiness passed from his stomach to his forehead; and the focus of his eyes grew blurred. Shaking his head from side to side, he slapped his cheeks, opened the two doors, drank a glass of water, raised all the shades, and stepped outside. Braced by the cold evening air, he then shuffled back to his desk, took a deep breath, and began to study a textbook article synthesizing the ethical philosophy of Immanuel Kant and the view of history delineated in *War and Peace*.

Within half an hour, C. J. dashed into the room and, flushed and shivering, threw his coat onto his chair.

"Looks cold," said Jack.

"Guess it might snow," answered C. J. "That's what the papers say."

"Where've you been?"

"Thinking," C. J. quietly replied. Smiling hesitantly, he yanked his red and white plaid, cotton shirt out from his beltless jeans, grabbed a brush from the bathroom, lashed his windswept hair, unparted, to his shoulders, tossed the brush onto his bed, and, pumping his arms up and down as if he were swimming through the air, started to pace diagonally between the corners of the central room.

"Where's that at?" Jack asked.

"What?"

"Thinking."

"Nowhere. Somewhere. I don't know. I'm sorry Kennedy got shot…. I wish it were spring. I wish I had a rubber soul."

"I wish my father would quit writing me to apply to the University of Denver Law School…"

Tensely gazing out the window, C. J. suddenly seized the ball of string from the mantel, snapped off a piece, and wound it about his fingers. "I'm leaving," he announced, then finding himself able to meet a silence from Jack only with, "I said that I'm leaving."

"I heard you. What do you mean?"

"I told you."

"A leave of absence?"

"Not a leave of absence. I'm finished. Tonight. Tomorrow."

"C. J., it's the second week in November. There's only seven months to go to graduation."

"I don't care. It's not what I want. I should have left a long time ago."

"I thought anthropology was working out."

"I was kidding myself. I never belonged here. I knew that at the start."

"But what harm would it do to stay until June?"

"This way I can still get the jobs people who don't go to college have. That's what I want. I should've done this three years ago. June would be too late."

"Have you talked with the Registrar?"

"This afternoon."

"It's definite?"

"Yes, definite. I won't be here tomorrow night."

"But what will you do?" Jack asked earnestly. In a complementary gesture of anger and self-restraint, he made a fist of his right hand and held it tightly against his left palm.

"What other people do. I don't know. Go to Boston. Work in the post office for the winter. Get enough money for a lobster boat. Start a carpentry apprenticeship. I don't know."

"You'll be up for the draft, C. J."

"They won't find out until July that I've left. Too much paperwork. I'll have figured out something by then."

"But Yale is supposed to send them our semester grades."

"They'll mail a set of incompletes."

"You could've gotten into graduate school. Anthropology. A government loan. A fellowship. That'd be a three-year deferment. That's reason enough to stay."

"Look," replied C. J. with suddenly evident fury. "They're killing people! Thousands of them! Killing them! You can hear them screaming every night on television. Because somebody decided not to go to college, or couldn't go, they're getting killed. And you know how much college is worth. You've said it a hundred times how they don't teach us to think really, how there's hardly one of them doing anything except passing the years away smiling, while we're getting killed. You've said all that yourself. Look how much good education does, look at it *really*, killers, napalm, and warheads all over, and the Senate with college degrees, two or three of them with enough courage even to ask why it's going on, not one of them willing to object to the killing at all, *object at all*. That's what college was worth to them, and if that's the way it is, and it is, I'd rather just let them kill me, too."

"I am not going to let you talk like that!"

"Being dead'd be better than joining their world!"

Motionless, they stared at each other; then C. J. grinned and said, "I, you know, I…" He knelt down, leveling his eyes with Jack's. "I'm sorry to leave you at almost the end. They'll probably put someone else in here. I asked them not to. But they wouldn't agree to anything. It might be a freshman. Maybe a transfer. It'll be hard for you. I know it's not what you want."

"It's all right, C. J."

"It's *not* all right."

"What do you expect me to say?"

"I don't know. I'm sorry…But I just cannot go on with it. Maybe if any of the professors were really doing something about war. But it doesn't touch them, and their being secure is all they care about. They pretend a lot of stuff to get their comfortable houses and their black maids, not black secretaries, no, all secretaries have to be white—that's how it is here, Jack—everyone waiting for police to use clubs to keep us quiet, so the professors won't have to look at what's at the bottom of their lives, so they can stay in their private corners where they don't have to see how beaten down they've been and how much they've lost."

"Couldn't you wait until January?"

"I don't want that kind of safety. If they're going to get me, I'd rather they'd get me now. It's not the same for you. You knew what you wanted when you started here. Knew it three years ago."

"No, I didn't. Not really."

"You think you can do a lot that's good with law, and maybe you can. You need all this to have a way to begin. Even if you've only got a little bit of certainty, it's more than I have. I don't have any. That's why staying on makes sense for you. They'll call me 'uncommitted,' but they don't talk about what they give us a chance to be committed to. They hide away in libraries where they know they won't have to see napalmed skins." Trembling, he sat down at his desk and cradled his elbows in his palms.

"Maybe we could get a place in Boston next year," said Jack, feeling as if ideas were battering against the back of his eyes. "An apartment. Secondhand furniture…"

"I may not be in Boston then...Besides there's Leah."

"You're getting a place with Leah?"

"I don't know. I guess I want to be by myself. For awhile, anyway. Working won't be much like school, that's for sure."

"Maybe it'll be worse than here."

"I've got to find out. I can't wait anymore."

"It's so soon. I don't...."

"Look, I'm not leaving the country," C. J. interrupted. "Not right now, anyway."

"You're thinking about Canada?"

"Other places, too."

"So am I."

"They won't draft you out of law school."

"They might. It's all changing. No one can tell. Anyway, I don't know how I'll do next year."

"You can get into any law school you want to."

"Yes, but that's not staying in."

"You aren't going to flunk. That's crazy."

"I'll be twenty-five when I'm done; they can still draft me for another year."

"This war'll be over by then. Maybe Bobby Kennedy will be president."

"Nobody'd ever take the nomination away from Johnson..." Jack replied, adding in muffled tones, "I don't, C. J., I don't know how I'll get on without you around. I really don't."

"Well," said C. J., bowing his head and darting his eyes upward about the room, "I would've felt like that if you'd left."

"Have you told your mother yet?"

"No, but she won't be surprised."

"I think my parents'd have heart attacks if they found out there wasn't going to be any diploma to frame."

"Yeah, probably. Or at least they'd have fits." C. J.'s words forced Jack to smile; and immediately both boys were gripped by convulsive waves of taut, crescendoing laughter; when one stopped laughing, the other started in again; and they laughed until they had forgotten what had initially provoked their spiraled outburst. Finally, C. J. said, "I guess I should start packing."

Sauntering to his room, he turned his bureau drawers upside down on his bed, tugged two suitcases from his closet, opened them on the floor, and not taking time to fold his clothes, rolled each item into a ball which he inattentively flung onto the window sill or into either suitcase.

One hand in a rear pants pocket, the other arched stiffly to his knees, Jack looked on from the doorway. He, too, had let his hair grow past his collar; and he shook his head repeatedly, inducing his lock to rise and fall, as he struggled for something to say.

"What're you going to do with that stuff by the window?" he asked.

"Throw it out."

"I could send it to Arlington."

"I don't need any of it," C. J. answered decisively.

"Maybe…" said Jack, "Maybe I shouldn't be in school either, C. J. How I am now, there's only theory. What I know, I don't really know, it's not part of me. I haven't experienced it. Poverty is theory. Courts are theory. Even people are theory. All I've done is read. So many words I've had to accept on faith…I get these feelings from some of the books, sympathy for people, I mean, but I'm not sure if how I can get to feeling goes toward how people actually are. It's been so sheltered here. It's all been words. Maybe, before law school, I should get more certain how people really live. Maybe I should find out from being with them instead of reading about them."

"Maybe," said C. J., slamming the lid of one suitcase.

"Last April," Jack continued, "it seemed like the government would have to listen to us, it seemed so obvious the war couldn't go on any longer. But now it feels like there's nothing anyone can do about it. I'm tired of writing letters and going to meetings. I don't know if most people even care."

"It's easy for us to have opinions because our jobs don't depend on keeping quiet. That's what makes me so mad about the newspapers always talking about what college students think. The other people, who are being most affected, don't ever get asked what it is they want."

"There's so much tied up in defending that no one knows what they're defending anymore," said Jack.

"It's going to get worse," C. J. added.

"You're sure they'll send the draft board incompletes in January?"

"I checked it."

"It's so crazy. All of it. Crazy. Going from eighteen to twenty-one old enough to be drafted and not old enough to vote!"

"My mother said once," C. J. answered, briefly looking up from his packing, "it's envy in a lot of them. 'Envy of the young,' she said. They don't want us to get the chances they didn't have."

"Nobody'd ever be likely to admit to that, though."

"No. No, they wouldn't."

"I wish there was something definite I could hold onto, C. J....something that would last...."

"Yeah, I...I don't know, I...What happens to me—sometimes, I mean," said C. J., shoving the drawers back into the bureau, "is I get out, get out of time almost, step out, so that ways that look silly, neckties and shined shoes, don't matter anymore. Trying to find something to believe in doesn't even matter anymore. The splashing of waves, thinking about the thousands of years they've been hitting against the rocks, sounding the same now as then, how unalike little bits of sand are when you look at them close, the color in mussel shells. All that's enough to hold onto. And it's always there, even though most of the time it's so hidden away there's almost nothing that can tell you to go find it. I take off my clothes and wade in shallow water at the edges of the tides, ducking my head, letting seaweed drift over me, seeing the different greens and blues, all fusing together, but separate still; and then, I can touch at whatever we've been that's lasted that's worthwhile...and the rest washes away."

"All I can think is that I hope there'll be time for other kinds of peace," said Jack. He sat down on C. J.'s cot, clenched his legs against each other, intertwined his ankles, and crossed his arms behind his neck.

"I don't know how to make the kinds of peace you mean," said C. J.

"I don't know either," said Jack. "But I'm going to work at finding out."

"That's where I'm not the same as you. Not the same at all..."

"I got stronger from being around you, C. J. I'm not sure what I mean. Some of your ways I took on as mine."

"Well, I did that with you, too."

"You're the best friend I've had."

"I'll be in Boston, at least for awhile. You can come up whenever you want," C. J. said, straining to close the other suitcase. Jack bent down, and the two of them pushed it shut.

"I hadn't thought about June yet," Jack said.

"I would've told you sooner, if I'd known."

"I figured it was on your mind. I didn't think you'd do it."

"You want any of the things I'm getting rid of?"

"I'll go through them tomorrow."

"Good," C. J. said with finality. Then he edged past Jack into the main room. "There's nothing more for me to see to here. I'm ready now. I'm going to take a walk. I've got to."

"I'll go with you."

"I'd rather you wouldn't."

"You sure?"

"Yes."

"Have you decided what time you're leaving?"

"No."

"Taking the bus?"

"Yes," C. J. answered, putting on his coat and inverting the collar. "Look, let's do this as easy as we can. All right?"

"All right."

"I won't even wake you up if I leave tonight."

"My mind's emptied out. I can't think of anything more to say anyway."

"Neither can I."

"Any messages for anyone?" Jack asked.

"No."

"Write me where you are when you want to."

"Yes. I will."

"Good-bye, then," Jack said; he sidled to his desk.

"Bye," C. J. replied; and quickly he was out of the door.

Jack, dazed and sullen, opened the textbook he had been reading earlier, glared uncomprehendingly at a densely printed page, pitched the book at the fireplace, supported his head in his hands, and ran his fingernails sharply across his scalp, stinging himself into semi-alertness. With a resigned, prolonged sigh, he then stood, flicked out the lights, took off his clothes, and folded himself into bed. Spent, numb, he sank his head into the mattress, wrapped a pillow over his face, and clutched another pillow to his chest.

As soon as he felt the bleak chill against his cheeks, C. J.'s body relaxed; and elation surged through him. All of the pent-up emotions and remnants of his many, halfhearted attempts at adjustment dissolved into a single strand of unchanneled eagerness. Letting his hair stream out behind him, he ran past the familiar shadows of the campus, sprinted along High Street two blocks beyond the library, angled left, circled the Grove Street Cemetery, and still running, trailed the train tracks off Lock Street for a quarter of a mile. When thick undergrowth forced him to slow his pace, he reversed his direction and headed toward the central business district of New Haven.

Happening on a juncture with another set of railroad tracks, he halted resolvedly, crouched, and after a moment jumped with all the energy at his command, intending to measure the number of wooden ties he could overleap. Immediately upon landing, however, he lost his balance, slipped, and in an instant was sprawling, limbs akimbo, on the cindery bed of the rails. Laughing loudly and panting, rapidly he pulled himself up, turned away from the tracks, and sped to the intersection of two of the city's main streets, Elm and State. There he paused, leaned back his head, and, shivering, briefly examined the heavily overcast sky. Then he faced west and dashed three blocks past City Hall to a small park, the New Haven Green. Quickly he stepped onto the now brown grass of its level ground and, seeing no one nearby, straightaway tumbled into a clumsy series of somersaults, almost as if he were trying to draw forth from the soil the final warmth of autumn. When at last he was quite out of breath, he got to his feet and dizzily stumbled toward the center of the park. Upon reaching an immense oak tree, he leaned against it, slid his back down its trunk, and, sitting, wrapped his legs about the hoary base of one of its roots. Idly, he then began to pluck pieces of dried grass from his coat and jeans; and as he held up each of the fragments for hasty inspections before sending them sailing into the air with snaps of his fingers, quietly he spoke aloud:

"It's a park. Where I am. I don't know where to go now. I can't tell what to do next. I haven't ever prayed before. I don't know if this is the right way to do it. I haven't ever known where You are. Are You?

"I don't see how You could've died if You ever were. Maybe You're behind all the fences we put up. I don't know where You are or what You are or even if You're there. But I want You to listen. Maybe You need to hear the words.

"I don't see how You could've let all this happen. They say we're not to challenge You. They say we're only supposed to accept. But I can't help challenging You. So forgive me, if You have to, for how I speak to You. But at least listen to me, because how can You let it be like the earth is flowing our blood out into the sky?

"I can't talk to You any other way but like I just did.

"See where I am? See what this is? We tie up little bits of your earth with walls. Isn't all this yours? Aren't we just on it for a time we're meant to sing through? Isn't that what You mean for us to do? Fall leaf colors and icicles calling out for notes, cottonwood seeds scattering, and see what we do with all the good You've made? Every church uses your name, while people tear at each other so much the earth all over is red from our blood. How can You let there be so many wounds?

"Where are You? Are You testing whether You're sorry enough You made us for You to decide to let it all end? But who would care for everything else, if we're not here? There would be no more songs.

"I don't know anyone who just accepts. I don't see how they could. Look at where we are now. There's hardly any goodness left. Why aren't You helping us?

"They section off your earth and call it cities and countries and stand their rows of armies on lines they draw that don't mean anything except keeping us apart and making us afraid, and in those fenced-up pieces where they sleep they cut themselves off from the skies and plant flowers and don't come out to see what You just let grow.

"I've been a failure by how people judge. I haven't fit in with them. I've lied and I've stolen and nobody's known about it and lots of times I haven't even seen why I should have stopped.

"But I know what You can do. I have waded through fields of your flowers. I've looked at the silver paths footsteps make in the sand. I've seen the red-gold tops of waves at sunset and smelled the evergreens where the skies are so full of stars nobody could help but only sing.

"If You'll let me find a way. If You'll show me how to go on. I'll fly You songs in the wind and make You laugh like You must at all the creatures that don't cause You anywhere near the trouble we do.

"Building up fences, hiding with guns in houses, killing by ways won't make us look direct at what we've done. Uniforms and badges they can call in a minute that turn what You've made into airplanes ready to rain what sets skin on fire. How could we be alive just for all that to be happening? I can't but talk to You like this because soon it'll likely all be more than any of us can bear.

"Their guns are in my face, and it seems as if I might have to hold one, when all I want to do is care for what You've given that's good. Do You want me to put away all I could be and get so ready to die it wouldn't matter whether it was now? I can't tell how to go on. I don't know any way to say it except I'm giving You the chance to show me what to do. I don't know if You'll take it unless I tell You about it. Right now is maybe when I'll need You most. My whole life.

"Forgive me if You should, but I can't accept what You've let happen. I can hardly even see the stars, ever a night, with what we've done to our air; and some days in the cities are so dark with clouds of smoke it almost starts to seem like the sun won't be out again. My mind is so confused I don't know whether I could have found You. I don't know if You're out there. I don't know if You are. But if You are, help me, because I can't fit in with what they're doing, and I can't see how You'd want me to.

"I don't know if You're hearing. I don't know if this is the right way to pray. I'm afraid, and I can't help but be when I look up at a dark sky and have to wonder whether it'll be ashes'll fall, or acid, or fire, or pieces of bone.

"It's not rainbows we need now, God.

"We need rain we can be certain's rain!

"That's what I know to say.

"Rain that'd make us sure again we could go on living and that there'd be food for us all and that we could be warm with rain-roof sounds we'd know what they were. And we'd not all be so afraid again.

"Let there be rain!"

For a moment, C. J. eyed the moon. Then he stood; and wanting to enwrap himself in the cold, he unbuttoned his coat and slowly walked back to the campus.

Whistling, he left the hallway door open so that a shaft of light would fall across the floor, crept into his bedroom, wedged a suitcase under each arm, and was nearly outside when he heard Jack's muffled voice asking, "Is there anything I can do?"

"Those three kites in front of the fireplace…send me two of them!"

8
Solstice Passed

1

Mr. Tetrao had suggested over the telephone that Leah join him for dinner on Ocean Avenue at the foot of the Santa Monica pier. Suspecting that a spot closer to the family home would lessen the likelihood of her father's attempting to deploy her in his wranglings with her mother, and, determined to maintain neutrality in her parents' regard, she had requested they meet instead late that afternoon at the Rancho La Brea Fossil Pits. Sounding as if he sensed her reason for preferring the mid-Los Angeles location, her father had agreed.

All week long, the balmy path of the winter sun had been diverting Leah from work on an essay required by one of her courses. She had become more inured than she had appreciated to cloudy Massachusetts skies and the modifications of apparel and attitude they had demanded. The widespread and florid emphasis on mild Los Angeles weather had seemed to her exaggerated when she was growing up; but after she had retrieved a straw hat from the back of her closet, donned a light jacket, and set out for a casual walk in the neighborhood of her childhood, she imbibed with the admiring eyes of a tourist the stable blues of the coastal horizon.

Hoping that browsing would stimulate a satisfactory organization of her thoughts on the assigned topic, she stopped first in a bookstore near the University of California at Los Angeles campus. During her three-year absence, there had been drastic changes in the styles of dress and arrangements of hair amidst the student preserve. Westwood Boulevard had become saturated with blue jeans, most of them tattered. Cotton, nineteenth-century farmwife dresses commingled with secondhand shawls. Makeup had vanished, but beads were everywhere. Carved driftwood and shells were alternately strung into emblems of studied disarray: necklaces, headbands, and belts.

Tense postures, however, belied the picturesque easeful garments and the unbound hair. A theme of underlying disquiet in the collegiate atmosphere was unequivocal and had two variations: fury tightened pliant callow faces into outraged grimaces veering toward violence; and brittle, purblind lassitude disguised itself defensively in evanescent semblances of communal rapture.

Surrounded by such colorfully muted discord, Leah found concentration impossible. Deciding to investigate the stacks of the downtown main library, she boarded a bus plodding east on Wilshire Boulevard, snatched one of the few remaining seats, and solemnly prepared herself for an hour's ride. Next to her sat a white-lipped, bland-jawed woman mantled, though matronly in years, by a blue halter, purple slacks, cordovan sandals, and mirrored sunglasses. Her arms were sheathed with unadorned, plastic bracelets; an immense, gold crucifix floated between her breasts. Her eyebrows were plucked into pencil-thin lines, and the tight ringlets of her carmine hair resembled a raw artichoke or a pineapple. As Leah contemplated the spindly palm trunks topped with umbrella leaves, the raucously blooming cacti, and the green patches of finely trimmed grass, all of which skirted the southern edge of Beverly Hills, the woman asked her in a high-pitch voice tinkling like a calliope, "Would you care to look at this newspaper?"

"No," answered Leah, thinking how rare such an offer would be in a Boston subway. "Thank you."

"It's not mine," said the woman, tipping her glasses to the end of her nose. "It's the *Herald*. Someone left it. I always read the *Sun*. More ads. Better editorials...You ought to put that hair of yours over your shoulder, you know. It's liable to get pulled, down your back like that."

"Yes, you're right," Leah said, compliantly brushing her hair away from the aisle.

"This is a local bus," grumbled the woman. "The sign says it's an express."

"I thought it said that, too."

"It does say that. Right on the front. You can't ever be sure. What do words mean? Half the time they forget to change the signs. I should write a letter. Maybe someone saner than usual would get it...The driver'll probably start skipping stops after awhile, though...Did you go to the rose parade this year?"

"No, I didn't," Leah replied.

"I bet you're disappointed you didn't. I never miss one. We used to be able to smell them all over the city a day ahead. Not anymore...the largest rose garden in the world is over at Exposition Park. The largest in the world, they say."

"I think I heard that once."

"Well, it has to be somewhere. The largest one, I mean. And I believe it's here. It used to be safe to go there. Not now. They don't care who they have to knock down to get at a purse, I'll tell you that. A friend of mine, someone climbed right over the front of her car, one of my girl friends, right over the hood, idling at an intersection, right across the hood, opened the passenger door before she could lock it, what are you going to do?, someone in front of your windshield, grabbed her purse. Cars all around. Nobody did a thing to help her. Middle of the day. I never thought Los Angeles would get like New York City. I've seen it happen...But, you can't find anything more beautiful than the rose parade. I don't care for football, though, do you?"

"Oh, sometimes," Leah said, lifting her hands from her lap.

"The parade is all I care for. I always get a place on the route. Early. Before the tourists. Television has brought so many more of them."

"Yes," agreed Leah. "Yes, it has."

"The largest rose garden in the world, right here in Los Angeles!"

Sirens wailed, as the bus lumbered by the corner of Fairfax Avenue. Two throngs of angrily shouting people were on either side of Wilshire, and upraised fists hammered the air. Lines of blue-uniformed police were establishing barriers on both sidewalks.

"I wonder what that was," said Leah, weaving her hands in circles.

"Filming a movie," said the woman. "Things like that don't happen in life. Not here."

"I don't know. A lot has changed lately."

"Not in the middle of a street. It was a movie...Why do you do that? Move your hands like you do. Every time you say something, you move your hands."

"I...I've gotten in the habit."

"You're not speaking sign language?"

"No," answered Leah. "No, I'm not."

The cramped bus was almost full; and the caged air smelled of sweat; but the driver continued to shout, "Step to the back. The back, please. All the way back." Near the rear door a black motorcycle jacket shrouded the bare, emaciated chest of a scowling man, who moved to the door and pounded it with his fists until it creased open.

"No one even tries anymore to stop people behaving like that on the north/south routes," said the woman, fanning herself with limp fingers. "'Downtowns' don't usually have this many people. The whole city must be exchanging holiday presents."

Silently pondering the alloyage of figures and faces in the bus and wishing she had brought along her sketch pad, Leah nodded—as the woman returned to the newspaper—and searched the crowd for traits that would identify geographic allegiances. She was sure that tourists, generally accustomed to more restraint in public conveyances, were perceiving the aggregate mood as friendlier than in other communities; but she was also convinced that the geniality was an aspect of a disengagement peculiar to Los Angeles, where rudeness tended to be more subtle than elsewhere, defenses more camouflaged, and loneliness more openly displayed. As a girl, she had often sat amongst people bizarrely cloaking themselves in voiced loops of their own words—people who would have been overtly shunned in the subways of Boston, but who had rarely occasioned any evident reaction from California commuters.

Intent upon relaxing for a few minutes after the long ride, four blocks past the library Leah rang the passenger service bell and stepped onto Broadway, feeling as she customarily did there: that she had crossed a national border. The carnival-like street was a festive meeting place for the aristocracy of the east Los Angeles poor. Lounging within sheltered doorways—hyphenated tunnels of recorded flamenco—buxom women chattered gossip in Spanish, laughed, and waved to mustached men strutting the sidewalks in neatly pressed shirts and tight, shiny slacks. A wizened matriarch, her gray hair cowled by a black cape, an arm laden with wristwatches, croaked incessantly, "No tax," while Leah hesitated at a tented vendor's stand, bought a chilled mango on a stick, hurried by a couple dancing beneath a pink neon sign that flickered Weddings Today, and—hunched over so the deep red, dripping mango juice would spill to cement which was both sidewalk and floors— angled into a fabric and clothing shop.

After verifying that prices, as usual, were higher than anywhere else in the city, she crossed the street and entered a vast, open market, a square block of glass counters tended by hawkers equally ready, she assumed, to bargain or to shortchange and inundated by suckling pigs, whole beef heads, unskinned fish, cuts of meat, fresh bread, and orange crates packed with vegetables and fruit.

The disposition of the multitude of shoppers, arms clenched about bulky paper sacks, was so infectiously buoyant that, unwilling to leave the enveloping bustle, Leah waved a five-dollar bill in front of a cash register, ordered a fried abalone sandwich and two warm, sugared churros, ate at what she knew to be a dilatory pace, advanced through the market to Hill Street, and there bought an iced lemonade. A block west, discarding her cup in a trash can at the edge of an alley bordering turn-of-the-century office buildings, she felt as if she were reluctantly re-entering the United States.

On the steps of the orange-faced library at last, she took a deep breath, checked her watch, unbuttoned her jacket, then meandered up a flight of stairs to a small room of poorly lit stacks sated with volumes pertaining to visual art. While gazing at a bulletin board by the doorway, she remembered, however, that most of the books could not be borrowed, had to be requested by title, and were stored on other shelves closed to the public.

Her browsing intentions twice defeated, she proceeded to survey the stuffy, achromatic room. At one table a ragged, stubble-cheeked, middle-aged man, his head thrown back, his mouth gaping, saliva rolling down his neck, reclined in a canvas and metal chair; although his vacant eyes were aimed at the ceiling, he was snoring. Enmeshed in a green trench coat much too big for him, a teenage boy cowered about the aisles in imitation of a television prowler stalking out a robbery site; his breathing was labored; from one of his ears swung a brass ring.

With the same dissatisfied lack of inspiration that had been troubling her since the start of vacation, Leah flipped through the photography entries of the card catalogue, slammed the drawer shut, and hastened to the stairway. By the time she arrived at the sidewalk, she was nearly running.

Seeing a bus in place at one of its stops, she scurried to its door and boarded without noting its destination. "Do you cross Alvarado?" she asked the driver.

"Ten minutes," he replied.

Unable to latch onto a handrail and feeling blood drain from her face, she hedged herself inconspicuously amidst the standing passengers until the driver's shout, "McArthur Park," compelled her to shove and apologize her way out into the sunlight. A bevy of tanned and listless men blocked the arched entranceway to the city park; and the moment Leah's feet met the sidewalk one of them sidled over to her, coiling his lips into a leer and lazing out a hand toward her shoulders. Instinctively she tightened her legs and arms into stiff dignity, held up a fist, and like an agile partridge outwitting a band of stupefied hawks, darted around and beyond the stone portal, and nimbly began to follow a path girding the park.

While she was deliberating what she might do in the remaining two hours before her scheduled meeting with her father, an elderly man dressed in a stained and wrinkled suit, his hair clinging sporadically to his gleaming head like thorns on a wet cactus, approached her and cupped out his hands. "Spare some change?" he asked with a voice caught and rattling in his chest.

"I don't have anything," Leah said.

"Twenty-five cents."

"I'm sorry."

"God bless you," said the man, as Leah brushed past him, only to encounter the outstretched palm of a youth in his mid-twenties who looked as if he had that week journeyed into Los Angeles from the mines of West Virginia. Bushy eyebrows and huge, purple, smacking lips swam in his slack, naive, plaintive face; he smelled of coal. "I won't try to fool you, ma'am," he drawled over toothless gums.

"I don't have anything," Leah interrupted.

"For a place to stay, ma'am."

"I really don't have anything."

"Peace," he called out after her, as she walked away on the sidewalk of Alvarado, a street that had long been a channel of erupting despair, an outpost where lifelong dreamers, California immigrants of all varieties, shared a usually recent recognition that they might be entrapped within the brim of a spiraling shaft that would engulf them, render them insensible, and would not echo the whimperings that would accompany the diminution of the likelihood of their ever regaining any hope. The majority of the denizens of the street were unaccustomed to despair; they had just begun to notice it. Whatever their age, there was a surprised, paralyzed spark in their tainted eyes, as they mutually discovered that some communities

would, henceforth, probably be unopen to them and as they prepared
either to grope through streets that would be darker and harsher than
Alvarado or to move toward avenues with more light. The routes of
penury had not yet become habitual to the shocked and stooped shoulders,
but convoluted mouths and trembling limbs admitted that only alternatives
void of affirmation might remain.

More repulsed than fascinated, Leah raced an almost empty bus until
it swerved to the curb. Feeling ensconced in a layer of dust, she sagged into
a seat opposite the driver, took a handkerchief from her purse, and wiped
her face and arms. Upholstery on several of the other seats had been
hacked apart with knives; penned, multilingual graffiti covered the walls;
two of the windows had been shattered and were held together by once
transparent tape that had turned brown.

In the rear of the bus a slight, oblique-armed, bitter-lipped woman,
apparently in her early thirties, strummed a guitar. Fixing her heavily
made-up eyes on Leah, she asked, her voice strident and piercing, "Since
they say art is supposed to celebrate particularity and similarity, is it obvious
that I haven't been involved with any art?"

"You mean," Leah nonchalantly asked in turn, "because so many people
pretending to be you would have improvised that same question?"

An unspoken reply of guitar chords merged with the arrhythmical,
percussive joltings of the ride.

"Let me off at the USC campus, will you?" Leah said to the driver. "I'm
not used to this route. I think you're going to have to wake me up, too."

"All in a day," replied the driver amicably.

2

Having by now again abandoned the expectation of making any progress on her essay, Leah wandered into the University of Southern California campus and—letting each toe touch her preceding heel in the mobile aspect of a grade school game—trekked along the deserted brick paths that bound locked buildings and wreathed a spacious expanse of grass, shade trees, and flowers. The New England-like atmosphere seemed, as it had in her adolescent years, disconcertingly medieval to her; it had an unashamedly imitative guise of borrowed architectural technique that was too bastardized for her tastes, too transplanted, and which she had come to think of as typical of California. Even the vacation tranquillity was unnerving; for it emphasized the dissonant bleatings of the surrounding cityscape which, lacking such a reposed contrast, would have sunk to the peripheries of her consciousness.

Playfully scrutinizing statues and scanning memorial plaques, she happened upon a waist-high portion of a marble column she had never seen before and which, according to an identifying marker, had been part of a Trojan temple. Kneeling, she spent the next quarter of an hour scratching in dirt amassed on the ancient column top a rough, fingernail sketch of the woman who had been seated next to her during the first bus ride of the day. When a clock chimed and echoed two o'clock, she stood and leisurely memorized the shapes of shadows cast by a barbed wire fence, which she trailed to the western boundary of the campus. There a gust of hot wind from the south whipped at her severely enough to compel her to walk sideways in order to cross Vermont Avenue.

Obstinately she persevered in roaming west, finding the disparity between the university and its community context to be stunning and perplexing. A block beyond a federal housing project, the neighborhood grew progressively desolate. The lawns either were overgrown with weeds or were little more than parched slabs of yellow earth. Small houses succeeded one another with such homogeneity they appeared to have been pressed from one rusting mold. Some of them were evidently unoccupied; vandals had splattered their infirm, sheet plaster walls with paint and broken every window.

After she had turned north onto a street intermixing ghetto stores and homes, she was swept ahead so forcibly by the wind that she scarcely needed to propel herself. In less than a minute, she became aware (her face blanched by the spurt of a fear she started to analyze immediately upon noticing the first hint of it) that enshadowed eyes were staring at her from some of the windows above the blighted store fronts. No one left any of the buildings or said anything to her; but it was plain, nonetheless, that her presence was creating an abnormal tension; and she increased the speed of her gait as rapidly as she could without manifestly being overtaken by panic. The peripatetic sounds of her heels hitting the concrete walkway caused a dog basking in an unfenced lot to yelp in fettered circles; and then a buzzing, as if from a mammoth, wounded hornet, took possession of the air. Instantly she looked up and saw a police helicopter slowly soaring directly above her.

Too frightened and disconcerted for further exploring, she sped toward Normandie Avenue, one of the city's major thoroughfares; but not until she had veered onto it did the helicopter alter its direction and disappear. Mystified, she flagged down another bus, and within ten minutes was back on Wilshire, this time traveling west. Green window barriers shielded her eyes from plate glass and steel shards placidly ablaze with midafternoon reflections.

3

To Leah's left, a black, iron fence enclosed a bloated pond from which primordial creatures had drunk and within which they had subsequently been trapped in tangles of roots and weeds that had proved merely to be introductions to inevitable, manifold drownings brought about by an ensnaring floor of tar. Installed within the fence were two, life-sized sculptures meant to symbolize all the errant victims. The face of one of the monstrous creatures, its body submerged, bespoke primitive, unalloyed terror. The other figure, helplessly extending its trunk to the engulfed animal, crouched precariously on the shore and appeared to be aware that any ensuing decision it might be able to act upon would inescapably be either damaging or fatal. The forms had been so vividly executed that they seemed quite alive, their suspended movements attributable to their desperate plights.

Curling the fingers of one hand about each parallel, vertical bar of the fence, Leah forced herself to look toward the water and its attendant quagmire, while she climbed a gently sloped hill that led to an exhibition of reconstructed animal skeletons salvaged from the tar-based depths. At the crest of the hill, she rechecked her wristwatch, took a brush from her purse, scrupulously smoothed her hair into an evenly flowing stream, then sat down on a level plot of grass in front of the museum. Experiencing the onset of a stiffness resultant from her lengthy walk, she crossed her legs, folded her hands together, rested them on her ankles, and again struggled to establish a train of thought for her essay. Her ideas hovered in shadows, however; whenever she neared an identification of them, they sank away from the sphere of her attention and dissolved.

While she was both noting that the wind had ceased and contemplating a possible premature return to Boston, she saw, standing below her at the bottom of the hill, her father. He wore a short-sleeved, rayon sport shirt, double-dyed in helixes of red and blue, and lightweight, lemon-colored, cuffless pants; a black leather belt, upbearing his swollen belly, accentuated the luminosity of the two garments. Leah had not inherited his height; but his hair was as black as hers; and though it had been carefully trimmed, it was longer than she had ever seen it.

"Have you learned to like parsley yet?" Mr. Tetrao asked, evincing, as he mounted the hill, the half-smile Leah had rarely known to desert him.

"That's something I'll never learn."

"College has certainly made you meditative."

"Is that how I look? I wasn't thinking of anything."

"Meditative. Isn't that what they're calling it now?"

"Meditation demands more discipline than I'm putting into anything."

"I've never seen you so, I don't know, reflective, I suppose."

"I was daydreaming. Really. Besides, my tan is gone. It's probably that…."

"How's your mother?" Mr. Tetrao asked.

"Busy," Leah replied, tightly entwining her fingers.

"I brought some fruit juices for us to drink. Grapefruit and pineapple. No added sugar. Want any?"

"Is it in bottles?"

"Cans."

"Drinking out of metal never appealed to me."

"Want one anyway?"

"I can't ever refuse you."

"Grapefruit or pineapple?"

"Grapefruit."

"When did that happen? the metal?"

"I don't know. Always."

"I guess I'd forgotten."

"We had everything in bottles. The issue never came up…."

"I could get you a cup from the museum," Mr. Tetrao offered, as he handed her an opened can.

"This is all I need. But thank you."

"You're much more than welcome," said Mr. Tetrao, lying down full-length on the ground.

"Watch out for your pants, Father," Leah said with unassertive tenderness. "Grass stains might have a hard time coming out of that fabric."

"I shouldn't have bought them. They're not practical. They're for someone younger."

"They look nice. I mean it."

"You think so?"

"Who needs cuffs? What good do they do?"

"All my life, until today, I've worn pants sewn with them; and I do not know," said Mr. Tetrao. The half-smile to which his mouth returned whenever he finished speaking would have restricted his face to blandness, had it not been for the trained compassion sparkling from his salesman's eyes.

"Tell me the truth, Father. Is there someone else in your life these days and nights?"

"That's blunt."

"Well, is there? You and Mother have never been especially secretive."

"No, there isn't."

"You look good. You really do."

"I think you should be eating more, Leah. Your eyes get deeper every time I see you."

"It's the sun being behind clouds five months of the year."

"Still glad you didn't go to the University of Southern California?"

"Gladder."

"Getting any seafood back East?"

"More than when I was living at home...."

"No grunions in Massachusetts, though," said Mr. Tetrao, speaking of a small fish that regularly leaves the sea to mate and lay eggs on a cluster of sandy beaches of California.

Leah released her hands, and they swept outward toward the fenced water. "You would bring grunions up, Father," she said. "Of all things here, they are what I miss...I haven't even found anyone with a boat there."

"You'll have time."

"Time is speeding up."

"For me, too," said Mr. Tetrao. "I remember, in high school, summer was an eternity! Then, for awhile, after college, a year would pass like a semester. I wouldn't plan it that way; it would just happen. Later on, I started thinking 'in five years' like I'd always before thought 'in a year'; and time would go by so fast that five felt like one...I suppose the only way I had of keeping up with all the family responsibilities was to learn not to notice the floundering that went with them."

"I didn't bring you any gray hair," said Leah. "You've got to give...what? me? life?...credit for that."

"No, you didn't. You did not bring me any gray hair," Mr. Tetrao replied, drawing the shadow of his can of juice into his eyes. "It's a relief seeing you now, Leah. It really is. To tell you the truth, it's nice finally to be able to feel I can let you find out what I'm not certain of. Don't ask me for a couple of more years yet what the best part of parenting was; but the worst part, by an inch, by at least an inch, was having to seem like I knew what I did not know!"

"I hadn't ever thought of that. I can see it, though. It must have been awful. Having to lay down laws you weren't sure were right just to get some order."

"Not just the rules. There didn't seem to be any other means of getting you to where you could decide things on your own other than to fill your head with ideas I'd rather have left alone or discussed. But...that's how the tools of personality get built. I didn't understand how intricate it would be."

"How strange it all is," Leah said.

"Unimaginably strange," her father agreed.

Sighing, Leah looked up at the sky for a moment then said, "I don't come close to knowing all the alternatives my life could have, and yet in the atmosphere of school I'm expected to have preferences, Father."

"I don't imagine anyone knows all the alternatives."

"You're no doubt right...."

"You've stopped acting completely?" Mr. Tetrao asked. With his right forefinger, he traced, as if he were practicing handwriting exercises, interlapping ovals on the grass.

"Completely."

"I'm sorry. You would've been good."

"Painting will be better for me."

"Less dependent on others?"

"Much less," Leah replied firmly, adding "I'm beginning to wonder if acting might not be a hindrance to the human race, anyway. Maybe it should be eclipsed by something. I don't think the theater really works without religion."

"'The theater,'" Mr. Tetrao repeated. He sat up and opened another can of fruit juice. "Your mother knows there's not anyone else, Leah."

"She didn't ask me to ask you."

"I'll tell you the truth," said Mr. Tetrao, his tones both ingratiating and intense. "Sometimes marriage can get like living alone. Two people functioning like one person. No more surprises. Changing gets difficult. It's easy to rely too much on what the other person wants to outgrow."

"Sounds depressing."

"Well...parts of it are. You should be ready. Bills make it so all sorts of griefs have to be covered up. To live well enough—I mean with a calm enough surface—to be able to put together the money for the eternal series of payments. You get sluggish. If the chance comes to make a change, you don't take it; the other person hasn't been aware you've wanted it...I didn't appreciate how much of my life your mother was managing. It happened by steps."

"She says the same of you."

"We needed some room. We were too close to each other. Even doing my own cooking is good for me, Leah."

"She's talking about getting a job."

"I hope she does. If she wants to. She won't have to. She won't ever have to."

"She's talking about real estate."

"She'd be good."

"It'd be hard, Father. It's been a long time."

"It's always hard."

"Are you still thinking about getting into journalism?"

"I'm looking at some courses, yeah."

"Where would you work?"

"Here."

"Magazines?"

"Probably. Television, maybe."

"I thought you hated television."

"I do. I do. Especially the news. That's why the possibility of working at it interests me. To get other perspectives into it somehow. I'm fifty-three, Leah. Life hardly looks like a string of accomplishments. I don't want to slip into regret until I have to."

"Good."

"Besides, what I know could be useful. I know the economy. Nationally. I know how California affects it. When people have never done anything but newscasting, salaries are what make the limits of their stories. It's the same with movies. It was that way with radio; so much could never be heard. Television is worse. It establishes a picture of reality for the rest of the people in the country who don't have the salaries that define what the picture can be."

"What are you getting at, though? What is it you want to hear talked about?"

"Oh, federal support of science. Directions it should take. Immigration laws. Things the news doesn't deal with unless it's from the vantage point of a typical, highest-level-income white male. Who gets which options in the economy. There's a lot about that I've learned from handling insurance hardly anyone ever knows. I've stopped more people's chances than I'd care to think about. There was no other way I could stay abreast of the prevailing money winds. It's a structure written in quicksand. Lots of lives get affected in ways they're never aware of."

"'Chances,'" Leah repeated. "I'm not sure what you mean."

"People don't get the policies, say, then they don't get the jobs or keep the businesses, can't afford the house, can't get the kids into college, get too worn out for promotions, can't get loans. It's all interwoven. The odds are heavily weighted, and the prejudices created their own scapegoats. Backs get broken to support the percentages. Rates and taxes in the rest of the country get higher to keep up with clever bookkeeping out here. Boys get asked to die to protect the property of the media staffs who can't remember yesterday and wouldn't know how to plan for tomorrow. Politics isn't exactly full of heroes, Leah; but broadcasting is even worse. There are not many people involved in it. That's one of the problems. A few on each coast. They reinforce each other's outlooks. They've got their islands of wealth, and practically nobody's available to take any steps investigating anything that might start showing what the real economic and political structures are. Their reporting emphasizes the decisions of all the petty leaders there are and that helps keep the leaders in power. The militaries and the local police forces get convinced they're supposed to support the leaders at all costs, and the lives most of us live go unrecorded. We get afraid to trust our perceptions, because what's usually talked about is not what's immediately around us. I think the audience would listen if they had a chance. It's hard to believe how much shafting is going on when you get exposed to only a couple of magazines and a couple of stations with the same sketchy versions of the news. Most of the truth is lost to everybody. It's not even the iceberg tip that gets shown; it's the shavings of ice. People with the knowledge I have tend not to want to use it for anything that doesn't keep the wheels turning so the power will stay in the same few hands."

"You don't think Mother would help you?"

"I don't know if she wants to. Or if she can. I don't expect she knows yet."

"It'll be quite a bit easier on her when you're more settled."

"Yes, but I wish it wasn't that way, though. I didn't want her life to revolve about mine as much as it did. Neither one of us could stop it..."

"Father..." Leah said, her fingers abstractedly playing with the brim of her straw hat, "Have you got another can of grapefruit juice I could have, by chance?"

"Sure," Mr. Tetrao said. "I can get another pack of them."

"I just want one more. There isn't too much time. I think I'm going to take a plane back early tomorrow."

"That's halfway through your vacation, Leah. I thought you could come by my new place sometime."

"There's a paper I'm supposed to be working on: I'm not getting anywhere on it here. It's three weeks late already. Anyway, I don't want to get too used to the sunlight. I think I've got jet lag. It feels like my shadow is still in Boston. I want to pick it up before classes start."

"Be careful not to take your course work for more than it's worth, though, Leah. Save worrying for what matters. Nobody's ever going to care about your grades."

"Easy for you to say..."

"What's the paper topic?"

"Photography...how it affected representational art at first. The instructor let us have a lot of latitude. I've never been so late before. I've got to lock myself in my room."

"That sounds like an assignment for 1920!"

"Yes, but he's a good teacher. He gave a lecture on warm and cold colors that was probably the best lecture I've heard at school so far. He's a graduate student. Hasn't gotten at all rigid yet..."

"Even so, Leah, there must be a lot of things you'd rather write about."

"There are."

"Maybe you should send him a letter. Tell him what you're thinking."

"Just write him a letter?"

"Sure."

"I'll consider it."

"What harm could it do?"

"You're useful for more than bills, Father."

"Tell him his topic's like guessing what Renee Descartes' views on abortions were!"

"I might," Leah said, smiling broadly.

"Does your mother know you're leaving tomorrow?" Mr. Tetrao asked.

"I only decided this afternoon."

"She won't be pleased."

"I just can't concentrate in all this sunlight, Father. I've tried. Really."

"You've become addicted to the East."

"I suppose I have…"

"…Leah…," Mr. Tetrao said, lying back down on the grass and turning over on his stomach. "I've been meaning to ask you…I would've thought you'd have wanted to go to the beach. Or the zoo, even. Why did you decide you wanted to meet me at this awful place?"

"I'm not sure, Father…I guess because it used to scare me a lot."

"Peculiar reason."

"Yes, but sometimes, if you go back to places like that, what's left of the fear goes away."

"Has it gone yet?"

"I don't know. I got really scared today, anyway. I was walking in a sort of mostly-no-white area by the USC campus. Exploring. Not talking to anyone, even. A police helicopter started trailing me."

"There was probably trouble in the neighborhood."

"No, it was trailing me. I'm sure it was. They're suspicious of anyone who walks, you know that. People in Boston are that way, too; but it's much worse out here. The police are the worst of all…I hate to be penalized for using my feet instead of putting more carbon monoxide in the air!"

Mr. Tetrao closed his eyes and slowly said, "More and more the city feels like the inside of a bomb. Tensions nobody can explain away. There's so much talk of Watts igniting again that people there may jump over the edge, get pushed over, I mean, by what everyone else is saying. The major moneymaking routes have been denied in some areas here for so long there's just not much hope left. Probably not enough to keep the rage hidden for even another year. The rest of the city knows it and is scared. It doesn't help that the kids from the ghetto are the ones most likely to be drafted. Circuits of wealth made so they won't touch Watts are the things I understand, Leah. That's the kind of knowledge I meant. People should hear it. In detail. Maybe I could even get water on the fuse."

"It seems to me more a matter of rechanneling the rage than stifling it, Father."

"Yeah, that...that's a good way to put it."

"It's not my phrasing. I got it from a doctor. A psychiatrist I know. You'd like him, I think. The way you've been talking...He reminds me of the sculpture beside the water there...Trying to help so many people stuck in all different kinds of tar."

"Are you seeing him often?"

"Not professionally. Did you think that?"

"I wondered."

"He's exciting to be around. Raises lots of questions."

"You were always one for questions, Leah...But, you were talking about these tar pits."

"Well," Leah said, tossing her head, squinting, "remember when I was upset, how you used to tell me about how the earth might be a molecule in a giant's ring, Father?"

"That was your favorite story."

"Yes."

"Of course, I remember."

"Well, sometimes I used to think of it—the earth I mean—as part of the face of a giant. The Atlantic and Pacific were his two eyes, and the United States was the bridge of his nose. The tar pits were a tear duct, and the land between here and the ocean was a little piece of skin...The giant was built weirdly."

"Giants often are. Giants often are."

"Yes," said Leah, smiling. "Often." She crushed her empty juice can with one hand and continued, "Water always flowed under the giant's skin, under the land, like a flood. That was so there might be a way for most of the animals to escape. The giant's tears would carry them to safety.... And those two sculptures would always come alive in my thinking. Usually everything else about the giant came to depend on them not moving at all, but sometimes I'd play with turning time around. A second for them would be millions of years for us. Instead of the same sun always rising and setting, every day would have its own sun—every day a different sun. If the earth could be a molecule, then that could be real, too. In their time the two animals weren't suspended; and the tar would probably disappear, like a mud puddle. The one in the water could crawl out. And they would both be saved...I still think of them, sometimes..."

"Found a tear duct by the Atlantic?"

"Oh, that was always Niagara Falls...And I haven't told you the best part."

"Are you going to?"

"Of course, I am...It's that at the bottom of these tar pits there was a sun."

"What did you say?"

"I said, 'A sun...'"

"Why didn't it melt the tar?

"It was too small, not warm enough," Leah replied. "But even so, it was what the giant and everything else in the giant's realm revolved around. It brought some light into the darkest part of the world, some hope that otherwise wouldn't have been there. Some perspective."

"Trying to imagine things into vaster perspectives doesn't work for me anymore," said Mr. Tetrao. "Even the skeletons in the museum should make that happen. But they don't. The years ahead of me are all I can look at."

"Better than getting ready to live them without looking at them."

"Yes. Yes, it is. I'm glad you said that. You're right. You're right...But enough of me, Leah. Your mother's going to be wondering whether to hold off dinner for you. Let me hear what you have in mind for yourself.

Painting's going to be difficult. Probably the most difficult way you could go. Especially at the beginning."

"I suppose what I'm doing lately is imagining myself as becoming something like a tribal shaman, Father. I'm sure that's what I'm doing. I'm surprised you got me to admit it. I'm assuming there'll be a need for professional observers and depicters for awhile yet. So other people can find enough clarity to keep on going."

"There's no question about that. There's got to be some light from a few of us. But that's always been true. Always will be, I'd think. So why did you say 'for awhile yet'?"

Shrugging suddenly, Leah replied with angry impatience, "I wish you could realize that anyone who was born after the atomic bombs were used is going to be different from the rest of you. Very different, Father. We've had to face the possibility of the end of us all every moment we've known. Most people your age haven't ever faced it."

"I can't get out of being in my generation," Mr. Tetrao said, lifting his head from the ground and glancing past the park to Wilshire Boulevard. "What do you mean? That we're relying on outmoded methods? Or have you given us up as...? What? Unworth your time?"

"I mean it's not painting that's important. It's using it to help find some way for us to survive. Maybe we'll be able to arrange our lives so most of us could share doing routine work, say. If we could develop more sides of ourselves, practically I mean, and understand better the structures around us by taking turns working in them, something like painting wouldn't need to be as specialized as it is now. More people could do it. A lot of the value of art is the activity of making it. I hate specializations. There shouldn't be any. They separate us so. They make us lopsided."

"You're sounding awfully vague, Leah. That's unlike you."

"Well, what do you expect, Father? For me—at the age of twenty—to have thought up a blueprint for utopia?"

"I'm used to more clarity from you, is all..."

"I know. I know," replied Leah with genuine weariness. "But so much is in upheaval now, Father. Not just for me. There are a lot of things I can't talk about easily. Especially since I'm spending most of my time painting. Words and colors are very unalike: parts of yourself get used that are close to being incompatible. Even though critics say there can be translations of paintings into words, anyone who actually paints knows there can't be. Good, finished work requires explanations, or more, requires guideposts; but I don't have enough skill yet to explain; and there's not much yet to guide you to. I don't want to give you impressions that aren't true, and I don't know how to give you any except a couple of incomplete ones…Sometimes, talking can be a violation." She stood and added, "I really should be getting back. There's packing."

"This soon? Are you sure?"

"We've got to be careful of saying things we won't want to remember, all three of us."

"Well…if you're determined to leave tomorrow," said Mr. Tetrao, standing and shading his eyes with both hands, "probably it's wise."

"I forgot to thank you for the print you had waiting for me here, Father."

"You like it?"

"Very much."

"It's the best print I've seen of it. The face in brushstrokes doesn't usually show through. I thought of getting you a late Van Gogh, one of those with the birds; but *The Old Guitarist* seemed closer to where you'd probably be…"

"It's wonderful."

"I'm glad."

"I don't think it's old age that it depicts, do you? or one man?"

"I'm not sure. Tell me how you're seeing it."

"I think that right then—right when he was doing that painting—Pablo Picasso began to understand that what seemed to be representational portraits might really be symbols of attitudes. Maybe even of archetypical attitudes. I think it depicts pure fortitude…Which I'm going to be needing a lot of...I...You were right, Father. It was a perfect gift. Especially for what I'm doing now."

"It's about time I did something perfect," said Mr. Tetrao, as he followed Leah down the hill. "What about letting me drive you home, Leah. It'll be dark before you could get there by bus. The shortest day of the year was, what? a week ago?"

"I never can remember," Leah replied. "That, and when daylight savings time begins and ends. I was an hour early for everything last fall. Or an hour late. Whatever it was. I should get an identification bracelet with those four dates engraved on it instead of my name...You don't think it would be awkward? Driving me back I mean?"

"I wouldn't go in the house. I'm sure your mother will understand."

4

The globe of the sun had no discernible outline, but its rays bourned a cream-colored oval which began in the west and increased in grayness, so that the eastern horizon was nearly black. The formation made the sky unusually rounded, domed, as if massive, cup-shaped, measuring bowls, layered within each other, had been turned upside down over the earth.

Some of the yellowed drifts heaped about the curbs of Huntington Avenue were so high it was impossible to be certain whether they covered shrubbery or consisted entirely of snow. Surface melting had occurred in uneven sheets of shining pools, and the street was veined with cinder-blackened tunnels. Several cars inched along the silver trolley tracks; but most vehicles were at rest, their chrome folds and colors concealed. Ferns of blue ice traced the car windows and glistened like illuminated, white-framed lace. In another hour it would be dark.

Since landing at the Boston airport early in the afternoon, Leah had barely stopped moving. She had flagged a taxi and ridden to her dormitory, deposited her suitcases in her room, changed her clothes, and in knee-high boots, a stocking cap, furred mittens, a honey-colored Hudson Bay coat, and a scarf wrapped twice about her mouth and nose, had immediately left for the Museum of Fine Arts. Gratefully, she anticipated that the freshness of her impressions of the East Coast and an intensity resulting from the loss of three hours would allow her that evening to compose either her overdue essay or a letter to her professor.

There was, moreover, on the front walkway of the museum a statue of a horse and rider she had been intending to examine for months. From a distance it had seemed to be a representation of a prayerful acceptance of all that being alive could possibly entail; but she had wondered whether elements of pleading or request or resignation might also have been sculpted into it. Its prominent location necessitated that it be an image capable of arousing variegated communion, and she sensed that studying it in proximity—in spite of the snow and the cold—would bring about the conclusive release of her thoughts.

Determinedly she scanned the lines alluding to muscle in the outstretched arms of the rider, and she searched for characterizing definitions, but there was too much ice on the molded human face for her to see the detail she had counted on investigating. Impatient, she rolled a ball of snow and threw it, hitting the white crusted screen but having an impact insufficient to improve her view. Assuring herself there were no onlookers and confident she could do no damage, she then rolled five more, tightly packed snowballs and, allowing her scarf to slip to her shoulders, laughing, hurled them in succession.

Her fourth throw finally cracked the hooded ice, causing it to plummet past the feet of the rider and, as if it were being defeated by sunlight itself, splinter against a cubed, supportive base. Yet although the head of the figure had now become visible, Leah continued to be unable, as she raptly circled the statue, to identify features portraying anything other than modest dignity, perpetual, reverent acquiescence. Satisfied, however, that she had made a gesture inclusive enough for her to succeed in relating the

dimensions of her assignment to the evolving latticework of her visual attitudes, she trudged back to the Boston University campus.

Upon entering her neat and comfortably equipped room, she plugged
a hot plate into an electrical outlet and held her hands over the reddening
coils. Next to her was a straight-backed, wooden chair; adjacent to it was
a metal desk bolted to the floor. A brown leather coverlet—strewn with
pillows of varying sizes—allowed a bed against the opposite wall to serve
as a couch. To the left of her desk, circles of brass fastened white curtains
to a rusty rod above a small window that enabled a view of nearby fenced
tennis courts and an adjacent, austerely lined gymnasium.

The floor of the room was carpeted; and more than half of it had been
spread with newspapers on which were tubes of paint, cans of pigment and
linseed oil, jars of brushes, a portable easel, drawing pads, a metal butcher's
tray for mixing colors, boxes of crayons, pastel chalks, and pencils. A T-square
and a collapsible measuring stick lay in balanced slants against a corner. A
sole bookcase contained only two books, both by the essayist and autobiographical novelist Eugene Webber, but was densely stacked with drawings
and sketches.

After stowing her coat in the closet, Leah positioned the hot plate in
her central line of vision on the floor, sat at her desk, withdrew a pen from
a drawer, changed her mind, took up a pencil, and opened a pad of lined
stationery. With the little finger of her left hand poised inside her mouth,
she stared a moment at the glowing spiral of the hot plate and then began
to write:

January 4, 1966

I had received an extension I have failed to meet. I'm going to
offer an explanation for my double delay and supplement it with
thoughts on matters pertinent to my own work. I realize I have
no precedents for doing this; but the content will suggest why
I'm choosing what will probably be for you (in our situations) an

unacceptable alternative, however meaningful and even necessary I find it. I think that if you would welcome an informal dialogue, it would prove more valuable to me than a simple essay.

Letting her eyes wander over what she had written, she erased "simple" in the last sentence, penciled in "commonplace," erased that, tried "predictable," glared at the last two words, erased them, ended the paragraph with "than an essay," and wrote on:

> I have found little enduring value in college course work so far. The student role rarely involves any kind of discussion; never does it allow genuine negotiation; contracts are obscure and heavily weighted on the sides of the faculty and the administration. Questions occur mainly in examinations prepared by assistant professors rather than being asked by students as daily adjuncts to natural learning. What happens within this context is that students are offered advice we are expected simply to accept; our evaluations of the advice are uninvited. Consequently many of our capacities for judgment are dormant and untutored. I ask you to consider some glimmerings of my thought. They by no means yet compose a philosophy, nor even an approach; but I expect they form the ground upon which my working philosophy will eventually be built.

'It should be as precise as I can manage to have it. I'm making it too tangled. He probably won't read past the first paragraph. Is it "framework" I mean instead of "ground"?'

> You asked us to write about the initial relationships of photography to what had been traditional, representational art. The topic was vague enough so I could satisfactorily have stayed within its bounds, but you seem to me to be requiring us to

pretend that controversies resolved half a century ago are topical. They were resolved simply by using cameras and thereby making much of what had been considered appropriate visual technique obsolete. That is widely understood. Such a request from you is almost an insult.

'It's what I think; and if it looks too exaggerated at the end, I'll rewrite it. I can still do the paper, anyway.' ·

It would have been more profitable for us to have been asked to trace the outlines of what has been done visually alongside photography since its invention. An assignment like that would have helped us plan where to go next in terms of constructive seeing.

Another improvement would have been an invitation for us to discuss the learning techniques that enable the leaps we make back and forth between the environment and representational works (photographic or otherwise). This would have let us analyze how responses vary according to societal context; it would have opened a door to reflections on "Eastern" perspective where the vanishing point is meant to be inside one's head; it also would have allowed us to study the consciousnesses of those adult groups (as reported by anthropologists) who have never learned to view colors and forms on flat surfaces as representations of other experience—people who, thus, always see only colors and shapes (even when they view photographs), no matter what was meant to have been depicted. Insights from such explorations would probably have refined our abilities to understand the natures of current, "nonrepresentational" pieces and would, perhaps, have enabled us to identify elements usually overlooked when considering representational art, elements that might always have been subliminally involved in communication processes. I refer to elements now primarily associated (consciously?) with abstract efforts. Without our being aware of it, might not representational images affect us in many of the same ways that nonrepresentational art does? Aren't all images abstract? Certainly what we call "abstract paintings" are often meant to *represent* feelings or ideas.

What we're being taught to think of as encompassingly human art forms stem only from "Western" traditions; we give no time to any other cultures. I am aware that the course material exists within a network of galleries and books and museums founded upon this same, unchallenged habit of terming visual techniques all-inclusive which have been truly associated only with a small portion of humanity; but, nonetheless, it rejects the attitudes and accomplishments of billions of people and is also indicative of insufficient recognition of efforts by some Western painters of this century to incorporate in a nonpatronizing manner methods of other cultures. I expect more from the university setting. Is an atmosphere of war responsible for the prevalence of this confusion of what is characteristically human with what is but one strand of our history?

I want to bring up a few aspects of current trends in painting:

The lay question, "What is it?", snickeringly asked in the presence of much of art since the advent of photography should be answerable by artists and critics alike; otherwise the question will continue to express justified derision. If paintings are to be other than arrangements of color, if they are to have symbolic functions, then the "What is it?"s should be treated with respect. Usually when people are so questioned, all they do is not answer and sneer knowingly, as if there is a knowledge with which only an elite is familiar. I wonder if that knowledge exists; if so, it should be communicable. Does the sneering result from a combination of apathy and hopelessness?

Surrounded as nearly all of us are by symbols, the expectation of verbal definitions, answers, is warranted; so are an examination and an evaluation of the uses to which commonly understood symbols are put within all communications media; for we are inundated by portrayals of experience that too rarely open doors to experience itself; often depictions become manipulatable substitutes for existential involvements.

Leah sharpened her pencil: 'I don't think I can reread any of it.'

Underlying the above objections and suggestions is this: after Western visual art ceased to be motivated and financed by religious structures and after it ceased to be primarily an amusement for a wealthy, nonsectarian minority, how much good did it do in encouraging the development of humane social institutions, networks, structures? Did it bring any salvation? Courses never put the works we study into historical contexts; and we never hear any judgments of art's effectiveness in enhancing the quality of lives.

If, as is sometimes said, Auschwitz took from us the right to compose poetry, then the events on every side which led up to the bombings of Hiroshima and Nagasaki obligate the conclusion that all the paintings and the sculpture and the courses and museums, reflecting, as they did the first half of this century, attempts to reach out to people living on every social level, failed to sustain or provoke human decency and may even have been terribly implicated in unleashing the horrors of war.

I'm not writing rhetorically. What do you think? Our lives are now ordered so that human survival is perpetually at stake. Can art help us at all?

This question and the attendant attitudes it suggests are, I'm almost sure, what the modern painter most often appreciated by professionals and lay public alike, Jackson Pollock, meant to shock us into asking and examining. Pollock's self-depicted anguish prevented "What is it?"s, because it was clear what he was expressing and why he used the means he did. He understood how permanently many forms of communication had been shattered by war. (The shattering concurrent with? the shattering caused by?) He appreciated meaninglessness; but he did not sneer at it; nor did he pretend that it was meaning; he depicted his anguish in regard to it; and maybe that's the only triumph any painter could have had during the late forties and early fifties.

Can we salvage from the wreckages that resulted from war visual techniques that will do any good? How can we develop new ones that will help us survive and live constructively? These questions are what most of the recent painters seem to me to have been incoherently asking. I think they have been struggling *to create, to discover, or both* a visual language, a means of sharing understanding that would be both clear and pertinent to all of humanity.

Some painters, of course, (I think all their work is worthless except as sociological data) equate comprehensiveness with science, mistakenly associate scientific methods solely with destructive forces, and have confused their detached, highly personal visual choices with symbols agreed upon by communities.

Is it clear to you I'm seeking the rudiments of a comprehensive visual language that would be cross-culturally meaningful and also humanely life-enhancing? I think it urgent we consider the attempts that have, thus far, been made to attribute linguistic qualities to colors and forms. We should, for example, be studying experiments that have been devised to discover how colors and shapes are perceptually linked with (symbolic of?) specific feelings

I haven't forgotten your discussion of the framework dividing colors into categories of warm and cold. But that's an inadequate and unproductively simplified, semi-linguistic sketch. It fails to take into account that many of our psychological/emotional associations are correlated with the varying weather of the environments we've lived in. For instance, after arriving in Massachusetts from my home in Los Angeles about three years ago, it took me a long time to alter the associations I had with colors as they related to temperature. I have subsequently experienced painted greens in manners far different from how I saw them within a semitropical climate. I've frequently heard newcomers to California complain they find the weather there colder than it looks.

Let me come back to school matters:

High schools often attempt to nurture development of many personality facets, which later fall into disuse. I think the goal of "producing" coordinated, multisided people is a good one and a necessary one; we should all be able to use many of our talents; hence, I think that the activities of making and means of appreciating visual art should be open to as many people as possible; we need an economy that would allow us, or even encourage us, to keep on growing.

College requires too much specialization. It is argued that such specialization will be economically necessary after graduation. But current ends of the economy I find often to be evil, insane, or both. I think we should develop global patterns for equitably sharing economic functions (especially those involving food, shelter, communication, and artistic endeavor) in order to attain sanity, decency, and the assurance of human survival.

I'm not suggesting renewed folk and hobby art, the dissemination of works by a few museum darlings, or more group mural projects. I mean the creation of viable structures within which a multitude more people would have time to engage in visual creation for the sake of enjoying the activity itself and in order to achieve a heightened awareness of our interrelationships with all that is.

As she put down her pencil, Leah saw that she had been exerting much less pressure on it than usual. Amused, she picked up her pen, signed her name, found an envelope, stamped and addressed it, and slipped the letter inside.

'Awkward and disjointed but maybe it has to be and it's certainly where I am and he ought to be able to help or I ought to know why he can't or won't. I'll reread it in the morning. Eight days from now I hope I can at least remember what I wrote, that's all.'

After placing the unsealed envelope on her windowsill, she started to brush her hair; but all at once she flung the brush to the floor; and with her pen she printed on a blank, unlined piece of paper:

> A long string————————————————————————
>> from a house key, lightning, and a federal constitution
>> to
>> ballistic missile systems and global symposiums

Holding a corner of the paper, she pinned it—so that her words would hang diagonally above the right side of her desk—to the wall containing the window. Depleted, but relieved, she then unplugged the hot plate and watched its red spiral slowly cool to black.

PART III

9 Soul Mates

1

The amber hues of the buildings, the streets, and the teeming sidewalks of Harvard Square were accentuated by the cloudless sky. Winter-pallid skin seemed to have been tanned prematurely; antique, brick fence posts glittered like freshly fired, raw pottery; even the reflections from the store-front glass, the chrome, and the windshields dallied between saffron and ocher. Cars rent the air with exasperated and ineffective honking, as late afternoon drivers adapted themselves to the dryness and lucent sunlight of the first days of the spring of 1966.

Tightening the lines of her mouth in mild irritation, Leah looked again at the number of a public telephone booth next to the subway entrance and assured herself she was where C. J. had asked her to meet him. Although she had unbuttoned her coat, she was sweating; her unshaven legs, however, were cooled by a gentle breeze rippling her green and white plaid skirt, as she became absorbed in examining the throngs of passing faces. The telephone had rung twice before she realized the sound was coming from the booth beside her. Surprised, she blinked, faltered, and picked up the receiver.

"H-hello," she said, stuttering.

"Shall I compare thee to a summer's day?" C. J.'s voice asked.

"Please don't."

"Sorry I'm late."

"Your whimsical sense of time is one of your charms."

"I brought you a kite."

"Where are you?"

"Across the street."

Intuitively she glanced toward the graveyard and saw him in a booth alongside it. His hair hung in shaggy waves over his shoulders; and his unbelted, white denims loosely hugged his hips. Three, huge, white buttons on the pockets of his blue, felt jacket and at the top if its zippered front gleamed like reflectors on a bicycle.

"Meet you at the corner of Brattle," he said, curving a hand southwest and tapping his knees together in mock applause.

"I've got to run for the light," said Leah. As she replaced the receiver, she heard a coin jangle into the return slot, smilingly retrieved it, then picked up a thatched picnic basket, and wound her way through the arrested flow of traffic on Massachusetts Avenue.

"I can't plan right," C. J. said, frowning, inclining his head to the west, and starting to walk. With one arm he held a bulky paper sack against his side.

"I did a lot of looking while I was waiting," Leah said, aligning her steps with his. "I need that. I've been staring at sketch pads so much my eyelids are stiff."

"The post office keeps docking me."

"Won't they let you stay longer when you get there late?"

"Timecard punches don't read excuses."

"Has anybody said anything to you about it?"

"No…they think I'm a magazine article. The supervisor wants me to cut my hair."

"Sounds like high school."

"Yeah, but instead of my mother getting a note from the principal, I may have to stop signing checks."

"…C. J., do you think the Beatles album is ever going to be released?"

"I heard it's getting a new cover."

"I heard that, too."

"It shouldn't take much longer."

"It's getting so I'm going by record store windows twice a day," Leah said. "Hey, could we get off Brattle? The people are wearing me out. I can't stop staring at them."

"Sure," C. J. replied. Immediately he shuffled onto a side street which coiled past porticoed verandahs, stained glass windows, and immaculate lawns studded with cobblestones, nineteenth-century sculpture, and enormous hedges.

"How far are we going?" Leah asked, swaying her head from side to side, her eyes preoccupied with the budding suburban greens that were struggling to replace a lingering residue of winter grays.

"About a mile. Are you tired?"

"No, but I wish I hadn't worn this coat."

"Want me to carry it?"

"You've got enough. I should've learned what to expect from Massachusetts weather by now…."

Unzipping his jacket and quickening his pace, C. J. asked, "Leah, do clouds ever look to you like taxicabs from other planets?"

"No, but sometimes they look like hair on clowns."

"Circuses make me nervous. I hate them."

"So do I. They remind me of political conventions."

"Elephants?"

"Chameleons…"

"Once I was sitting on a bus…" C. J. began.

"The date can be forgotten or unmentioned, but the where I must know," said Leah. "You've been so many places."

"Boston."

"One of the trolleys that doesn't take passengers underground?"

"No, a bus."

"Go ahead."

"President Kennedy was standing in front of me. He was a Senator then. I recognized him because of the 1956 convention on television. A kite was next to me. Taking up a whole seat. I said, 'Sir?' He didn't turn around. If he answered, I didn't hear him. I tapped his back and asked him if he wanted to sit on my kite. I couldn't think of anything else to say."

"Was it one of those kites with the Declaration of Independence printed on it?" Leah asked, laughing loudly.

"Maybe. It was one I bought."

"For forty cents in a black ghetto or ten cents in a white ghetto?"

"Ten cents in a white ghetto."

"What happened next?"

"He said, 'No, I do not want to sit on that kite.' Completely serious."

"And he stood for another stop?"

"He stood for two more stops. Even though I put the kite on my lap..."

"Maybe it was one of his brothers."

"Yeah, I didn't know he had brothers then. Maybe it was..."

"It sounds like one of the three of them, for sure, though."

With his free hand C. J. pushed a low overhanging branch up out of their way. "Whoever the people are who own these trees," he said, "they don't expect anyone ever to walk here."

"They play golf and go to health spas...."

"You know what?" C. J. asked slowly.

"What?" Leah answered with an obvious combination of carefulness and lack of hesitancy.

"My salary is higher than my mother's."

"That doesn't surprise me."

"I get so angry when I think about it."

"Good."

"She won't take any of my money."

"Did you expect her to?"

"Yes."

"Maybe she'll change her mind," Leah ventured.

"I hope so," C. J. replied, adding in tones that denoted incomprehension rather than contempt, "…It feels here, it feels like people are sitting inside the houses terrified their doorbells will ring."

"You're right. There's hardly what one thinks of as a neighborly aura."

"It's like a flock of forts…."

"Sometimes…" said Leah sadly, "on the news…I'll see South Vietnamese huts with fishnets strung out over a river and with communal gardens on the shore. How people live there makes such perfect sense. I get afraid that's why we're destroying them."

Kicking pebbles into the street, C. J. transferred his package to the arm between himself and Leah, and stepped ahead of her.

"How's the apartment?" she asked.

"I got a table."

"Oh, good, C. J. What's it like?"

"Rectangular. Solid oak. I had to have them deliver it from the second-hand store. No chairs yet."

"Been using your laundry line?"

"Sometimes."

"Things smell so much better that way. Even in the city."

"One night I was too tired to bring it in."

"Was it there in the morning?" Leah asked.

"Yeah," C. J. answered. "Some of it was a little stiff, though."

"Still on a sleeping bag?"

"My back's getting molded to the floor."

"What about cooking?"

"I'm used to it. There's no problem. I did so much at home. The shopping makes me want a car, but maybe I'll get a bicycle. Things'll be better this summer, though. The landlord said I can have a garden in the backyard."

"That's wonderful. It almost makes me envious. Know what you're going to plant?"

"Not yet. It's harder than I expected. Figuring it all out. Growth times and shade and watering."

"That's the kind of thing we should've learned in grade school."

C. J. nodded vehemently, then asked, "Leah, the piece of a tree, the part that's not hit by light, say, the western side in the morning, is that called a shadow?"

"I don't think so," Leah replied. "It's in a shadow, but it's not a shadow. That's one of the hardest parts of landscapes to draw. It moves so quickly. I don't know what good it does to draw it, anyway. All those hours to get the pretense of a moment. Growth is what I want to understand how to convey. Not just growth, but the best directions for it to take. Maybe that's too ambitious. I don't know. C. J., am I making enough sense?"

"It helps when I see what you're doing," C. J. replied, uncertain whether he was lying.

"I meant portraits, more than landscapes," said Leah, her tongue stumbling. "Making a portrait that would show what a person might become."

"I guess I'm not exactly sure what you mean."

"That's all right. Half the time I don't know myself what I mean lately."

"You're experimenting," said C. J. "So lots of ideas have to be unformed for awhile."

"It helps me just to get some of my thinking said, even if I'm incoherent."

"I like for you to talk about your work, Leah."

"I know."

"I want to do more than listen. I'm not sure how to."

"Trust whatever you're thinking."

"Yes, but you're almost the only one who wants me to do that."

"You've been talking better than I have been these past couple of months."

"Better than at Yale anyway."

"Tell me what else you're doing. Have you started painting the apartment yet?"

"Yeah.... It's going to take longer than I thought, though. I don't want to get asphyxiated."

"I've been feeling that, too. The ventilation in my room is terrible. Even oil paints get impossible to breathe around. I can't use any sprays there."

"Metal sprays, you mean?"

"No, fixatives, glosses, that kind of thing. Some of the drawings are good enough now to save. Just so I can refer to them later. They're not for anyone else yet…C. J., is it going to be light enough?"

"The streetlights should be on soon."

"There are streetlights there?"

"Not exactly, but…you'll see."

"I always wonder where they turn streetlights on from," said Leah, continuing to sway her head from side to side.

"It's automatic. Dark-sensitive timers."

"Are you sure?"

"I'm sure."

"So much that happens, it's hard to tell who's doing what."

"Yeah, I know…" said C. J., as he steadied an index finger in the breeze. "Leah, if you promise not to laugh, I'll tell you what I've been thinking about in most of my spare time."

"I won't laugh."

"Light bulbs."

"Thinking what about light bulbs."

"Whether they could be in different shapes. Different colors. Throw all sorts of patterns around instead of pretend to be sunshine. I want to know if they're usually the same shape because they have to be to work or because so far that's how it's easiest to make them."

"Found out anything?"

"I got some physics books."

"Are you remembering enough calculus?"

"Mostly."

"Keep working at it."

"Yeah," said C. J., hooking a thumb around his belt buckle, lowering his voice, and peering behind them to make certain they were unseen.

"You're going to have to follow me through the trees at the end of the block. Tell me if I'm going too fast. There are lots of bushes."

"I wonder why it's so hidden."

"They don't want people having picnics and flying kites there is why."

"One of these times you're going to lead me into a jail sentence."

"It's safe. You'll see. It'll be brighter than on the sidewalk. Be as quiet as you can, though."

As soon as they silently had crossed nearly twenty feet of untended grass, C. J. heaved his package over a camouflaged fence made of three wires staked parallel to the overgrown earth, forced the wires far enough apart so that Leah could creep between them, bent over, squirmed past them himself, and, grinning, allowed them to snap back into place. He then led the way up a rough, gradually inclined mass of boulders, weeds, and compactly planted trees.

"Let me take the basket," he whispered, as he stopped in front of a knoll twice his height. "Careful of the dust getting in your eyes, Leah."

"My shoes are getting full of gravel," she replied. "I've got to get them off soon." Her coat strewn with dry leaves and her hair disheveled, she followed closely behind him, as he arched his body, bounded up the hill, and pointed fifty feet below to a barbed wire fence encircling a donut-shaped, treeless, sandy beach and a small, shallow lake. In the last of daylight the surface of the undulating water glowed like a summer field of ripened wheat.

"You can't see the opening from here," he said. "Come on. We can slide to it." Simultaneously they fell to the ground and careened to the bottom of the eroded slope. Without a pause, he went confidently to the fence, wrestled with it, pried loose a corner, and rolled it to his waist.

"I'm the hinges," he said.

"So how did you find the gate?"

"I tested for it a whole afternoon. I knew it had to be somewhere. They probably use it only for repairs."

"Repairs of what?"

"Pipes."

"I wonder why they don't have a lock."

"This way hardly anybody sees it."

"You're sure we can get back out?" Leah asked, as she crawled through the narrow hole.

"I'm sure, Leah," C. J. replied, supporting the fence with his back and slithering beneath it.

Flushed and smiling, she slipped off her shoes and stockings, set them on top of the basket, and lightly took hold of his elbow; skittishly exhaling a yell that echoed in a boomerang path, he edged closer to her; and arm in arm, they walked to the verge of the water.

"It'd be good here," he said. "The wind is from the west. Mostly."

"Fine. I'm hungry," she replied. She put down the basket, opened it, took out a blanket, tossed it high in the air, caught it as it began to unfurl, and spread it upon the damp sand. Meanwhile, he hastily pulled two kites from his sack and started to assemble them.

"The sky always seems so much lower here than it does in California," she said, taking off her coat. "I wonder why that is."

"Can you paint the difference?" he asked. With one eye closed, he adjusted the bridle angles of both kites.

"I don't know..." she answered, opening two bottles of spring water and handing him one. "There's a thermos of herbal tea if you want any later."

"The lake's going to make the dark seem brighter soon," he said. "You'll see."

"Are there any fish here?" she asked, removing cellophane from four sandwiches.

"I don't think so. Too many chemicals. It's a storage pit. The water gets piped to covered reservoirs. The rest of the treatment's done there."

"All the pipes and wires!" she sighed. "Doesn't it sometimes seem to you like we're strangling ourselves with them?"

"Yeah..." he answered. "Yeah, it does...But only sometimes." He unzipped his jacket and dropped it with forced casualness onto the blanket.

As he rolled up the sleeves of his baroquely patterned, blue and turquoise shirt, Leah said, "C. J., I've never seen you so dignified. You look about five years older."

"It's the first time in my life I've had any extra money."

"What a magnificent shirt!"

"Thanks."

"I mean it."

"I know."

"You're right about the dark getting lighter. I can see it already. The fence looks almost phosphorescent..."

Settling the two kites in the sand, C. J. lowered his back to the blanket, tightened his upright knees, and playfully asked, "...Leah, is Zen when you think you understand, somebody arrives to show you that you haven't understood?"

"I guess so," she replied, breaking an eggshell on the handle of the picnic basket. "As long as you keep on trying to understand, C. J."

"The egg peeled right!" he said solemnly.

"Yes..."

"No matter what methods I use, I can't ever figure out what to do to make sure they'll peel right."

"Me, too..." she said. She threw a grape into his mouth. "Just when I think one way works best, the shells start sticking again. It must be us. The human race has to have discovered by now how to deal with shelling hard-boiled eggs."

"You'd think it," he replied, munching a sandwich.

"Hey, I got a reply from that instructor whose course I flunked."

"It took him long enough to send it."

"I'd stopped waiting."

"I'm glad your letter did something, anyway. It was a good idea...Did he tell you anything that helps?"

"I'm not sure. What he said was, 'How many people do you know who have heard of Jackson Pollock? Sincerely, Tom Miernan.' That's all."

"Are you going to write him an answer?"

"I don't know yet."

"At least he signed his first name."

"Yes, and it's not as if I'd sent him a self-portrait he'd returned with 'This doesn't look at all like you and that's the best part of it' printed across my cheek bones."

"But, still, though, I mean, what did...What do you suppose he was implying?"

"Mainly, that I'd better realize how isolated I am. He's right...You remember how it was in high school. People around us knew basically the same things we did. But that isn't true anymore. It had honestly never occurred to me before that most adults haven't read any art history books. I've even been taking for granted they've read the same ones I have. I've been getting a specialized knowledge without having noticed it."

Delicately she dipped a strawberry into a container of sour cream and then into a bag of brown sugar.

"I wondered how that was going to fit together," C. J. said admiringly. "Did you think it up?"

"No, it's what we used to do at home. That's how we spent a lot of Sunday nights a long time ago. Sitting around a table listening to the radio and getting ready for the week. Usually I'd get sent out for more strawberries. I don't know why we quit doing it."

"Television, probably."

"Or maybe things like that always disappear when we grow up, C. J."

"Yeah, maybe," he replied. Reaching into the paper sack he had carried, he quietly added, "Oh, by the way, I have something for you." Taking out a white cardboard box, he set it on her lap. "It's a present."

"Not even my birthday!"

"I hope you like it."

"To kites!" she said affably, as if she were proposing a toast. Once she had lifted the lid of the box, however, her eyes grew perplexed; she felt her cheeks pale; and she pressed her hands to her mouth.

"It's a portable easel," said C. J.

"I know what it is; but it must've cost a quarter of your salary for a month!"

"That's all right."

"Can you really handle that much?"

"For awhile, anyway."

"I didn't expect to have one for a couple of years," Leah said, holding the accompanying instructions close to her eyes and beginning to read. "It's better than the one school's been letting me use. I'm hardly ever overwhelmed. I'm overwhelmed. Or at least I'm whelmed, if that's a word. Thank you, C. J."

"Besides, you're better than a bank," C. J. replied. He poured a cup of herbal tea, stretched out his legs, and put the weight of his shoulders on his left arm, which he trussed stiffly behind him. "...What banks do," he said. "What they work from, is people having their salaries the only thing they can see. They can be sure of the numbers, and that gets to be the only scale they have. It happens right off. It's happening to me. They don't relate money to how they get it. Not even to how they spend it. They don't have enough time to. The numbers are what they care about. Not what work they do or what they buy."

Gazing at the sky, he began offhandedly to pile handfuls of sand into irregular mounds, while Leah, attempting to encourage him to continue his rambling stream of words, bowed her head and sat motionless, as if she were coaxing a chipmunk into eating from her hand.

"They don't say anything that might get in the way of higher numbers," he went on. "They have unions to keep the numbers going up; but the members don't talk with the leaders any more than they used to with the managers; and they don't really talk with each other, not about anything besides numbers. If you're not in the union, they separate you and wear you down. They say 'the government' like it's something different from them, like it's something they can't affect. Maybe they can't. I don't know anymore. I'm so away from the sun, I forget it's there. Some of the people at the post office say how stupid I was to leave Yale; they think it's not having a college degree has kept them from getting what they want. Which is higher numbers. Never anything about how they spend their time. Grouped together making what we don't need, telling ourselves we need it, getting used to what we don't want because it has a price tag on it. Then time is gone. Spent in routines. All we did was add the numbers up. So why even have lived?"

He leveled the mounds of sand with one swoop of a fist.

"I don't mind the routines," Leah said. "But I mind about the chance to choose them. I don't think routines are always deadening. You have to make them serve your purposes. I'm not doing much in courses right now, but my grades are the best they've been. Just because I'm putting papers and exams into little, weekly slots. I've decided school is basically paid-for, free time. I suppose what I'm learning to do is make my own routines; I want to know how to use them for what I'm interested in, for what I'm passionately interested in; I want to know why I have them."

She finished the last of the grapes, crumpled the ragged stem, dropped it into the picnic basket, swathed her arms around her knees, and rested her head sideways on one elbow.

C. J. lay back and covered his face with his hands.

"A lot of what's around us is ugly, granted," Leah continued. "I've been trying to decide whether to depict it as it is or to paint it somehow to suggest how life could be changed, how life could be made better. I'm trying to get a sense of what my intentions should be. Making mirrors that show us as we are doesn't seem to me enough. We need more guidance, if we can find any. Windows aren't enough either, because the looking-through doesn't take us far enough. Art should be like a door, so people could go where they haven't been, so they could envision better places, so there'd be better places. It should depend on a language that would be purely human, using every kind of perspective there is, if it has to. Not that I have any idea what a language like that would involve...C. J., am I sounding vague?"

"No, I know what you mean," C. J. replied, uncovering his face. "Something that could cross national lines and lines of time and be understood by almost anyone."

"Yes," said Leah firmly. "Yes. I don't see how else we can survive."

Standing, C. J. dug his feet into the sand and leaving behind him a two-furrowed trail, slouched to the water.

"Fly against the wind, not with it," he said.

Moving slowly, he unbuttoned his shirt, returned to the blanket, and picked up one of the kites. "This is called an Eddy. It's made of cloth. The spine and the crosspiece are the same size. Yours is a diamond. It's made of plastic." Facing the wind, he took off his shirt, folded it carefully, set it on Leah's coat, unwound several yards of string, and pitched his kite into the air. Angling backwards then, he yanked at the line. "Just do what I'm doing," he said. After fingering for a moment the transparent face of the other kite, Leah stood and gingerly cast it over her head. Instantly the clear, plastic film coalesced starlight into a narrow, cloudlike shaft that radiated first to the earth, then as the kite rose, to the water. "Let it out slowly," C. J. said. "Pull at it to make it go higher. If it starts to fall, run toward it and take in the line."

"I didn't think there'd be enough wind tonight."

"It never takes much. There's always more than we feel. Air likes people to play tricks on it. Don't be afraid of it, or the wind will find you out. Bluff if you have to."

"I thought kites needed tails, C. J."

"Tails are usually for beginners. I figured you'd do better than most people do at the start. You don't need much coordination, but you can't let off concentrating. In a few seconds, we can tie yours to mine. They'll go higher that way."

"It's pulling more now. Is the wind getting stronger?"

"The further away from you it flies, the more tension there is…I've got about five hundred feet out. I'd better hitch mine onto yours. It looks like they'll be less likely to run into each other that way…"

"Should I let mine go higher?" Leah quickly asked.

"Just keep it stable," C. J. answered. Narrowing his eyes, he broke his line, guided it to hers, and tied them together. Light reflecting upward from the sheet of plastic faintly illuminated the cloth of the other kite. "This is called a Lark's Head Hitch," he explained. "If it's made right, it won't come undone through anything." Testing, he released his hands and stood back.

"Hold it tight," he said; but already the kites were spinning; and the next instant they plunged, steadily gaining momentum, toward the lake.

"I lost it," Leah cried out. "I lost it!" Grabbing the string, immediately C. J. began to run a snarled path along the beach, his face frozen in ardent contention. The plastic kite was nearly down; and the cloth kite was falling fast, when suddenly, imperceptibly, the single line grew taut; and both kites righted and lifted. "It's almost a thermal that's caught them," he shouted. "If I can hold it, they'll be all right."

"My hands…" Leah said. "My hands lost the balance."

"I should've warned you!"

"It happened so…I don't know, so…"

"Wind is like the tide, Leah," C. J. said, as he returned to her side. "It's playful until it's cornered you, then it'll fight. What you have to do is join it."

"They seem fine now. I hope nobody else sees them."

"They may go so high we'll have to use the second line, too. If they come down, they'll probably land on some professor's roof!"

"So tell me what are thermals, C. J.?" Leah asked, handing him her ball of string.

"Pockets of warm wind. They're good for launching. You can't depend on them for long, though. They rise straight-up, but they don't go very far."

"…C. J., this is all making me wonder where the satellites are now. I haven't thought of them in a long time. There used to be so many of them."

"Yeah, I know. Maybe the orbits got larger…"

"By the way, did you notice the light in the city this afternoon before the sunset?"

"Everything was orange for awhile."

"But not the sky."

"No."

"Why do you suppose that was?"

"Dust, probably, from the ground being in between snow and plants," C. J. replied. He steered the line to Leah, held it a moment to be certain that her grip was tight enough, then let go, and threw himself onto the sand. "Let it out easy," he said, "and let me know if it starts to loosen."

"I can hardly see them anymore," Leah said, standing on her tiptoes and extending her arms.

"Leah?"

"Holding the string is like feeling music, C. J."

"Leah, do you think I..."

"Say it, C. J. What?"

"Do you think I love you? Is that what I do?"

"I don't know. I don't know how to know. Whatever it is, it's equal."

"Equal."

"We have this much. I don't know what it is. It's what we have. That's all I know."

"I'm going to quit the post office before the trial period's up. It won't hurt anybody if I leave early. They must get a hundred applications a day. They'll never put me on as a regular."

"Why not?"

"They hire people like me for six months to give the other ones something to complain about at the times they have to do something like scrape off a pile of mail a peanut butter sandwich someone has accidentally dropped in a mailbox instead of a bin for garbage. I don't think I'm in a real trial period at all. Besides, I want to be outside. I want an apprenticeship. I could get one in June. Jack's moving to Cambridge then. Maybe I can even start in May if it's warm enough…I want to touch something only from me, Leah; that's what I want. I want to stop being a collection of how everybody else is. I think I could do that with carpentry. Or with any kind of construction work. I don't feel like I'm myself very often lately. I guess I haven't ever felt much like myself."

"C. J., I…C. J., would you take the line now?"

"Let go of it."

"They'll fall."

"No, they won't. Not for quite awhile. I adjusted the balance to prevent that. And, anyway, they wouldn't land here. They're too high up at this angle for that."

"I don't want to take the chance."

"I shouldn't have asked you to," said C. J., getting up, flicking sand from his back, and clasping the string.

"The more you feel like you're being yourself," Leah said, "the more it helps me." So lightly that he was uncertain whether it was his own hair he felt or the pressure of her fingers, she eased her hands, palms outward, onto his chest. "I'll tie the line to a fence post," he said.

"They'll stay in the wind?"

"They'll stay in the wind. I fixed the balance for that, too."

With both hands free he turned to her again and saw that she had unbuttoned her blouse; resolutely she edged her shoulders out from beneath it and with graceful abandon dropped it to the blanket. Tethering his arms to his sides, he leaned forward and grazed her lips with his own in what was more a test than a kiss.

As they wavered, both of them innocent in their uncertainties and confident of their desires, memories of their separate pasts assailed each of them: the gradual forming of her breasts, the undiscussible spasms brought on by the fortuitous touch of a stranger, the monthly headaches, the expectations; the shaving of his cheeks, the breakings and deepenings of his voice, the soaked sheets, the rumors.

Balanced unsteadily on one foot, intending his fingers to be as light upon her as hers had been upon him, he glided his hands over her breasts. Seeing on her contented face the effects of his languid caress and remembering, then, their other times together, the contours of their silences, their conversations, the yearnings they had brought forth for the other to consider, he began to relate his hands to what he had shared with her, to what he knew of her; and he fondled her breasts more circumspectly, less exploratorily. Aware of his uncertainty and pleased by it, she enfolded his back with her arms and drew him close to her.

Tranquil and relieved, they lowered themselves in unison onto the blanket and pressed against each other, their lips so tightly entangled that for a time both of them found breathing an intrusion.

Reaching past his hips, his self-assurance increasing, he rested a hand on her knees and, trembling, followed the taperings of her thighs upward, allowing his forearm to fold back her skirt until he felt smooth cloth enclosing her skin. Holding his thumb and little finger outstretched, again and again he traced the lines where the cloth met her legs, letting his other fingers strain and subside, finding a rhythm, as, basking in the cool air and in his touch, she unbuttoned her skirt and let it fall.

After a suspended moment of quiet and mutual awe, he got up on his feet, lifted her hair to his waist, then knelt and brushed his open lips over her stomach. With a temerity that surprised her, she curved one of her hands on his distended pants, unzipped them, and spread her fingers inside.

And so they lay, their movements becoming ever more expressive, as both of them determined the patterns whereby their energies would meet and combine.

"They want me to protect you," said C. J.

"I know they do."

"But they want me to do it in the wrong ways."

"Don't let them trap you. The kind of protecting you don't want to do is what they count on to shape us into their killings. It's hate they build, and they call it 'caring.' I want you to be as you are."

Embracing a concurrent pause, breathing in easy harmony, intently they eyed the still cloudless, but fuliginous sky.

"Let's run," said C. J. "Run all the way around the lake."

"Yes," Leah replied, laughing, jumping up.

Without looking back at their clothes, they set off, keeping pace with each other at first, glancing toward each other and toward their translucent images on the rippled surface of the water.

"What about the kites?" Leah asked, dazzled by the canescent risings of his muscles.

"The wind will hold them," C. J. said, starting to speed ahead of her, inclining his head back, questioning.

"Don't wait for me. Go as you want to."

Pumping his arms up and down, whisked onward by her trailing laughter, he ran as fast as he was able and did not stop until he had circled the lake. Panting, sweating, he then dove into the blanket, as if it were a down-filled pillow; and the compliant sand beneath assumed his shape. With wet eyes, he turned over on his back and searched the shore for her, finding her, at last, stooped near the fence, then running, flowers in her hands, her hair flying parallel to the ground.

"Purslane, they're already blooming," she said, as, still lying on his back, he caught her in his arms. Bracing herself on her palms so that only the tips of her breasts touched against him, she kissed his forehead and said, "We're an us, you and I, an us, whatever."

"Yes," he said, "whatever." He placed his hands solidly on her hips, pulled her down upon him, and, hesitating, lifted her so high that their bodies almost separated; but she stiffened; and she stretched her legs the length of his. "Stay, C. J.," she said. Stroking her back and looking past her shoulders at the two kites a quarter-mile above, he thrust his hips up, hard.

Merged within and upon each other, their bodies quickening, it was not merely that they were engulfed by the transiencies of lambent passion; neither were they envisioning nor adhering to the specific outlines of a future for themselves nor for anyone else. Rather, it was, as it could not have been for any people at any time throughout human history until but twenty years earlier, that they were straining somehow to preserve the possibility of the future itself.

C. J., his arms widespread, grasping the sand, quaking hips by turns shoving, then settling back, as Leah twisted upon him, her hands tugging at the hair about his neck and her own hair tumbling down her back, over him, and onto the blanket, as together they turned in an arc, thought only, Don't stop.

2

His elbows at his knees, his legs apart, and his head propped in the cup of his hands, reluctantly he watched her dress.

"It's as if silence were illegal outside the fence," she said. "What time is it?"

"About ten," he answered, groping on his pants and contemplating a cluster of dried leaves snared, like crushed plaster, in a hollowed fork of a dead elm.

"I lost a kite once," he said. "When I was a little boy. It stayed in a tree for nearly a year. I never told anyone it was mine."

Distractedly she shook sand from her shoes, wedged her feet into them, looked up at the sky, and said, "I want to go now. I want to go, C. J. Will you take up the gate for me. Let me out alone. Do you mind? I don't want to be in the city with you. I don't want to see it with you. Not now."

"We could stay until morning. I'm going to call in sick anyway."

"Don't worry. I've got to get back. I'll be fine."

"It's a long walk."

"I want to walk alone. Really I do."

"We can come here another time."

"It won't be the same."

"Somewhere else."

"Somewhere else."

After he again had opened the space through which they had crawled, when she was on the other side of the fence and standing, she shaded her eyes with her hands, upturned her head, and gazed at the two, distantly anchored specks.

"Against the wind," she said, her arms rocking the picnic basket.

"They flew well."

"Don't forget your jacket, C. J."

"You could still stay."

"Thanks for the easel."

"Use it."

"Yes, C. J....yes. Good night."

"Good night."

"The sky is lighter now," she called back, as she crept beyond the summit of the knoll. "Lighter than it was."

Alone, slowly rewinding the kite string, he ambled among the triangular, honeycomb shadows of the fence and hummed what seemed to him nearly a dirge for all of humankind.

10 Solicitations

1

"Take me to Idlewild Airport," said Mr. Tane, fully aware the New York airport had been renamed for President Kennedy soon after his death.

Torpidly the driver spun his taxi away from a La Guardia Airport platform, lazed his arm across the top of the front seat, honked at nothing, and replied imperturbably, "It *is* difficult, isn't it? keeping your own mind in the midst of whatever the majority decided." His brown hair was trimmed into a crew cut, his face closely shaved. He wore a blue cotton work shirt, carefully ironed, and brown polyester slacks. His frame was compact and wiry.

"The New Haven shuttle," said Mr. Tane.

"Having to go along with what you don't want. Not let it change you. Always has been difficult."

"His election was enough of an aberration. Covering the nation with his name was madness."

"She lives in New York now. You've probably heard that. Lots of rides will ask about her."

"He would never have been reelected."

"Of course, they're sheep mostly…sheep is all they are. The polls make the opinions instead of the other way around. That's how I look at it. Back in the thirties, no money, people didn't have anything to lose, they'd say what they thought. Get angry about it. Not now. A good depression would start everyone thinking again. I can tell the way talk will go by looking at the polls in the morning. People take on for their own what they read their opinions are."

Passing the mythic New York City landmarks he had been familiar with since his youth but had never expected to see, not even when he had purchased airline tickets months before, was as dreamlike and satisfying an experience as Mr. Tane had imagined it would be. Traveling two thousand miles in five hours had occasioned in him the intense thrill that one-tent carnivals had always brought to his rural boyhood summers. Jack had been so accustomed to airplanes, even as a child, that his flights had involved no comparable magic. The universalization of the automobile, Mr. Tane remarked to himself, had undoubtedly been more exciting in his own youth than the perfecting of flight had been in his son's. The lack of stable association with place was becoming more inevitable all the time; it was probably even a bond among people nowadays instead of the primary characterizing trait of outcasts it had been in the first years of the century. Flight had made the entire nation a city for the apathetic, for the careless. Sheep, as the driver had said, bearers of bland uniformity.

It was June of 1966. The previous fall, Mr. Tane had purchased a membership in a Denver health club and there, through regular swimming, had reduced his weight. By January he had felt he had both regained the energy of his early manhood and channeled a reserve of vitality that would make the upcoming decade his most productive. For the first time in his life he had few financial burdens. During the spring, Jack had been granted a federal student loan and, in addition, had been awarded an academic achievement scholarship applicable to law school tuition. The last mortgage payment on the family house had been made in February. A leveling-off of local construction needs had not occurred. Mr. Tane's contracting business was prospering, and he was drawing up plans that would enable its extension to the western edges of Denver. With Jack handling the legal affairs of the company, he confidently expected to be among the wealthiest men in Colorado before his seventieth birthday.

"My son is graduating from Yale," he said. "It's a wonderful time."

"That must've set you back plenty," said the driver.

"Yes," said Mr. Tane, his tone more comradely than he had intended. "My wife and I never hesitated to sacrifice."

"It'll be worth it to you."

"We wanted to see him safely on his way at the beginning. He's going to law school next. To Harvard."

"Harvard. I have a lot of them as rides. Seems like they spend most of their time getting haircuts and taking plane trips. He won't worry your bank account again. That's certain. You can worry his."

"In three years he'll be returning home."

"Home? With a Harvard law degree?"

"Not to the house, of course. I didn't mean that," said Mr. Tane, wanting silence. "To his state, his people. To Colorado."

"Colorado," the driver whistled. "I get rides going there. Skiers mostly. Though why they don't use Vermont or somewhere else close instead is a mystery to me. The newness out West, I suppose. And then, too, Bobby Kennedy got that part of the country in the papers going down the Arkansas River in a raft."

"I'm afraid I wouldn't know about that," said Mr. Tane.

"Colorado. You must've been all for Senator Goldwater for the presidency two years ago. Even before that I'd guess."

"Yes, certainly."

"Most of my rides, I hate to tell you, but I will, most of my rides would laugh about him. Just laugh. You probably don't like to hear that, but it was true. Nobody thought Johnson would turn around and follow Goldwater's foreign policy like he's doing."

"That is to his credit."

"Does your Yale son agree with you there?"

"I have no doubt that he does."

"Don't be too sure. Not the way they are these days. We're on one side; they're on the other. Most of them taking drugs from what I hear. From what I see, too. Around Columbia. 110th has gotten to be like 125th. Hair down to their butts. In everybody else's beds. Girls swearing like sailors once would have been ashamed to. It's all that noise from England, you know. And the extra dollars. You'll see it. Dealing drugs right there in college. The brightest of them along with the rest. They don't know what those degrees would have meant to us. They've had all the chances anybody's ever wanted, and they're turning into no better than bowery junkies. Tearing up draft cards and stirring up the coloreds till it makes me wonder if Hitler didn't have a lot of the right ideas, and I never guessed I'd be thinking that, never, don't often think it now; but sometimes the sight of them is enough to make me wonder if I should've joined up with *that* other side…. Discipline doesn't mean a thing anymore. Smelling like haylofts, boys with necklaces, wait'll you see it, it'll make you sick, fancy necklaces over bare chests, ribbons in their hair, expecting to be treated like normal people. The circus wouldn't have them as clowns. There's a limit to what money will make me do, and I'll just not pick them up. Even if they've called ahead, I'll check in for another ride. Not everybody could do that, but twenty-two years means something to the company. So when I drive off, leaving them standing on a corner with their beads and their flapping hair, I don't hear anything about it. The dispatchers send in a rookie. I won't stand for it in my cab. You're lucky if your son has the sense he left home with."

They had been planning the trip for a year; or rather Mr. Tane had been planning it, leafing through brochures, juggling dates and hours, seeing to it that his office would run smoothly in his absence. As he had described the alternatives and had made the decisions; Mrs. Tane had nodded and smiled and agreed. Hotel reservations had been made since January. Theater tickets had been purchased. They were to spend a week in New

York City, touring the Statue of Liberty, Grant's Tomb, the Empire State Building, and the Riverside Church, four days in New Haven, attending graduation ceremonies, ten days in Boston helping Jack resettle, visiting Faneuil Hall, Paul Revere's home, and Plymouth Plantation, and next were to fly to Washington, D.C., where Mr. Tane had scheduled conferences with their senators. After a stop at Mt. Vernon, they were to board a return flight for Denver.

But in February Mrs. Tane had mentioned her long-standing dislike of airplanes. They would take a train, her husband had assured her. No, she had replied, she could not sleep while traveling. They would drive then, he had said, stay in the best motels along the interstate. That would be too tiring for him, she had insisted. In March he had made airline reservations and had attempted to speak no more about the trip. Mrs. Tane's uneasiness had not dissipated, however. In April she had begun to depart nightly for her bedroom immediately after finishing the evening dishes; her cooking had become careless and her housekeeping clumsy. Able neither to fathom nor to soothe her, Mr. Tane had taken to maintaining later office hours and had often come home to find a cold supper on the kitchen table and his wife's room dark.

On the first of May, Mrs. Tane had said she would feel better if he would agree to go on the trip alone. He had waited; but she had become adamant; and finally he had canceled the majority of their reservations, retaining only those for his own single-accommodation, reduced stays in New Haven and Boston. Her mien of weariness had persisted; but she had said repeatedly how relieved she was at his decision; and he had convinced himself it did not matter that she was staying behind. He, after all, had been primarily responsible for the twenty years of family events leading to the celebration; it had been his ingenuity, his boldness, his steadfastness, that had provided the many comfortable configurations of their three lives; therefore, the seven-day trip would be a seemly reflection of his triumph.

"My son is graduating from Yale," he said to the stewardess, who was showing him to his seat on the brief shuttle flight to New Haven.

"You must be very proud," she said with professional friendliness.

"Yes," he said. "Proud." But as he watched the boroughs of New York City fade away from him, he felt more than proud: he felt regal.

2

"I want to know what light is," said Mrs. Tane insistently, tapping her blanched fingers on a soft, green mat, which covered a desk separating her from the town librarian, a bespectacled man in his mid-thirties whose face had been molded by the responsibility of his work into an appearance of unchanging earnestness. "I want to know what some of the differences are between sunlight and electric light." Frequent, lengthy, secret noon meals in Denver the past four years had caused Mrs. Tane to gain forty pounds; the flesh on her waxen cheeks was distended; her freckled arms sagged out from under her short-sleeved blouse. "Surely you can recommend a book that will tell me."

"It's a rather complicated subject, Mrs. Tane. I'm unqualified to answer you. Perhaps the main library in Denver. Or better still an adult education course. Can I show you our school files? You might contact one of them for the summer semester."

"The time for schooling is long past. Are there no books you can direct me to? no pamphlets? no magazines?"

"Only a few highly technical journals, Mrs. Tane. I'm sure they'd be too complex. The simplest sounding questions are often the most difficult to answer."

"Computers, then," said Mrs. Tane. "I've read about them in the newspapers. They're talked of more and more. Even in the comedies on television they'll be mentioned. But I don't understand what they are. It all happened so quickly. There wasn't time for me to learn. Something on computers."

"There again, Mrs. Tane, I'll have to refer you to Denver. Our resources here simply are not extensive enough to help you. The budget doesn't allow the purchase of all that we'd like to have…"

"Are they improper questions I'm asking? If that's what you think they are, please tell me. I don't want to be the cause of embarrassment. I've been busy with other things for a very long time."

"Not at all improper," replied the librarian, accustomed both to encountering middle-aged desperation disguised as casual questioning and, feeling he had no alternative, to trying to direct it to metropolitan sites he had come to expect probably would be left unvisited. "I only wish we could be of more assistance."

He spoke with such finality that Mrs. Tane lowered her eyes and fumbled out the door. A gust of hot wind lashed at her face, and she ran to her car and turned on the air conditioner. Remembering the number of times she had driven past the library in order to gain sufficient courage to enter it made her shudder; and as she arranged her curls in the rearview mirror, a momentary, grotesque vision of herself approaching people on the street to ask them the nature of light or the uses of computers skirted her thoughts.

For four years, Mrs. Tane had so regularly been placing in her bureau drawer the inner portions of Jack's letters that she had long ago ceased considering giving any of them to her husband. Again and again she had reread them, using them to partially fill the emptinesses in her life that her son's absence had created. During his first three years at Yale, when he had written often of his course work and had even included sections of his term papers, she had found herself unable to comprehend many of his ideas and had been bewildered by his unfamiliar terminology. Her early replies had been laced with laboriously composed questions, but these had come to annoy Jack, and he eventually had responded that he had already delineated as much detail as he could afford to in his rare spare time and that she should address her questions to his previous letters as well as read succeeding ones with more care.

Transferring to his mother his irritations at professors and their questions and failing to appreciate how impossible it was for her to grasp the causes of his anger, Jack, in his second-year letters, had periodically complained about the inadequacies of his Colorado public education in relation to the prep school backgrounds of many of his classmates. Mrs. Tane had been tempted to present her husband with these passages; but fearing Mr. Tane's anger and suspecting he would blame the Yale environment and perhaps even discontinue tuition payments, she had decided to go on grappling with them alone. When Jack had announced he would be in school over the summers, she had been sure, since he had never displayed any gratitude for the two decades of her provident routines, he had enrolled for the extra classes in order to stay away from her husband and herself.

The past year, his letters had become more strident, grimmer, and had pertained more to politics than to his course work or to his life in Colorado. His handwriting had become cramped, and some of the pages had contained barely more than horizontal straight lines. The paragraphs that had been legible had been loosely knit sketches of what he had deemed to be the proper role of the university in social affairs and frightened diatribes in opposition to the growing military involvement of the United States in Southeast Asia—an involvement Mrs. Tane recurrently had heard her husband applaud.

Wanting to understand what was being discussed, she daily that year had been viewing afternoon television news. Reports of the war had predominated, and she had found them strikingly different from the heroic accounts that had ruled the newsreels of the forties. Whatever the words of the commentators, she had been able to locate no heroes in the graphic pictures from Vietnam. She had seen only more destruction, only more sorrow.

After listening to and pondering the conflicting, war-related statements of diplomats, educators, and religious leaders, she had come to the conclusion that there would be no possibility of her resolving the opposing views of Jack and Mr. Tane; and she had grown certain that the family reunion in New Haven would be marred by dissension. If human rights are self-evident, she had wondered once that spring, how can so many people not be discovering them?

There were other items of televised news, however, that had alarmed her more than had the reports of the expanding war. Films taken during the aftermath of the deployment of the atomic bombs had been shown and had been supplemented by interviews with survivors of the explosions in Hiroshima and Nagasaki and by examinations of the unexpected, delayed effects of radiation presently seeming to be resulting from what had been said to be the pure science for, as well as the initial testings of, nuclear weaponry.

Following her solitary viewing of these documentary segments, she had hesitantly asked Mr. Tane whether the plant actually was as harmless as it was commonly assumed to be, whether it might have adversely affected the air or tainted the water supply. He had replied that her doubts were nonsensical and her anxieties baseless. Since from the town's beginnings its residents had understood that it would be impossible for such questions to be publicly raised, there had been no one else for her to ask.

The rock garden in front of the Tane house was being weeded by a yardman in his early twenties, face and arms deeply and unsafely tanned, as Mrs. Tane drove partway into the garage, shifted to reverse, and parked beside the yardman's van, quite battered but clean, in the driveway. Upon entering the kitchen, she opened a can of soup and ate it without diluting it or putting it on the stove. The telephone rang, and she stared at it until it stopped. Aware that her car had not passed a night outside the garage since its purchase, she went to her room, undressed, and sank into bed, prepared to lie there until morning.

Counting on being able to think uninterruptedly and deeply for an entire week, as even a minimal facade of composure and tranquillity would be unnecessary prior to Mr. Tane's return, she spent the rest of the afternoon letting her mind roam over what she knew of the lineaments of her community, arranged her memories of the town's twenty-year development. Noticing out her window that twilight had begun, she asked herself for the first time the question that her distress of the past months had steadily been readying her to frame: Why are they making more, when what they've made can already end the earth?

3

Mr. Tane pressed one hand firmly on his billfold in his jacket pocket and gripped his valise with the other. Acrid, humid wind tore at his coattails and forced him to squint, as he looked through a runway observation window and scanned the airport waiting room.

Wearing a new suit, which had been shipped to him for the occasion, his year's growth of untrimmed hair swooping to his lapels, Jack stepped from behind a pillar and said, "Hello, Father."

Blinking spasmodically, Mr. Tane turned and held out his hand. "Son! Son!" he said. "It's fine to see you, son. You needn't have taken time out from your work to greet me."

"We agreed days ago that I would meet you, Father."

"Even so, I don't want to be an interference."

"There are no more classes. Everything is finished now," Jack replied, pronouncing each word with decisive precision, his posture rigid, his manner politely restrained. "I've been looking forward to seeing you. I'm certain you'll be no interference. Shall we go to the luggage return?"

"This is all I have, son. I had intended to take much more with me; but when your mother made her decision, you know, I decided this would be enough. I hope I won't be displeasing you with a lack of variety in dress."

"I'm sure you won't, Father," Jack said. With quick, sharp movements of his arms and shoulders, he guided Mr. Tane into the parking lot. "You're looking quite well."

"I feel well. Never better," Mr. Tane replied.

"How is Mother?" Jack asked, as if it were expected of him.

"Busy as ever," said Mr. Tane, beaming. "She just couldn't find the time to be away, son. Didn't want to leave the house in someone else's hands, you know. The arrangements were all made, all made, but no matter, she didn't feel she'd be able to manage. I wish you could have seen her these past weeks. So proud of you she could scarcely think of anything else."

"There was no reason for you to come, Father. It's a needless formality."

"Nonsense, son. It's a great honor."

"Perhaps it seems that to you. To me it's merely an inevitability," Jack said. He opened a rear door of a rental sedan and pointed inside. "I don't think I'll unlock the trunk. We'll be at the hotel in a few minutes."

"You know best," Mr. Tane said. Elated and self-assured, sanguine, he patiently lifted his valise into the back seat. "You'd rather I sat in front, wouldn't you?"

"Of course, Father. Why would you think otherwise?"

"The highways are so different here. So much more crowded than at home. I don't want to disturb your view."

"I've been up and down the coast, Father. I'm quite used to the traffic."

"A passenger does make a change in driving, though. With your mother beside me the first year of our marriage, I recall that it was almost like learning to steer all over again. You must've heard about our 1938 Studebaker."

"Yes."

"You rode in it yourself. But I'm sure you don't remember..."

"How was the flight?" Jack asked, swerving onto the highway and trying to keep his tones empty of all emotion.

"Miraculous. Just miraculous. I hope you won't smile at me to hear that. I've known few times as exciting as landing in New York City. One wouldn't forget that easily...Watch the lane on your left, Jack."

"You needn't direct me, Father."

"I didn't mean to intrude," said Mr. Tane. "You're on your own after all. On your own."

Jack smiled, then said, instantly regretting his words, having resolved to move through the days ahead without expressing any attitudes that might trouble his father, "The world falling apart, and they have us putting on crazy hats and looking like all the pieces fit where everyone wants them to."

"These highways are one of the greatest things ever to have happened," said Mr. Tane, quite as if Jack had not just spoken.

"You know about the scholarship, Father, of course."

"You're very fortunate, son. Your mother and I couldn't be happier. We would have been glad to have kept on helping you until your training is completed, you're aware of that, but I'm sure this is a better way. They couldn't overlook your talent."

"Always the getting ready," said Jack, shaking his hair away from his eyes. "That's all I've ever done. Junior high school getting ready for high school. High school getting ready for college. College for law school. In law school it'll be getting ready for the right firm or a private practice. I'm starting to wonder if anything is ever going to happen. All I've ever done is wait."

"Time goes more slowly when you're young. You'll be grateful one day for your preparation."

"I can't even be sure I want to go to law school," Jack continued. "With the draft the way it is, it hardly feels like I'm deciding. The truth is, I still don't know what a lawyer does. They make it a secret society, and you have to go through all the rites of joining it without anyone telling you what membership involves."

"Three years will pass soon enough."

"I don't want to have to find out I've wasted them," said Jack. He twisted the car into a parallel parking space. "We're on Malley Street now, Father. The Hotel Taft is half a block west. On the corner. I probably can't get closer."

"This will be fine."

"I checked the room. It's all set up and everything. Do you want me to come in with you?"

"It's nearly three o'clock. Several hours before we need to think of dinner."

"It's really five now, Father. You'd better change your watch."

"That is their measure," said Mr. Tane with a genuine trace of studied disdain.

"You haven't brought the whole state of Colorado with you!" Jack exclaimed, clenching his fists on the dashboard. "When it's five o'clock, it's five o'clock."

"You're used to this time, son. I didn't consider."

"I'm sorry," Jack said suddenly contrite and puerile. "I didn't mean to explode. It'd be fine to eat later, Father."

Darting his eyes, Mr. Tane nodded, got out of the car, and retrieved his valise from the back seat. "Do you want me to come up, or do you want me to stay here?" Jack asked again.

"Whatever you wish."

"I'll stay here, then."

"I'll join you as soon as I've seen to the room. I'm sure it will be more than satisfactory," said Mr. Tane; and down the sidewalk he strode, appearing to his son more vulnerable, less imposing, smaller than he could ever remember having seen him, than he could ever remember having expected to see him.

4

"I wish you wouldn't do that," said Jack. His father had been offering a patricianlike smile to every group of people they passed as they walked amidst the ivy-covered buildings of the Yale campus. "It's not a small town. You've got to keep a distance here."

"They're your friends, Jack," said Mr. Tane, feeling his stomach rebel at his unaccustomed seafood and cheese-soufflé dinner. "I must be cordial."

"They're not my friends. We only occupied the same space," Jack said. He cleared his throat and pulled at his necktie with exaggerated irritation. "I don't even know the names of more than thirty people here. This has not been an environment to encourage friendships, Father; and that is an understatement."

"I hope you understand," said Mr. Tane, missing in his sustained enthusiasm the bitter edges of his son's words, "that it's still not too late to change your mind and attend the University of Denver Law School. This Eastern bustle can't be good for anyone. I'm sure you could be accepted for the January semester, Jack. There are people, you know, who consider Harvard one of the most humanly out-of-touch citadels in the nation."

"I may come to consider it that myself. I'm not sure I'll stay through it all. But you've forgotten about the draft, Father. The way call-ups are now I'm not allowed the extra time."

"I'm confident something could be worked out."

"You can't pull any strings with the draft board," Jack said.

"I'm sure that reason would be listened to."

"If they appreciated reason, they wouldn't have those jobs. You make Colorado sound like another country, Father."

"It's the states that give validity to the Constitution after all, son. It is to them we owe our greatest allegiance."

"That's completely untrue. Excuse me if you're offended, but it is. It's the federal Constitution that guarantees each state a right to a Constitution, and each state that gives the communities inside them authority to exist. You've got it backwards."

"I fear you've been far too influenced by the Supreme Court's attempt to replace justified variations in local procedures with a uniformity of condition."

"I was already tired of hearing you tell me that three years ago, Father. What you say is truer internationally than it is for the United States. That's what Kennedy meant by 'freedom for diversity.' Not that Johnson pays any attention to international law."

"We must respect the decisions of our leaders, especially in times of war," said Mr. Tane. "Even though we may disagree, we must trust their judgments are informed by access to material that can never come to all of us. The communist threat has been successfully met, thus far; and we must continue to meet it."

Bringing his feet down hard on the stone path, Jack replied, "I cannot believe you still think as you do. After all of this. The red menace. Domino theory. Next you'll be complaining about David Lilienthal and the United Nations. Every respectable authority there is maintains that Vietnam has historically been an enemy of both China and the USSR, and yet you and so many others like you keep insisting that what's really a civil war is some kind of noble struggle for all of humanity. Napalm is being dropped so often I don't see how any of you sleep. Even the nonalliance of China and Russia disproves what you say about monolithic communism, but no realities will change the system you all carry around in your heads like a plague. That's what it really is, a social plague. It's enough to make anyone crazy who tried to comprehend the difference between what you're saying and most of the facts. And yet you have all the power."

"I continue to urge you to trust in our leadership," said Mr. Tane. "I must insist upon that. How long would my business last, do you think, if I shared with the lowest-level employees the material which comes across my desk? They trust my judgment. All of them. Rightfully. That's why the company is effective."

"It may be effective for construction; but it's also an autocracy, Father. You hold the strings for so much of what your men can do, I often used to wonder in high school how you could say they were free..."

"You're set on Harvard, then Harvard it is," said Mr. Tane decidedly and calmly. "Your mother and I will be behind you wherever you are. We're confident you'll do the right thing."

"...I do want to do what's right, Father," Jack said. A strain of sad longing wound through his words. "But that means instead of what's profitable. It often means that. When you talk about 'us' you mean the people you know; at most you mean the people of the United States. But what I mean by 'us'—and I hope somehow I can make this clear to you—is everyone, all of humanity. My concerns are for the earth, Father. They have to be if we're going to seriously consider the faint possibility of our survival. Right now there's enough food and shelter for all the people alive, but there aren't the means of distribution. I want to help bring them about. That goes beyond politics or at least demands a new kind."

"I admire your humanitarian concerns, Jack; but you must also appreciate that doing the right thing will inevitably be accompanied by an improvement in one's economic position. That is the essence of the free market. That truth has provided for you all your life."

Loosening his necktie, Jack wearily replied, "This war makes every discussion an argument. Not just with you. Sometimes I feel like it's driving me crazy. I wish I could get away. But there's nowhere to go. There's nowhere that's safe anymore..."

Offhandedly Mr. Tane glanced at his wristwatch and said, "I should be heading for the hotel, son. I'm sure you have much to do to ready yourself for tomorrow."

"Not really. I'm just anxious to have it over with."

"You'll want to stop at the barbershop in the morning," Mr. Tane said tactfully and with warm innocence.

"What do you expect me to do?" Jack then burst out. "What do you want from me? Do you want me to start turning on my headlights during the day along with the suburbanites who support the war? Do you want me to start doing body counts? My hair is going to stay like it is. At least something about me is going to remind me of the possibility of integrity!"

Startled at last, Mr. Tane quickly replied, "I had no idea you felt so strongly about such a simple matter. Your appearance is your own affair. I had only meant to be helpful. Your best interests were my concern; they always are."

Angry, confused, and tired, Jack found himself at that moment very much wanting to believe his father's avowal: yearning for comfort, nearly as if he had cried out at night from his Colorado bedroom, he faced Mr. Tane and addressed him with a childlike dependency he was never to display again, "I wish I could go back to being sure of what I knew, Father."

"All of us are frightened at your time of life," said Mr. Tane tenderly. "It is the challenges themselves that produce the readiness."

"They'd better," Jack said without smiling.

5

"I recognize those buildings from my map," said Mr. Tane, looking past a footbridge to a row of lights on the other side of the Charles River. "That would be the Harvard Business School."

"Yes," Jack morosely replied.

"I've been thinking about tomorrow, son. I want to get you started in Cambridge on the right foot. I've decided to buy you a new wardrobe."

"I don't need any more clothes, Father."

"Nonsense, Jack. You've been too absorbed with schoolwork to pay attention to yourself."

"I dress as I want to dress. I don't want to wear their double-breasted uniforms."

"It's time to be realizing that your appearance will have much to do with the nature of your clientele. You're no longer a boy; you must dress as a man now."

"Clothes like that are demeaning. I don't want the kind of practice they'd bring. I don't want to forget that lots of people are hungry, Father. I'm not going to let myself become that kind of lawyer."

Continuing to look across the river, settling a hand on his son's back, Mr. Tane said, "I commend you again on your humanitarian concerns. They are obviously very meaningful to you. I don't suggest you give them up. But you must take care to remember that the struggles of work are the best remedies for the conditions of the poor. Artificial medicines expand existing tendencies toward overdependence."

"There's nothing that can convince you that the worthy don't always win, is there? No matter what the rules, they always rise to the top."

"There is little in life that can defeat those with initiative, son; just as there is little that can be of help to those who suffer from innate laziness and lack of pride."

"I wish you could see how so often it's a matter of not having had a chance, Father. The interrelationships of justice and privilege have got to be altered. They've got to be altered everywhere. Constructively altered. Peacefully altered."

"You mustn't allow your studies to bring you the conviction that you're aware of the qualities of lives with which you have had no real contact, Jack."

"There's no need for you to tell me how much I don't know, Father."

"You must be careful to keep in mind how remarkable it is that democratic institutions have lasted as long as they have in the United States. You mustn't forget to give traditions their due regard."

"I'm going to be there to serve the people who want change, the most necessary kinds of change, the best kinds."

"Of course, too, conditions in Colorado are quite unlike these on the East Coast. The truly ambitious left this area in the western migrations of the last century. Those are your forebears. You and I are in their debt..."

Leaning against the stone railing of the bridge, Jack turned his head to the southeast, peered at the lights of Boston, and asked, "Father?...Is it worse to live in the United States paying into the federal budget than it is to live here not paying into it?"

"I'm not certain I understand the intent of your question," said Mr. Tane.

"I mean the war, Father. West Point. The Air Force Academy. How does all that make you feel? It's hard to claim that murder is the evilest of crimes, when that's what everyone who pays taxes does, a degree removed, but murder all the same."

"We naturally would appreciate the additions to our incomes that lower taxes would assure," said Mr. Tane.

"That's not what I'm talking about, Father. I mean the direction, not the amount. I mean the responsibility. It's a matter of self-regard. It seems to me that being an active part of the budget would lower yourself in your own eyes, when you think of all the death it's paying for."

"I don't know if I understand you yet, son. I don't know if I want to. What you say may be true, but on such a luxurious plane of high thought that it can hardly be considered meaningful in the everyday world most of us inhabit...You're reminding me of something I learned years ago, Jack. I know it's true, because I heard trappers tell it themselves. They said there's one sure way to kill a wolf, and that's when there's snow-covered ground, to cover a knife with blood, stick the knife in the snow with the tip of the blade pointing out, and wait for the wolf to smell it and come up and start to lick it. After a minute or so, the blade cuts the wolf's tongue, and the two bloods combine. Then the wolf gets flustered, you see, not knowing where the blood is coming from. It cuts itself again and again, and finally it dies from swallowing its own blood. That's what you make me think of, son. You're cutting off your tongue with your own words. You've got to organize yourself more stably, so that you can proceed as effectively as you have been until recently."

"I'm just wanting us all to live better," said Jack.

"I fear, though, that you're more trusting than is good for you."

"Trusting! Yes. Trusting. You don't trust anyone, do you, Father? Not anyone at all."

"Of course, I do, son. I trust your mother. I trust you. I trust my co-workers."

"You probably trust them more than you do Mother and me. But it's not trust really. It's more counting on them. You count on them to do what you order them to do. Subtly order, but order all the same. You don't see Mother and me as we are. You never have. You do whatever you can to make us into the people you want instead of letting us be the people we are. That's why Mother didn't come with you. She knew you would have forced her into doing whatever you wanted, like always. I admire her for staying in Colorado."

"Your mother and I have no regrets, Jack."

"You don't admit to mistakes. Whenever you change your mind you say you've always thought that way. You depend on the people you work with more than you do us. But they're not your friends. You haven't had any friends. Not once in my memory since I was very young has anyone visited you in friendship at the house. You don't belong to any clubs. You never do anything with anyone like fishing or even going out to dinner with another couple."

"The nature of proper loyalties is more complex than you can realize at your age, Jack. Time tempers all relationships."

"That's why I didn't have any friends," Jack replied. "Because of you. I couldn't learn how to have any. You were afraid they'd interfere with your social status somehow. It was the same for Mother."

"I'm sure I never stated anything of the kind."

"You didn't need to. It was said by what you did. It was in the way you moved. Mother and I both understood it. That's why I read so much, Father. No one could ever be with me. You wouldn't permit it. You talk all the time about freedom, but you can't stand disagreement. What you say doesn't relate to the rest of what you do. You don't know how to discuss; all you know how to do is insist. You talk about how other people have made their own decisions, but lots of times you've backed them against the wall so much that there's been nothing left for them to do but what you've wanted. Whenever you thought some decree of yours about me should be enforced at home, you'd have Mother do it; and you'd pretend you didn't know anything about it, all the while lecturing about freedom of choice. It's not freedom when you arrange the circumstances so the only choice people have is not even to think about what they might have preferred. If someone starts to go against your will, you drive them almost crazy, but indirectly, so no one could ever pin you down to it. You talk as if the American dream and the reality of the United States are the same thing, but they're not. They're not at all. And it isn't relevant anymore whether you believe what you say, because your life is a complete contradiction of what you are always preaching!"

Mr. Tane's shoulders had fallen into unintentional intimations of vexated exhaustion. With pleading eyes he shifted his gaze from the somber buildings of the Harvard Business School to the incensed face of his son, and said, "I'm sure you'll feel differently by the time you've returned home."

"My home is the East Coast now, Father," replied Jack. "I'm not going back to Denver to practice law. I'm staying here. You want to be able to hold all the strings of my life like you do Mother's, so there won't be anything you can't predict. But I'm not going to let you do that."

"You're talking without having thought, Jack."

"No, I'm not. It's definite. There's more I can do here. There are more people here who think like I do. The war is bringing us together. Your generation has almost succeeded in destroying yourselves and everyone else. You've used your technical skills to build fortresses all over the earth. I don't know why you've done that, but you have. We're going to find a way to live in spite of you. There's only one human race, and that's what's important. We're going to find peace."

"I have listened to you for five days, son. Your manner has been as disturbing as your words. My patience is almost at an end. It's foolish and dangerous to talk as you do. The weaponry of the United States protects the last hope of any reasonable person anywhere in the world. Apart from that, which is quite enough to merit our gratitude, your life would have been a good deal less comfortable without the structures of our defense."

"What are you talking about, Father?"

"Surely you must have sensed by now that the plant has been central to our military achievements."

"I don't..."

"It's time you understood, Jack—and, of course, you won't yet find this information in the newspapers and the magazines—but, you're old enough now to know with respectful and necessary silence that from its inception the plant has been not only one of the largest and one of the most essential nuclear weaponry production centers in the nation but also the most thoroughly developed site the earth has for researching the possibilities of solar-powered weapons," said Mr. Tane, thoroughly confident that his long-delayed disclosure immediately would impel his son to begin to reconsider and eventually to abandon many of the views he had acquired during his years at Yale.

Staring at his father through the warm evening air, Jack, slowly taking steps backward on the river bank, said, however, his voice shattered, his tones emblems of amazement and horror, "You have made me sorry I was ever born!"

6

'Never a hungry moment in his life. Never a night he couldn't sleep. Never an obligation he couldn't pick for himself and put down like a pair of shoes that had stopped meeting his fancy. Not one day of work and twenty-two years old.

'The best student ever to attend the high school. The principal told me that. Said there'd be nothing to worry about with more like him. Could've gone to any college in the country.

'I didn't want to see his face for another hour. I should have bent him over double and whipped him until he bled, put him on my knees and taken a hairbrush to him until he couldn't stand...

'I made it too easy for him.

'All the way along.

'I wanted to save him the unnecessary.

'He should've been working at sixteen.

'No knowledge can take the place of sweat.

'He thinks I'm finished. Thinks he's got what he can from me. Well, let him watch. Let him wait until he's forty before he's half as well off as I am, even with all he's drained away. Let him find out what a mortgage is. Let him find out about down payments. Let him know the years when there's nothing to do but face the bills however you can, feel your hopes falling away in pieces, too tired, too tired even to dream.....

'It was death used to do the weeding out early. But now they stay on. The weak drag us down. Storing up the faculties and the government.

'It's medicine has made those survive it would have been better if their weaknesses had brought them to early graves. The politicians propose a guaranteed annual income. Is the farmer guaranteed rain?...

'And I have tried.

'Done better than most.

'But how do you explain putting the lines of nature in the buildings of our lives when it's clothes outgrown overnight and hairdressers on Saturday and car payments and washing machines, cheap lumber and careless work, employees supporting each other with union demands, courts always there to back them up, push buttons, built in weeks what should take half a year, not caring if it lasts, none of them seeing how the houses could be tied into the land, always their own little plot, not knowing how the separate parts should fit, do fit, could fit, put up for the quickness of it, not for the building itself, not for the doing.

'It's a wonder I've done what I have.

'Could've made more money if I'd tried to do less.

'Land is land to them. They miss all its smells and its colors and its sounds. Weather is something happens somewhere they don't live. From house to car to job to store to school to church to restaurant, light and temperature always the same.

'Something goes wrong, it's me to blame. Never the unions owning up to mistakes. Men who made them long gone. Five years the most they'll stay anymore. Down payments themselves and off to the cities. Working faster and knowing less.

'Looking at me like I'm finished.

'Summing me up.

'But let him watch now.

'Let him start to think about what I could've done if he hadn't been there, always taking, never an offer of help, never a word of thanks. Never having had to lift anything heavier than a dictionary. I should have whipped him until he bled. I want to see that smile of his face a paycheck. I want to hear how he judges me then.

'She won't own up to mistakes. Always taking his part. No reason even to tell her. And it's mostly her fault. I should have seen it coming. And I would have, if she hadn't always been there standing between us. Sleeping her life away like it was over at fifty. Everything paid for now, but what does she care of that? Everything ours to be used. But she's had it all along.

'No more comprehension of money than any woman...

'I can't see how it's wrong to want gratitude for the time of my life. No one could say that was wrong. Not the paying back, but just the simple appreciation you have a right to expect. Maybe no one can be grateful when it's been made as easy as it has been for the two of them. And if that's so, it's a sad thing for us all. Because what is it to have lived, doing what you can, nowhere near what you wanted at first, but all the same what you can, what is it to have lived, when the ones you gave it all to don't do any more than look at you as if you're finished or lie back and act as if they're ready to die?...

'It was best at the beginning.

'When there were only the plans.

'Watching him crawl along the floor so glow-eyed it made me want everything good for him.

'As if he'd be different from the rest.

'It must be one of nature's tricks, because the older they get, the further away they go, and the more they've taken from you, and the less they want to give back.

'There's so much I never would have put myself through if I'd known there would be this to follow. Just when the old plans come at me again with the old gladness, he steps away like I'd turned into a hollow, dried-up gourd. I can feel the aches of the first years still, if I let myself. Most of my life they've had as if it had been their due, but what did either of them ever accomplish to let them think so much had been owed them?

'Twenty years ago it was only prisons held his kind of talk.

'Denying his heritage.

'Making as if people in huts in Africa, don't know what a machine is, are good as a roomful of engineers.

'Like as if all we've built has been nothing more than an arrowhead and a pottery pitcher.

'Getting drafted, that would cure him soon enough. Make a man of him in short order. Put him in with boys never used toilet paper, and there'd be no more going on about city poor and such. He'd learn quick enough what the flag means. He'd learn obeying again. If I thought it possible any law school wouldn't achieve the same thing, I'd speak to the draft board myself...

'...But...how fine they all looked at the ceremonies.

'Bright as you could wish for.

'Put the rest of the world to shame.

'Look at England, how much she's lost.

'And us soon landing on the moon.

'If we could get this far, pressed as most of us were when we started out, who can consider where we'll go with them, with all the advantages they've had? And whoever would have thought I'd see a son of mine graduate from Yale College?

'There's not much my life has lacked. What a man has reflects his ways. No amount of being given is ever going to·make it like earning it yourself. A person cares for what he's earned.... She'll want to know all the details of the campuses. It's good I got to see his room. Larger than she and I had at the beginning, but no need to burden his mind with that. No need to mention it to her either. Nothing worthwhile ever comes from privation.

'She'll ask me to describe all the sights. And plenty of the men at work will want to hear, too. I'll have to be careful not to repeat the stories. The principal, the teachers, and such.

'He'll be wanting new clothes after he sees how the others are dressed. I must get a side of beef tomorrow. No need for him to make it harder on himself than it will anyway be. I'll send him a check in a few days. He's not a boy anymore, and I must remember that.

'A side of beef will fix us up fine.'

Cheered by deep blue mountain sky open about him on every side, already attuning himself to the accustomed, vast silences of his home, Mr. Tane, having returned to Colorado a day early, parked his car next to the yardman's van in front of the garage, entered the house, and walked down the hallway to his wife's closed door. Assuming that she was asleep, although it was late afternoon, he walked back to his room and began to unpack his valise. Hearing a door being opened or closed, he went to the kitchen and there found Mrs. Tane in her nightgown and robe, standing beside the entrance to the steps leading to the garage. He kissed her cheek and with a florid smile, as sounds from the van filtered into the room, said, "The Yale campus is greener than any place you've ever seen. One thing New England has is trees."

7

'I always see it first.

'When they don't know themselves they're making the signs, I see what they're doing.

'I watch it grow as they pull me to them.

'So that when they know what they've done, when they see how they have been pulling, I am there. Not know as they know their life, but as they know what they are not, as they know what they have lost or have always wanted but have never had, are sure they won't have, sure they shouldn't have. What they've turned into dreams, that sure. Them not seeing how they reach to me any more than they can ever see their own faces.

'Them used to giving the same looks before, the same signs, but used, too, to not having the signs seen. Sure of the not-seeing always around them, so that when I'm there it's their own dreams they find nearly. It's never me. It's all the other times of dreaming at once in me.

'Someone, which they never thought they could, even that much, someone, holding them like they never thought they'd be, they find in me. Someone not me. Because dreams are too hard upon them. And after, they can't keep the touch of my face in what they hardly remember.

'I was young when I was little, and when I stopped growing I wasn't young anymore. But they carry the being-young too long. They hold it, so as to stop the power when it should be growing. They turn it to dreams more than to the shapes of their bodies. Then they give up the thinking they will find.

'I never seek them out. They always pull me to them. I see how they're pulling before they know it themselves, and I get ready long before they take sight of their own signs.

'Once or twice with me is the closest they'll ever come to finding what they dream. And afterwards they can't be sure I was there...

'She was so old you couldn't see her eyes for the folds of her face. She drew me to her house and took me inside where the adobe made it cool, and set me on a little grass rug by the water pump, so that it tickled my feet, giving me cookies, saying, "Stand there." Only that, watching, there more often, until I'd grown, just "Stand there." Drawing me in with honey and dry crackers, not saying any more words.

'Until she knew I wouldn't be growing any more.

'Then she pulled me to her room. She took hold of my shirt. She was so old she soon wouldn't ever get up again. Sheet of skin with bone almost sticking out, so you could see the edges of the white of it. Fingers moving all out-of-touch with anything except the moving, not reaching anymore. Not even a voice anymore. Breakings. Like the sound of eggs cracking open. Hatching. "Stand there." And I did. She took down the trousers, so as they were, and held me. Twice more she did so.

'And then it was so she wouldn't have me into her adobe again.

'For I was grown.

'And she'd seen.

'Seen what there would be and what she was leaving.

'It was from her I learned to tell the signs.

'Only I didn't know it was the spirit was moving in me. I didn't know how close was the hand of the Lord. Until a couple of states and lots of them more, touching me, and not just the standing. How it began, the Spirit in her hands. All the empty spaces I'd filled in their lives, all the dreams I'd turned into. But I didn't know about the meaning of the Lord until after the pastor had locked the door like I knew he would when I saw there in back of the chapel, knew he would because he'd been giving the signs. And I'd waited until he'd know it, not moving toward him of myself, waiting until he had me stand there, a white cross behind me, him kneeling in front of me, his dreams talking like I wasn't there and the same time like I was the Savior Himself.

'I looked past where he was and saw the light broke up by the windows, making the chapel like there were a dozen suns and every one a different color. I saw that and heard him talk and felt the cross solid, and then I knew for that it was the Lord at work in me, the wakings of my ways. I knew it not so as anyone for could have told me it, but so as to feel it all through me. And I couldn't for to doubt His presence again.

'It's the spaces of their loneliness should have been filled when they were just-grown the Lord puts me into, uses me to hold. All twisted in dreams they are. So bent about themselves, if it weren't for someone to touch them and fill them for a time not for long they'd crack each other open with their broken selves broke all the way. The Lord uses me to carry them to enough of His peace for them to go on with only their dreams so to know how their hearts turn...

'Somewhere, they could fall upon me. Some of them. Enough.

'And even though I know for it may come so, I won't be ready.

'Even though the Lord has shown me that's how I might go unto His arms, I won't for be expecting if it does.

'Sometime having stayed too long, they could come to me. Come together. In their shame. Someone having seen, or someone having told, thinking me someone else maybe, thinking me someone who has never been, likely. All of their faces hard for the doing, them not knowing the Lord will be waiting for me. In a kind of dream it will be for them all, that they'll never need talk of again. Hiding what was me in a river or under a rock. Used so will I be by the Lord...

'Ever since they took the land, they've made us apart from them.

'So that even when there's the birth certificate to tell them where I was born, that's the last the government ever heard of me. Mestizo I am, I am always to them, for to how I look and what they do not ask. As if a stranger they do not think a person. When I am with them they talk their dreams, them not knowing what I hear is not just sounds to me. Not just sounds. In spite of words they could know behind my mouth for them not to hear, I am mestizo to them. They never think, they never know, they never guess, I've taken their every cry as an offering for the Book of the Lord.

'I never move but that He uses me, and I have never gone against His will but always do His bidding in ways no one could tell me of, but ways I know from Him.

'Hired for work for a time. Soon to be pulled on again. They think I do not know what they save. But it's me so doing the saving more, since the government has not heard of me since I was born. More I get than I could if they knew I was born on the land they took and called theirs and will not have for long.

'It's the knowing I won't be there to stay lets them pull me to them. Not the me for to put into their life, but someone only having been there. Not the ones for who hire me and count on what they save. Not often them. But the ones beside them. Ones left alone in the houses. Ones left alone in the schoolrooms after dark with a few clothes over the desks of children. Eyes burning and bodies moving fast and hard upon me. Them hardly knowing I am there. And never me, but someone. Holding me to them. Never me going to them.

'Howling quiet like birds on waters, behind secretary desks, unlocking me into rooms of ones pay them, holding on my mouth their hands, legs on tops of desks of bosses, janitors gone home, not even a candle, talking, making I'm the one sits at the desk in the daytime, not knowing I'm hearing every word plain, so for the Lord can get it writ. Moving my fingers upon them to fill the spaces enough, so as they won't for to set the rooms on fire.

'Them reaching like they should have right when we were just-grown, being told they were young, stretching it out too late, past time to begin. Being told so by some librarians and music teachers, they that find me in the dark, reaching at me as someone not who they want to touch for long. I hold their sorrows and the Lord gives them more comfort than they've had in their lives. So by day they can stamp the dates on the teachers' books and put songs in the minds of those waiting too long when they're just-grown.

'Or it will be the ones just-grown themselves, them feeling their skins pull, and everyone around talking them their bodies aren't doing what they are. Just then, when they're out for some touch at all. And the Lord gives them a taste of what they lost when their people started the ruin of the land was ours. The boy just-grown waiting in a car often as not new and often as not his, waiting there with the door open, and in I get, knowing what

I'll see, him sitting there, shivering, pants down to his knees, wanting me to do it all, him wanting to find where to send the power come new everyone tells him isn't there. Having seen me seeing him moving toward me long before. Or the girl just-grown standing beside the road in clothes show every bit of the shape they tell her don't matter she's tended, feeling the burning they put no words to. Into my van, and right off her unbuttoning the breasts, her leaning over me, her half crying, her not knowing how to bend to the burnings they tell her she does not have. Twisted already he is, she is. But not so much yet twisted to be only the colors of their dreams, as they pull down the earth for to make a mirror of their own loss.

'Boy and girl, they run quick, say, "Yes, it is." Not alone they know it anymore. What they've found by me told isn't there by ones waiting behind the windows alone. Now shown it by the Lord they know it is, me offered in the face of their redemption.

'It's then I have to leave.

'For always they'll be wanting an end of silence by winding themselves too long around me, so it's me who gets can't breathe safe in the air of their words. Giving them just-grown the touch, in the cornfields and the haylofts, and on the lakeshores and down a ways from the roads by the streams. Leaving fast and further than from the others older than me, though it's me who seems older. A county away is enough with them. But not for the ones just-grown wanting to prove it is to the ones told them the power wasn't there.

'Find me again if they want, a county away, the ones older than me I seem older than. Them freed by a couple of miles, more than knowing I'd be soon gone. Freed more than the thinking I didn't know the words of their sounds freed them.

'Just a county line.

'It's then the paths of the Lord are hard. Then that I cry for to turn toward Him most. To fill the space in my soul I almost get to for want them to stay in—a county line away—like as if they were the salvation itself in flesh.

'But when they go back, and they always do, crossing the line where they come from, the nurse, pulling on her stockings and repainting her cheeks, the new widow calling me by his name that's dead, her getting what he never gave, the politician accepted a speech-giving where he knew where I was, him hitching on his pants and rinsing out his mouth, when they go, I see clear again the hold of their dreams on their souls, making it so they cannot ever touch anyone for anything but someone they can count on soon going away, so they'll never have to know it wasn't part of a dream.

'But the ones just-grown need more than a county line.

'And sometimes a city will fall across the tracks of my van, or I'll head into one easy, wanting to find it out again, wanting to know by seeing what I already know to remember. I'll leave the van by the side of a street. My things tied up in a towel laid in back. And I'll start in to walking, knowing anybody sees me will think mestizo-speaking-no-English. Not ever think I'm one from who they took the land as that.

'And soon what I'll see'll be the car'll slow down and drive past. It doesn't matter where. The apartments all rowed, or the houses with gardens or the high buildings. Drive past, then drive past again. Hand held out of it, as I keep on walking.

'It never takes long.

'The open door and five minutes walking again.

'Even though it's the dreaming they'll be feeling, the touch has awhile. But the cities, it's faster and harder, and it sometimes hurts, and I see then it's only the ones most likely to be saved He brings me to, and the others He's readying them all for the everlasting sorrow you can see the signs of in what they've done to the land they have never known for to use as how it is. The dirt on my hands running over the lips of the few might be saved is the closest any of them ever get to the earth. And that's why the blood hardly runs in their limbs and even as it does, does so with such twistings up, you'd take to think it maybe shouldn't and maybe soon won't.

'Money they'll offer in the cities I get to without ever really meaning so. Like as the Lord found my direction for me. And money's what sets them free, making me anyone to them. Where a block away is the same as a different county. I take it, because, doesn't a parson? Most of what you can buy are their roots solid as stone, poisoning the dirt their hands do not touch. I take their money for the Lord like any parson I know would, and I use it like my van was a church where the glass makes it there's a dozen suns of different colors shining through it....

'I have seen them cut their own bodies into bloody shreds was like cherries left too long and hit by the robins. Seen them scratch beneath their clothes into what might not heal, striking at the power as if their own blood could deny its name. Trying to get out of themselves what they're told when they've stopped to grow is not there. Jesus wept for such as that, and His tears shine in my eyes for the comfort and the leading of the way. His tears in my eyes for them such as have taken from themselves all grace, save only my touch for to bring it and give them the only peace they will ever live....

'I know how it could happen.

'For I have found them have gone before me as they are not. Me pulled on by the word into paths were theirs. Found them in smoke-black shacks laid over with fresh lumber left to stay out as no one would but for to hide a common shame. Skulls sticking out from breaking-moss boulders not deep enough to have been a year uncovered over from the rain. Put in quick by hands soft and scared. The Lord Whose Presence is always with me and from Whom I never stray has offered me these signs of how I will embrace Him.

'I have seen already how their eyes would open wide like as they are when they've come for to know the signs they've given. All the crying-outs we've never learned how to give melted together in hard little points that would glow at me like the sun in the desert. All those points coming out of their eyes. Them knowing what they're doing and why they've come to do it is how they'd come to me. All together. Them wanting for to rid themselves of what they've all along told themselves isn't there. Signing away their own souls forever like they've signed away their lives. *Not* for to see they're sending me straight to my reward....

'The ones who took the land do not know what they were made for. Do not know to feed in their needs off the oceans and the unplanted grasses and the roots and the berries in their seasons. Move north and south with the sun and leave the metals only to shine from the rocks for the glory of the Lord. Hold their limbs around each other under the stars and in the shades of their comforts.

'A man was made to be a prayer all the times of his wakefulness. And all so were made.

'Made so by the Lord.

'But they have turned their own natures away from themselves and have filled the earth with the supports of their twisted dreams and have failed all the while to mind the supports of the Lord, which are written in the leaves and in the clouds and within our hearts.

'Torn asunder the very supports of the Lord.

'They tell themselves they can count on what they made themselves into because they decided it and should know. But all they have is the shells of themselves, so it gets to where what they said wasn't when it was, isn't anymore, and they lose their own souls.

'I am twenty-four years old and have lived in seventeen states in the last eleven years, been thought a mestizo-speaking-no-English in every one, my birth certificate from the first one, and the government may not ever again hear from me.'

11 Soul-sickness

"Colin?

"Hello...no, it's that I was surprised you answered your own phone.

"It probably would.

"Standing in my room with my hand on my windowpane thinking that if I leave here today, I'm going to have to get my winter coat out of its plastic bag...I wondered if by any chance you'll be free at all this afternoon. There are some things I want to talk with you about. I'd like to come by.

"That's no problem. I should be back before dinner, anyway. I've got a kind of class tonight.

"No, it's on the campus, but it isn't exactly with the university. A group of us get together to do figurative drawing.

"I already have the address. I'm good at wheedling them out of telephone operators.

"Yes, it is.

"Colin, someone down the hall has a record or tape or something on of a song I really love. Would you hold the line for a second, so I can open my door?

"Just a second.

"Okay, I'm back, thanks.

"It's called *Urges for Notes—And the Rest.* It's the longest song I've ever heard. It really is.

"Tom Rush.

"No, he didn't. Someone named Joni something did. I heard she's from a town in Canada called Curtain-Falls-Flat-on-the-Marches…and that's all I know about her.

"Yes, I was out last weekend. I'm going to make a point this year of remembering the colors until spring.

"I don't need any. I've got the route all planned. I can be there in an hour.

"Yes, good. See you soon."

Quickly Leah pushed her door closed and put on a trim black skirt, patterned nylons, a bright red, long-sleeved blouse, her newest shoes, and a coralline, abalone shell necklace. Frowning, she then removed her coat from its container in the closet, meticulously arranged the vertical lines of her clothes into a guise of staid formality, snatched a small leather hand purse and a note pad from her desk, and, not stopping to check the lock, dashed out the door.

While getting off a bus at a corner unfamiliar to her, she eyed a penciled map and then walked the length of a dead-end street to a curved, brick wall cleaved by a steel postern which opened onto a gravel path lined on both sides with shoulder-high spruce trees. Certain she was in the right place, although she saw no buildings as yet, she unbuttoned her coat and, looking down at her feet, rushed along the path. Gradually and symmetrically it widened into a courtyard garden encircled by two- and three-story nineteenth-century brick and wood cottages. The upper stories offered no hint of how they were being used, but most of the street level spaces were taken up by an assortment of small shops. It was an architectural island, unusually well tended. Unpretentiously, it suggested both a suburban commercial center and a rural English village. Even the air seemed clean.

Delighted, Leah surveyed the store front signs, went into an ice-cream parlor, bought two strawberry cones and after wrapping them in napkins, found the entrance to Dr. Tsampa's building. Seeing no elevator, she proceeded to climb three flights of stairs to his attic office.

"Colin?" she called in front of his partially open, numbered door.

"Come in, Leah. I left the door ajar for you."

"Don't move or the walls will look like a measles epidemic," Leah said, shutting the door behind her. "I hope you like ice cream."

"Proximity has made it a weakness," Dr. Tsampa replied. He sat, smiling sadly, on the sill of a screened window which framed a courtyard view.

"With your weight you don't need to call it a weakness. Call it a fondness."

"One ice-cream cone a day is a fondness. Two a day is a weakness."

"Suit yourself. I hope you like strawberry."

"Second best."

"What's first?"

"Chocolate."

"Another time."

"I won't forget."

"It's like an explosion of peace here, Colin," Leah said, expansively handing Dr. Tsampa her coat and examining the room, an uncustomarily large expanse of pure space, white-walled and red-carpeted, containing virtually no furniture. "However did you find it?"

"Came upon it unannounced one summer day."

"How long have you had it?"

"Five weeks."

"I wish you'd let me know. I could've helped you fix it up."

"There's still more to do. I suppose there always will be…What do you think of it? Can you tell me yet? Be tactful, but don't spare me the truth."

Licking her ice cream, Leah wheeled in a circle and said, "Give me a few minutes."

"There's no hurry. I'm going to be here a long while. I'm sure of that," Dr. Tsampa said. He seemed to be making a decided effort to appear alert, but his inflections repeatedly turned into wearied and rasping monotones, and his eyes were rimmed with gray. "Have you heard the new Beatles album yet?"

"At least a hundred times. I mean it. At least a hundred."

"There's another one coming out next month."

"Oh, yes, I know," said Leah. "I feel like I've never waited for anything as long as this one. I was afraid they might be breaking up. I kept trying to believe the tales about it being only the cover keeping it unreleased. I guess they were true…It's awfully different from any of their other ones, isn't it?"

"Every one of them's been different."

"Yes, you're right. I suppose that's what's so amazing about them."

"It's a little uneven, but I like it a lot, anyway. Some of the arrangements keep reminding me of Bach. I wish I knew why. I don't have enough of a musical vocabulary to be able to identify the reason…"

Suddenly frowning, Leah said, "Colin, excuse me, but do I actually see you eating ice cream with your teeth?"

"I'm afraid you do."

"Doesn't it make you feel like someone's scraping a fingernail along a blackboard or a greenboard or whatever they're being called in grade schools these days?"

"It's a long-standing habit," Dr. Tsampa replied, chewing in placid demonstration.

"I really can't watch you. My back starts to jump."

"Sit down, if you want, while you look somewhere else," Dr. Tsampa said, guiding her to a yellow-cushioned, swivel chair and then resting one of his shoulders against a sturdy, wood-slatted shutter jutting perpendicularly from the window frame. "Things can get loud in here sometimes. The shutter works better than curtains. There haven't been any complaints yet. I've got to keep the neighbors as unfrightened as possible. Patients tend to pick up on the fear, if there is any; and that gets to be a strain on everyone. It's especially unfair to the ones who weren't responsible for it. By the way, it's 'chalkboards' these days."

"'Chalkboards'…from the color to the tool. An improvement."

"Yes."

"Where have you hidden your desk? That's the first think I looked for?"

"It's at home. I wanted to see what would happen without it."

"So was your back getting stiff from elbow-leaning?"

"Yeah, that, but, too, not having it is something of an experiment. Patients were tending to feel like they were on an assembly line. Always on the side of the desk right where the last patient had been. Having to take the same position the next patient would. I wanted to try some informality. There's enough space here to allow moving the chairs around. I may bring the desk back. I don't know yet."

"You need some plants."

"They're on my list."

"There's so much light here. It's wonderful. Almost anything should grow," said Leah, sitting with her back arched away from the chair and her knees close together. "What about the neighborhood? Are there any other doctors in the circle?"

"A few. Not many. The zoning is multipurpose. I like the variety. My other office was too insular. This is insular, but in a better way. It's more cosmopolitan."

"Did you get out of the last lease?"

"With some extra cash, finally, yes. Thank you for asking. People don't usually think to."

"What about the patient load? Are they managing to locate you here? Roxbury must be new to a lot of them. It is to me."

Dr. Tsampa eased himself into an overstuffed cushion on the floor, crossed his legs, and lodged both hands between his ankles. His curly, brown hair was neatly trimmed; but its part, which had never quite succeeded in being a clear line of division, edged irregularly along the left side of his head; and quarter-inch hairs stuck out from his neck immediately above the base of his otherwise clean-shaven beard. The corners of his mouth were markedly rounded, and each of them was propped outward by tiny pouches of flesh which seamed his cheeks and fell toward his chin when he spoke. He wore a candy-striped sport shirt and checked cotton trousers.

"There's been quite a turnover," he replied. "I've had to take on more private patients. My schedule hasn't adjusted at this point. That would have been true without the move. The halfway house was shut down two weeks ago."

"That's terrible, Colin! It must've been terrifically hard on you," Leah said. "I'm sorry to be so trite. But I can't think of anything else to say."

"There's nothing else you could say. I learned long ago that the times that are the tensest are apt to leave us with only the trite to rely on. It *was* hard. It still is."

"What happened? Something to do with the administration?"

"No, it was that the federal funds weren't renewed. The war is taking over the national budget. Most of the patients had to be rehospitalized. I hated that. I had to watch them retrogress right away. There was nothing I could do...But tell me about you. What are you up to these days?"

"Painting is wearing me out," said Leah, looking toward the window. "It's not the techniques that are getting to me; it's trying to understand what my intentions ought to be. I think if I hadn't met you I would just have told myself to trust my subconscious."

"Can I help?" Dr. Tsampa asked, his tones softer, less restrained, than those he had used when asking the same question hundreds of times a month for more than a decade.

"I'm not sure."

"Tell me about the figurative drawing."

"We meet three nights a week. There are eight of us and a model. The university won't allow it as formal course work but will provide the space."

"Sounds typical."

"Alumni contributions," said Leah. "Is it always the conservatives who give the most?"

"That's what administrators usually assume."

"I did not know how much censorship there would be in college. I really did not. So many irritating, little controls."

"Is there a new model every week? Something like that?"

"We've had the same one every time. I don't mind. There are lots of poses for her to use and lighting changes to make and different mediums to work with. It's so awkward, though. It's a standard arrangement with easels in a circle and all; but that means it's like there's a sign up which says, 'No eroticism permitted.' It should be more intimate. The pose is always static; but even so, mainly what I'm seeing is the motion of relationships people in the group have with each other. That's what interests me. That's what I want to express somehow. The ways we look at each other and at the model and why and even what each of us is noticing. It's amazing how different eight people's drawings can be and still recognizably be referring to the same person in the same pose. But I'm already tired of doing the stock renditions of anatomy artists did three centuries ago well enough for no one ever to do again. I think I must be going through something like you did in medical school, trying to find a decent balance between approaching a person as unique and as a representative, sort of, of everyone, Colin. What I want to get at are the proper limits of objectivity, and I keep coming back to relationships. Figurative drawing usually seems to me to deny them. It's too one-sided. It's almost like turning a person into a cadaver. It really is. It stresses moments and avoids all the processes that lead up to them and stem from them. It treats people as products.

"Maybe portraits should have an element of self-portrait in them, too; something on them partly drawn by the model; maybe they should be done mutually. I don't know. What I'm sure of is that my capacities to see are increasing; painting and drawing will do that for anyone. That's the most important part of it all. Words can't get at a lot of what I'm seeing. That's why I'm stumbling so much when I talk. I've learned new coordinations, and they've jumbled my old ones. I can hardly even use color words anymore. Especially when they're applied to something like hair or eyes. I see so many shades now. So many separate tones that used to all blend together and be labelable...Colin, excuse me for going from one subject to the next like this. My mind has been a bit unglued lately. Not unglued exactly, but roaming about more than usual."

"I'm following you," said Dr. Tsampa. He relaxed his back against another cushion and loosely stretched one leg toward her. "What you say reminds me that in my first year of medical school, when we were dissecting, dissecting cadavers, Leah...we were never given any information about who the person had been. That's the usual policy, but it seemed to me unwarranted then, and it still does. It's a denial of social relationships that's similar to what you were describing. And social relationships have quite a bit to do with health. Some professional approaches don't seem to me sufficiently to take into account the fabrics of our environments. Instead, what they do is conceptually stem from the assumption that patients are living in kind of solitary limbos. Like the one your group puts the model into. Attitudes supporting approaches like that begin to form the very first year of medical school. You're right. I agree with you. We need a lot more delineations of relationships."

"Yes, but, what I'm trying to tell you, partly, mostly why I'm thinking so much about relationships—and I don't mean that it's an unimportant reason—not at all, Colin, but...I'm starting to see how isolated I could be after graduation. That's what's really on my mind...I don't know if isolation is necessary for whatever kind of art I want to do or antithetical to it. I mean my own isolation. I've got to decide as soon as I can what sort of situation is going to be best for my processes of painting. The faculty at school seems absolutely incapable of offering the slightest bit of economic or legal information. Even basic copyright routines never get mentioned. I'll need an income from something that hopefully can fit in with the artwork or at least not conflict with it too much, and I wanted to ask you if you think a job in a hospital might be good for me. Something like being a lab assistant at Boston City."

"It'd be difficult to find anything. These times most of the positions are being filled by conscientious objectors."

"Yes, of course. I hadn't considered that at all."

"Don't give it up as a possibility, though," said Dr. Tsampa in a carefully reassuring manner. He stretched out his other leg. "But what about looking for commissions, Leah?"

"I don't think I'll be ready for that by summer. I really don't. I start to panic whenever I let myself think about it."

"Have you investigated getting a teaching certificate, then?"

Leah stood and stepped to the window. Pushing the shutter back and forth and watching its lined shadow expand and contract across the floor, she said, "There's a graduate student I know. He was an instructor of mine a year ago. He's seeing school from both sides, trying to figure out what he'll accept as a professor. He isn't really sure it'll be any of it. He wants the income; but he doubts the demands, especially the demands that aren't ever stated. He'll ask me if I approve or to approve of something or other in the university structure, and often I can't, and then he doesn't approve, and then later on he does again. I'm certain what he's doing is deciding whether he's going to paint or not. It isn't a simple decision, but it does mean settling on the one thing or the other. I don't think teaching can ever be effectively combined with the doing. I really don't. I've got to find some combination; but as far as I can comprehend any of the alternatives, that's the one least likely to help me."

"I guess you'd have to be associated with an institution of some sort to get a foundation grant."

"Yes, they're almost all that way. Sadly. It's the dependability-of-mediocrity syndrome."

"You're not thinking of going back to Los Angeles?"

"No, I'm going to stay here for sure, Colin. For sure. I really don't see how people ever manage to spend the rest of their lives in the places where they grew up. I couldn't."

"Well, it seems, then, that the only thing for you to do is to put in as many applications as you have patience for and after a few weeks or months or whatever, days maybe, take the job with the most money and the fewest hours. I can't suggest anything else...I certainly think you're wise, though, to be planning as much as you can now."

"But it's not only the length of time of the work; it's also how what the work is will relate to my painting. I want the two things to enhance each other, if they can," Leah replied, observing the transparent, windowpane reflection of the shutter. "I should tell you that I've been getting a bit afraid lately, worrying about it all. For one thing, classes have never taken up anywhere near forty hours a week. So far, I've had few routines to have to handle. Very few."

"There's much to reasonably fear, Leah. If you tell yourself you're not afraid, you'll get more afraid. The best thing to do is keep sight of what you fear."

"'Afraid.' It sounds good to hear that word said by someone else. People don't often talk of being afraid anymore. They say 'paranoid' instead. As if they're pretending everything's fine and that it's crazy to be afraid. Have you noticed that? You probably have. Probably oftener than I have."

"There's more than enough to fear," said Dr. Tsampa.

"Colin," said Leah slowly closing the shutter and gazing through it out the window, "there's someone I know. I'm concerned about him. He left Yale about a year ago. It was the middle of the fall term of his senior year. He worked at the post office for awhile, and at the end of the spring he got into construction work. Carpentry mostly. Which is what he wanted to do...Bought his own pickup...But no one will let him have any responsibilities. They don't want to give them to him and have him be drafted the next day. He's been with three companies in about that many months. Every time I see him, he's more discouraged. He doesn't have any plans at all for dealing with the war."

"What about trying to get a conscientious objection status?"

"Yes, but when you apply for that you have to demonstrate a belief in God; and he says that's too private a thing to have to tell them."

"I'm sympathetic with him there," said Dr. Tsampa, looking at his wrist-watch. "Whenever the Supreme Court decision on that comes, it'll be too late for him among so many. Freedom of religion in the United States, unfortunately, usually means some form of Judeo-Christianity or silence."

"Every choice he has looks like a bad one to him. To me, too."

"Tell him," said Dr. Tsampa, again looking at his wristwatch, "that I'll write his draft board a letter saying he's psychiatrically unfit for military service."

"Do you need to talk with him?" asked Leah, surprised at Dr. Tsampa's offer, although she had expected him to make it.

"No, that won't be necessary, Leah. If that's what he decides he wants, just give me his name and the address of the draft board."

"What about it being on his record?" Leah asked. She pushed the shutter quietly to the wall.

"It'll be there. It may matter. It may not. He'll have to take that into consideration. If the war goes on much longer, I'll likely start doing the same thing for as many of them as I can. Everyone in his position is going to have an objectionable record to some future group."

"Aren't you apt to find yourself in court, though, if you write many letters like that?"

"I don't imagine I'll be risking anything…"

Taking a step away from the window, Leah said, "You're in a strange mood today, Colin. Really. I've never seen you so depressed. Is it mainly the closing of the halfway house?"

"It's that, and it's…there's a good deal about which I'm making up my mind right now. News broadcasts as well as the office. So many issues are flaring up these days that being noncommittal is probably immoral except as a process of preparation. Having to focus on acquiring private patients means that I have to alter some of the major intents of my practice. I can't be as oriented toward environmental conditions as I want to be. At least for awhile. The government is tying my hands right when so much is occurring that I might have taken advantage of."

"Or been an advantage to."

"Yeah, well, I…I'm very tired, Leah. I'm sorry I can't disguise it."

"You're making me want to count the petals in a field of daisies and clover. There's a sadness hanging over the room, even with all the light and the informality. I noticed it right away."

"Happiness is rare here. It always will be. It comes, if it comes at all, only at the end of a long series of sessions. Hopefully it continues in other spheres; but if it does continue, I'm not ever there to appreciate it. The office has to be hospitable, but it can't be homelike enough to cause people to want to linger too long. It can't be too easy a space, but it can't be too formidable either."

"You need a table. A small one. Medium height. Even if you don't use it, it'll be good to have for people to look at occasionally. Driftwood maybe. Redwood. Something with a rugged beauty. Unfinished."

"I'll put it on my list. I've got to get a small heater, too. The building was made for a coal furnace. No one's said anything, but I'm pretty sure the conversion to gas hasn't worked out very well. The landlord kept trying to convince me to take an office that had a fireplace..."

"You didn't have a dictaphone before, did you?" asked Leah, walking past Dr. Tsampa to a ceiling-high corner bookcase laden with hardcover books, magazines, journals, notebooks, and the dictaphone.

"I got it about a month ago. My impressions were flying faster than my typewriter."

"Is it working out better?"

"I don't know yet. I haven't had time to play back most of what I've recorded. So far it's like having part of me outside myself. I feel like I'm mutating."

"You're still keeping up your other journal, though? the written one?"

"Yeah, but lately, to tell you the truth, I've been wondering whether it's been worth all the hours I've spent with it. I'll have what seems to be a new idea, but then I'll go back through the old entries, and I'll find I wrote the same thing or its opposite years ago, and I'll be unable to remember ever having thought either one."

"Well, that's a good reason to have a journal, isn't it?"

"Sometimes I suspect that the errors of selective memory may be healthier than accuracy," Dr. Tsampa replied, standing, yawning, and walking toward his office coatrack. "I have a patient coming soon, I'm afraid,

Leah. I wish I could talk with you longer, but I've got to use the next few minutes getting ready for the therapy session. I always do that, if I can."

"Yes, of course. Thank you for so much of your time. I didn't really expect to be able to see you."

"I hope you don't feel you were wedged in."

"No, not at all," Leah said, as she buttoned her coat. "Really. It feels like you must be handling your scheduling miraculously."

"Anything else about the office?"

"No, nothing I can think of yet anyway. I was afraid you might ask me for a painting. It's too soon."

"Yeah, I...I figured that'd probably be the way you'd feel."

Uplifting one hand in a wave of good-bye, Leah reached with her other hand for the door, opened it, and turned back into the room.

"Colin?"

"Yes?"

"If I tell you one of my favorite things you do, will you promise to keep on doing it?"

"You won't tell me what it is before I promise?"

"No."

"Because if I knew what it is I'd stop doing it if I hadn't promised?"

"Maybe."

"And there's no other way to find out but to promise?"

"Not from me."

"All right, I may regret it, but I promise. If I can manage to do whatever it is I'm promising, I'll do it...Now tell me what it is I've got to do."

"You've got to always wear shirts with frayed collars!" Leah said, laughing and looking directly into Dr. Tsampa's eyes. She put her arms around his waist; but as he started to pull her to him, she stepped through the doorway.

"Have they really always been frayed?" he asked.

"I'll call you about the letter," she said.

12 Solace

1

The October moon seemed lower to Jack than an hour earlier when it had been an oversized scarlet disk outshining a clouded pool of sulfurous yellows and tarnished greens that had been the setting sun. As he tried and failed to open an unwieldy security door without its creaking, he raised his eyes a final time to the sky, stared a moment, and then entered C. J.'s apartment house. Glancing at a row of battered, padlocked mailboxes, all of which had black numerals inked into slots meant for name cards, he walked to the rear of the front hall, and, taking the steps two at a time, lithely mounted five flights of stairs. Breathing heavily, he opened another door, indifferently constructed of plywood, and began to feel his way up a wanly lit, narrow passageway, which, although it joined only two floors, turned twice upon itself. As he slowly climbed the cramped, dim steps, he used the fingers of one hand to steady himself, tracing them along a wide line of luminous, unsanded plaster patching, so consistently cracked and shredded away from the wall that near the top of the stairs there was a hole large enough to enclose a fist.

Vestiges of stained wallpaper showing through successive layers of paint that had peeled, fallen, and been ground into coarse fibred remains of carpeting on the warped floor caused the landing to resemble a misshapen, uncompleted jigsaw puzzle. A fly scudded across the ceiling and buzzed loudly with the anxiety of autumn; and a centipede lumbered a scalloped path over a pile of wadded newspapers. Wearing, brown corduroy pants and a matching jacket and cap, Jack, with his long, sandy hair and a newly debonair mien, which partially reflected a strenuous, four-month-long effort to disassociate himself from the roughhewn style of his father, was a semblance of a young English lord from the seventeenth century who had gone vacationing through time. After knocking on one of three doors and waiting more than a minute, he tried the easily turning knob and, unzipping his jacket, let himself inside.

The preceding gloom had always before been immediately counteracted by light from windows that covered half the wall opposite the hall door and bracketed a screened entrance to a porch hidden from the front sidewalk by an overhanging extension of the roof. Sometime within the past week, however, thick, green drapes had been installed. Since they were stretched forbiddingly the length of the wall, streetlight flickering in above them served only to sate the room with malformed shadows, amidst which Jack stumbled, as he waited for his eyes to adjust to the surprise of darkness.

The apartment had originally been designed to serve as quarters for servants. The floor, consequently, had been laid with planks of soft pine, which through the years had been sanded and revarnished with such regularity that the landlord had adamantly maintained the wood could withstand no further refinishing. Nonetheless, C. J. had been given per-mission—without restrictions—to renovate any other aspects of the rooms. Subsequently, he had painted the living room wall bordering the windows white, the opposite wall black, the two other walls a pale green, and the ceiling, which he had worked on last, a flaxen, aureated yellow. Most of the multicolored lines of juncture had been successfully evened; but the yellow paint had dripped onto the walls leaving blemishes that, having not as yet been repaired, had taken on the appearance of cords of melted wax.

Next to the hall entrance was a six-tiered bookcase constructed from splintered boards and precariously balanced, gray cinder blocks. Its shelves were haphazardly lined with books concerned with various phases of carpentry, several dozen record albums, a portable stereo hinged with small speakers, and an assortment of rocks, shells, and pieces of driftwood.

On the other side of the bookcase was an upright automobile seat, functioning comfortably and almost attractively as a couch. The previous spring C. J. had retrieved it from an alley and had covered it with a loose piece of imitation leather, which was held in place by a knotted strand of fishnet. French doors, each missing several panes of glass and painted a muddied bronze mixed from the other colors, were centered in one of the green walls. On either side of them were an unshaded floor lamp less than five feet high and an overstuffed footstool, permanently pocked with indentations from the many feet it had soothed on its circuitous path through apartments and stores specializing in used goods.

Running the length of the fourth wall was a boatlike, aluminum frame, manufactured for outside use, within which floated a supple, hand-woven hammock. Pillows of assorted shapes and colors were beside it within easy reach on the floor; and a poster-sized, photographed seascape had been taped to the ceiling directly above it. Adjacent to the end of the frame nearest the intersection of the black and green walls was a kitchen entryway, partially blocked by a wood and canvas, patio chair.

From the middle of the ceiling there hung the cankered skeleton of a crystal chandelier, most of its pendants having been broken or hocked by a succession of tenants, all of whom had attested to a gradual razing of gentility in the neighborhood. No attempt had been made to disguise the fractured state of the fixture, and its sockets were empty. Beneath it and occupying most of the rest of the room, was a rectangular, wooden table, more than eight feet long and nearly half as wide. Scattered upon it were saws, hammers, screwdrivers, a tape measure, an electric drill, a plane, knives, boxes of nails, tacks, staples, and screws, sandpaper, bottles of glue, and a stack of crumpled, oily rags.

As soon as he was able to see the contours of the furniture, Jack listlessly pitched his jacket and cap toward the footstool and walked through the kitchen to an adjoining bathroom. While returning to the living room, he faintly but distinctly heard a muted trumpet playing the duple meters of improvisational jazz and was looking for its source when C. J., holding a portable radio, swung open the French doors and stooped through them. He was barefoot, at least a week unshaven, and wore a torn, tar-encrusted tee shirt tucked into faded blue jeans cut off above his knees. Splashes of paint had been neither brushed nor washed from the tangles of his uncared-for hair but had amassed about his shoulders like burrs in the mane of a horse. His elbows were black, his ankles scratched and bruised, his fingers blistered, and his neck layered with dirt and dried sweat.

Yet in spite of his shambling, unattended-to appearance, he exuded health. Five months of outdoor work had lightly browned his skin, tightened his muscles, and rounded his frame so compactly that there were no longer any tentative or agitated qualities in his movements, as, saying nothing, he glided across the room to the automobile seat, sat down, and instantly became motionless, save only for his toes, which tapped an unceasing counterpoint to the barely audible, prerecorded jazz.

"Hey, C. J.," said Jack, sidling to the bookcase. "I hope it's all right I let myself in." He glanced at the phonograph spindle, found it heaped high with records, and began methodically to transfer them into their jackets. "I didn't want to go home to Cambridge again. I needed a night off." Unable to find the jackets for two of the albums, he put them back inside the stereo, closed the lid, picked up a piece of driftwood, and rubbed it mechanically between his palms. "I wish you'd get a phone..."

In the four years of his friendship with Jack, C. J. had appeared steadily to have been growing more adept at conversation; but he had continued to be subject to occasional, protracted periods of extreme taciturnity, which Jack had patiently learned to cloak in streams of his own words. Although C. J.'s current interval of near silence had lasted longer than any of his others—since midsummer he seldom had offered even a gesture of greeting—Jack had waited as before while talking on alone, certain that nothing he might do could force or elicit any immediate replies, certain, too, that C. J., when he would start to speak again, would probably for a brief time use the telegraphic style of his boyhood, then haltingly would add complexities of form and detail, and finally would deliver extended, rambling monologues, several of which would be delayed responses to specific statements he had heard many days earlier.

"I thought Yale was competitive, but it seems like a commune when I think about it in relation to Harvard Law School," Jack said, wondering whether C. J. straightway would make a cryptic comment. "It's not just that classes meet oftener or that they're longer," Jack continued, having weighed C. J.'s failure to reply. "It's that every minute depends on the last one. If I miss anything, none of what comes after it makes sense, and I have to borrow somebody's notebook and trace back to wherever it was I left off. Everything links together more than anything did at Yale. The whole atmosphere is much more intense. It's like learning a new language, even though it's mostly English. It's all so specialized. I'm not sure how much of it is necessary. But there's no way I can skip any of it and expect to be able to keep up.

"I try to separate out what's training my mind in what seem to me like the right ways, disciplining it, I mean, and what's really more meant to be indoctrinating us. I don't want them to develop prejudices in me without my knowing it. But it's difficult to pinpoint that going on. It happens so gradually. And there's so much history tied up with every new definition and every new principle."

Having by now assured himself that C. J. would be spending the rest of the evening listening, attentive, mute, Jack set the piece of driftwood back on its shelf, angled through the darkness to the hammock, sat down in it, and kicked his shoes to the floor. Arching his hands behind his neck, he relaxed, lay back, and leisurely contemplated the faintly illuminated, photographed seascape, as he again released a flow of spontaneous talk: "Every class, there's more to memorize. You have to learn the minutest details because the next argument might hinge on one of them. It's not questioning or challenging they expect; it's more developing a technique. It's like learning how to play basketball using a tennis ball, when all the time you have the feeling someone's going to prove you're supposed to have used a football. It's all so formal and well-laid-out that it's disarming, and it's hard to object to any of it. There's such a gap between that clean logic and how we live, though, that somewhere along the way I know there's going to be turnoffs I'm not going to want to take. I'm not sure yet how to recognize them. I mean I'm going to want to be prepared for them and understand them, but not take them. Quite a bit of it came from the worst kind of politics, only everything's so well ordered, by the time it gets to us, that it's easy to keep forgetting the origins. Facts and opinions get merged together more often than in any kind of writing I've read. Footnotes of a section in a book you opened by chance can change the whole presentation of a case, since almost every argument depends on what's been argued before.

"Anyway—as far as I can tell—I'm doing all right…There's a kind of beauty to some of it, I've got to admit that. There really is. The kind of beauty the framework of a suspension bridge has. Or icicles hanging from the edge of a roof.

"There's a lot more talk about the war than there was at Yale. The United States press just doesn't deal with international law. There really is a good chance Johnson can be tried as a war criminal. Even some of the professors think that. Cambridge isn't anywhere near as provincial as New Haven was. Harvard must be the best place for me to have gone. So much of what law is based on happened because of people from there. I've got access to documents that haven't ever had copies made of them.

"But I wish I could get to the beach or somewhere. I don't have time for anything besides studying. And my mother keeps sending me these strange letters. I don't know how to tell you about them. She'll get on this track I suppose is philosophical, these long hints, sort of, about justice and helplessness and sacrificing; only I can't understand what she's trying to say. In her last letter she asked me to mail her a book explaining the theory of relativity; and on the next page she'd written 'Doesn't it have to do with us?' That was all there was on the page. She keeps wanting me to let her know everything I can about Vietnam. She's decided she's against the war, and in every letter she asks me to help her keep my father from finding out about that."

Still looking at the ceiling, Jack paused to gather new thoughts; but as he prepared to begin speaking again, C. J.'s voice came searing through the air: "Could it ever occur to you I may not be interested in every detail of your life?"

Startled, uncomprehending, Jack lurched his feet to the floor and peered across the room. All he could see, however, was the enshadowed outline of a featureless shape that did not move.

"Your concern is always for yourself," C. J. said, his tones staccato and shrill. "You never give me any at all…I come up here wanting never to leave this room. I come up here not ever wanting to see another human being again. And you walk right in as if you can go anywhere you want to, and you expect me to listen to you describe every problem you have ever had. What's it going to take to make you realize I live a life of my own?"

"C. J., I don't know what else to do when you don't talk."

"Listen to me!"

"What? Listen to what?"

"This psychiatrist…"

"What, C. J.?"

"This psychiatrist Leah knows said he'll write my draft board a letter saying I'm crazy…"

"Have you ever met…?"

"…and she thinks I should have him do it."

Before either of them could say anything else, C. J. silenced the radio with a slam of his fist.

And then he began to cry.

His tears were the tears people may usually have strength enough to shed only twice in their lives—tears that have little to do with grief or with physical pain or with passing frustrations or even with self-pity.

Such tears are apt to occur in the presence of a witness; but since they fall in part because of the recognition that there can be no diminution of the sadnesses from which they initially spring, they symbolize neither a demand, nor even an entreaty, for consolation. They are not tears of unique sadnesses, but stem instead from sadnesses similar enough in lives otherwise quite varied, sadnesses widespread enough, to contain within them—once it is appreciated what common sadnesses they are—the geneses of two bridges that are fundamental to most human interrelationships: the bridge of compassion and the bridge of accommodation.

The young may weep, as C. J. wept, soon after they have first learned not only that life will be unlikely to bring them what they have secretly longed for and dreamed of, but also that even many of their heretofore unchallenged expectations will probably not be realized. The tears often cried at these commonly experienced times of painful discovery are not, however, expressions of rage toward entrapment in a maturity deemed unworth the soon-to-be-forgotten sorrows that have accompanied physical growth. Though they are tears reflecting the onslaught of sadnesses resultant from the unforeseen, sudden, unambiguous defeats and cessations of manifold childhood hopes, more importantly, they are tears signifying the reluctant acceptance of personal limitations and of real possibilities; they are tears of acquiescence. Because they bring with them the twofold revelation that they serve to demonstrate the weight of the sadnesses occasioned by the loss of unwarranted anticipations and that they cannot mitigate those sadnesses, they are tears the young usually shed only once.

Many of the elderly may weep nearly the same tears, and again they may usually weep them only once. Their tears are not caused by awarenesses of approaching death nor by regrets nor by bitternesses nor by wearinesses. Instead, they are tears proffered as testaments that the early unhappinesses, those that had been partially responsible for acknowledgments of the necessary limits of particular lives, have not been alleviated by the ensuing years, but all along have been there, been there within the geography defined by sighs and wistfulnesses, been there to forge compassion and to support accommodations so prevalent, so customary, that defenses of them are seldom considered obligatory. The elderly are no more prepared for their testamentary tears than are the young for their tears of acquiescent recognitions. And during the times such tears are shed, whether by the young or the old, they are shed so forcibly that it seems even the marrow of one's bones is being torn apart and dissolved.

When at last the thrashings of C. J.'s limbs had subsided and the plaint of his sobbing had ceased, when his tears no longer fell, when all that could be heard within his apartment were the two sounds of breathings, Jack was the first to become aware of the already crescendoing transposition of their mood. He could have eased then away from the arms that more than a quarter of an hour before had been convulsively flung about his waist, but he did not. Even when he was sure that C. J., too, felt the shiftings and risings of the currents of their stance, still there was time for Jack to step back, there was time for C. J. to unclasp his arms; but neither moved. And soon the protracted moment of their shared and intentional immobility had been too prolonged for either of them to have any doubts that agreements had been made with every unmade movement toward separation, too prolonged for either of them to be surprised when Jack lowered himself through C. J.'s arms, or when C. J. slid to the floor, drawing Jack with him, too prolonged for surprise even when, unmoving again, they lay with their bodies slack against each other and their legs entangled, lay with their hands hesitant and uncertain, lay waiting to be guided by the rhythms of their mutual regard.

2

Smelling bacon and hearing it spatter, Jack crooked his neck over the edge of the bed, searched for a clock, located one, was unable to read its luminous dial, reached for it, held it close to his eyes, and still clinging to sleep, found that it was nearly three o'clock in the morning. Feeling at once settled and disarrayed, comfortable and chaotic, at peace and beset by turbulence, he slipped into his pants, crept past the French doors and to the kitchen, pulled one of four wooden chairs away from a collapsible card table, sat down, and attempted in shy wonderment to discover a place on which safely to focus his eyes. C. J., wrapped in a robe and wearing sandals, stood solemnly hunched over the stove.

It was a large room, a remnant of the turn-of-the-century years when a kitchen had functioned as an essential meeting place for all the members of a family. The walls and ceiling were the professionally painted orange they had been the day C. J. had first seen them. A single strip of terra-cotta linoleum, cracked at the edges, was stretched across the floor. Affixed to the ceiling over the card table was a chained, rectangular light fixture containing two fluorescent bulbs; additional light came only from a round, porthole-like window above the refrigerator.

Against the entryway wall was a spacious and sturdy cabinet, its lower shelves dense with labeled jars of vegetables C. J. had canned during one of the intervals between his construction jobs. On its top shelf were two sacks of small potatoes, a sack of onions, and a bowl of dried corn. Close to the stove, in a corner of the room, were a hoe, a shovel, a potato fork, a hose, a watering can, and an almost empty bag of fertilizer. Next to them and opposite the cabinet was a broad, metal sink, multipurpose and imposing, beneath which were assorted cleaning fluids, soaps, buckets, and a loose mass of dirty clothes.

Confining his gaze to the surface of the table, Jack shook some salt from a cardboard container into his hands, passed the grains back and forth in a series of arcs, and did not reply when C. J., adroitly holding each piece of bacon directly over the gas flame for a second of singeing, said in a voice without intonation, "Prosperity is paper towels."

After lowering the flame, pouring most of the grease into a tin can, and filling the frying pan with slices of frozen hash brown potatoes, C. J. crossed the room, opened the refrigerator, brought out butter and ketchup and strawberry preserves, set them on the table, then relifted the bottle of ketchup, and, before replacing it, held it above his head as if he might bring it down hammer-hard on the top of one of the chairs.

"I've stolen things," he said.

Again Jack made no reply.

"I said, 'I've stolen things'," C. J. repeated, walking backwards to the sink and balancing on it, keeping most of his weight on his feet.

"I heard you," said Jack. "What do you mean?"

"That's what I've always done. I used to check out library books when I was so little I could hardly read, and I'd tear them up and say I'd lost them. I'd go to somebody's house, and there'd be something of their parents I'd want, and I'd take it. As soon as I was grown enough to go into stores by myself I already knew what I could do, and I did it. I did it anytime I felt like it. Nobody ever caught me. I couldn't see any reason for something to be there and me wanting it and not to have it. I couldn't ever see any reason for cash registers. I'd tell myself, 'So what, all the adults around are bored out of their minds with their jobs anyway, whether it's the making the thing or hauling it or selling it or being a cop, so why not take it?' And now that I've finally got enough money to pay for things, a lot of times what I've done is still just take them. I've taken them like I always have. Half my tools I've walked into a hardware store and walked out with nobody knowing…Maybe most people can't see any reason for things being there without taking them, but they don't take them because they didn't learn to early. And because they're so used to being bored they don't ever want to do anything that might upset the boredom. I know that's why they have wars. They have wars to protect their own boredom on both sides of cash registers."

"You've stolen things. Why are you telling me?"

"Because I've lied, and I don't want to, and I don't know how to stop, and I want you to help me."

"When, C. J.? When have you lied?"

"At Yale I lied a lot."

"Everyone did."

"That's not what I mean. I don't mean putting into term papers somebody else's ideas like I'd thought of them myself or pretending to be interested in a lecture I didn't care about. I mean saying I'd been where I hadn't, saying I was going to do what I knew I wouldn't, making up whole stories I'd tell like they were the truth…The year after I was out of high school, it was one story like that after another. Hitchhiking saying I'd been places I'd only heard about, saying I'd done what I'd only thought of doing…People'd let me know things about themselves, things that'd happened to them, and later on I'd tell somebody else what they'd said like it was me I was talking about."

Staring at the small, circular window above the refrigerator, C. J. hesitated, waited until he was confident that Jack for a third time did not intend to reply, and then continued to grope past the edge of his months-long silence: "In school at Arlington I'd look through the windows and try to compare what we were getting told with what was outside. But that wasn't what the teachers wanted us to do. We weren't supposed to test any of what we heard or even what we read. Everything always got talked about in the same way. Whether it was something supposed to have been happening that year or was history or was a theory in science or a formula in geometry. All they wanted was to hear back from us what they'd said. Nothing had to be proven, because whether any of it was true or not wasn't what mattered to them. What they thought was important was the power they had in making us do what they wanted. A lot more important than what we were supposed to be learning. I'd not say it back, and after awhile they'd stop trying to get me to…Mostly it seems like what people talk about is what they don't really know. They repeat what they've heard like they did in school. I want to talk so as to be sure. I mean somewhere inside me that's what I want. That's the best of what

I want. What people say together is how they think things are, whether anything is that way or not. I want to trust what I'm saying, even if it can only be 'good morning' and 'good night'."

"I always gave them back their words," said Jack. "I never thought to do anything else. Never."

Shifting his eyes toward the ceiling and nodding, C. J. returned to the stove, blindly spooned the potatoes onto two paper plates, poured the bacon grease back into the pan, and turned up the heat. As the grease began to steam, he looked down at it, broke six eggs into the pan, and smiled as the whites sizzled, bubbled up, and turned brown. He then speared the eggs with a fork and lifted them onto the mounds of potatoes and bacon. "I've never known anybody else to cook this way, but it's how I like eggs to be fried," he said, putting the plates on the table. "You don't have to eat them, if you don't want to."

"They look fine, C. J."

"They're going to taste like plastic."

"I don't care."

"I don't want anything to drink. Do you?"

"No."

"Anything else?" C. J. asked, settling into a chair.

"I'm all right."

"Maybe I shouldn't have told you. About the lying."

"I'm glad you told me," said Jack. "But, C. J., I don't know how you could've lied that much at Yale. You almost said just a minute ago that you hardly ever talked then."

"That's partly why I didn't. Whenever I'd start to, I'd likely be making up whatever I was telling…"

"I guess I trusted people more than you did. I don't know. I…C. J., ever since my father was East…You hear about the ignoring in the towns beside the concentrations camps. You hear a lot about that. It seems so close to impossible. But home seems even worse than those towns do to me now. How can I think any other way? There's the same ignoring, the same pretending, the same lies, the same following tracks nobody questions, the same doing incredible evil people have convinced themselves is good, or at least is necessary. So much of what I am is what they made me. I don't know how to separate myself from all of it. And I want to. I've got to. Only it's like I'm trying to use my right hand to amputate my right arm. Things seemed so normal there, so peaceful even. But when I think about what's been going on all along, it feels like the top of my head is about ready to fly off; and sometimes I want it to, C. J. I don't know what to say about lying, when I look at how much of it I've been around. Lies are what built that town and what kept it together. My father says he didn't have any choice. They'd all say that. But it didn't have to happen the way it did. They made their choices themselves.... We can face what went on in the towns by the concentration camps, because that's all far enough away from us. What happened where I lived...there may not be anyone left to judge."

"I don't think you can do anything about it," said C. J. "I think just living out however long we'll get to and trying not to let them in your way is all there is."

"I don't agree with that. I don't agree with that at all. Not only there, but everywhere else it's going on, whatever country it's going on in, something somehow has got to force them to reverse what they're doing."

"It's too far gone. They've taken away every reason there ever was to plan for anything at all..."

"C. J., what about the draft? What *are* you going to do?"

"Let them send me to jail."

"Five years?"

"There's nothing else left."

"Maybe they won't start to classify you until you're twenty-four. You could be in the Peace Corps by then."

"They won't wait that long. I might miss it by a couple of months, but that'll be enough. I can feel it coming."

"If you had a letter like that written for you, the people you work with would find out about it, wouldn't they?"

"Sure they would...They'd find out about it right away...And that'd make it easy for them to call all the changes coming at them crazy. I'd be making things worse for a lot of us, not just me."

"If you could get across the border, there'll be amnesty when the war's over. There has to be."

"The Canadian government claims there's too many gone up there. People already are beginning to be shipped back to the United States."

Loosing an extended sigh of grim and explosive bewilderment, Jack pressed his palms flat on the table and said, "Every week, most everybody hears the words for almost every kind of killing and dying. If there are ways of talking about how people are supposed to care for each other, I don't know what they are."

"Do you think we can find any?"

"Do you think we should try to, C. J.?"

"Yeah, I...Yeah, probably. Probably."

PART IV

13 Solicitous Exchange

Numbly C. J. sat down on a bench, stuck his legs straight out to the sidewalk circumscribing a pond on the western flank of Boston Common, leaned back, momentarily relished the cool of the breeze on his neck and shoulders where until that morning his hair had been, removed from his shirt pocket a ballpoint pen, opened a loose-leaf notebook, and printed on the first page: *To Whom It May Concern.*

Resigned and less afraid than he had been earlier in the day, he looked at the words, crossed them out, tore away the page, crumpled it, tossed it into a nearby trash can, and on the next page printed:

October 23, 1966

Dear potential other people:

'If I go slowly, I will not have to change anything. I don't want to have to copy it over. However it should be, I can get it that way, so long as I do not go too fast.'

Closing the notebook, he stood, and as cautiously as if he carried a reliably accurate dowsing stick, paced a straight line toward the easternmost corner of the pentagonal park. Counting his steps, he stopped walking at forty-five, grazed his fingertips against the bark of a maple tree beside him, found the warmest side of the trunk, smiled, eased himself to the ground, and reclined full-length on a patch of bluegrass and clover, stubbornly green in the late October chill.

'I've never seen anyone painting them again. Not up there or anywhere.'

After trying out various positions and estimating the durations of their comforts, he rolled over onto his stomach, hooked his left arm under his right shoulder, inclined his outstretched feet toes-downward, opened the notebook, and again began to print, using every other line of the page:

> I am writing to you from Boston Common. Before me are reminders of the history that has provided the reasoning allowing you to control much of my future. I am writing to you because you have this power, although I have not met any of you and am unable to find out any of your names. I do not even know how many of you there are. I only know you are more than one.

Putting down his pen, he weighed the possibility of getting up and taking his notebook to the Park Street Church half a block away, decided to stay where he was until he had completed his writing, seized a fallen twig, and used it systematically to remove the signs of autumn from the green carpet surrounding him, stabbing dry leaves and bunching them together with elaborate and playful care. As soon as he had succeeded in clearing all the space on every side of him for as far as he could reach, he pushed the stick into the ground close to his left shoulder, took up his pen with his right hand, and went on:

> Likewise, all of us whose lives you have the authority to affect are almost anonymous to you. I am using my constitutional right to fill in some of the gaps the statistics to which you have access rest upon.

In spite of our mutual, virtual anonymity, I am asking you to consider certain aspects of the nature of our shared humanity. The translatable word *we* can apply to all humans.

Having arrived at the end of the page, he ripped it away from its spiral binding, held it up in the air, and read it intently. Finding the words so carefully printed he was certain there could be no mistaking any of them, he folded the single piece of paper and lodged it in the back of the notebook.

'I better not tear any more out or the breeze'll take them. Like it was turning skywriting into clouds.'

Because I have been out of college for nearly a year, I am sure you are currently considering my classification. I am also sure there is little, if anything, I can say that could change the ways you affect so many lives. But even so, the common bonds of our humanity compel me to address you as well as I can, using the complete truth in so far as it is related to your anonymous power over me.

'I wouldn't need much land. Only enough for a small garden. Anywhere on earth. So long as things would grow. Lots of wild plants are good to eat. Just because farming took everything over for awhile, we don't have to keep on getting food only from that. It doesn't have to be one or the other. We gave up too many good ways of surviving and stopped too many people from doing what we should start in doing again ourselves. The size of land I'd need would be less than most backyards.'

I'm supposed to fit myself to you. You're not supposed to fit yourselves to me or to any of us. You've already done a lot to me, and you haven't had to contact me directly to do it. I've been trying to find out how to make a decent life, and all I've had to turn to have been the uncertainties you've caused. I can't put off any longer telling you how much of nearly one of my years you've had.

You have made it impossible for my employers to think I'd be staying. So there's almost nothing I've been able to learn from any of them. My nights have been taken up with wondering what to do about you whose names I do not know, nor how many of you there are.

I am unable to flatter you or try to convince you of anything by making light of what we're involved in together. I want you to know you have left me only the capacity to offer you contempt for what you do and who you must be to do it.

All that our common humanity will allow me is to give you my contempt and to explain it.

'I would use a set of tetrahedrons like Alexander Graham Bell's. Only bigger. Four-sided pyramids with two sides open. If they were strong enough, the pyramids could be the rooms of a small house with the windows already built-in. Whether the rooms would fly would depend on how many parts there were more than on the size. Make it out of spun-bonded olefin. Nothing can tear that. It'd be better than a tent. There couldn't be enough snow to weight through olefin.'

All over the earth when I was born there was blood.

When I try to think how many people that blood was from, I wonder how any of you who were around then can know anything for yourselves but sorrow and shame.

Fear has been ruling our lives for as long as I can remember. And maybe it's really been terror, not fear. There's not many who could face it being terror and still go on living. Hope has been making the difference between terror and some of the fear for sure, and maybe the hope has just been from pretending.

There's been so much fear that most people have kept tied up inside themselves opinions they've had about anything. Lots of times people have been afraid to find out what their opinions even are. You make fear. You use it like it was decent. I'd like to be able to give you something else instead of my contempt.

I know what you assume I am, which is my name and my age and that I'll do what you'd tell me. I know you expect me to close my mind up completely out of fear, so you can let yourselves think I'm another of the ones who wants to defend you. The truth of you making us do it, you don't look at. That's how you get an illusion of self-respect. Which is like buying a present for yourself and pretending it came from somebody else. Except what you're buying with is our blood that's still inside us; and our blood can't bring you anything, if you put it on the earth, but more sorrow and shame. I hope I can find some way to show you that, whoever you are.

I also know what you want me to become. I know you want to cut me off from my better self before I've had a chance to use it much. You want me to join you in your shame. I will not let you force me into doing that. If you try to make me join you, you can succeed only in driving me further away from you and from the people you represent. My contempt for you has already started to spread outward to those who give you leave to do what you do.

You cannot help but make me think that wisdom and humane concern are not guiding the lives of those who are older than myself. You make me wonder if there can be wisdom any-where anymore. You make me wonder if all wisdom bled from us during the time I was born. How can a man who has killed, as you would have him, ever be wise? Or ever love again? I know that now there are many fathers who have killed. But I cannot look to them for wisdom. I think they long ago gave up or had taken from them their capacities to love. When they were my age and facing anonymous figures such as you in all their nations, they joined you by paying the price of their hope in their own futures. Since then they have made a science and an art devoted to the destruction of themselves and of us all. They are the burdens of their children, as you seek to make us burdens for those who might be born.

I don't have to carry your shame yet, and neither do most of the people whose lives hang upon your decisions. We still deserve so much more than you offer us that our only alternative is to find each other without regard to your national boundaries and assure ourselves first, of the possibility of a future, and then of worthy lives within it.

I cannot submit to your demands for the betrayal of myself, and in this inability I merit the respect of whatever can remain of the best of your humanity.

Laying aside his pen, C. J. turned over on his back and, large-eyed, gazed upward at a thick, gray lid of clouds and smoke.

'I wouldn't need to be on the water. Just near it is all. Even a pond would do. One kite for fishing could last me all my life. If it was made out of plaited leaves and bamboo, it could be used on any water there is and'd go further than the longest casts ever could. It wouldn't take many kites like that for plenty of people to be able to live on a supply of fish that'd increase because all the tools the kites would stop the making of would help clear the waters again. Except for the water already lost forever for anything to live in.'

Sitting up, he crossed his legs, rested the notebook in his lap, and continued:

Most people have no capacity to negotiate how they spend their working days. Wages and prices kept them caught long enough at the beginning for them to lose a sense of wanting to do what they started out wanting. In this basic way what you say and they repeat about how free we live has not much reality in the details of lives. People get home so dulled by unchosen routines that they can't bring much charity to anyone. People treated with pretended respect at work bring pretended respect back to their families. Not many of us can take pride in what we do. A lot of us know how unnecessary so much of it is compared with what we need. You take advantage of this lack of pride just like you take advantage of fear. And you turn them both into narrow kinds of loyalties toward a small number of people inside a national boundary. You use the same methods whatever country you belong to. You try to make us forget the most important loyalty there is, which is a loyalty to everyone alive. It is my loyalty to you that can grant you only contempt.

Lots of people around me are so confused and afraid and lacking pride that they judge themselves and each other not by what they do or by the quality of what they have but by how much they have of what they do not need and do not use. The goals you represent are so wrong that people lose sight of decent goals. All they can think is that a higher price tag means a better-lived life. That's looking at the size of the steps without giving any thought to where the staircase is leading.

Also, a number of small-to-large businesses and wider-or-narrower-than-national organizations have already taken up (which means more than "have supported") your methods and may soon be adding nuclear weapons to their stockpiles of pistols and rifles made for murder or wounding rather than for getting food.

'Something like a geodesic dome. Built so the pieces could be taken off and flown. Part of the walls made of Marconi sails. Vents doubling as windows. A wau bulon over the door shaping the top of the entrance like a new moon.'

I sit here in Boston Common very aware of the small bit of human past relating me to you. I think how much of that past has to be ignored to accept what you make out should be glorified. I know the racism that makes the United States at least two countries. I remember the fires of our cities these past summers set by people tired of hollering that what you say about equal opportunity isn't true. I remember how much of the land making up this nation came from broken treaties, rifles, and empty words. I suppose you're so used to knowing about promises no one intended to keep that you can read about the sorrow connected with those broken promises as easily as you read the scores of basketball games.

I sit here and think of Thomas Jefferson saying that a standing army is something no nation should have. The way it is now, that's pretty much all we are: one big standing army defending only the routines of its own defense.

What you're doing is readying us to use what we've been paying for and building since I was born. What you do serves to open the way.

People have always said that new weapons would function as deterrents to using them. But the weapons have always been used after the spaces of time people have taken to ready themselves for the using. Exactly like you are readying us now. People said the same thing about dynamite that you say about nuclear weapons. I think you are readying us to use those nuclear weapons, because you will not face the shame of the deaths and miseries you have already caused. The only way you can see to end that shame is to end yourselves and the rest of us with you.

I am obligated to speak of the present conflict you are forcing people to participate in. Getting elected on a promise not to bomb North Vietnam, then right away sending in the planes, the President treated us all like the people of the Great Plains were treated. Since his election we have been involved in such a confused tangle of misunderstandings with so many different stories told about what is going on where the troops are, that it's likely none of you even know who the enemy we're supposed to be fighting is. It's likely we're creating the enemy ourselves. In other times such ignorance would have been incredible; but in our times it's just another in a series of happenings we've made ourselves used to, no matter how monstrous they are. That you require us to accept your ignorance as knowledge and ask us to kill for it is what fuels your shame.

'Or it could be a cygnet. Big enough so that in the right wind the whole house could fly. And I could rig a box kite like a lobster cage. Put grain inside. Send it up from a field. Angle it close to the woods. Reel in a quail.'

I wouldn't deny that some people in other countries are a threat to me. But so are you a threat to me. It's the putting together of people within borders to which they give their loyalties that is the main threat to our common survival. You are some of the ones who do that putting together. At the same time, people like you in other countries are building against our power and each other's power, and emphasizing separate loyalties, instead of facing how alike we all are and finding ways to live well together.

I don't know why it is that the majority of people this century have chosen to obey you instead of looking at their similarities. But so far that's what most people have done. I'm not going to.

We should have pride stemming from being decently human instead of having a pride based on wherever we happen to be living. The human race is a commune that hasn't yet recognized its nature or found its linking forms.

'I'd experiment with the weight of the wood and the coverings of cellular Conyne triangles, so I could turn them into shelves that'd be sturdy and light.'

If the way of life that's talked of in the United States is really best, then that should be showable by power of reason. People shouldn't have to be napalmed into agreeing with what we say.

Our one chance, not only for decent survival, but for survival itself, lies in developing international law. Since the United States, in its violations of agreements relating to Southeast Asia, is threatening the existence of this network of law, what you are asking is that I participate in further damaging, if not in eliminating, the only hope there is. This I will not do.

I've backed away from most commitments in my life because your examples made me know only what I did not want to be. What you mean by courage is really the loss of the capacity to go one's own way. You mean the ability to carry out orders whatever they are, be they given on a battlefield or in a factory. And you mean using our capacities for violence. You don't associate courage with affections. I do. Affections are the roots of real courage.

Having been born in the blood you shed, how could I have anything but distrust toward your forms that purport to give religious and legal sanctions to my affections? There are others my age who distrust you as well. I write from a strength starting to exist because of relationships with people for whom I care. We are discovering what we can and should do to enhance each other's lives. We are discovering what obligations to each other we have. Your social forms aren't needed to release or guide our affections.

There is a vivid contrast between what you want me to do—kill—and what I am learning to do with others—combine affections with pleasure.

I have written of your shame and sorrow and have offered in opposition my working toward an integrity based on an identification with the purely human. I have contrasted forms of power with forms of friendship and love. I cannot accept your turning around of standards—a turning around that amounts to saying it is bad to murder a person in this nation but good to murder a person in another nation because the latter murder has been done by a warrior with proper loyalties. There is nothing courageous or noble about deaths on battlefields. Such deaths result from the failure to work together. The failure to build with and for each other. What you glorify is the cutting down of a tree instead of all the years it took for the tree to grow.

Murder is murder. In every case it removes us further from our better selves. In every case deep-seated feelings of guilt are merited. You ask me to ready myself for such guilt. I will not do it. Nor will I accept the load of guilt I am sure you would require of me for the ways I have thus far learned to care for others.

With a free heart I am giving you evidence that in the midst of such a whirlwind of fears as all of us know and you continue to fuel, there can be tenderness coupled with honesty. I send you signs of the future to which I will not bring the guilt that would result from what you would have me do. What strength I have is a gentle strength, a loving strength; and it is gaining integrity. It is a strength based on mutually discovered insights. No matter how you misview my strength, you are going to succeed in warping it only in your own minds. The images you demand we apply to ourselves do not fit us, are based on denials of large portions of our natures, and turn the good we might do into evil. You ask us to feel guilty over pleasure and to kill with clean consciences. What you ask is obscene. That lots of you, if not all of you, combine asking us to kill, with your going to church on Sundays or synagogues on Saturdays is likely insane.

Everyone needs everyone else in order to survive. We can never know what an individual life will give to the rest of us. Destroying that life eliminates the possibility of what that life can bring. Damaging it weakens the possibility. That is why war is wrong.

'I'd take an H-form three stick. A small one'd do. Put a string between the bottom two spines. Fold a piece of rice paper in half and glue it over the string, so the two paper edges would flap. Tie on a set of bells and some hollow chimes. At the top attach two parchment disks, so they'd rotate and set off sticks that'd strike miniature drums strapped to the frame. Wind would carve the melody and height would adjust the volume. Different-sized, carved whistles, placed just right, could even make a scale.'

Every day we grow less able to breathe and to see. The earth is hardly real to most of us anymore. Some places already the black rains do more damage than would a long drought from which the land could at least someday find renewal. It's like we're turning all that's around us into a tomb. Just when we've got things arranged so as to be able to negotiate a couple of more contracts, add a few devices, then have the chance to pick up a phone to reach anyone on earth, you make it look like it'll all have amounted to an unmade call. You want us to fire rifles when we should be learning languages to use for exploring each other's ways and for sharing production techniques of necessities. You hold onto ideas that crush inspiration and love, and you want us to preserve those ideas by destroying what's different instead of learning and teaching with each other all over the earth.

You make us unwilling to look at the simple truth that hungry people could eat if we would share with them what we let rot or do not grow when we could. Those people we might be helping, even those in our own cities, get desperate, they're so hungry. That's when you make out they are the enemy. But the enemy is yourselves. Because of what you do not face and do not choose to do.

The prosperity of the United States has been tied up with both the political ideas and the abundance of land. You give the ideas too much credit. You refer to what's spoken of rather than to what's practiced. You say it's the ideas you're fighting to protect and bring to other nations, but you're really fighting to keep the abundance of the land for yourselves.

If there is a scale of human savagery, you and your counterparts in other countries make up the most savage group there has ever been or probably ever can be, even though you're often removed from the results of your savagery and from open participation in it.

Being civilized is to represent the best that humankind has managed. To think of yourselves as civilized is to deny all human standards of decency. You are involved in attempting to bring about the end of humanity. Nothing could be more savage than that. You can sit and read 'attempting to bring about the end of humanity' and not feel anything, because you've probably known you've been doing that for a long time.

How can you think of yourselves as civilized when you've almost eliminated many of our possibilities for goodness and awareness and proper construction of tools and social forms? Your armaments don't represent the maintenance of strength. They represent the greatest possible folly. Your power over us, not just in this nation, but in many others as well, has reversed progress. The existence of your weaponry has more than begun to make it evident to anyone who can still think about what you have done that what you mean by being civilized is being in a sorrier state than what you call 'undeveloped people' could be in or could ever have been in. You are the true savages.

I will not let you shape my will.

Every person will add to the destiny of us all. If each one took a course similar to mine instead of to yours, there would be no more war.

In spite of how you make it look, war always comes from individuals collectively deciding to fail to meet their proper responsibilities to each other. It is only after the battles that you throw people back on themselves and show them what they have given up and lost for the rest of their lives.

'Cut patterns into a brayer. Ink it. Roll on one design over all the surfaces or a separate design for each section. By making more cuts or holding the brayer in a different way, I could change the look of the whole house whenever I tried to. There'd be no end to patterns.'

The Nuremberg trials provided an insufficient indictment of war. The precedents of the trials were helpful in emphasizing individual responsibility. But they also served to leave in dark, unjudged shadows the acts of people like yourselves, so that you would not have to publicly or privately confront the implications of your guilt and so you could continue on in apparent innocence with your, at best deluded and at worst evil, ways and preparations. It is with initial acceptance of war as necessary that one's guilt begins. One's capacities for good, properly responsible decisions end when allegiance to wrong goals is given.

The Nuremberg precedents make it appear that a passenger riding in a car heading north could still be going south by turning around and looking backwards. I'm not going to get inside your car. I'm going to walk in the opposite direction.

If those of us on all sides do as I am doing, your triumph over us will not be possible anymore. It's always been you, wherever you have been, who have had the victories over the rest of us, no matter how much you've made it seem like it has been separate nations triumphing over one another. Your victories always begin with getting us to join you. You convince us to agree to put national boundaries above our common humanity.

I will not let you use patriotic slogans to force me to fail to recognize the quantity of your power and its nature.

As the bells of Park Street Church pealed out three o'clock, C. J. realized that he had not noticed their ringing at any time during the hours of his writing. He could feel the final sentences inside him but did not know what they would be. Nor did he yet know whether he had been composing pages he would tear up as the day cooled to evening or pages of a letter he would mail inside a large, addressed stamped envelope he had folded into his jacket pocket before leaving his apartment. He did not yet know whether he had been intending to communicate his thoughts or to clarify them for himself.

Drowsily he set his pen on the grass, relaxed his fingers, ran his hand over his shaven head, and watched two children on bicycles circle the pond beside him. Colored crepe paper streamers tied to the fenders rose and fell in the wake of their sidewalk path, as Boston prepared for the first snow of fall.

People need very little: food, shelter, and clothing. The means exist now to provide these for everyone alive. Doing that should be our common goal. I would like to work with you toward this goal. We could increasingly define the limits of what we know and abandon the ignorances that have impeded the processes of scientific discovery and have aligned so much of experimentation with death. We could loosen the patterns of social relationships and, through explorations and dialogues and agreements, could create new forms of abiding loves and friendships.

You ask me to participate in ruination and waste, but what I ask is that you begin to help create and find the best means of our common survival. You will always have your shame and sorrow and guilt, but there is no reason for you to go on adding to them. If you desire that we should come to suffer as much as you and that our hopes should be beaten down as much as yours have been, I can only ask for your mercy, not only for myself but also for all those whose lives you affect.

My challenge, and it is yours as well if you could accept it as such, is the creation of a humane civilization limited only by earth.

'A Char-volant carriage drawn by two kites traveled well enough on dirt. It'd work better on the roads we have now. I could use it to get from the land to the water and to the fields by the woods. There'd be no pollution, because the wind would be the only fuel.'

What you do maims those it does not kill so much that their sleep is unquiet. Their consciences cannot give them peace. The human mechanisms for destruction are called forms of defense in every nation; but the processes of building and maintaining them, coupled with the threat of using them, have almost eliminated the possibility of having much that they are said to defend.

Again, I would like to be able to offer you more than contempt; but until you cease your slaughter I cannot. I will struggle against you and against what you represent however I can, but you will not reduce me to using your methods. Our common humanity demands that I oppose you, but not that I fight you. I would like to work with you, but I cannot do so until your goals and techniques are transformed into ways of living that would serve our survival.

You can get me killed, but you cannot break my will.

Standing, C. J. stretched, scratched his back, bent down, picked up the stick with leaves he'd earlier impaled, and tossed it into a branched fork of the maple tree. Then he ambled to the edge of the pond, soaked his hands in the water, shook his fingers dry, and wearily walked to the western end of the Common. Empty of emotion and with no capacity for further thought, feeling only the absence of his hair against his ears and on his shoulders, he there stopped and stared across the street at the Massachusetts statehouse for nearly five minutes, before opening his notebook and reading his own words.

By the time he had finished reading the last page, the streetlights were on; and the chapel chimes had tolled seven o'clock. Still undecided what he would do with what he had written, he began to wander south in search of a grocery store or a restaurant. But when he arrived at the corner of Beacon and Walnut Streets, he saw in the gutter a muddied newspaper containing an upturned photograph of a young Vietnamese woman whose bones were scarcely all that remained to support her outcry. Without reading the adjoining headline, for he had seen—as by October of 1966 had a probable majority of people in the United States—many such pictures and had read many of the words accompanying them, he turned around, climbed back up a two-block-long, Beacon Street hill, stopped upon reaching a postal box bolted to the sidewalk in front of the statehouse, and balanced his notebook on the top of the box. After signing his name on each of his printed pages, he tore the pages away from the binding, folded them together once, put them in the envelope, and sealed it.

For a moment he contemplated returning to the bench by the pond and there tearing the letter into shreds. But the night was cold. He was hungry. And he wanted to get home.

Resolutely he opened the mailbox, dropped the envelope inside, walked east a block along Park Street to the subway entrance, and joined the blending crowds of the terminal.

The following month, C. J. received in the mail official notification that the members of his draft board had, on the basis of his letter, unanimously determined him to possess insufficient sanity for military service.

14 Soul-force

1

Amid the wake following the transfer of a residency from one community to another, it may not be very unusual to experience a temporary disorientation wherewith the myriad dilemmas of relocation are accompanied by brief interludes during which the features of strangers and memories of faces familiar in former surroundings become merged in such a way so as to make it appear that acquaintances from the past have inexplicably associated themselves with the new environment. Such perceptual discomfiture may customarily wane after several months, when enough introductions have been made, enough names have been learned, for the community newcomer to begin to feel at home.

In connection with moving from Connecticut to Massachusetts, Jack had been subject over the summer of 1966 to this variety of confusion of person and place; he had assumed it to have been a normal, transitory side effect of the processes of reorientation and had been neither bewildered nor discouraged by it. During his first term of law school, however, his intervals of dislocation, instead of subsiding, had increased in frequency, lengthened in duration, and taken on other forms. While acquainting himself with the Boston area, he had often seemed to recognize not only

students he had known at Yale, but also people from his distant past
whom he had not thought of since leaving Colorado. When attending a
concert or a movie, he had upon occasion become erroneously convinced
that some of the performers had been anonymously mingling with the
audience. In subways he had sometimes misapprehended passengers
whose images he had been under the impression he had seen on television
or in magazine advertisements. Twice he had initiated street corner
conversations with people whom he had erred in believing had been
referred to in legal cases he had been studying. Eventually, he had been
forced, simply by the frequency of their appearances, into full awareness
of his sustained tendencies toward mistaken identifications; and when
alone he resolutely had vowed to put an end to them. Nonetheless, each
time he had allowed himself to re-enter the crowds of the city, he once
again had suffered the selfsame misjudgments.

As the semester had progressed, Jack also had come to experience
recurrent, numb lapses of memory, forgetfulnesses that had become
more pronounced and inclusive with every attempt he had made to
defeat them and that finally had grown so encompassing they had
reduced him to virtual insensibility at the times of his examinations. It
had been, therefore, no surprise to him when his semester grades had
consigned him to the lower quarter of his class. By the beginning of the
new term in February he had lost considerable weight; his cheeks had
become sallow; and he had acquired the habit of continually keeping his
head bowed, intending thereby to assure himself that no one would be
able to look into his eyes.

Having persisted in his explorations of materials devoted to religious
subjects, he had focused his attention largely on imported variations of
Eastern mysticisms relying on meditative techniques to affirm a sanctity
unavoidably diluted across the geographical, epochal, and linguistic distances
separating the ancient sources from the contexts of novice practitioners in the
United States. He had not been alone that year in his newfound emphasis.
For within a social atmosphere characterized both by national news magazine

covers rendered pictureless to display the question "Is God Dead?" and by newspaper statements of petition reading only, "In the Name of God, Stop the Bombing," diverse religious approaches attributed to the East had been impermanently adopted by an uneasy multitude of Westerners, many of whom had reluctantly decided that the traditional three faiths of their heritage had been having no salutary effects in Southeast Asia.

Public statements on any side of issues once said to be pertinent to the deployment of United States troops in the spiraling war had apparently nearly ceased by January of 1967, perhaps because many people had by then become aware that contradictory versions of the nature of the struggle had been placed into circulation by numerous, diverse sources. An exception in this news-media-portrayed climate of support or opposition without explanation had been the Reverend Martin Luther King, Jr., who had announced at winter's end that in New York City on Saturday the fifteenth of April he would lead a march from Central Park to United Nations Plaza where there would be a rally at which he would deliver an address expounding a theme meant to clarify the interrelationships among the allied phenomena of racism, militarism, and poverty. He would, he had said, seek to consolidate people from every sector of the national population into a potent union of rational and effective protest.

Late in the afternoon on the day before the scheduled rally, Jack spontaneously decided to attend it, having earlier heard that within an armory in Harlem sleeping space would be provided for anyone, a rumor widely circulated on the Eastern Seaboard. His car, unasked for, had been shipped to him by his parents several months earlier; but he did not feel well enough acquainted with New York City to drive it there; and so he quickly took instead the subway to downtown Boston, got on a bus, and at nine-thirty that evening debarked at the Port Authority Terminal in central Manhattan.

The anxieties of law school had melted away from him during the lulling ride; and he had been substantially heartened by the gossamer prospect of the formation of a broad coalition that would be in harmony with, that would espouse, his own highly abstract concerns. Along with thousands of others, he had been drawn toward Central Park, hazily gripped by the conviction that a multitude of inequalities and attendant torments were shortly to disappear in the midst of a nonviolent but vast and speedy revolution—a revolution that would bring about at last the triumphs of justice and love and friendship and peace.

Leaving the bus station lobby in a mood of intemperate reverie dependent not only upon his denial of the depth and intensity of his multifarious rage but also upon his mistaking, for the probabilities of what will happen, lucid analyses of what should, he noticed that for the first time in months he could raise his eyes; and there seemed to him no reason at all for the best and most abiding of his dreams not to become realities on the morrow. His mind hummed with the thrill of considering equitable distributions of affluence and the development of social structures that would assure universal dignity by tapping the untold creative potentials within every human soul. Only a brittle innocence, too sophisticated to be termed naïveté but radiant enough to resemble nobility, kept his chimerical state from becoming ludicrous, as he proceeded to do what at the time they had been roommates at Yale he had heard C. J. repeatedly say a wealth of anthropological evidence might suggest it may be rare for a person at any time in any place to do: he proceeded to take the explicit, central tenets of his culture seriously.

"Can you tell me where the Harlem armory is?" he ebulliently inquired of a man huddled against a darkened window frame on West 41st Street.

"Oh, yeah sure," answered the man, street-wise and world-weary. "You just take the 7th Avenue subway to 125th, get out, and walk east. That's all you've got to do."

"Thanks a lot," said Jack, feeling himself to be partaking of a sublime goodwill that forthwith would enwrap all the corners of his life. "I appreciate it," he added, thinking, And what is a stranger then, but yet another face of God?

"You just walk east," said the man, as he pointed to a subway stop. "Just keep on heading east."

Always before, Jack had found the Times Square subway terminal a maze of tunnels, lights, and arrows to be moved amongst as quickly and as anonymously as possible; but there was time for ease now, time for relaxation; and after calmly descending the entrance stairs, he wandered slowly from sign to sign, smiling benignly, pleased by the sight of all the people destined to be awestruck that their near fatal irrationalities had possessed them for so long.

With neither pride nor arrogance to demean his expectancy of a massive communion that would preserve and augment individual liberties guaranteed by political assumptions and religious traditions, and with an innocence both restricted to benighted dimensions and strengthened by an unawareness of the fragile qualities of its own scanty discernments, he soon arrived at the 125th Street subway stop and stepped outside.

Being in a section of the city with which he was thoroughly unfamiliar served at once to heighten his sense of mystic involvement with immanent and lasting change. Indeed, he felt he must surely be commencing the successful separation from his past that he had been longing to achieve for almost a year. Since there would be plenty of time to sleep, east on the island being no further than a shore he had seen on other nights, though assuredly from locations south of 110th Street, it was merely a minor irritation to him when he realized that, thinking he had been beckoned on by enclosed neon, he had been heading west for a quarter of an hour.

As he neared the Apollo Theater twenty minutes later, having both reversed the direction of his path and quite lost his capacity to recognize that he was very tired, he told himself confidently that if he should be unable to find the armory, he could after all knock on any door, or ring any bell, request shelter of any passerby. For does not everyone, he thought, need, at times, warmth, rest, and a welcome based solely on anonymously shared humanity? And will we not be prepared at other times to give whatever it will be in our power to give simply because we will be aware of someone else's needs? Are we not all brothers and sisters, pursuing happinesses authorized by self-evident and providentially graced truths?

After maintaining his eastern course on 125th Street for more than an hour, he was no longer sure whether he was in a business or a residential district or even if there were such distinctions in Harlem or for that matter if there were such distinctions in all of New York City. But ahead there was a sign blinking *Cafe*, and although the window beneath it was heavily curtained, the doorway on the other side of it was lighted and open. Inspired, ingenuous, and serene, Jack ambled off the sidewalk and through the doorway.

The walls, furniture, and curtains of the room he entered were a deep red and turquoise aggregate seemingly sewn together by a wide, golden thread. A sole saxophone player lullabyed patterns akin to those of the jazz associated with James P. Johnson. Sapphire silk and amethyst velvet, held in place by silver and gold chains appearing to Jack to be more swept onto bodies than worn, had been creased into combinations of elegance and abandon. Feathers were looped from tops of heads to breasts, and flowers were pinned to many of the lapels. Pink and white striped sport coats edged over black leather pants intercepting parti-colored shoes shined so brightly they configured upon the floor a glowing, mosaical pattern.

As Jack stood in the doorway, there was a second of silence, so brief a pause that, although during it most of the eyes in the room had impassively converged upon him, he had been unaware that he had as yet been observed. Seeing an empty table near him, he went to it and, watchful, waiting, silently sat down in one of its chairs, bowing his head.

After several minutes of finding himself unattended by any of the waiters moving about the room, he finally raised his head and asked, loudly enough for a corpulent and affably chuckling man at a table next to him to hear, "Can you tell me something?"

"I don't know," replied the man with apparent friendly unconcern. His huge, round cheeks dominated his face. His eyes sported beneath his forehead like sunning insects.

"Can you tell me where the armory is?"

"He wants to know where the armory was," said the man to a hovering waiter, who answered with an eclipsed nod. "The armory!...Give this boy a glass of cold water. He looks about dried out. You want something to eat, boy."

"I don't think so," said Jack, exhausted, amiable. "Water'll be fine."

"He said a glass of plain water'll be helpful, sir," said the man to faces that had become attentive on all sides of him and Jack. "Well, now," he continued, "I'd guess you to be a college student. You a student in college?"

"I was in college," said Jack, loosening his coat collar. "...I'm at Harvard Law School now."

"Harvard Law School. He says he's from Harvard Law School. You bring me any bill this boy gets for himself. Any bill at all."

"I really don't think I want anything. I just came in here to...get my bearings...to.... I came to New York to listen to Martin Luther King, Jr. talk tomorrow. That's why I want to find the armory. I need a place to stay."

"'Sleep at the armory,' he has said. Sleep at the armory! Martin Luther King, Jr. will be speaking somewhere tomorrow. Wants to know if I'm going? Wants me to come with him...Well now what do you expect that that King going to tell us this time, young man from Harvard Law School?"

"I suppose," answered Jack earnestly, "he'll say that if enough of us get together, we can end war, end racism, end poverty, end all wrongful prejudices. That if enough of us get together, we can build a civilization based on friendship, and trust, and creating together. I suppose he'll say some of the ideas behind the Declaration of Independence and the Constitution can be translated into how we live, if we want them to be."

Gradually letting his acicular teeth be revealed, the man turned then, stood, and fully facing Jack, asked with a voice filled with sudden surprise not just at the presence of a white face in the restaurant but even more at having himself in a moment of unusually quick intensity been touched by the extreme sincerity Jack clearly radiated, "Oh, *yes,* and oh, why is it all at once I can't tell who you are by the white of your face?" Throwing up his hands, abruptly the man unleashed in a kind of paroxysm of amazement a yell so titanic it immediately incited a nearby companion to jump to his feet, point both his fists toward the ceiling, and let out a second yell. In an instant the two bellowing forms were joined by another man, small and grizzled, who convulsed his limbs and loosed a series of huge sighs.

Changing racial mores were producing that year many similarly bizarre reactions throughout the United States, as long-standing energies of hate, submerged but habitual, collided with newly wrought impulses toward trust (and even affection) starting to bridge in often unusual ways hitherto seemingly impenetrable barriers between peoples.

Jack, however, now felt himself not in any way at all to be breaking through racial barricades but to be recoiling in fear, not in a fear of the three figures before him, nor even in a fear of the dangers inherent in the city, but rather in an all-embracing fear that wrenched through his limbs with a throb it seemed to him must be audible—a fear that had been redoubling inside him since the previous June; and on he sat, dazed in mute suspension.

It was as if he had been climbing a mountain, had reached the summit, and had discovered the view of the environment he had intended to unite himself with to be an array of enormous, interlocking maps, many of which had all at once blown away, revealing the overview of a terrain so different from what he had expected that his capacity to rely on the fabric of his own consciousness, on his own habits of judgment and perception, appeared inviolately to be deserting him, to be vanishing in a self-consuming vertigo evidently potent enough to be capable of eliminating any possibility for reorientation.

As the tumult continued, transfixing the other patrons, as well as the staff, and threatening momentarily to break out amongst them, the lone musician, habituated both to defining and being subject to the disposition of the room of his profession, meandered with his saxophone across the floor and, continuing to play, stood between Jack and the doorway. His bloodshot eyes glittering with a mixture of conclusiveness, exasperation, irony, amusement, and compassion, he lowered his instrument to his chin and stabilized the hush his proximity had invoked by saying, "Don't sleep at the armory, boy; it's too cold there for that. You'd best go on home."

Instantly sliding off the chair and out the door, beginning to walk, Jack had no thoughts, no intentions. In supplanting every other emotion, fear had left him but the resonances of a hollow indifference delimited by the conviction, a normal accompaniment to overriding fear, that none of his past concerns were going to matter to him for awhile. Hearing footsteps behind him, he did not look back, but started to run, angling away from 125th Street in a frantic, zigzag course.

The faint sounds of disembodied voices in conversation, rather than his pounding heart, finally impelled him to slow his gait by forcing him to realize that his frenzied motions had doubtless been highly conspicuous for many minutes on the otherwise deserted sidewalks. Shaking, he held to a lamppost until his breathing grew calm. Then silently he united his path with shadows, following their semblances in lieu of heeding the grid of the streets, moving with primeval instinct toward safety and warmth, even if that meant moving only toward the morning.

While he hurtled onward, all sense of direction gone, the separate compartments of his memory seemed to be acquiring lives of their own, to be liberating themselves from their anesthetized states, and with turbulent momentums to be shattering their walls of division, making him a helpless spectator, as elements of laws of the United States boiled over and combined with Taoism, as chunks of philosophical treatises were shredded by mathematical formulas, as the personages of history mingled amongst contemporary politicians and the members of his family. With an ensuing discord of unintelligible sentences swirling through his mind, he saw on an upcoming corner a phone booth and in a surge of hope, quickened his pace, not noticing until he had lifted the receiver that the severed cord dangled to the sidewalk.

Rage—however socially unacceptable it may be—is seldom purblind; it is, moreover, a worthy opponent of fear. Thus, when the dangling cord immediately ignited Jack's rage, he was not entirely hindered. Dimly comprehending, as he walked on, that at that moment his rage was probably his most reliable inner strand, attached as it was to matters external to him he had been reacting to over a long period of time—racism, militarism, the deceptive atmosphere of his boyhood, he haggardly gave it leave to govern his senses and to orient his course.

But the judiciousness of his rage had little time to be verified. For he had not traveled more than five blocks when a clap of thunder ripped apart the clouds and a rain, which throughout the next day would be apportioned into intervals of equivalent duration, began to fall, establishing at the outset its unorthodox qualities.

None of the sporadic intervals of the rain were introduced by warning drops. Nor did they end with diminutions of energy. They consisted, instead, of stable sheets of water, which descended with uniform intensity and which were dissociated from each other by brief, trucelike haltings. Each sheet seemed to be of equal density. And while they fell, the unrelentingly black sky appeared to have become a roof lined with immense aqueous shingles that were being disjointedly released in a symmetrically punctuated deluge.

The first sheet of water soaked through Jack's coat with ease, causing him to stumble in astonishment, so that the second sheet tore at him prone on the sidewalk. Groping to his feet, he again started to run, careened into an alley, and as if darkness itself might bring shelter, ran on until he descried the side entrance of a vitiated tenement. Leaping up its cement steps to a partially enclosed, wooden threshold, he dropped his shoulders to the floor, wedged his head into a corner, and lying amidst the shadows and the rain, fell asleep in the shrouded aspect of a battered toy in a dilapidated realm where all things, even silences, had been broken.

2

Across the United States there were to be many more antiwar gatherings in upcoming years than anyone may have suspected in 1967. Already the events of protest had come to reflect an increasing hopelessness in regard to altering the course of the war. Often people attended the rallies more to keep their consciences intact than because of expectations that their presences would affect government policies. Each rally grew more rigid, sadder. Each brought more rhetoric, fewer discussions. And each had its own ethos, which was never planned or anticipated but which, nonetheless, was apparent long before most people had arrived at the scheduled place of meeting.

The predominant mood of the kaleidoscopically factioned crowd convening in Central Park on the morning of Saturday the fifteenth of April, 1967, was that of a bizarre festival destined to play havoc with the nightmares of countless, suburban parents. Giant, grotesque, papier-mâché effigies of governmental leaders were carted over the grass and disposed of in makeshift coffins. Skin was painted into illusions of disfiguring, unbandaged wounds. Scores of men and women intimidatingly costumed as warlocks, demons, witches, and vampires danced in procession. Blood-filled pillows were tossed back and forth and emptied into leaking vats.

Although a number of people within the enlarging assemblage were being offended by the highlighted, multiform images of a laughter-denying hysteria, the decision to come to Central Park that day had frequently been determined with painless seriousness rather than with agonized disquiet, and most of the mobilizing gathering stayed on.

Clutching his draft card in his right hand, glancing at it from time to time, but making no move to join any of the groups of men pledging their willingness to share jail sentences and fines, Jack stood alone, contemplating the piles of burning cards that flared amid cheers from throngs hedged round the park. His stance was adamant rather than violent, indicated that he was not to be trifled with rather than that he was aloof, as he felt a hand gently touch the back of his coat.

"Do you want a match?"

"Leah?"

"Have I gotten that thin?"

"Yes," answered Jack, bowing his head and summoning every trace of self-control he could muster.

"Yes, you'd like a match, or yes, I've gotten that thin?"

"Yes, I'd like a match," Jack answered. "It's been awhile since I've seen you."

"I suppose there should be some sort of ceremony," said Leah, holding up a matchbook.

"There's no need for any. It's not an eternal flame."

"These fires seem to me to be making a more suitable memorial. Perhaps it's improper for me to be thinking that."

"It's not improper. But it's probably not true. For every fire, there are lots of stories prepared about how the draft cards got lost or stolen."

"Got your story ready?"

"Not yet."

"Sure you want to go through with burning it?"

"Yes, no," replied Jack, so fatigued and unsettled he was surprised he was able to talk. "What does it matter?"

"I supposed you were considering all the possibilities. I've been watching you for half an hour."

"Why did you wait so long to come over?"

"I didn't know if I had the right. Perhaps you can understand that. Also, if you'll forgive me, you look in the worst shape I've ever seen you. How did your coat get so muddy?"

"I woke up this morning in an alley."

"An alley," Leah said. "Yes."

"It's good to see you."

"Thank you. I..."

"Are you waiting for the speech?"

"I don't know. I was."

"Want to go to the Statue of Liberty or somewhere?"

"The Museum of Modern Art, maybe. Really? An alley?"

"I think I want to get out of the park. I don't want to hear him talk in the rain. Maybe it's cowardice I'm feeling."

"Could be. But, then, there could be some wisdom in your cowardice," said Leah, aware of Jack's dislocation but subscribing it principally to his ordeal of deciding what to do with his draft card. "All right, yes. Let's do leave. Maybe we'll find an Irish-Catholic wedding with tables full of corned beef and cabbage and soda bread. We could pretend to be guests!"

"First the light," said Jack.

"Am I aiding and abetting?"

"Oh, at least."

"To the wind!" Leah said, lighting a match.

"To the wind!" Jack repeated, as he let the burning paper fall upon the grass to the sudden cheer of the people gathered nearby. Shrugging and tentatively beginning to lead the way to Central Park South, he added, "I have never seen such rain."

"Nor have I."

"Are you here for the weekend?"

"Some people I knew from the theater left me their place. There's room for you tonight, if you want. The way the sky has been, the storm could start in again any second. It feels like a time for arks! Maybe we should go to the apartment now. I...Jack, where was the alley?"

"I can't exactly..."

"The building they're in isn't too far from here, using subways."

"I couldn't sleep now anyway, Leah."

"But what about last night?"

"I got lost looking for the Harlem armory. I guess that's how I ought to put it."

"Is that what happened?"

"Leah, I don't...I don't remember enough to say more about it now."

"Then that's enough said."

"And I'm fine."

"I can't do anything but take your word for that, Jack."

"Really, I'm fine. I…I'm just trying to fix this all as real in my mind. I guess I've spent too much time in classrooms. Sometimes I feel like I should've tried to answer all the questions in my mother's letters instead of having gone to college. That's the truth."

"You should tell her that."

"She wouldn't understand what I meant."

"I do, I think…Being in school can be like living in a cellar without windows. Taking turns at periscopes. Is Harvard Law like that?"

"Yes, but the periscopes have colored cellophane over them."

"What about all the time at Yale you worked with the Wagner Act? Was that any help?"

"A little bit, I guess. I don't know if help is the right word. It made me aware how often people think what's internally justified in this country is warranted everywhere on earth…One of my professors calls it the 'whatever-is-good-for-the-United-States-is-good-for-human-nature syndrome'."

"Yes," said Leah, attentive to the spectral reflections in the pools of rainwater amidst which they were walking. "We've kept ignoring values other people have had for centuries."

"One Law School Forum I went to, can you believe this, the topic was, 'Is There Justice in the Military?'"

"Oh, I can believe it easily," replied Leah. "It's another example of people in higher education assuming a discussion can occur in isolation."

"The program had 'Biochemical Religious Sacraments' listed as the next month's forum."

"Did you save a copy of the program?"

"No, I didn't."

"Oh, you should have. It almost sums up the times."

"That's not the sort of memory I want to preserve," replied Jack, confident he could go on speaking but uncertain how much further his deadened legs would be able to carry him.

"It's surprising to me," Leah said, now verging on playfulness, "but I'm starting to regret school's almost over with. I'm more frightened than I had expected to be."

"I can appreciate how you feel," said Jack. As they turned onto Avenue of the Americas, he shook his shoulders back and forth in an attempt to thrash himself into alertness. "I barely made it into the second term. So much is happening, I can't concentrate on the work."

"I suppose that's more admirable than being able to shut most everything out. I don't know anyone who has a decent balance."

"Neither do I."

"I must say it's good to be away for a couple of days…New York always makes me feel like Alice in the Forest of No Names."

"You'd better keep in mind that Wonderland isn't Wonderland to those who live there," said Jack. Seeing they were approaching a vendor with a steaming cart of food, he added, "Leah, I haven't eaten anything since yesterday. I'm going to get a warm croissant. Want one?"

"Sure do," Leah answered, half-curtsying in a parody of coquettish charm. "With orange marmalade, sir."

"Something else, too?"

"No, thanks. Not now."

Jack smiled stiffly, as he ordered and paid; but when he was given two croissants and change, his face became livid; and, his voice quaking and angry, he said to the vendor, "It was a five I gave you!"

With artful graciousness, the vendor impassively waved a dollar bill in front of his hand-painted sign and said, grinning, "A one, sir. A one, sir. A one."

"Oh, well," said Jack, "if it's that important, keep the four dollars. Just keep it."

More amused than startled, taking Jack's arm and continuing to walk with him south on Avenue of the Americas, Leah said, "I got used to short-changers in Los Angeles, Jack. It must've been quite different for you."

"Different, yeah, different," Jack replied, handing Leah a croissant filled with orange marmalade. "Thievery in Colorado involves bigger things."

"More romantic? Or do I have the wrong century?"

"I imagine you do," said Jack. "I imagine you do...Leah, tell me something."

"At your request."

"Does hair stop growing when it gets as long as yours?"

"In effect it does, yes. Why? Have you been waiting ever since we first met for it to touch my toes?"

"I did wonder if it would. Could mine get that long, do you think?"

"I suppose so. If you're patient enough."

"Patience," said Jack, finishing off his croissant. "Even for hair!"

"Yes, I...It does sometimes seem as if everything we want is being dangled in front of our noses in the future, doesn't it?"

"Then by the time we get what we'd wanted, we want something else..."

"I'll tell you what, Jack," said Leah, smiling in an attempt to show she was savoring the last bit of her croissant. "Whenever I think about patience, I think about the Staten Island Ferry."

"Why's that?"

"I hope you don't mind stories of childhood."

"I don't mind."

"Well, in a park near where I lived in Los Angeles, there was a model of the Statue of Liberty. It was very small, made of bronze. Or copper, maybe. After I finished first grade, we took a trip to New York. And when I saw the real statue, I momentarily thought it was the same size as the model. Isn't that amazing? Lots of things must've happened like that, I suppose. We probably forgot them right away. But the reason I remember that one is that I had dried apricot candy on the boat that time. The taste stayed with me; and I kept pestering my father for years, wanting more of the candy. He'd always tell me to be patient. Then my senior year in high school, I was East looking at colleges. We went on the Staten Island Ferry again, and the candy tasted exactly the same…Last time I took the boat, though, they didn't have it anymore…."

"…The Museum of Modern Art is around the next corner," said Jack, so abruptly and distractedly that Leah instantly doubted whether he had been listening to her. "Do you want to go sit in the courtyard or something?"

"I don't think so," she replied, beginning to wonder what methods she might use to induce him into accompanying her to the apartment where she was staying and noting he seemed oblivious to the discordant sounds of traffic, which were appearing unmistakably to her to be beginning that day to express all of the harshness of war and the tensions of protest against it. Leaving the sounds unmentioned, she suggested as buoyantly as she could, "Let's go to Times Square," adding, "The sky would cause anywhere to be depressing today, even the museum. Besides, the croissant has made me hungry."

"Times Square, then," said Jack. Making a decided effort to appear at ease and buoyant, he added, "My parents always used to celebrate New Year's Eve two hours early when 42nd Street came on television."

"All the little images of the big things we finally get to and are at times disappointed by!"

"I'll tell you what happens to me when I'm in New York," said Jack, again appearing not to have been listening. "It's not Wonderland, it's the reminders of how much I've had all my life. Forty people probably occupy the same amount of space in Manhattan that my father and mother and I did at home."

"I expect there are compensations here," Leah said. "You've got to be careful about comparing yourself with a set of theoretical attitudes that you ascribe to…"

"Yes," Jack interrupted. "But, you see, I'm trying to consider the directions I want my life to go. How else am I supposed to find out what I want to do, except by remembering what I've known and comparing it with what I can only guess at?"

"On the other side of those walls," said Leah firmly, "there are strengths that aren't readily apparent, joys even. They couldn't have happened any-where else or under any other conditions. I think that for a long time you've been tending to confuse your own dissatisfactions with how other people feel, Jack. But perhaps I don't really know you well enough to make a judgment like that."

"Say what you think constructively, Leah. Maybe you're right."

"I didn't intend to insult you."

"I don't feel insulted."

"...I know what you mean about how hard it is to plan, though," off-handedly Leah said next, as they walked alongside Rockefeller Center. "I'm only now learning to trust my own decisions. There hasn't been much encouragement for that. I'm sure there hasn't been much for you either. And yet it might be worse for women...I suppose I'll stay on in Boston. I considered moving to Manhattan; but there are too many painters here for me, with as little confidence as I have."

"What've you been drawing these days? Abstract things?"

"Human figures mostly," Leah replied with an air of fragile subtlety. "It's still experimental...The sorts of experiments that are rehearsals."

"You mean you're using models?"

"Not specifically, no. At least not so that anyone knows I've been watching them. What I tend to do now are composite images."

"Composite images...Something like double-exposed photographs?"

"Yes, sort of..."

"I don't know, Leah...It may not seem to you like you have much confidence; but I wish I had anywhere near as much a hold on law as you have on all your art."

"What I've been working on has changed quite a bit lately, though. I'm not sure where it's going anymore. All I really know is that I'm becoming much more sympathetic to people than I was. A lot of people. It may sound peculiar, but the closer I get to graduation the more I see how easy it's been for us to criticize. Because we haven't ever actually done much of anything.

Any of us. Mistakes are easier to see from far off than accomplishments. That's what I was getting at when I was talking about the ways people live behind all the walls. When we have to deal with the problems they've already settled, I expect we'll have more appreciation for what their decisions have been. I don't mean to ignore all the ugly ways of surviving there are. But even so, the strengths people have are becoming more obvious to me now. I guess I'm looking for them more than I was. Trying to use sketch pads to show something of the realities of faces makes people appear more awesome to me than they did before. More admirable, too."

"Are you thinking about going back to California at all...?"

"Sometimes," answered Leah, certain now that most of her words had not been heard by Jack and suddenly realizing that his movements had come to border on being those of a stagger. "Over the holidays my parents treated me as if I were a little girl again. They really did. It's tempting to let them keep on doing it. But I'm sure I won't."

"Are your parents back together now?"

"Yes."

"How is that working out?"

"Things are...I guess everything's pretty much like it was before they separated, Jack. I'm disappointed and glad at the same time."

"Wasn't your father thinking about getting out of...the public relations business?"

"It was the insurance business."

"Did he...get out of it?"

"No, he didn't. I'm not sure how serious he ever really was about that possibility."

They had reached Times Square; and as they walked beneath a golden band of changing letters announcing the news of the day, Jack, his shoulders drooping and his chin pressed to his chest, lunged sluggishly toward the sidewalk, his memory so numb he was unaware he had been on the same street corner fewer than twenty-four hours before.

"Maybe we should get on over to the apartment," Leah said, careful not to appear oversolicitous. "Do you think you could get some sleep yet?"

"Honestly, I'm fine," Jack insisted in a thin, unsteady voice. "You said you were hungry, Leah." Darting ahead of her, he pointed above them to a sign saying Hot Food Always, then opened the door of a small restaurant, stood in the doorway until Leah with reluctant resignation passed through it, and followed her inside, where immediately he slumped, facing the walls, into a chair at a table in one of the corners.

"It looks like we're going to have to order at the counter," Leah said, positioning herself opposite Jack in order to have a view of the entire room.

"I don't want anything but water. And a couple of lemon slices."

"It didn't occur to me I would be eating alone."

"I've been doing some fasting recently. I don't get hungry as often as I used to."

"Sure you don't want something else? Besides water and lemon, I mean."

"I'm sure."

"I'll...order...for us both, then."

Aware Jack would be offended by any attempt she might make to point out to him his unmindful state, Leah slipped out of her coat, stepped to the counter, ordered, and scanned the restaurant. There were fewer than twenty tables. Most of them were taken up by one person, nearly half of whom sat only with soup bowls and something to read before them. The undecorated walls were coated with plaster that had been painted a single shade of cheerless brown.

"This place is a triumph over decay," Leah said, returning, tray in hand, to the table.

"What'd you get?"

"It's the special plate. It's supposed to be soybeans and brown rice...."

Sitting down, then, and handing him his slices of lemon and glass of water, Leah noted that Jack seemed to have become calmer, more regardful. "You know what?" she asked, intent on diverting his thoughts from obvious public events of the day.

"I don't know much of anything right now," he replied, his composure already proving to be short-lived. "What?"

"In Los Angeles there are more earthquakes than you find out about here. They don't often do much damage, but you have to be ready for the room to shake without a warning. We say it 'thunders underground.'"

"That must be nice in a way, Leah. Shocks. But predictable."

"I'd hardly heard real thunder before I moved to Boston," she replied, absently stirring her beans and rice with a fork.

"...Leah?" Jack began, the fingers of both hands rigidly linked about his glass of water, his shoulders curved forward, his hoarse and splintered tones increasingly unable to disguise his disquiet, "Do you ever think, or wonder, I mean, or does it seem to you like it's possible that...before we were born...the souls of people...made plans for us to meet and to, I don't know, resolve the...to meet."

"I hadn't considered it," Leah answered. "What're you getting at?"

"Sometimes things will happen, and it'll feel almost like I decided a long time ago that they would."

"You mean making agreements before we slide down a tunnel into life? Something like that?"

"The same as preordained, but we're the ones who planned it somewhere else."

"I really haven't ever gotten into that sort of thinking," Leah said with finality. "I don't want to, either, truthfully." Turning to the window, she added. "Mr. Tane, I guess this is just not our day! It's raining. Raining again."

"Yeah," said Jack, slowly sipping his water. "Seems like we'll be here awhile."

"It's that sort of place," Leah sighed. "My guess is that everyone else is a regular. They're molded into their chairs..."

"Leah, it's funny, isn't it? I mean that what you and I have is a friendship based on mutual relation."

"You mean based on C. J."

"Based on C. J."

"I suppose we should talk about him."

"I suppose we should."

"...Whatever this all is," Leah said, glancing out the window at the rain, "we're in it together."

"Yes..."

"And we can't go on preserving feelings for a world we envision. We've got to bring them to this one. I'm not sure how yet. We've got to, though. That much I'm certain of."

"But, you see...when...there...C. J.'s draft board...didn't..." said Jack, his hands trembling and his voice the token of a dispersing composite of irreconcilable observations, intentions, and pleas,. "At law school...they wouldn't...almost everything I have to read, I...goes against..."

Hoping the intensity behind her words would guide him into coherence, Leah said vehemently, "Whenever I think of what C. J.'s draft board did without even talking to him, I get so infuriated I almost never want to hear anything about the United States again!"

"A year ago," said Jack with momentary clarity, "the letter he wrote would have given him a jail sentence."

"I know."

"There are too many cases to prosecute now.

"They wouldn't have talked with him, either, if he'd have let that doctor friend of yours send them a letter."

"Yes, well, I never would have suggested what I did, if I'd known then what was at stake."

"There's no way you could've known."

"It's not that I didn't understand what C. J. thought about the war and the draft. I did, and I agreed with it. It was how he felt...that I couldn't...How he would've felt. What I wanted was to keep him alive and out of jail. It might have seemed all the same to the draft board, but in some ways I'm certain he feels better having been classified with a psychiatric deferral because of his own letter than if it had happened because of my friend's. At least this way, he gets to hold onto what he thinks. Which is a minimal amount of comfort, I know."

"I…Leah, I thought for awhile his draft board might be right."

"I didn't. I didn't at all. Ever. But I can see how you would have. I'm sorry you had to. There's nothing basically wrong with C. J. I'm sure he needs your faith in him, though. Mine, too."

"It's been hard on him at work."

"Very hard. It'll be a long time before that'll get any better…He talks so often of leaving the city, Jack. That might be a good thing for him to do. He might find less prejudice somewhere else. He might be happier, if he made a break with…"

"He hasn't said anything to me about leaving," Jack interrupted.

"That surprises me."

"He didn't say anything about leaving Yale either, though, until about an hour before he was gone."

"Yes, and about an hour after he got to Boston."

"I didn't know he's been thinking about leaving," Jack said slowly. He lifted his head from his chest, stared at Leah, and for the first time that day she saw the distended pupils of his swollen, blackened eyes. "Jack," she said, reaching for her coat, "I think we probably ought to be getting back to the apartment."

But Jack—in a sudden moan that diminished into a barely audible whisper—replied only, "The pigeons. The pigeons…they shouldn't have been tanned." Then his eyes closed, his hands stopped moving, and his ashen face dropped, limp and insentient, to the top of the table.

3

"Of course you're panicked. Anyone would be.

"You understand I can't possibly answer from a professional standpoint.

"A year ago I might've suggested that. But not now, Leah. What happened to him is happening all over the country to people in his situation.

"It sounds as if you needn't do anything until the morning. I expect he'll have forgotten most of today by then. I think you should remind him…You were lucky a cab would stop for you!

"No, but if he appears capable of hearing about it, that's when he should.

"On the contrary, I don't think you're to be faulted for that. It would be easy enough for you to be putting all the responsibility or lack of it onto him. That's what many people would be doing right now…And they'd be telling themselves they had his interests at heart in doing it.

"I can't think of anyone offhand. But if you need someone—and I can't stress this enough—from what you've told me that should be a last recourse, but if you're sure it's the only thing to do, then call me tomorrow.

"I mean that a person can be forced into an unnecessary hospitalization by someone else's distress, Leah. And an unnecessary hospitalization can helix into the ruin of most, if not all, of a person's future.

"That much is clear. He's worn out. The rest sounds to me like the dilemmas of life to be met alone or shared with friends rather than with a doctor. Sometimes something like this is a necessary part of acquiring the strength to build a kind of base for one's integrity…It may prove to have been a purgation.

"A base for integrity, yes.

"I think so.

"No, there can have been both a camouflaging and a kind of last-ditch effort to construct an outpost of coherency. Verbal lucidity can appear to continue on until just before the moment of physical collapse.

"Oh, I…I'm listening to a recording of Mahler's Tenth Symphony right now.

"He did, but he finished a first movement and left some fragments.

"Yes, it has been.

"I heard parts of King's talk on the news. I meant to tell you that. I think it probably was one of the most significant speeches of this whole era…. Actually, I think it's a good deal better than Lincoln's "Gettysburg Address." It bases what's valuable about the United States on pacifistic nonviolence instead of on war.

"Yeah, it's still falling.

"Neither have I.

"Of course.

"There's no reason for you to worry about that. Thank you for calling, Leah.

"Good night."

15 Solemnity

"How many times have I told you?"

"How many times have you told me what?"

"How many times have I told you to take the scrambled eggs off the heat fifteen seconds sooner?" said the waitress, as she put six plates of food onto an oval metal tray.

"It's your feet, not my timing," replied the cook, flipping pancakes with a spatula. A white chef's cap sheltered the brushlike stubbles of his hair. His apron was stained and matted.

"I could do your job and mine together and still have time to spare if I had to," the waitress continued. "You should have to be tipped! That'd put a stop to bacon grease in the cooking oil."

"There's never a complaint from the first shift."

"That's because they don't wake up until they get out of here. Besides, there's two of them to do the tables I do by myself."

"That's your choice. All you have to do is say the word, and you'll be sharing steps with feet have had forty fewer years of whining on top of them."

"I'd take every table, if they'd let me, low as the tips are in this place."

"I'm going to stand right here and work out how many steps there'd be in forty years," said the cook humorlessly. "Yours get slower every day. And if you used the window like you're paid to, I'd stop hearing complaints about lukewarm baked potatoes."

"If I waited to use that window for every list of moneys due, you'd be running so many trips back and forth from the grill that by four o'clock, you'd be stuffing chickens with frozen strawberries," the waitress replied. Impatient and cheerless, fractious, she grasped the tray with one hand, adroitly affixed another plate at her elbow, and bustled out of the kitchen.

It was Monday, April 24, 1967.

Keeping her eyes partially focused on the entrance to the restaurant, Leah discreetly appraised across the table from her the melancholy face of Dr. Tsampa, who, motionless, gazed attentively at C. J., sitting alone at a third side of the table.

"So what am I supposed to think of William Butler Yeats saying that all people can do is embody truth, they can never know it?" C. J. asked. "The only reason I read his autobiography is because they keep talking about him like he was so intelligent. Do they hold their jobs by making authorities out of people nobody can understand? He was an old man when he wrote that, too. Is that wisdom? We are what we are, and we can't ever know what that is? Can you tell me what I'm supposed to do with that?"

"I presume," replied Dr. Tsampa, "he meant that all assertions should be tentatively offered. We get tired and hungry. The rest is enigmatic."

"Yes, but what that came down to, in effect, was having to have the opinions of the people who had mostly the wrong kinds of power over us," said C. J., balanced on the two rear legs of his chair, his head touching the wall. "I am so sick of hearing how valuable doubt is. I don't need to hear it again from you."

Tapping a pencil on her note pad, the waitress approached the table. "Would you like to order yet, or do you still prefer to wait?" she asked.

"Perhaps we should order now," said Dr. Tsampa.

"I'm sure he'll be here soon," said C. J. "Let's go ahead."

"Then what can I bring you today? Miss?"

"A toasted English and a pineapple sherbet," said Leah solemnly.

"Honey or jelly?"

"Honey."

"Something to drink?"

"Lemonade," Leah replied. She smiled perfunctorily, rested her left thumb against her upper front teeth, and slid her chair closer to the table.

"Bean soufflé for me," said Dr. Tsampa. "And a side order of mashed potatoes," he added, wedging his menu in a spring-holder between himself and C. J.

"Something to drink with that?"

"Water will be enough. Thank you."

"And you, sir?"

"Chef's salad," said C. J.

"What kind of dressing would you like?"

"Italian."

"Crackers?"

"Yes."

While with a single nod the waitress issued a firm demand for enough silence to allow her immediate departure, C. J. lifted his glass of water, shook it so that the ice clinked against the glass, and smiled at Leah, who, pale and tense, was staring at the center of the table.

"I feel like can't help but memorize…" Leah began at the same time that Dr. Tsampa said, "I didn't mean to…"

"Sorry," said Dr. Tsampa.

"I feel as if I'm memorizing all of this," Leah continued. "I didn't realize it was going to be an occasion. I suppose it couldn't help but be. Thank you for coming, Colin."

Leaning forward, touching the legs of his chair to the floor, his manner too defensive to be regarded polite and too genial to be considered threatening, his eyes angry and detached, his gaze steady without being antagonistic or drawing attention to itself, C. J. took up a paper napkin, started to tear it into confetti-sized pieces, and said, "Yes, it's nice to have an emissary from the realm of official adults in here, Doctor. Where they eat around campuses has been a mystery to us…But I still don't understand what you're saying. Is it that you think we should always be examining everything? That we should always be investigational or something like that?"

"I simply meant that the strength with which a person holds some convictions can prevent one from holding other convictions that would serve as self-enhancing complements," said Dr. Tsampa. Glancing at the unlighted window that opened into the kitchen, he loosed a discrete sigh and pinched between a thumb and a forefinger the skin behind his right eyebrow.

"I know you're going to say I'm self-righteously prideful and arrogant, but the truth is that what you do seems to me like trying to walk up Pike's Peak on skis. I don't even like to ski," C. J. said. "I don't even want to learn to like to ski." He tossed the remnants of his napkin to the floor and then asked with a voice subdued, but nonetheless, adamantly insistent, "What about you, Leah? What do you think?"

"That you recognize the dilemmas more accurately than Colin does, at least right now. Although it's probably a difference of your emphasis. He sees constantly so many of the minor ones, and he deals with them. Excuse me, Colin, but I..."

"No, Leah," said Dr. Tsampa. "Go on. I'm sure I need to hear this."

"You're right, C. J. I think you're right. Unless the major problems are eliminated, no amounts of compassion and intelligence are going to be enough. But identification isn't enough either. You're having no effect. You don't want to have any. You think no one can have any. And yet it seems to me that your approach might be combined with Colin's, because otherwise..."

Wearing a green, pocketless, long-sleeved shirt, scrupulously creased blue corduroys, and white shoes, Jack, manifesting a placid restraint similar to, although less intense than, that of the convalescent who is evoking and emanating a benevolence necessary to the healing in process, had opened the door and was walking toward them.

"I'm late," he said, arriving at the table. "Sorry."

"No explanation needed. Good to see you," said Leah with intrepid civility. "This is Jack, Colin. Colin Tsampa. Jack Tane."

As Dr. Tsampa began to extend his right hand, he was interrupted by the waitress, who, dour and indomitable, served the lemonade, the sherbet, and the salad. "Doctor, hello," said Jack, sitting down opposite C. J.

"I'm afraid we went ahead on Colin's account," said Leah. Resolvedly she anchored her elbows on the table, braced her back against her chair, and pressed her fingertips together.

Holding his water glass against his forehead, C. J., one eye closed, peered up at the ceiling, laughed, and said, "I think it's safe to say that the doctor is the only one of us who has an account...."

"I'm aware I'm indebted to you, Doctor," said Jack, his words slowly paced and temperately spoken. "I sort of had a...psychological avulsion..."

"Bean soufflé and an order of mashed potatoes," the suddenly reappearing waitress nonchalantly said to Dr. Tsampa, who impassively removed his plate from her elbow.

"I'd like a mushroom omelet," Jack said quickly. "And Hawaiian Punch," he added, as the waitress turned from the table and hurried away.

Having delicately bitten away the end of the paper covering her straw, Leah blew the rest of the paper through the air to the wall above C. J.'s shoulders, attempted a grin, then said, "That was the only gesture I could think of that'd be like a toast. I hope it was enough."

"It was enough," said C. J. "Whatever you do is enough..."

"I'm sure you were placed in a difficult position by Leah's phone call, Doctor," said Jack.

"I hope you'll continue to prove my judgment to have been correct," said Dr. Tsampa. "...In your regard."

"It was a relief to get things more in the open. I feel much better now. I'm sorry it had to happen like that. I guess I'm sorry it even had to happen. But at least I don't have to use as much energy hiding struggle as I did. Do you know what I...?"

"It's seldom acceptable," interrupted Leah. "To let on that one is doing it. Struggling. Why is that, Colin? It should be. Acceptable."

"I don't think I…" Dr. Tsampa replied. He lunged his head high above his collar and held his mouth open, as if he were asking for mercy or for inspiration or for both.

"Too complicated," said C. J.

"For lunch…" added Jack.

After sipping her lemonade through a brief, wordless pause, Leah pushed aside her uneaten sherbet, inhaled deeply, and then brusquely and precipitately, her reluctance entirely undisguised, said, "Look, the three of you, I'm not sure how I got myself into being a hostess…I did, though; and I can't get out of it. But…please, please, oh don't expect me to be a moderator, too!"

"What I meant to suggest was the fragility of our political and economic institutions," Dr. Tsampa said immediately, primarily addressing C. J., "rather than their ambivalent natures. I meant also to request that you consider the many aspects of institutional invisibility."

"Fragility I've heard enough about. I don't need to hear again that I'm dangerously impatient or some other equally faddish diagnosis. Deferred dreams. All that. I don't care whether institutions are fragile or strong. I'm going to get away from as many of them as I can, get away from them by leaving them. I tried to get away from them and still stay inside them, and I can't do it. I don't even want to anymore."

"When, C. J.?" asked Jack.

"Before my next rent."

"A week?"

"Less," replied C. J. "…But what do you mean by invisibility, Doctor?"

"Perhaps you cannot now appreciate, although everyone usually ought to of themselves, how miraculous it is that you lived beyond infancy. I speak as a doctor. I ask you to recall all of the vaccinations you have had, merely them, and to consider how much time it took to develop them, to consider what calamities they have prevented. I ask you to appreciate the miracle of grocery stores. And I am well aware that new generations have difficulty in doing other than taking for granted or despising the realizations of the dreams of their forebears. Nonetheless, I would rather see you a clerk arranging oranges in January for the benefit of, among others, an eighty-year-old woman who had scarcely seen an orange, much less an orange in January, when she was your age, than to see you abandon this admittedly, in some respects, inadequate and even, I agree, wretched and, at times, debilitating community. I ask you to consider the miracles of water faucets, always warm beds, and a dependable system for sewage disposal. I do not mean that our institutions do not need tampering with. I only ask that you consider how much you have relied upon their invisibility. I expect that you have had every advantage anyone can have had in these times, and I suggest you ought to be thinking of repaying those who were responsible for allowing you to have known so many satisfactions and to have been presented with so many opportunities. Their work has been largely anonymous. Well done. Invisible."

"Survival is not enough, Doctor. In spite of all the advances...especially in medicine," said Jack. "It's the quality of survival that's important. We all should be able to get what we want without wrongly exploiting each other."

"I agree with that, but an extraordinary array of luxuries makes it possible for me to do so."

"I have not ever had the advantage of being shown how to love," replied C. J. "And I would guess that's been true of the four of us...I don't think a survival like that is an advantage. You say everyone is basically decent. You say they haven't had time to reflect. But it doesn't take all that much looking around, or even effort, to see that people have attached this basic decency, just working decently providing a home like you say, attached it to mechanisms that are going to bring about the greatest of indecencies. People know that. Nothing is done. I want to leave. I want to leave while there's still a little bit of time for me to mind the wind, Doctor. You haven't convinced me I have any obligations of the sort you've talked about."

"Where, C. J.?" asked Jack.

"I'm getting in my truck," C. J. replied. "I'll know where to park."

Left? Right? Will it matter how? Leah rapidly asked herself. With? And then she glanced at the wall behind her and scarcely moving her lips, whispered, "Yes."

"Leah?...Can you predict how much time you'll need before you can be sure whether or not to go on for good with your painting?" Jack asked.

"The best I could do would be to set a limit line. Three years. Five years. I haven't done it yet. I hope I don't have to. I'm going to need solitude, but I'm not sure how much or for how long. There's going to be a temptation to sacrifice isolation, not sacrifice, run from. I don't have enough strength for much being-alone right now. Besides, I don't think anything good ever happens in art except from caring about someone else, at least someone else. That's who it's for. The best art and science involve gestures of love, whether they are recognized gestures or not. You talk about social repression, Colin, granted, I agree with you in many ways. Art functions often to stabilize the repression it portrays a struggle against. What I don't want to have happen is to achieve the ends I've aimed for in the work and then find out that other people are using what I've done to circumvent what I value. I want what I make to be utilized in ways that will be consistent with it."

"That's a fine and mature attitude," said Dr. Tsampa. "I wish it were more common."

"Maturity!" said Jack, tapping his spoon against his chin. "Isn't that mainly a matter of finding out we've been, I don't know...duped, I guess? Duped all along, duped in a sophisticated way, yes, but duped all the same. Isn't that what the three of us are supposed to realize now? Aren't we supposed to go on the other side of adulthood and start in duping, so that in a few years we'll be so used to what we're doing we won't know we're doing it anymore? Isn't that basically what maturity involves?"

"No, it isn't," replied Dr. Tsampa firmly, a strain of spontaneous hopefulness creeping through the sadness and habitual patience of his tones. "I assure you there are other alternatives. A goal of my work is to increase the number of them and to strengthen the structures existing in relation to them." He gripped his fork close to his face and glared at it. "I sometimes think it would be better for all of psychiatry and psychology to be economically classified as research and that the results should be disseminated as quickly about the earth as possible, more widely than any other category of information with the exception of linguistic essentials…"

"I think…now let me start again," said Leah, as the waitress silently delivered the English muffin to her and then his glass and plate to Jack. "I think we must create environments where we can develop our own kind of maturity, our own integrity, if we can't find any support within what we have around us. That's what we've done in a way." She looked at the corner of the table between Dr. Tsampa and C. J. "At least I feel that. It's been the two of you who have given me the chance to get a sense of myself I could never have had otherwise. Your faith in me. We have to devise our own groundworks, if they aren't already there to hang onto. I don't mean only imagine them, unless there's no other option. I mean build them. So that we can build our best selves. Internal struggle isn't enough. There have to be external opportunities."

"Identity," said Dr. Tsampa, "has to be granted by others to a significant degree. But those who grant it can be altered in the process, induced, I mean, to aid one in becoming the person one wants to be, so that one can eventually be recognized as such, although perhaps with the many regrets of too late."

"That's true, Colin. But even so, what you say about research isn't enough," said Leah, her gaze fixed directly on C. J. "The intents of research ought to be proper. Pursuits of truth are by no means always justifiable. The goals should also be humane. They often aren't. That may be largely why there isn't more sanity currently. Acceptable conceptions of sanity can never be anything but humanely constructed and potentially inclusive of all people. Perhaps that's what you think. I…I really don't know anymore."

To Leah's right, formidable and stolid in her billowing white uniform, the waitress stood, trayless and plateless, holding the check. "Something else for anyone?" she asked.

"No," said Leah with abrupt calm. "No, nothing. I'm sure we're all fine. Thank you."

While the waitress adroitly was placing the check in the center of the table, C. J. darted an intent look at Jack, then said, "When I was a boy, Doctor, I remember sitting at home trying to think about all the people who had been responsible for what was there. Everything involved in the making of it all, the different steps of the transportation, the selling. I didn't do that often, but I did sometimes, and I tried to figure out how to be worthy of those people. I could not sit there and do that now. Something happens. Maybe it always has to. The things get more important than the lives. Having them, buying them, and not using them, not being able to use them all, yet still making more of them. Especially not sharing them. It's like you get so you won't give up assumptions that make you accept what you don't want, and when you accept enough of that, you forget how to grow...There's very little I want, but I can't get it here. Please don't tell me I'll change my mind. Maybe I will. But please don't tell me that now."

Dr. Tsampa smiled and said, "I would not presume to do that. You have a certain grace and may accomplish more than you will be aware of or intend." He shoved back his chair, loosened his belt one notch, and stood. "If you'll excuse me, I must soon be elsewhere."

Picking up the check, C. J. turned toward the entrance to the kitchen, stretched his legs out on either side of the table, and said, "There isn't that much anyone can change. You have to adjust or leave."

"Perhaps you're right," answered Dr. Tsampa. "I hope not. I truly hope not...At any rate, I...I wish you all well." As Leah dazedly watched him vanish from her window view, the waitress, seemingly oblivious to the taut silence at the table, deposited a pitcher of ice water in front of C. J., who, shading his eyes with his left forearm, rolled the check into a cylinder with his right hand, and said finally, "I can't help it. I just can't help it, Leah. I think he's pathetic."

"He *was*, C. J. He was pathetic.... part of the time," Leah replied. "He wasn't when I first knew him, though. Not ever...But, yes...he *is* now. At times. That's what some of his lonelinesses have done to him.... And *pathetic* is a word it's almost impossible to say without disgust. I heard your attempt; and I'm glad you made it, because he is also a source of encouragement to more people than you or I will probably ever meet." Imperceptibly she was already starting to stand. "One of the three of us should say this, and I'm going to: that was our youth. There, that's been said...And when it comes time for regrets, whenever that happens, but when it happens that we begin to look back, in five years, ten, seventeen, then let us agree to be done with regrets by thinking only this—even if that means being done with memory—let us think, let us think only: we did not take the time to build palaces in the sand.... Fly your kites, C. J. Oh, fly your kites!" Clutching the top of her chair, she turned, took a deep breath, and without looking back, sped out the door and hurried along Massachusetts Avenue, until she was walking at Dr. Tsampa's side. "'Advice, remember that I offered it,'" she said. "It would've been consistent for you to have ended by saying that to us, Colin.... It's not completely your fault. Perhaps it's not even partially your fault. But I cannot be around you again for a very long time, if I can ever be around you again at all."

A moment later, alone outside the restaurant, Jack surveyed Harvard Square and at last discovered C. J. sitting upon the sidewalk by the graveyard across from the subway entrance.

With his hands in his back pockets, Jack wove through the traffic, crouched at C. J.'s side, and said, "There's no use putting in more words. I've got to resolve all the ones I have. I'm quitting law school. There's no way I could pass the exams; they wouldn't do me any good, if I could. For awhile I've got to just breathe and be in the sun. I'm going to leave with you, C. J. I'm selling my car and storing most of my things and coming with you."

"That gate wasn't ever locked before," C. J. said, grasping two, black vertical bars of the graveyard fence and pulling himself up from the cement. "Why did they do that?" He kicked the fence, kicked it hard: "Why'd they go and do that?!"

16 Solar Motion

1

Spring, 1968

'It would've been so nice for us to have taken the land that had the lake. Wouldn't that have been nice, though? He wanted to swim every rainless summer's morning, just as he had as a boy. That's what he wanted. If there had been only the property to consider, my, what neighborhood picnics we could have had!

'It would've been so good for Jack. So very much better. He could've had his friends stop by to fish. Stop by to ice-skate. Idle away in a clubhouse, as boys do. There was nothing here for any of them, after all. What was there?

'But the lake was too far away for anyone to see what my husband meant. That's why we settled here. That's why we stayed on. The soil was better around the lake; but the town coming made my yard more expensive, even then. He needed to have a house would show them his dreams. The way he talked, those first years, none of us would hardly be able to tell the difference from the earth and the buildings, it would all fit together so well.

'We could yet have moved to the land with the lake, started again, when Jack was seven or eight. But even though it would have been a better place for the neighbors to come to, and they would have, it would have seemed like we were moving away from them. And that they would have resented.

'Even while it was working out there would have been so much more to offer them welcome.

'We are farther away from there here than we would have been there, though it seems like we're closer... .

'It was the deciding to have it be a little bit better than theirs to show them what he meant, made it so they couldn't visit, couldn't call, couldn't write, couldn't ask, couldn't answer.'

As she had done every morning for more than a decade, Mrs. Tane knelt in front of her grandfather clock, reached inside, took out the other clock, wound it, checked its accuracy, and put it back in place, its dial unable to be seen.

Without looking at the piano, glancing instead within the array of her shadow boxes, and arranging her thoughts as if she were by turns praying and addressing an imaginary friend, she walked to the opposite corner of the parlor, opened the drapes, and stared down the front yard, past the town, all the way to a huge cloud of smoke that already had formed in the air directly above Denver.

'It used not to happen until afternoon. Every day it wraps so gradual, they don't see it there. You'd think they would, but they don't. Because of the sicknesses of their eyes.

'And all...

'It was so good Jack left just in time. Just in time. So like him. Because who knows what would've happened to him if he had stayed?

'I could not have stood sitting here and watching parts of Boston burn, setting their own homes on fire, and have known he was there. They say it's still black to the ground in Los Angeles and Cleveland; and, of course, you can see it's the air makes them do it. They're suffocating, but all together, so they don't know each other's chokings for their own. Don't hear each other's stranglings for their own. Left when he did. Right when did...

'Father would have kept them out if he could have.

'I don't mean the colors. No. I mean the people. *Any* people. "Bringing us what we've come to get away from," he'd say. And, too, none of us knew then how many there would be or how badly they'd been used to living. So as what they'd want we wouldn't have settled for.

'"They didn't know the land from where they'd been," my husband used to say. "If only they could be heeding to the housing and not be carrying their ways here. Not now. Not when the dream can take hold. The dream they wouldn't let happen there."

'But soon it was plain he'd have to be content with here. Not all of Denver. Or even a part of it. So it became to make what happened here show the city. Just as we should show the town.

'Only the town didn't ever see.

'They saw, but they didn't see-understanding-see.

'And that's what I had to...was him explaining away how what he wanted was not turning out, having to hear him say it had turned out when it was long past when maybe it could have...

'There was a time, when Jack was seven or eight, when I no longer had to be between, you see. Between my parents and my husband. When we yet could have taken the other land. It could have been ours. When that space of time passed, what I had to be, was between him and. Between him and Jack. Between my husband and my son.

'Just the little bit of time.

'The time between being in-between.

'It was not enough.

'He never knew, doesn't know it yet, that the people you're ambitious to prove yourself to are dead or don't care by the time you've done something to show them. And the people your own age are only envious, think you've taken what should have been theirs, or are bragging about what they've done better than you. And the young aren't gladdened either, they want what you have for themselves, or they want to get away. From you. From me. Jack did. No one ever shows anyone. You'd think they'd catch on, but they don't.

'Not that my father was scornful of my husband or how I came to live, not that at all. He didn't care anymore. Even at the beginning. He was too tired. It wouldn't have mattered to him if I'd been the mayor's wife.'

Humming snatches of songs from her early childhood, Mrs. Tane walked past the window, past the wall of glassware and knickknacks arranged on open shelves, and just as she had planned for more than two months, picked up the sand dollar C. J. had presented her nearly five years earlier. Fondling it in both her hands, she carried it under the antlers to the recreation room and sat down in a cane chair positioned so she could look through the wall of glass.

'Much of the snow will melt into the streams today. The farmers will be pleased. The trout will grow fat.

'But, no, it will not rain...

'Judge my husband, oh, Lord, if You judge any of us at all, by the view of those mountains from this room.

'For that is what is left of how he worked out the only dreams he could find.

'I do not know whether I am Your instrument or whether I am denying You. Look now, and You will know. You cannot help but know. All I am able to do, all I can, is trust I am following Your will. I have pleaded with You for a sign. There has been nothing. All I can do is trust. If You judge us at all, You must judge that I trusted in You. You must...

'It was such a nice, flat land. He wanted an apple orchard there. Wanted potatoes and corn. Wouldn't that have been nice? By the lake? Without the rain? Today?...

'I suppose, you see, I suppose it was that none of us thought there would be another war. That was our heritage. There was the newspaper photograph of my mother in front of the Equitable Building in Denver when it was over. Not her alone. In a crowd. But her all the same. Holding a flag. She almost carried me there herself that day, she told me, there was such joy.

'All we ever read, all we ever said, all we ever knew was that there would be no more war. None of us were ready. We'd heard, of course we had, the stories from Europe, the reports?, but we were apart from that. Half the world did not seem to depend on us then. None of us were ready until it began...

'There should never have been an American revolution. Wouldn't that have been nice, though? To have been protected by a King and a Queen and those centuries instead of all this...all this confusion? If we're going to have rulers, we should have them.

'The President in Berlin but sixteen years after the end of it. As if it were like the first and we were ready to forgive and accept. But that fooled no one. We had already known that, and there was nothing to do but ready ourselves for war and stop it only by always being ready for it. That's what we said. We were not going to think again it would not happen. We would be ready for it whenever it came.

'And so have we been. So have we been...

'Isn't it strange...how separate the house became from the town? Isn't it?

'Not so as a visitor would call it strange, but newcomers always find out after awhile, though nothing is ever said.

'It would have been different if they'd wanted his dreams.

'Or maybe it wouldn't have been different at all.

'Maybe a family always has to be apart from all the others...

'Over and over, my husband would say it was a slave system in the factories; and the new housing'd change them. Make them proud. But then he didn't say that anymore.

'Not anymore.

'Because where else was he to get what he would build with?

'There wasn't time for him to use in the ways he'd wanted to—ways he'd dreamed of—what they made. Not time for him to show them how he thought they could be.

'So let him be judged by that window. Because it is what he meant for everyone somehow to have...

'Isn't it peculiar how separated we became from the life of the town?

'If we had started again, they would have said by the lake was farther away, even though it could have made them closer. That's how people are when there's a change like that. When there's a moving to a lake, the neighbors put everything they couldn't talk about before into something else, making the change sound way more than it is, when it might even be less hard for them to visit than it had been before.'

Still holding the sand dollar, she walked along the hallway, turned into the kitchen, opened the oven, removed a fresh loaf of bread, and set it on a rack to cool.

'It was the fountains I wanted most of all to see. Wanted in that little space of time when I was other than between. All the ancient fountains with the statues, with the lights. That's what we'd planned. We'd counted on that. It was the thing to do. There was no doubt of it.

'And then there was the war and Jack and the house and even when Jack was small, we'd talk of it yet, because most of the fountains—isn't that odd?—most of the fountains were left after the bombings. We'd see the pictures. We'd talk of going ourselves when Jack was through college.

'When Jack was through.

'We talked so in that little space of time. Because that's how we'd planned it. But when it was sure we couldn't move to a swim every rainless, summer's morning, then we didn't talk of it again...

'The house took us over.

'It wouldn't seem that could happen, but it did.

'And it was the war was what made us used to not having opinions. There had to be so many secrets, how could we judge them? Even when we knew the secrets, not completely, no, but enough so as to be able to decide, there wasn't any question that the ones who truly, truly, knew the secrets had to be knowing what to do with them. For who else could? It isn't that we agreed to them, like Jack always says, even though I know how it must seem to him, it's that we gave up the chance to have opinions because we thought it was all so complicated only a few people would be fit to decide and naturally they'd decide what was right. We got our not knowing what they were doing mixed up with our not judging where they were heading. We let ourselves make it the same thing.

'No.

'No.

'No.

'It will not rain.'

Just as she had, time and again, during the previous two months, she lifted a metal bread box from a shelf beside the stove, placed it on the kitchen table, examined it, and transferred it to the sink. After filling the bread box with water, she assured herself that the metal did not leak, dried it, and put it on a waist-high shelf by the door opening onto the steps to the garage.

'If one of the two of them, only once, had ever offered to cook a meal.

'But they couldn't have.

'I arranged it so they couldn't have.

'Mother told me I should sit down at the table every night as if the food had been prepared by someone who was off in the kitchen eating alone. That's how they expected me to be. The house demanded it.

'There was the year when Jack was twelve. How old was I then? Let me think. And I saw all those decisions ahead. All those decisions I would have to keep on making. As I had.

'Without any of the decisions ever being acknowledged, you see.

'Acknowledged.

'And I got the notion of calling the neighbors, making plans to clean each other's houses and cook each other's dinner casseroles. And salads. And desserts.

'It wouldn't have taken any more time, and wouldn't it, oh, wouldn't it, would not that have been...relief?

'It seemed such a good idea.

'It made me happy just to think of it...

'It would have been better, though, if I'd kept on thinking it only.

'Because after I'd phoned so many of them, always having to make up an excuse for the call, without ever saying what I'd meant to, I had to have done with that idea.

'Have done with it.

'What holds the houses together is counting on them being separate.

'You wouldn't think it'd be that way, but it is.

'What holds people together is them keeping apart from each other.

'...Of course, Jack's father had more opinions than I did. That's only natural.

'But even so, his opinions rested on that giving-up we did, you see. That giving-up I told you about.

'You've already forgotten what I told you, haven't you?

'All of his opinions were different from...different from what he'd given up having opinions about.

'Or nearly all.

'That's why he couldn't ever talk with Jack.

'Not talk.

'Not really.

'That's why I was between them.

'A wife has to support what a husband decides, you see. Otherwise nothing would get done. He builds your world for you; and all you have to do—that's all—is live in it. He has to think he's doing everything he's doing for you, because you can't do it yourself. And no one ever says that that's what makes you so you can't do it. That right there. You don't make out a list of presents you want and send it to everyone you know, do you? You trust them to decide what it is you need, and then you do what you can with it. If it's not what you need, you tell yourself, (at least it exists and is here), and that's that...

'Wouldn't you think the way the planes and the television are now, they'd put tape recordings from one country onto a plane and send it to another country and then everybody would find out what each other is like, what we say, we could truly be it, and there'd not be a war again?

'They don't use the planes and the television for that because it would be almost the same as cleaning someone else's house while someone is cleaning yours. It makes sense until you think about how people are, and then you know it wouldn't work. Countries hold together by being separate.'

Stepping out onto the patio, Mrs. Tane for a moment gazed up at the sky; and then she faced the mountains in the west.

'Jack used to ask why "purple majesty" and I'd say, "Sometimes they're purple, you wait and watch and you'll see." Of course, he was right. The song was from that sort of late summer day when the land is dry red and the sky is blue without a drop of water in it. Late in that summer day. The sounds of the words make it seem like mountains are always that color. I suppose it doesn't matter, though, to anyone except who's around them...

'It was not me who broke my husband's dream. Not me.

'No, You cannot put that upon my soul.

'I did all I could to suppose what he wanted. Maybe I could've changed him. Maybe I should've. But I cannot be faulted with making life so very much less than he expected.

'It became that way.

'It happened.

'And after...there was nothing more to do but keep on. If there was a way to keep on without pretending his dreams were his plans, You did not show it to me; and I cannot be taken to task.

'...He said on my birthday...he said fifty-two years should be like fifty-two weeks. Said I should be starting a second what I'd had the first of.

'Is that nearly what You are having me do?

'Should it be nothing?

'Will it rain today?'

Sighing repeatedly, she re-entered the house, went to her room, used one hand to pick up a cardboard box from the floor, and carried the box through the hall to Jack's room. There she lifted out of the box and up to Jack's bed his grade school drawings, all of his letters, and the remaining totality of his school papers, which she had arranged to show his progression from printing to writing to typing, from addition and subtraction to multiplication and division to calculus.

'The little gold and silver stars we keep on expecting, even though they never come again! If Jack had too many stars, I did as well. And why not? Gluing on those stars helps us begin the times when no one looks anymore at what we do.

'I wanted a little time to know him.

'He had taken the halest years of my life, and I wanted a little time to find out who I had made.

'So there was nothing to do but be between them or not know him.

'Should I have chosen not to know who my son had become?

'It was hard enough to read his words and hear his father say the other side as if it were all and mine, too.

'...Are you laughing at me now?...

'If I am not Your instrument, I cannot understand why You made it so all there was was left for me to do was look at what we've done here. Look at what we've done here. Look at what we've done here. That's why Jack's handwriting turned into lines. He wanted words to match the rest of what is. "How can the reason for the weapons go when the weapons are built so to last?" he'd write again and again. "And if the reasons someday go, will there have to be new reasons because of what has been done there? Because of what has been made?"

'We thought we were giving up our opinions to those who were looking out for us.

'But there's no reason to think that anymore.

'We cannot think they are doing that.

'What we said was, we thought was, although we knew it wasn't. And that is how the children were raised...

'It will come to Jack to want to be more grateful than he'll be able to be. That's how it came to me. I hope it does not come to all children like as that. It makes us so alone. Seeing ahead they'll want to reach us when we can't be, 'most exactly how we wanted to be reached when we weren't.

'Do we all have to be that alone?'

Sighing, she shut the door of Jack's room and went down the hall to the guest room. Lying upon the bed, she held the sand dollar in one hand above her breasts and pressed her other forearm against her open lips.

'On such a day as this, if it had been a Sunday, we would have gone to the City Park Lagoon. Already there would have been lemonade, and we would have ridden the paddle boats. How lovely that was! Parasols. All of us in white dresses with green and red sashes. All of them in blue neckties and black shoes...Childhood is the time for friendships. Only we cannot ever tell them that...

'If there had been but one person I could have shared this with. If there had been one person I could've talked to.

'One.

'But, you see, we made that impossible at the beginning. Quite impossible. Who could I have gone to? Where?

'We accepted early on the pretending that anyone who really looked at, really knew, what we do here, could not stand the knowing. We did what we did with eyes said too much to face. That's how we stopped the talking.

'How else could livings have been made by them all?

'How else?

'How else?

'...Every year, he and I, we tell each other the weaknesses haven't come to us yet. And they haven't come when so we say. But then for a minute, we rest. Even celebrate, a little, how much of our strength is left. And when we get up, begin again, it is harder to stand. We can't breathe as deeply. Something has gone. Just as we had been having our gladness it had stayed...

'There's so much I've always done for him he'll have to learn to do for himself. But it will be better for him. Just because it will be so hard, you see. I know him.

'There will be that to do.

'He will have no choice but to do it.

'And that will take hold of what otherwise would have been a slowing-down. His mind would have had nothing but for to wander. There would have been no place for his hands or his legs to go. You wouldn't think it'd be that way, but it would be.'

Balancing between her breasts the sand dollar, she closed her eyes, confidently fell asleep, woke up in an hour, just as she had planned, and gradually quickening the movements of her limbs, walked to her husband's room.

'Father used to tell me our shadow separates from our body. Shadow goes in one direction and body in another. For awhile we don't know which one we are. I used to ask, "Can you tell me now which one I'll be, so I'll be sure right away and not have to wonder?" He'd say, "Sooner than you expect, there'll be lots of things you'll know how they'll happen; but you won't be able to know that one. Not as you are, you won't, you won't, not as you are, you won't."

'They will try to explain away instead of reading, and likely they will convince themselves they have explained away with whatever stories they settle on.

'Though there will be nothing to make stories from.

'Nothing about me has ever seemed any different from any of them to any of them.

'Nothing.

'Nothing at all.'

Placing the sand dollar upon her husband's pillow, Mrs. Tane said aloud, "I do not know why You have selected me to bear this. I do not even know whether You have selected me. I only know I bear it. I cannot ask You to look into my heart again. There is no more time now. I can only trust I am with You. That is all I can do."

'Yes.

'I will leave him this.

'He will not know what it is, nor where it came from. But he will tell Jack where he found it. He will ask Jack what it is. Jack will remember where it came from. Jack will tell him what it is.

'Neither of them will soon know why I left it.

'For a long time, Jack will wonder why.

'And when he's ready, he will understand. He will understand from this.

'That what his father and I did, we did together.

'He'll not be able to praise one of us and blame the other. Not then. He'll understand we made each other who we became and cannot be judged separate from each other.

'Salvation in life is so shared I don't see how even You could judge us separately. Which is why I suspect You may not judge any of us at all. There are the goodnesses we managed because of someone else. I do not know what more there is of love. We make each other how we become.

'I don't know any longer whether it was right or wrong.

'All I know is that we kept the secrets together.

'Jack will understand.

'After awhile.'

Having once again entered her own room, Mrs. Tane put on a green summer suit, buttoned the jacket, reached underneath her bed, and pulled out a large thermos jug. After carrying the jug to the kitchen and down the stairs into the garage, she placed it on the back seat of her car, then returned to her room, where she lifted and for a moment cradled in her arms a lidded, nearly knee-high, wooden footstool sturdily constructed more than a century earlier to resemble a tree stump. Next she took the footstool to the kitchen, opened its lid, carefully put the bread box inside, closed and fastened the lid, carried the footstool down the stairs, and set it on the front passenger seat of her car.

Again she returned to her room. There she removed a heavy, full-length, gray winter coat from her closet, hung it loosely over one of her arms, took from a bureau drawer a thin, foot-square package wrapped in cloth, and picked up her purse. Retracing her steps through the kitchen, she compared the time of her wristwatch with the time of the kitchen clock, opened the stairway door, paused, closed the door, walked down the stairs, and opened the driver's door of her car. Upon placing her coat on the back seat next to the thermos jug, she seated herself behind the wheel, rested the cloth-covered package beside her between the footstool and the seat, and put her purse on the dashboard. Then she started the car, opened the automatic garage door, backed out into the driveway, closed the garage door, and drove to the access road leading to the plant.

Turning, she followed the access road for a quarter of a mile until she arrived at a guard station, where she stopped the car and opened her window.

Through thick, bronze-tinted glass blurring his features she saw the guard's lips move expressionlessly, as he pointed toward an octagonal speaker on the outside of his booth. His voice sounded as if it were coming from a radio.

"Afternoon, Mrs. Tane."

"Good afternoon, Bill."

"What can I do for you?"

"Has my husband been by, Bill?"

"Not today, Mrs. Tane."

"I scarcely know how to explain. I hope you'll be patient with me, Bill. It's our son. You know him. You know Jack."

"Certainly, Mrs. Tane. Fine boy."

"He's been taken sick, Bill."

"Sorry to hear that, Mrs. Tane. Nothing serious, I hope."

"Apparently it is. He's unconscious. The doctor has called three times today from the hospital. Naturally he wanted to speak to my husband. There hasn't been an accident. It's a sickness. The doctor thought it best not to tell me any more. I got in touch with Mr. Tane's office right away, of course; but my husband has spent the day in the Ft. Collins area, apparently, checking over new building sites. They simply haven't been able to find him, Bill. He didn't have any specific destination. I've had nothing to do but wait. He did mention over breakfast that he'd be having a conference here at four-fifteen, so dinner would need to be delayed. There was a note at the office, too, about him being here at that time. I would've called, but I had no idea who the conference would be with. And no one at the office knew that either, which, of course, they wouldn't, since he was coming here. I thought it best to drive out myself and meet him. I hoped he might have arrived early. He often does that. That's his way. I know it's an awfully unusual thing to be asking, Bill; but this has all been terribly hard to manage; and I wonder if I might drive in and wait for him in the lot."

"I'm real sorry you had to handle this alone, Mrs. Tane. You go right on in. Just as soon as I see him, I'll let him know where you are. I'll be glad to. Never you mind."

"I'm grateful for your kindness, Bill. I couldn't think of anything to do but explain what had happened. I expect I should go to the southern section. It looks quite open. My husband will have no difficulty finding me there."

"Well, now, Mrs. Tane, that area's for the next shift, now. There aren't any formal parking divisions, as you'd say it; but it usually works out that way. This shift will be ending in fifteen minutes, ma'am; and the next shift starts an hour from then. About an hour from now, some of the people will begin streaming in sure. There's always some overlap, Mrs. Tane. Never much, but always some."

"I'd not want to be in anyone's way. I'd prefer not having to explain my presence. You understand, Bill."

"Certainly, Mrs. Tane."

"It would seem to me best that I drive to the open section and wait there. If by some chance my husband should be delayed, I'll leave for home in forty-five minutes, so as not to be any problem for the next shift. I have the doctor's phone number. He'll yet be on duty in the hospital then. In case of my leaving, I could give the number to you. You'll still be here, won't you?"

"Oh, yes, ma'am."

"I do so want to learn, myself, what is wrong as soon as I can."

"You drive on in, Mrs. Tane. I'll direct him to you."

"And I've brought some mending, Bill. The lining on my winter coat needs attention. I hope it'll be acceptable for me to set to work beside my car. I haven't had any fresh air all day, one phone call after another; I should keep my hands busy so the time will go faster."

"That's just fine, Mrs. Tane. You go on in."

"I'm real grateful, Bill."

On the other side of the guard booth, a metal gate immediately swung open; and Mrs. Tane drove past it, then maneuvered through the vast, concrete lot. Upon parking at a spot she judged to be roughly equidistant from the booth and the main entrance doors of the plant, she rolled up her window, unwrapped the package next to her—thereby revealing a piece of cardboard to which firmly had been pinned a small needlepoint canvas, and folded the cloth that had covered it. After putting the cloth in her purse, she placed the canvas-pinned cardboard between her back and the driver's seat, got out of the car, and looked through the windshield.

Satisfied that her needlepoint words (upon a background of black and white checks, she had sewn in red:

One. To show
How bright
The light
After, will eyes ever see?)

could be clearly read, she then opened a rear door of the car, removed her coat and the thermos jug, set them on the concrete, and opened the front passenger door. After taking her purse and the tree-stump footstool from the car, she locked all four doors, sat down on the footstool, lifted her coat onto her lap, checked her wristwatch, and, certain that only her head could be seen by the guard, waited for five minutes with her gaze affixed to the plant entrance.

Just before the shift was scheduled to end, Mrs. Tane stood, raised the cover of the footstool, unscrewed the lid of the thermos jug, and poured kerosene from it into the metal bread box. As soon as the thermos was empty, she took up her coat, dipped it into the kerosene, and, as if she were washing a quilt, rapidly swirled it with her hands.

Within half a minute, she put the coat on, buttoned all the buttons, and wiped her fingers on the cloth that had enclosed the needlepoint. Drawing from her purse a waterproof cylinder, she glanced at the sky, then opened the cylinder, turned it nearly upside down, shook out a wooden match, knelt, and, in a crazed and wrong act incapable of achieving any of what she thought of as its humane purposes in the cause of peace, struck the match upon the concrete.

As the workers were spilling out the doors and winding solitary paths in the directions of their cars, in sudden motionless silence they beheld moving toward them a six-foot flame.

"How did that get out?" shouted an assistant manager of the plant, under the impression what he was seeing was a device related to studies of solar-powered weaponry taking place deep within the interior of the buildings.

2

Fall, 1968

Although icicles hung from the cabin roof and the last of the nearby leaves had fallen to the frozen earth, the sun had quickly melted the first marauding snow, thereby unveiling a transitional loss of most autumnal colors. With one exception, all that had endured, while the totality of resignation that was the land struggled to remember the sustaining shapes of longing, were skeletal browns casting lineal shadows on naked, reddish-yellow surfaces, tense and smooth. The snow, however, had done more than eliminate most colors from the landscape: it had shown the end of their lambent reign to have been the sun's method of camou-flaging a diminution of its own capacity to bring warmth.

Mr. Tane had been impelled to drive up the tortuous, mountain road more by a desire to see the evergreens surrounding the little cabin than by the hope of finding his father; for at such a time each year the unyielding patch of green offered the comfort of a promise that eventually there would be a thaw and an accompanying reawakening. Not until he was through the door and sitting in one of the cane chairs, did he apprehend that there was no other place for him to be, no other place where he could be. Across from him his father whittled, as dusk captured the room.

Whether sitting or standing or moving about, Mr. Tane's father had always seemed to be listening to faraway sounds that might the next instant necessitate his departure. Even when he was motionless he did not appear at rest. He seemed always to have temporarily alighted, to have stationed himself unpredictably in the aspect of a sly, hungry coy-ote. His habitual unquiet was partly constitutional, but it also resulted from his being accustomed to living upon land that was rarely level. Most of his life, he had used his feet more to cling with than to step. His arms had frequently been ready to circumvent the impact of a fall. His coordinations, moreover, were not separate; for instead of carrying his weight solely on his legs, he had learned to move in the midst of the uneven terrain with a complex agility dependent upon his continually employing all of his body in rapidly variable positions. Because he relied on them for numerous, daily activities, rather than because he meant to use them for communication, his white-knuckled hands were his most prominent feature. His energy was usually so focused upon them that the attention of others was drawn to them as well; and whenever he made one of his habitual sudden leave-takings, his fingers would leap away first, as if beckoning him to follow.

"Woke up one day this summer and couldn't find my chisel," he said quietly, beginning to speak of the gravestone he was carving for himself. "Realized I must be dead and that everything'd forever be the same, only

I wouldn't know what'd been set up above me. Then I found it, the chisel, right where I'd put it, holding up the window. Wedged it in there so I wouldn't have to hammer in another pulley…Forgetting like that made me think I'd best finish carving my name. Figured I'd wait until spring to start the 1886." Expecting no reply, Mr. Tane's father laid aside his knife, fumbled beneath his chair for a plaid, cotton jacket, and circumspectly draped it about his shoulders, saying, "The way I look at it, son, people started in to thinking death and taxes are the only things certain at the same time they collected up together and stopped paying note to what truly is certain. Which is that the sun will seem to rise in the morning and that most every night will have a skyful of stars lighting up the colors of the spaces around them. Sleep isn't all we need for the next day. We need sleep having been brought on by watching the shiftings of the heavens." Resuming his whittling, he added, "Guess Jack has left."

"Yes."

"Guess he wasn't much help."

"No."

"Guess he couldn't be."

"No," Mr. Tane answered in a voice barely more than a whisper so tired it sounded almost as old as his father's. His shriveled body was huddled within a wrinkled suit. His cheeks floated wan and slack over his jaws. The sallow skin of his forehead had collapsed into his eyes, forcing their darting motions to give way to incessant blinking. His arms lay limply at his sides.

"He doesn't have the least idea how young he is," said his father.

"I suppose that's always true at twenty-four, Pa."

"Twenty-four."

"Twenty-four."

"Well, son…when I was about his age, I wanted to attach myself to some great big project I'd know couldn't ever get finished, so as I could count on working at it the rest of my life. Never did learn how to finish something and get on to something else. That's a common fault around these parts. It's sure, though, there's no telling anyone anything at that age.

All they can give mind to are our failures. I was that way myself. So were you. Probably's just as well he's gone. Might not seem like it, but probably is…I know this much, and not much more; if they turn out the way we want them to, it's likely to mean we've killed the spirit in them. Not anything for you to think you can do with him anymore."

"No," Mr. Tane said. He leaned forward.

"You aren't trying any longer to pretend you didn't lose what you started out wanting, are you, son? You know what I mean, don't you?"

"I couldn't very well be trying that, Pa. Not now."

"I suppose it had happened by the time you were born is the truth. So as what you wanted wasn't apt to be. All that freedom and harmony with the earth never to take place.

"A couple of years into the century. That's when I began to see how it was probably going to go. People were worn out when they got here, so they crowded in together, and who could blame them? But they stayed together long after they had to. It needn't have gone the way it did. The land could have been divided up smaller. They could have kept on heeding to their own food. But they chose to turn to the machines, instead; and some of the machines made it so the few people who had the land'd get more of it and get to be even fewer. Pretty soon nobody could hardly remember it not always having been most everyone buying their food from not more'n a handful of farmers and ranchers, when you think how many of us there got to be out here…If hunger gets separated from the growing and the picking of what a person eats, there's no end to disconnections…What you wanted had a chance for awhile there a half-century ago, though even then not likely east of Chicago." Slipping his knife into a rawhide sheath attached to a corner of the copper mantel of his fireplace, he continued to speak, as he inspected his whittling in the last of the daylight. "Still…I'd say what you've been's a patriot, son. You and your notions of building. I mean that in admiration. There haven't been many patriots, and patriots don't often turn out to be the same as winners. Most people don't hanker after other people trying to tell 'em what they might be if they would."

"In a month or so, when what was started then is finished, I will have no business left, Pa. None at all. I won't get any more. I can't start over again. Not here. Not anyplace. Even so, I'm soon going to have to go somewhere else."

"Now that ain't exactly true, son. It's true enough. But not exactly true. You could start over, but no one'll let you. Sure not here. Probably not anywhere. Not many men know how to keep on working at your age like you do. It's them that'll make it so you can't. There's the truth of it."

"I realize that, Pa. That's their disgrace." Slowly he brought his hands together for a moment, then he let his arms fall back to his side.

"You know," his father said, "when I was...small...I ain't sure why I'm telling you this, son, but when I was...younger than Jack...I'd see the old folks around me...and there'd be so many things I'd want to ask them...But I wouldn't, because I didn't want to remind them how much more time I had ahead of me and how little they had ahead of them. Then when I got older, and they were gone, I'd remember them; and I got started to thinking maybe they'd been sitting there waiting for me to ask, wanting to tell but not able to without the asking. After awhile I got afraid that's the way it'd been. And now that's the way it is. You'll find out when you're my age how little history usually gets told. Sometimes I'll run into a youngster out walking along a stream, and I'll get to hoping I'll be asked to tell it, or some of it even. But I can see that look on their faces of wanting to know but not wanting to remind me. So it all stays inside to join the rest that never got carried on. Mostly, the best stories we get in life are the ones we don't have a chance to tell..."

"If she had said something. If she had said anything. If I had known what she was thinking."

"You would have stopped her before she was done with her first sentence. I don't mean to be harsh with you, son. But there's no reason to let on now you would have heard her."

"I don't know what I...I don't know."

"Your obligation is to stay on and remind them. That's what you've got to do. There's no doubt about that. If you leave now, if you ever leave, she'll be easier for them to forget. It'll be easier for them to think all she wanted to do was die. The sickly see such agonies and deaths as hers as signs of their own mad victories. She was half-crazed, but so is most of the town. I told you that fifteen years ago, and it's far worse now. All around the earth there's a disease gets strength from not being talked about. Surely what happened to her must have shown you what her sickness was. At least you, son. Surely you've let her have that much of a victory. You oughtn't to take that from her, too. She was beyond knowing that we don't *ever* die just because we expect to. Even with her, something else *could* have happened, even at the very last moment. Something that somehow might have helped her make a way to build on what health she had left. You should remember that....And what do you imagine is out there on those government lands with the fences around them? Where do you think those train tracks from the plant lead to? That hasn't been a site of research. It's been a place of unholy studies and insane production. People lying they're doing science, like they've always lied when weapons designed to be aimed at anyone have been meant to get put together. Real research values all human lives. Values our environment...I truly can't see as how much good can come from blaming yourself, son. But you oughtn't to leave her memory to them without you to try to explain it—explain it almost like you were explaining...them to themselves."

"I loved her as I could, Pa. As I could. I don't know what more to think than that."

"It's time for you to be looking ahead, though, son. Past time. I'm not suggesting it'd be anything but a miracle for folks in town ever to take sight of what they've done. And for them to change...People with government contracts, they're likely to follow paychecks and the letter of the law even if it goes against every minute of their days. They tell themselves it's the will of us all they're doing, though they know nobody'd ever say that to their faces. They'd kill everyone in a prison or a concentration camp without looking back and call it the necessary testing of a new bomb, if they were told to."

"There's been talk of moving the plant further from Denver, Pa. Maybe to another state."

"Which would accomplish nothing! It doesn't matter where it's done. Since '45 there's been just two paths: to handle the knowledge as they have handled it or to stop the construction and make agreements of non-use that'll last forever. Even Harry Truman understood that much. Yet the only way those people have been able to put out of their minds all those things would likely be set off was to keep busy producing more of them. The plant makes some of the people in the penitentiaries of this state look like a collection of saints. And that's the sorry truth."

"I don't know as I have the strength for staying on. I don't know as I truly care to. I don't know as to what I could do."

"You owe it to your wife's memory and to your son's future to find out. There's no way getting around that. You have no choice but to keep on here. Unless you want to live out your last years with most every bit of yourself gone. Those are hard words. No other words'd do."

"They'll say I've lost my mind. You know they will, Pa. They're probably saying it already...Even if I do stay, I'll have to sell the house."

"Grief is appropriate for death, son. But not for loss of property. And the only way to comfort grief is to offer to share it. That's what I'm trying to do."

Bending down to the floor and untying his shoestrings, Mr. Tane coughed, cleared his throat, and, raising his voice, said, "Pa, I don't think I can go home tonight. Not tonight. I don't think I can."

"You're welcome with me, son...You're welcome for as long a time as you need. No one'll be bothering you, that's sure. I don't know as I even remember the last time a car's been up that road."

Aware that his father usually slept fully clothed, either in a sleeping bag unrolled outside beneath the overhang of the roof or sitting up by the fireplace in a chair, Mr. Tane nodded, stood, languidly walked to the couch, and stretched himself out upon it, his hands pillowed behind his head.

"Well, son...you know, if it ever does happen, if we do unleash these madnesses again and for the last time, I hope some of us make it through it. I may be a fool to hope that, but I do. And I hope one of them has...a guitar."

"It's been a long while since I've heard you play the guitar, Pa. Play it. Play it, Pa. Play it like you used to."

"Can't help but play it like that. I haven't learned any new music for more decades'n I can count with one hand. The old songs have been enough for me. When I first set to them, it's certain I couldn't have guessed how long I'd be hearing them."

Deliberative and forebearing, Mr. Tane's father went to the cabinet, took out the guitar, tuned it, edged to the window, sat upon the sill, and unassumingly began to strum. His instrument had been more than a solace to him, more even than a companion: it had been nearly an additional limb. He considered it more important to his health than exercise, valued it more than his legs, and regarded it as the primary reason for his longevity.

The songs he played had all been composed before the advent of radio. Most of them were centuries old and had never been written down, instead had been passed from fingers to ears in Europe and from there been transported by solitary strums and picks across the Atlantic Ocean, where they had been adapted to the rhythms of sea shanties. For awhile the songs had almost been put to rest in the work of establishing the fields of New England; but when the United States had begun to expand Westward, they had been revived by voyagers needing both entertainment and sources of inspiritment, been carried to the Mississippi River, and after again having been altered, this time by chords of spirituals, finally been scattered—often as the sole reminders of the communities homesteading players and listeners had abandoned—throughout the arid Great Plains.

Mr. Tane was familiar with the melodies he heard, as he attempted gradually to relax his frame. But he had been unaware of the skill his father had acquired in his many years alone—his many years removed from most of the cacophony of twentieth-century civilization. The music arising, flowing, from the guitar was neither mournful, nor sad, neither joyful, nor happy. It was not ironic. Nor did it evince the patterns that accompany or induce work. Dissimilar as the songs were, they all manifested but one element: simple, unrefined vibrancy. They evoked no emotions, referred to no qualities of land, no seascapes, no fluctuations of the air. They advocated neither resignation, nor endurance, nor triumph, nor even celebration. They advised nothing at all, save delight in partaking of the purely musical process that had spun them neither from humility, nor pride, but rather from a tradition of involvement solely with the manifold variations of sound.

The old man played long past the time when his son's anguished limbs had assumed the stolidity of sleep, played a blending of harmonic strands so distinct in counterpoint that it seemed quite as if there were two guitars. After stopping momentarily to spread a sheet over the comatose form on the couch, he went out into the night to a rocking chair at the rear of his cabin, sat down, and played once again, strumming uninterruptedly and indomitably—until his fingers were too cold for him to go on. Breathing with a steady, unobtrusive regularity that was a semblance of sempiternal calm, he then loosened the six strings of the guitar and balanced it against the clapboard wall behind him. After unbuttoning his jacket, he wriggled his arms out of its sleeves, reached beside the chair for a blanket, wrapped it about his legs, then buttoned the jacket—his collar upraised, the sleeves dangling, his arms folded upon his chest—and turned his eyes, at last, to the stars.

'How was it Jacob Sky Bird used to tell it? He'd let out that yell. "Y— Waa—Se." Which meant he was aiming to tell one of those stories. Not stories they were to him. Explanations they were. Though not exactly that either. Seven brothers there were. Back when his tribe began. Or soon after. Comanche he was. Or Ute. Or long after his tribe began. But anyhow, way before now. Seven brothers and one sister. Or was it seven sisters and one brother? No, it was seven brothers and one sister.

'One of the brothers, any one of them, was always supposed to stay home with the sister. This particular day it was the youngest brother's time to be with her; and for some reason, daydreaming I guess it was, he wandered off to a canyon where no one could find him. So the second brother, he stayed with the sister for awhile. But something the second brother ate, knotweed stalks it was, disagreed with him; and off he went to the medicine man who gave him a chufa leaf potion that put him sound asleep. So the next youngest brother stayed; and it was a bad day, because he up and got bit by a prairie dog; and straight off he went into such fits the other brothers had to knock him out cold. The fourth brother, he got picked up by a giant eagle. An old enemy of the family put the evil eye on the fifth brother, hypnotized him into walking smack into a lair of rattlesnakes that was sunning themselves right at the entrance to a cave of wolves. The sixth brother found all this hard to take and got roaring drunk. The last brother, by mistake, he tumbled into some quicksand and was sinking fast just at when the Comanches or the Utes, whatever the other tribe was, started pouring lickety-split into the campsite, so as the sister, she had nothing for to do but howl out to the Great Spirit for mercy and aid and whatever else the Great spirit could come up with.

'Well, fortunately now, the Great Spirit heard her and looked down, or around or wherever a Great Spirit looks from, and gets this scrawny, old weed to growing right in front of the sister. She grabs onto it and sets to climbing. All the while it's growing fast, the Great Spirit helps the seven brothers out of each one of their predicaments and puts all them brothers up in front of the weed, which by this time has become a tree and is still growing. One by one the brothers begin to climbing, too. And pretty soon all eight of them look down at the tribes below, so far away, seeming like ants, so high was the weed. All at once—it was the Great Spirit did it, had to have been—all at once the seven brothers, the seven brothers they turn into the stars of the Big Dipper and the sister she becomes the North Star.

As the tree is disappearing, the Comanches and the Utes are so wonder struck and amazed, they vow to leave each other alone ever after; and then the Great Spirit real patiently explains in a language everybody understands that the two tribes'll go on in peace like that forever with the eight stars to remind them of how it once had been between 'em....

'Or maybe it was ten brothers, and they became the Herdsman and the sister became Arcturus....

'Long dead now is Jacob Sky Bird. Long Dead.'

Yawning, the old man closed his eyes, resting his chin on one of his shoulders, and prepared to meet the morning. Screaming from the cabin soon awoke him, however. Instantly alert, he got up, vaulted to the window, and peered inside. Assured after several minutes that his son, though thrashing and moaning, slept on, again he settled back into the rocking chair, squinted, and examined the sky.

'I can't recall if she became the North Star or Arcturus. That'd have depended on how many brothers she had. Unless, of course, three of the stars were already there, somehow or other, or got put up later on.

'However it goes, it's quite a story...

'But...for me to have to sit here, sleepless, wondering whether some so-called astrobiologists might have gotten it into what's left of their minds to try to turn my son's dying wife into a...my God, into what?...a perpetually living sun?...now, doesn't that just...now, doesn't that *truly* just...beat *all*?

It was nearly dawn.

PART V

17
Solstice Upcoming

1

She was slightly more than a block away from him. Her face was hidden by a bag of groceries which she carried with both hands. Her hair was cloaked in a scarf. Nonetheless, he recognized her walk and her manner of swaying her head from side to side. Not until they were fewer than ten feet from each other, however, did she see the glint in his eyes; and when she did, she stopped, transferred her grocery bag to her left arm, put her right index finger in her mouth, raised her hand, and said, "Southwest."

"Squalls, probably," he replied. "Off Cape Cod."

"Thermals?"

"Too late in the year."

"Did you know I live on this street?"

"Yes."

"You've had all the addresses?"

"I think so. I've been calling long distance information every few months."

"And when there was no more phone?"

"My Mother got in touch with your last landlord and sent me the forwarding address you'd left."

"But you weren't certain I was still here."

"I checked the mailbox day before yesterday. I came by yesterday, too. I wasn't sure I should knock. I hoped we'd meet."

"You didn't know what my living arrangements are."

"I didn't want to intrude."

"I am living alone," she said, taking his arm. "How many of my addresses did you have?"

"Eight."

"You missed one. Probably the first-year move the phone company let me keep my same number for."

"Four that year, then."

"Yes," she replied. Without looking at each other, they continued on in the direction she had been walking. "And you never called?"

"No."

"I didn't expect you to."

"I understood that..."

"I knew we'd see each other again," she said, smiling. "If....".

"So did I."

"I even thought it would be soon. I've been almost waiting for you. What brought you back to Boston?"

"My mother died," he said quietly.

"When?"

"Ten days ago."

"Ten days...All over the United States," she said quietly, "people were sitting down to Thanksgiving dinners and trying to forget what was flying over us in Kissinger's global alert, 1973 style."

"The man next to me on the way here kept claiming the planes couldn't really be up there. I'd ask him, 'Why does it say what it does in the papers, then?' And he'd just smile like there were some absolutely obvious...for the press to be reporting what wasn't true."

"It was worse than the Cuban missile crisis. At least for me. That combination of unreality and of being inured to it all," she said, then slowly adding, "Had your mother been sick?"

"No," he replied. "Her death occurred at her home…There's nothing for you to feel you have to say."

"I know," she answered. "My father died, too."

"When was…that death?"

"Seven months ago."

"Had you seen him recently?" he asked.

"I'd talked with him on the phone a week before. He sounded the best I'd heard him in a long time. He said, 'I can cry. I can laugh. Everything isn't lost.'"

"How's your mother?"

"She's moved to a condominium in Palm Springs."

"A retirement place?"

"Not officially. But, yes, in effect."

"My mother didn't want a funeral. I was glad of that."

"The ceremonies don't seem to make it all more comprehensible."

"No…"

"What's going to happen to the apartment?" she asked.

"Someone has already rented it. I finished cleaning it out today," he replied. "I just didn't ever think of seeing it the way it is now, empty rooms. I didn't really appreciate that the two of us were the only ones who used all those things."

"I suppose the law firm already has a replacement for her, probably one they'd been grooming for a few years…."

"Yes."

"Where is your luggage?"

"At the train station."

"You're leaving tomorrow?"

"I…"

"You don't have a ticket."

"I don't have a ticket."

"Want to see my work?" she asked without a trace of a suggestion as to what the answer should be.

"Oh, yes."

"There's quite a bit of it. You'd better prepare yourself."

"I want to see it all."

"All but the one I'm working on now," she said, her eyes sparkling.

"Agreed."

He smiled then, a radiant smile enveloping his face, the kind of smile that can occur only when one realizes that in spite of a long absence, one still matters to someone else very much.

"Do you live in your studio?" he asked, as she stepped off the sidewalk and headed toward the red-brick facade of her apartment house.

"You'll see," she replied. "Come this way."

Continuing to smile, he followed her along a flagstone path to the side of the building, where she silently unlocked a door. After angling through a dark passageway and unlocking another door, she led him into a sunny, triangular courtyard, a fourth the size of a football field.

"It's almost an atrium," she said. "I'm the only one who gets to use it." Pointing to a metal bungalow, she added, "That's where I live. It used to be a storage bin. It's a single room...but I guarantee it's going to surprise you. Wait here a minute, will you? I want to get what I'm working on turned to the wall."

"There's no hurry. I have no plans."

As soon as Leah had disappeared inside the bungalow, C. J. stuffed his hands into his back pockets and ambled about the courtyard, whistling.

He had gained more than thirty pounds, but all of it had been translated into trimly hewn muscle. His shoulders had broadened and become rounded. His hips had widened. His legs no longer hinted at an energy coiled within them, but instead reflected an unpretentious, calm strength. His evenly clipped, tawny hair swept modestly past the lower edge of his collar; and a thick, unbrushed lock shaded his eyes.

"Now we're going to take this very slowly," said Leah, standing in the doorway. "Let me have your coat. Nice coat. Sheepskin?"

"Yes," he answered, scraping brown boots on a welcome mat, closing the door behind him. In his heavy, black work pants and red cotton shirt, he seemed to Leah to be as out-of-place in the city, as if he were a muskrat in a swimming pool.

The room was rectangular, approximately twenty-five feet wide by sixty feet long, and had been painted entirely white. Built-in shelving appeared at first glance completely to cover the fifteen-foot walls. But after a moment C. J. discovered that hedged amidst the shelves of one of the walls were an electric stove, a refrigerator, a sink, and a radiator. The floor was unadorned, gray cement.

In front of the appliances was a yellow kitchen table. Four wooden chairs, all with arms, were in place about it; and upon it was a glass bowl of fruit. In one corner of the room was a double bed with an ornately carved headboard. At its foot were a stepladder, a portable record player, and an open, unabridged dictionary. Between the bed and an adjoining wall was an easel holding a canvas, which had been aligned so that its face could not be seen. Next to it was a metal stool four feet high. To the right of the entrance were the only other objects in the room: two, identical reclining chairs.

"No television set," C. J. said.

"I had one, but I got rid of it during the 1968 democratic convention!" Leah replied, clearly very proud of her sparse arrangement. "For awhile, I thought of getting another table to sketch at; but I got conditioned to using the floor."

On the ceiling had been temporarily positioned an array of spotlights, which complemented three skylights, one above the table, one above the bed, and the third above an empty portion of the smooth, solid floor.

"The white walls make it brighter in here than it is outside. But when I want to, I can paint in the courtyard, too…I meant it, C. J. There's quite a bit of work here. It's all on the shelves in the order I did it. Don't start looking yet, though. It's going to take me at least half an hour to get ready for this. Are you hungry? I am. Would you like some kind of lunch?"

"Lunch would be fine," C. J. said, sidling into a chair at the table, narrowing his eyes, and peering up at the skylight directly above him. "This is perfect for you, Leah. Perfect. How did you find it?"

"A difficult process."

"It must have been."

"Ads on bulletin boards in laundromats and grocery stores all over Boston. The newspapers. Trailing every lead I came across. When I first looked inside here, there were shelves everywhere. But the landlord was tired of people leaving their belongings when they moved, so he agreed to take most everything out and to put in the stove and refrigerator. The bathroom and closet were here. And the sink. And radiator, fortunately."

"What about the skylights? I've never seen three of them in one room before. They're certainly ample."

"Some skylights make worse kinds of light for pictures like mine. So close to direct sunlight that fading happens fast. But these are a special kind of glass that keeps out what's harmful. Or most of it.... the landlord told me he'd have them installed if I'd sign a three-year lease. So I did. He even had everything painted, C. J. I was expecting to do that myself. I'd done it in so many apartments already."

"Have you been here a year and a half then?" C. J. asked.

"Closer to a year."

She had taken off her shoes; and her long-sleeved, white blouse was loosely draped over the top of faded blue jeans, which clung tightly to her waist. Rapidly she chopped an onion, a tomato, and an avocado into a green plastic bowl she had first partially filled with mayonnaise and spices.

"Avocados," said C. J. "...I picked them for a time when I was eighteen."

"Where was that?" asked Leah, slicing a loaf of whole wheat bread.

"Texas. I didn't work very hard, though. People take a fondness to anyone that age who's traveling. They don't ever expect much from them."

"I'd live on avocados, if I could afford to..."

Deftly she heaped the avocado mixture over the slices of bread, sprinkled on dried chopped mushrooms and a mixture of cabbage and broccoli
sprouts, put all the sandwiches on one tray, and set it on the table. Then
she poured two glasses of water and sat down. She had completed the
entire process in less than three minutes.

"Well," C. J. asked, large-eyed and amiable, "who in the world is
Gerald Ford?..."

"The Vice President," Leah answered, adding with seriousness, "of not
every Omaha."

"You didn't know anything about him either?"

"Nothing. For a few minutes there, though, I must say I actually
thought Nixon was going to nominate his own wife!"

"Ah," said C. J., laughing and lifting a sandwich from the tray, "but
they have the same state of residency."

"I expected him to announce he intended to direct the Congress to pass
a constitutional amendment eliminating that requirement. Something
similar happened in Alabama, after all. And besides, the war had already
thrown aside so many laws, anything in that realm seemed possible."

"It's as hard to know what's going on now as it was three years ago,"
said C. J. "I'm not really sure that war's over yet. In '71 it seemed to have
ended. And then it hadn't again."

"Yes, and accounts of veterans en masse dumping their medals onto
the lawn of the white house aren't likely to be included in high school
textbooks, are they, C. J.? If people go back to calling it all a conflict, I
am going to emigrate...."

"I guess there just got to be too many troops in Southeast Asia not to
call it a war," said C. J. "Even though it wasn't ever declared."

"Oh, yes, C. J., that's right. yes. I'm...I'm in a distinct minority, I'm
sure; but in spite of all his disregard for the law, I think Nixon's become a
scapegoat," said Leah. "I mean that. The most unlikely scapegoat anyone
could've picked, but a scapegoat all the same. We're busy getting rid of

him instead of dealing with what's been happening these past ten years. The processes of forgetting are well under way."

"Not many people are paying much mind to it, so far as I can tell. To the break-in at the Watergate, I mean," C. J. said, finishing his sandwich and reaching for another. "It's the press is making it look like that's what we're thinking about. Jack says the way they're reporting it makes it obvious how much is left out of histories that get written from mostly using newspapers, magazines, and committee hearing reports. The betrayals of trust the reporters are obviously making turn the whole means of reporting into something as awful as a lot of what's being reported."

"People don't talk as much about any kind of politics as they did ten, eleven years ago. I suppose none of that will come back," Leah said, adding firmly, "We've learned how little power any of us really have."

"Or ever will have," C. J. replied more resignedly than grimly.

"…Now that I think about it, C. J., Boston has changed quite a bit since you left. You must be finding it awfully hard to navigate yourself through it all."

"I hardly recognized downtown."

"Government Center, you mean. Yes, it's the kind of complex that the day it was dedicated looked like it'd been up for twenty-nine years…"

"I can't help but be sorry a lot of buildings that I knew have been torn down for new ones," C. J. said musingly. "Even though I knew it all would be that way…Leah, I…Leah, these sandwiches…they sure are a lot better than the food I'm used to."

"Than what I'm used to, too. I made the mayonnaise myself. Drop by drop, it's an exercise in patience. I used olive oil. That's what you're tasting."

"It's the best meal I've eaten in a long time," C. J. answered, sighing and wiping his lips with a finger. "Have you become a vegetarian?"

"Pretty much so…" Leah replied. "At first it was from economic necessity. Every month I'd feel like I'd pared my grocery list down for the last time. But the next month I'd take even more away from it, wondering each shopping trip how I had managed to be so blithe when I could pick out whatever I wanted...Then I began reading...about how being vegetarian appears to be a lot healthier than any other way of eating. About how organic food requires a lot less energy to produce than any other kind. And about how the ten million children estimated to be dying every year could live if, among other things, we started raising crops instead of livestock on part of the land...I have meat or poultry or fish about once every six weeks now. I don't like them much these days. Five years ago I thought I had to have one of them every night."

"I don't often have beef anymore. I have been eating a lot of fish, though...."

"Which makes me think, C. J., the restaurant we used to go to isn't there anymore. It got torn down awhile back."

"No more nights full of talk and watching graduate students, then. That's too bad."

"Have you been out to Cambridge at all since you've been here?"

"No."

"It was like a battle zone, four, five years ago, that time. Broken windows boarded up with plywood...New buildings are on all the campuses now. The city put in a crosswalk for pedestrians over Massachusetts Avenue. The drivers are happy. And the subway is going to be added onto pretty soon. So *that* square isn't going to be the end of the line much longer."

"The way it was then...it seemed so permanent. I guess that must always be true of what's around you when you're in college."

"Yes," Leah agreed. "It did seem permanent. All of it. And at the same time there was so little to hold onto."

"Yeah, but now, though, it seems like there's even less. At least it's harder than I had any idea it'd be for me to feel comfortable. In the city, I mean. A lot harder, even though on one level I don't really think of people as living in the country or the city but as living all together on the earth and lately in space...But I didn't know how used I've gotten to the open sky, Leah. I've forgotten how to sit in a subway. Hearing, too. I'd forgotten how much we have to block out here. The first three days I was jumping at all the sounds."

"I can imagine," Leah replied. "It must be incredible for you…" Her eyes beginning to glow with curiosity and confidence, she carried the tray and glasses to the sink. On her way back to the table, she lifted a handful of her hair over one shoulder, tossed her head, and settled her hands in the front pockets of her jeans, saying, "…Well, you can start looking at my drawings and paintings now, if you want. By the outside door. Take the ladder. There's an attachment on it to support the canvases. You'll see how it works. At the top of one section go to the top of the next one. Same at the bottom. Stop and lie down on the floor, if you get tired. And don't feel you have to say anything. I really mean that. It's quite enough for you just to look. I may be watching you. I probably won't be able to help it. Will that make you self-conscious?"

"I don't think so."

"Tell me if it does."

"Do I go to the bottom or the top first?" C. J. asked, dragging the ladder into the corner by the door.

"The bottom."

As C. J. bent toward the first shelf, Leah went to the phonograph, turned it on, placed a recording onto the spindle, and adjusted the volume.

"What's the music?" C. J. asked.

"*Mass*…. Have you heard it?"

"No."

"It opened the Kennedy Center for the Performing Arts in Washington, D. C."

"Yes, I read about it. Some people were saying that government agents were translating the Latin to see if antiwar messages had been coded into it."

"However that all went, it's the only music after, after…how many albums could it have been by now? thousands?…They collect up in most of our lives, and bring back all the times we've played them. Then all at once, they don't sound the same. Not because they've been damaged, but because we've changed. We can't understand why we ever wanted to hear them. But we don't toss them out. They pile up unlistened to, like unopened scrapbooks. They become quaint, and we begin to suspect that we've become quaint ourselves. It must be going on all over the world. We're the first ones it's happened to. We spent so much more consecutive time with them than our parents could have with their music...But what I started to say was that out of all the albums I've heard by now, this is the only one that has ever come very close to making me cry. And it does that every time I play it." Her voice cracking, she added, "Though usually not this soon." Quickly climbing down from the ladder, C. J. took a step toward her; but she waved him back to the drawings and paintings, saying, "No, I'm all right. Go on looking. It's...it's that what I do is seldom viewed by anyone else, C. J."

The first shelves contained hundreds of realistic images of human faces Leah had sketched using chalk, oil crayons, colored pencils, and pastels. They were drawings tracing the development of a skill that gradually had become almost photographic. The perspectives and colorings were traditional, but the range of age and emotional attitude was extensive.

As C. J. proceeded along the wall, the adroitly executed, yet simplistic and undistinguished, sketches evolved into a far more intricate series of acrylic portraits on paper. These grew ever more exploratory and soon came to include peripheral representations of photographs and mirrors, each of them delineating variations in age, mood, or circumstance of a central facial image. Intermingled with this group of variform studies were several paintings—Leah's earliest compositions on canvas—that made use of surreal, architectural backgrounds largely consisting of multiple, tiny, limned windows, each again containing a different lifelike semblance of a primary figure, thereby producing an impression that the person depicted was being judged both by memories and self-expectations.

There then occurred a fundamental change in the utilization of color: interlapping, similar-sized likenesses of one face had been painted onto the same surface by means of nearly nonobjective, segmented tones, lines, and shades. The technique had slowly been perfected and eventually had

resulted in an illusion of superimposition presenting the viewer with precise considerations of the manners varying emotions exist in relation to
each other.

The next shelves held only canvases; and oil paints had been employed on
all of them in order to compare juxtaposed objects usually analogous either
in color, shape, or function: a snail shell had been compared to a dried
flower, a parking meter to a postmarked stamp, a necktie to a passport, a loaf
of bread to a sponge, the front of a schoolroom to a television set.

As soon as she had mastered enough procedures appropriate only for oil
paints, Leah had returned to portraiture, utilizing nonlifelike pigments in
a doggedly experimental manner, while relying on her earlier methods of
illusory superimposition; and after a time, by means of consistently
associating distinct clusters of colors with particular feelings and separate
attitudes, she had managed to accomplish the construction of an elemental,
visual idiom. Her subsequent works seemed to suggest that every emblematic
model she had portrayed, each in a series of paintings, had stood before a
succession of mirrors, each of which had been tinted a different color and
then been shattered into the prismatic, slivered components of what
resembled meticulously pieced together puzzles. Although the mosaical
configurations were investigations of the attempts people make to resolve
some conflicting aspects of their lives, whenever an arrangement of tones
and shapes seemed to be approaching a balance·indicative of peaceful
harmony, grotesquely distorted fragments would come to dominate an
ensuing, segmented depiction of the same figure. The inevitability of this
having happened would then at once be seen to have been implicit within
the previous, complementary studies of that specific personality. What
had thus been chronicled were struggles apparently being waged for their
own sakes rather than for the sake of resolutions of the contradictory
facets of individual consciousnesses.

It was late in the afternoon when C. J. completed his viewing of the
final portrait. He had moved the ladder the length of two walls and most

of the length of a third. After standing for a moment in silence, he turned, faced Leah, and said simply, "Thank you."

Leah eyed him.

Then she began to laugh.

"What?" he asked, sitting down beside her on the floor. "What?"

"It's just that that's all I wanted you to say. That's all I needed. That was six years, C. J.; and it feels peculiar to have to tell you this; but I will, anyway. For reasons mostly beyond my comprehension, when people find out what it is I do, it doesn't usually occur to them to ask to see any of the work. Isn't that incredible? If it does occur to them, they think they're supposed to make all kinds of comments fitting me into this or that trend or that they're supposed to marvel at how much effort I put into it all. They think they're supposed to trace influences on me as if artistic inspiration is a twin of the Olympic torch. Put me in the supposed line of development big money in art depends on: impressionism, cubism, abstract expressionism. The line that ignores most of the people on earth and denies that two-thousand-year-old art can be as valid an influence on an artist as what was done ten years ago. Progress and artistic development just aren't the same thing, C. J., and neither moves in straight lines. Nor are they subversive. And creativity isn't the same thing as originality. Really, the whole idea of calling a few artists major is ridiculous! Some art is of some interest to some people at some times; and that's all there is to it. Works get forgotten, shut away, rediscovered—and all that artists can do is create as well as we can, whenever we can, how we can, for as long as we can, where we can…It's incredible that people cannot accept that a painting is merely to be looked at…Yes, C. J., you're welcome!" She linked her fingers together in her lap and continued, "It's strange, but this whole time, I haven't missed you. I had no doubt about your being almost right next to me…Watching you look just now at my work made me aware how patient I've become…. I fairly constantly expect rejection. I have little reason to expect anything else. I patiently try to get people to talk…and I find out how I've been misunderstood this time…and I see whether I can manage to have the person stay around long enough for me to make myself clear in whatever their terms are."

"What're you working on now?" C. J. asked, lying down with his back on the floor and sliding a pillow under his head.

"The painting you can't see."

"Ah."

"It's on the easel."

"No questions?"

"Only that one."

"I guess it was easier to ask about the future than to...than to try and tell you what I think about what you've already created."

"Yes, but...I don't want what I do to be...overemphasized. Even by you, C. J. Almost anything else that can be seen is more amazing than any visual art can ever be. Paintings help seeing, help quite a lot, should help; but they shouldn't be substitutes for the rest of experience; they should enhance it...I want to offer psychological insights more than I want to produce pure studies of light. That makes me completely unfashionable. At least for now...What I see is always going to be bound up with English, but to some extent I can identify emotional qualities that words can't indicate. So to label my works as studies in fear or kindness or something like that would bring the same distortions to them that words bring to everything else. Not distortions, but the same set of simplifications...That's why I left everything untitled. Colors are so very different from words. Because of time, you see. The durations of one's relationships with a painting depend upon the choices of involvement. Something that's framed can be glimpsed or be looked at throughout a life. But a book demands the time required from the first page to the last. Books can't be encountered all at once, whereas colors have to be, usually..."

"What I liked the most..." C. J. said, "is that the characters...is that what you'd call them? Types?"

"Not archetypes, that's for sure. They're too grounded in the present for that. I started out trying to establish types; but later on, I got interested in how people vary, how we influence each other, what happens when the types meet. I suppose that's what makes you think of them as characters, especially the last ones. Yes, characters, I'll settle for that...What was it you began to tell me, though?"

"The expressions...no matter what they are...there's always a trace of wondering in them...That's what I liked the most."

"Oh, I see that in people, C. J. I see that. Do you think I'm being too sympathetic?"

"I don't know. I hope not."

"The techniques are imaginative. They're mine. I'm proud of them. And I try to use them to depict realities. But it gets difficult knowing whether I'm being empathetic or rationalizing. Lots of times I worry that I'm fantasizing what I want to see because I'm too afraid to criticize what I do see."

"My mother used to tell me that my father, when they first knew each other, would say that criticism involves the obligation to suggest alternatives."

"I certainly agree with that. I'm working on being able to offer ideas for paths people should take. I can't do that yet. All I can do is observe and portray and hope I'm being accurate," Leah said, rising, walking slowly to one of the reclining chairs, sitting down, and beginning to rock. "C. J., I'm getting tired of talking about me. I want to hear about you. How have you lived? Can you tell me? Some of it? Do you still have the same truck?"

"Yes, still the same truck," C. J. replied, rolling over on his stomach. "I haven't done much thinking about the past, until these last few days. There hasn't been much reason to. I didn't realize how much less I trust to chance now than I did even two years ago. It took awhile to learn how to plan."

"You didn't much want to plan. When you left."

"No," C. J. said. He pushed his lock away from his eyes and lifted himself up onto his elbows. "When I left here, I wanted so much to be wherever I was going I didn't want to take the time to get there."

"So where did you go first? Do you remember?"

"We just drove. Just drove, Leah. I made most of the decisions. It isn't that way now. But it was then. It was Jack thinking I'd be able to decide that let me do it. I needed his thinking that. I couldn't ever have done it alone. I didn't know that then."

"Traveling must've been new to him," Leah said, tossing a pillow from hand to hand. "It wasn't to you."

"It was more than it being new, though. It was...Well, you know how he was then."

"Worn out. Completely."

"Yes, but also—so much it was hard for him to know whether it was...real. Not because he'd been imagining, I mean, but because of...how he grew up, Leah. What he grew up in. It wasn't until we'd stopped a few places before he started getting any kind of a sense of confidence, I think...he'd just seemed to have had that before. He didn't really have it..."

"He probably couldn't have."

"No."

"...Where was it you stopped, C. J.? What did you do?"

"We drove straight from here to Pittsburgh. I've always liked Pittsburgh. It's an honest city. The atmosphere. It's obvious what happens there. It isn't hidden. The neighborhoods are mostly like what the areas around depots are in other cities. There's a sort of smell of coal in the air, and that gave me the idea of going to West Virginia and finding out about work in the mines there. So that's what we did. The trains in Appalachia move real slow. Through the mountains. Boxcars. Open. Filled with ores. One of the engines heading along beside a road we were on, I yelled out to the conductor asking where we could get jobs. I didn't know much about unions then. Didn't really consider them. I've had to learn a lot. Where they're likely to be. What you have to say to get hired. Shouting back and forth like that, the conductor told us about a town. We went there, and what it turned out to be was a railroad crossing near some mines. Houses spread through the hills. We got hired right away, loading boxcars. Eight, ten hours a day. It was good for Jack. He needed something wouldn't make him think much about whys and hows and all. We found this abandoned shack up on a slope-sided coulee. Lines of property seemed hazy to me then. With all that, things didn't work out too well. We got on each other's nerves…Sometime that fall, I don't know exactly when, I guess we'd been there about four months, we drove up to the dock; and there was the county sheriff fingering his club, the foreman with him. That was the end of loading boxcars."

"They didn't have to say anything?"

"No…Their faces were enough…But we should've been ready for that, though. It was getting on toward winter. The work was going to be way less. We had to be run out of a couple more jobs before we got on to when being fired was likely to happen and know to leave before it did. It was November, I remember now, because the next place we went was Duluth, Minnesota. There've been so many stops I've lost track of them all. But a reason I remember that one is because we had Thanksgiving dinner in a boat restaurant on Lake Superior. Duluth is kind of like Pittsburgh in that it's clear what goes on there. Steel production mostly…We found work stacking beams in the supply yards…Even when unions are strong, like they were there, there's almost always something to do for people who don't belong to them. You can get hired so long as you don't want it to last. And you've gotta look enough like you know what you're doing to satisfy everybody that you might've done it before. But neither one of us much liked being in the city. We heard of a resort the owners wanted someone to stay through the winter at. Look out for thefts. Do a little bit of upkeep. We took it right away."

"Minnesota. That's where lots of lakes are."

"There's snow there, too. I didn't have any idea how much there'd be…Hadn't learned yet to find weather reports about where I was going…Oftentimes, we couldn't move the truck. Drifts eighteen feet high!…We kept on there until spring. That was a good time. There was space enough for us both. Lots of books in the office. We read quite a bit. Jack got interested in wildlife management, fisheries, that kind of thing;

and whenever the roads were cleaned up and dry enough, he'd take off for a reserve area. Ducks or geese. Or for a hatchery. I did a lot of reading in geology and crop management. Irrigation. I liked doing that. Easing up. Knowing I wouldn't be examined on anything. My mind got freer. I'd look for what I wanted to find out, instead of what somebody might be expecting me to have memorized."

"Did you do any ice fishing, anything like that?"

"It was pretty much a reading time is all...I suppose, though, that's when I started learning how to plan. I studied books of maps, guessing what the lay of the land might be. Traveling after that wasn't traveling unaware. March came, and I wanted to get back to the ocean. That was good with Jack, so we drove down to New Orleans. Following the Mississippi all the way. It's just a trickle to begin with up in northern Minnesota. We got hired on a shrimp boat, and things seemed to be going fine, except after awhile it was plain we were either going to have to do some pretty convincing pretending or find ourselves being awfully hated. As far as Jack and I were getting on, things were great, but..."

"That wasn't about to be appreciated by a lot of Louisiana fishermen."

"No."

"Attitudes like that would've surprised you very much. Me, too. Then. We thought those kinds of battles ended with haircuts."

"Yeah..." C. J. responded. Then he stood, went to the sink, washed his hands, and sat down in the other reclining chair. "Leah, it was there in New Orleans Jack got a telegram from his father...it said that...his mother had died.... So we drove up to Colorado. It was more than that she had died, Leah. She had...Leah, she...she had set her body on fire in the parking lot of the weaponry plant by their town."

"Oh, my God, C. J. My God!"

"Jack was right off collaring folks on the street, trying to tell them why she'd done it, knocking on doors, making phone calls. Everybody shied away from him real soon. To them it was the United States he was attacking. He'd keep saying it was the weapons plants everywhere his mother had meant, but nobody was...nobody was..."

"Identifying what's purely human," said Leah, unsuccessfully searching for C. J.'s eyes with her own, "keeps coming at the bottom of the list of our priorities. I'd hoped pictures of the earth from the moon would change all that. Maybe they would have by now, if war hadn't been that much to our mind.

"...Let me put this together for a minute.... Eugene McCarthy in New Hampshire, President Johnson announcing he wasn't going to run again, Martin Luther King, Jr. dying, and Robert Kennedy. Jack was walking the streets trying to.... Where were you, C. J.?"

"I stayed in Denver. I think I must have been renting in the cheapest rooming house in the city. It was originally a miners-of-gold hotel. I decided I'd wait to see what was going to happen and try to get some money together, so I did factory work out of a bunch of temporary agencies. If you get tied up with just one or two, they'll make it so you earn the least possible money on which to survive. That way there's nothing for you to do but keep with them. The neighborhood I was living in was sort of like the Times Square of the Denver ghetto. Five Points, it was called. And after about a month I figured out that since I was the only white person around, the other people had been thinking I was a dope dealer and had been waiting for me to start in selling. Things were getting tense. Jack finally realized there wasn't anything more he could do at his home. He wanted to go to the Chicago convention, but I talked him out of it."

"You started driving again?"

"Yes."

"C. J., would you like some herbal tea?"

"Yeah, I would. I feel kind of...kind of thirsty."

"I'll heat the water," Leah said. She got up out of her chair, flicked on a spotlight set at an angle to illuminate the table, then turned on a burner under a teakettle, handed a cup with a tea bag to C. J., and sat down again opposite him.

"You'd gotten up to telling about the summer of '68 everyone hates to remember," she said. "Five years ago."

"Yes."

"Go on."

"We were on an old road in Kansas. July, it must've been. Anyway, we saw smoke seemed like was coming out of nowhere. We pulled off the road and drove toward it. Found a factory. There in the middle of the plains! Not exactly a factory. It was a place where bread companies from all over the Midwest would ship their pans to every once in awhile to get them cleaned and coated with this rubberlike stuff that makes it so the bread'll fall out easy. They weren't pans like you'd think of, though. More like great big muffin pans. Holding twenty or twenty-five loaves. I've forgetten how many. Maybe it was forty. The people who ran the place needed work done, and said we could live out in a barn that was nearby. There everything was way away from any cities, which was what both of us wanted. Working ten or twelve hours a day. Vats of boiling cleaning fluid. Ovens as big as a garage...This fixative stuff'd get on our arms, and we'd have to dip them in soapy water, which hurt a lot at first—until our skin got layered right...Swinging across the ceiling on ropes from one operation to another. It was the closest-to-wild civilized thing I'd ever seen. Tens of thousands of loaves of bread depending on us...Sometime in September we decided we'd better get settled early that fall for winter. So we drove through the Southwest, trying to figure out what we'd do. And that worked out to be pretty much all we did. Every town we'd drive into, if it would look like we were going to stay, the sheriff would soon be standing in front of the truck. There was likely to be a thing going on involving him and whoever owned the hotel and whoever needed chores done, so people like us'd get paid as much as would take care of our bills, until the work nobody else'd do was about finished; and then the three groups, they'd get together and let us know it was time for us to be going somewhere that wasn't near. We kept that up for a good while. Paying some taxes, too. From town to town. Oklahoma, New Mexico, Texas, Arizona, Utah."

"What kind of work were you doing?" asked Leah, standing, turning off the burner, and pouring boiling water into C. J.'s cup, then into another for herself.

"Construction, mostly," C. J. replied, as Leah again sat down across from him. "Roofing, especially. I couldn't even lift a batch of shingles at first. But I got so I could throw them up from that pickup to the rafters...I enjoyed that period. Wandering. What we were doing made some kind of sense. Enough. Nice being up high. In the wind...Spring of that year we started camping out. But it was real hard keeping clean and taking care of food. And no one else wanted us to be around very long. People who drift get adjusted to being used for keeping in line the ones in the regular crews by making 'em remember how easy it is to get laid off. There's jobs we would've stayed on longer for, but we couldn't. Small towns tend to favor permanent roots."

As C. J. spoke, whenever he would describe a situation or outline a dilemma, he repeatedly would raise his right arm with his palm toward the floor; while shifting into explanations of the solutions that had been resorted to in solving any problem, he would turn his hand over. His manner was both easygoing and firm.

"We kept on like that into '70, talking with lots of folks, farmers mostly, checking out when there might be work, what it would be, what's planted and harvested where, exploring from the dirt roads that usually weren't on any maps. Stumbling onto lakes. Abandoned mines. Most of them marking dreams of a century ago that never came to anything. Sometimes there'd be a commune had taken over a few of the buildings."

"Did you feel like outsiders in places like that, too?" asked Leah, removing the tea bag from her cup. "I hope not. I don't see how you could've."

"Yeah, but we did, though," said C. J., removing his tea bag and handing it to Leah. "More so even than in the small towns. People our age, all in a group, were suspicious of us. They had their own visions, I guess you'd...say. Couldn't stand being challenged."

"Did you find any communes that seemed like they were going to last at all?"

"No, we stopped even thinking of that as a possibility. Most of them folded before they'd been going a year.... I suppose some are still around, though."

"C. J....what about dinner tonight? How does a cheese fondue sound?"

"...You're going to have to explain to me what it is."

"You haven't had one before?"

"I haven't even heard of...What is it? Cheese...?"

"Fondue. I'm sure you'll like it. Let it be a surprise. It takes a long time to eat. If worse comes to worst, there's a restaurant a block from here."

"Yeah, okay. I trust you."

"You'd better, C. J. You'd better," Leah said, getting up, walking to the sink, and taking her still partially full cup with her. "Keep on talking. It'll take me a while. Be sure and let me know if you want some more herbal tea."

"Leah?..."

"I can feel it coming. It's going to be about the paintings, isn't it?"

"Yes."

"Maybe I'd better finish off my herbal tea first...No. No, I won't. All right, C. J....What?"

"All I can really tell you about them—and it doesn't seem like enough, not near enough—but I can't say any more right now than that what's radiated from you out of those skylights seems to me worth what the sun has radiated in through them.... And I'll look for the wonderings..., Leah."

"Oh, that's enough for you to say," Leah replied. "That's quite enough, C. J....Thank you." Turning immediately to the refrigerator, she removed a melange of vegetables, cheeses, and spices. Her movements were as precise as they had been earlier when she had prepared lunch, but they had become more subdued. When she sat down at the table and began to cut the vegetables, she appeared to be studying their shapes and colors, all the while continuing to listen to C. J.'s words, which steadily wound about each other across the now darkened room.

"...Early in '70 we got the idea of hiring ourselves out for odd jobs. House painting. Refinishing. Plumbing. Real estate agents were good help for that. There'd likely be something they'd want fixed up one way or another. That turned out real well. We could set our own hours. Not have anybody over us. Jack and I got so we worked together without any hassles. Sometimes one of us would take on a job alone, and the other one would go off somewhere. We kept that up for about a year.... By then, we had enough money not to have to be desperate; and we met a farmer in southern New Mexico, started talking with him like we did lots of other ones. He had a cabin nobody else was using. Said we could live in it. So we did. I guess we brought in a little more money to the country store. Gave people something to gossip about...We were there five months. Fishing. Hiking...It was desert land. The smell of sage all around. We learned how to get water from a cactus. I did a lot of reading. Botany. And I got an idea on mushrooms. Gathering them and selling them by roadsides...We did that for a few months. Traveling. We got used to being outside, got to be able to predict the weather pretty much. Know where prairie dogs'd probably be. Snakes. Coyotes. Mosquitoes. What to steer clear of...About a year ago, we were on some Wyoming grassland. Searching for mushrooms. The land there has the same kind of feeling the ocean does, Leah. The Great Lakes, too. That holy combination of always being the same and always changing. A rancher drove up and asked us if we wanted to take on his sheep for him.

"We said we didn't know anything about sheep; and he told us that didn't matter, there wasn't much to learn, it just needs people would be willing to stay with them...there's more to it than that, but not much more, really...Sheep have got to be watched, or otherwise they get into all kinds of trouble. If you aren't careful, one of them'll fall off a cliff and get trapped on a ledge halfway down, or stray into a shallow brook and end up stuck in the mud, chewing a poison plant."

"That's what you've been doing for a year, then?"

"Yes."

"Do you have horses?"

"They gave us a jeep. It works better. It'll go over anything. And two collies."

"How many sheep do you take care of?"

"Around eighteen hundred...June to September they get herded to the mountains. October to May we drive them along river valleys. They travel about ten miles a day on the average. Shearing's done in the spring. That's where my coat came from. In the fall they'll graze on the stubble in fields. Get the soil ready for winter. One of em'll eat the grass for less than a sixth of an acre in the time it'll take a cow to eat the whole acre. Some grasses'll increase with the grazing you said a little while ago we perhaps shouldn't have...I don't know. I'll have to give it some thought...The sheep are picky when they have a chance to be; and usually the increasing grasses are the ones for which they don't have much taste. Rams'll weigh about 175 pounds. Ewes about 140."

"Is that where Jack is now? Wyoming?"

"Yes, that's right. He's close to the Tetons."

"How did they find you ten days ago?"

"Helicopter."

"What about Jack and the draft, C. J.?" Leah asked hesitantly, measuring spices into a bowl with one hand and stirring melted cheese with the other. "Whatever happened with him?"

"That's unfinished."

"I forgot that it can go on for all of you until you're old enough to be presidents of these United States. I'm trying to improve myself in terms of memory. I recognize my need to...."

C. J. lowered his eyes and said, "You know, seeing you now makes me remember I didn't really intend to be as alone as I've been. I didn't expect it. We go lots of weeks without even seeing anyone else. Sometimes I've thought about hitching up with an archeological team. Or a geological survey outfit, maybe. For the contacts with the people and.... That kind of work might be better than what we did before. Most of the jobs, at least it's been clear what was supposed to be done. And I've been able to do it. The less money I can get by on, the more I know about food and land, the freer I am...It's funny, but when I was in anthropology at Yale, I used to read about tribes of hunters and gatherers, and some of how they lived seemed reasonable to me, more reasonable than quite a bit of what was going on around me. It's weaponry plants that seem uncivilized to me...I've done a lot of makeshift hunting and gathering myself during the times we weren't working anywhere. I probably know more about soils and what grows wild than most farmers do. I've had to learn it. We were hungry. We also had to keep moving on. With how the energy situation is getting to be, nobody can be sure how many ways anyone's living now may be passing soon. I'd rather know how to cook mission bell roots so they taste like potatoes or how to make flour out of cattail leaves or tea out of sumac than learn most anything I can. I feel safer with the kind of knowledge I've been getting." He stood, shuffled to the table, and sat down in one of the wooden chairs.

"I want to hear about the people you've met," said Leah, breaking a loaf of French bread into small pieces.

"I've got a lot of stories by this time."

"Tell me some of the best of them."

"Yeah, all right...I guess I remember especially this one old man in Utah. Said he'd fixed his horse up with the shoes on backwards, so as he could hide from the draft in 1918. He'd gone into the woods and hadn't barely seen anybody since. The tracks made it look like he'd ridden out instead of in. Most of his clothes were made out of animal skins he'd sewn together. He hadn't ever heard of television. Kept thinking it was like a phone where you'd see who you were talking with...People like that, after they're sure you're serious about wanting to know, they're willing to help you along, teach you. I found out a lot from him about food...Then once in Arizona, just after sunrise, we met a Navajo family, who were having breakfast near the Grand Canyon. They took us to where they lived. Caves dug out of a cliffside. Like Mesa Verde. Only simpler. Made me think of you, though, there was so much color. That's where I learned how to stone-grind flour and bake bread on a slab of rock." Drawing a hand through his lock, he added, "I almost wrote you about a place in Wyoming where we ran into a man and his wife, both of them in their seventies. They made sculptures. But only of each other. Completely realistic. They did the whole process themselves. From getting the rock, down to the last chiseling. They'd been doing that for twenty years."

"That's wonderful, C. J.! How many sculptures were there? Did you see them all?"

"Yeah, there were about three dozen, I guess. They were spread over a field of clover. Life-sized mostly. Vines had crawled up onto some of them..." Sighing, he stood, then walked to the shelf containing Leah's collection of phonograph albums, began to thumb through them, and lowering his voice said, "Thinking about that...makes me realize...makes me realize how I've not been accomplishing much of anything yet, Leah. At least in what you might call an applied sort of way. I've started some experiments in growing, though...Pure science is what it is, really...I must have about forty plots planted around Wyoming and the Southwest in out-of-the-way places no one else is likely to find...I don't know exactly what any of it's leading to. But I'm happy doing it. Trying to figure out what effects soil conditions have. Altitude. Climate. Water. I've done quite a bit of transplanting. Cross-pollinating. One garden I've already got some third-generation hybrids...So far, it's like my questions are flowing with the curves of the land and the twistings of the weather instead of with any particular kind of ideas I want to test out. Understanding what I can about natural processes seems to me a main reason for being alive. It's science I'm doing, and that means it's trying to find knowledge that'd benefit people—benefit people ecologically. Knowledge that'd have nothing to do with any kind of weaponry. It's taking me a long time to find my way mainly because so much of what got called science at Yale was what's behind putting together what may end all our lives..."

"What about songs, C. J.? Are you still writing songs?"

"No. Not lately. I probably will again sometime. I just haven't been in the mood. Jack plays the guitar, though. He plays it quite a bit. He's gotten good. He'll strum four or five hours at a stretch. Music comes easier outside than it does in a building. It's like the other sounds call it up. I'd swear the birds sing with that guitar. There's nights I'd even swear the locusts do...Jack's been doing some writing. He's working on an article about civil employment. For a legal journal. He's been talking about going back to law school in a year or two. I think he'll do it...."

"...And kites, C. J.? What of kites?"

Nonchalantly tapping his fingertips against his cheeks, C. J. returned to the table and sat down, saying, "I've never been inclined to have the sort of maturity that lets people who worked on the atomic bombs be predicting now that the human race has twenty-five more years to survive, Leah. Science didn't make that state of affairs. Evil did. And ignorance. And insanity. Kites can be there either for good or for evil; and I'll never get too old to fly them...For me, they're...for gestures...for *good* gestures...toward some other ways of living. That's what they've always been for me...It used to seem they couldn't help but bring me friends. But they haven't. They haven't at all. They do the opposite. They separate me. More every year. I'm sorry. Sorry for other people. There's so much peace peace that'd be easy to get to, if we all just would."

Nodding, Leah put a salad bowl, a tray of bread, and a pitcher of ice water in the center of the table, arranged two place settings, and stepped back to the stove. "I would've asked you about kites right away," she said. "I was afraid to, C. J." Silent, smiling, he reached for the pitcher and filled their glasses with water, as she turned away from him and withdrew a cheese fondue pot from one of the shelves. "This fondue pot is where I keep my money," she explained. "Whenever I happen to have any." Licking her lips, she wiped the pot clean, poured steaming cheese into it, and lit a flame in an open-ended metal cube underneath it. "We're about ready," she said, not seeing until she had set the pot on the table that C. J. had flinched backward in his chair and was trembling involuntarily.

"What's wrong?" she exclaimed. "What's happened?"

"Every time I see fire…"

"I should've realized, C. J."

"There's no way you could've."

"I didn't think."

"It started happening right off," said C. J., breathing heavily and forcing himself to look at the flame. "Seems like it's going to stay with me."

"Do you want…?"

"No, nothing. I'm fine now."

"You're sure?" Leah asked, sitting down.

"Sure."

"C. J., I'm sorry."

"Yeah, well…it's no…Tell me what we do to eat."

"Just…just put pieces of bread on our forks and take turns moving them around in the cheese. It's the cheese with the least cholesterol I could find, the least sodium…Anyway, if the bread comes off your fork, you lose a turn."

"Sounds simple enough. Can I have one practice?"

"Yes, but only one."

After spearing a piece of bread, he swirled it in the cheese and grinned; but as he lifted out the fork, the bread fell away.

"Timing. You have to feel it. Have some salad and watch me," Leah said, pointing her fork toward the ceiling. "C. J.…… I want you to know I didn't count on being as alone as I've been either. It's been necessary. Not so much for developing my techniques of making art as for learning how to see. That's a different process for a woman, very different, because most of the images we've had have probably been from men. That's all we've had to rely on. We've had to think of ourselves as men have seen us."

"What about when the fondue pot hasn't had cheese in it, though? How have you gotten along?"

"If I tell you what I did, you'll probably be able to relate it to what I was painting when I did it."

"Good. I'd like that."

"I'm not going to be giving you an examination on the relationships between the work and the life."

"I didn't expect one," C. J. said, laughing. "Start at the beginning. Tell me what happened after graduation."

"I got a job as a clerk in a clothing store, C. J. Starting the very next week. Drew at night. You know what it's like when you first have to handle the routines of shopping and cooking. Laundry. Even though no one would be apt to be around, you think it's because you're breaking free of them. Getting independent."

"Yeah, that's pretty much what happened when I left Yale," C. J. said.

"I'm sure it was," Leah replied, as she transferred a cheese-soaked piece of bread from the pot to her plate. "That all lasted about three months for me. Time then appeared so slow, compared to now, it seemed like three years. I moved twice, was proud of myself after every paycheck. But finally I got it into my head that life couldn't go on being like school had been. And one Saturday morning I woke up, had a bowl of cereal, went back to sleep, got up in awhile, had another bowl of cereal; and I started feeling that that's all that would ever happen. All that ever had happened. Even my memories seemed like a set of filing cards that didn't apply to anything I'd done or would do. They just accompanied the endless cycles of naps and cereal…What are you smiling at?"

"Thinking about you with a bowl of cereal for eternity."

"Oh, but, pretty soon I took the garbage out; and I was sure I hadn't done that the first time…"

"And so that's how you learned about the importance of sleep."

"Yes, and these days, whenever I begin to think that all that exists is what's in front of my nose, I take out a box of cereal and remind myself I probably haven't been feeling with my back for three or four hours!"

"I'll keep that in mind, Leah," said C. J., relaxing again, unbuttoning his sleeves, and folding them to his elbows. "It may come in handier for me than you might think. The remedy of remembering to feel with my back...So what'd you do next?"

"I had a little money saved. I quit the job and tried to paint full time. No one was interested in my work. I clenched up, wondered whether I knew what I was doing. Classes weren't there to complain about or get supported by. I saw how little I'd actually done those four years...I ought to've said that *almost* no one was interested in my work. Tom Miernan was. You knew about him. I had him as an instructor. He flunked me for not writing a term paper."

"I remember."

"It was his last year of graduate school, C. J. We moved in together in September."

"I'm glad. I'm glad you did. I'm glad you didn't have to be alone."

"Yes, there was that. But I leaned on him more than I should have. I knew I was doing it at the time. I was scared. In spite of everything I'd done to try and get ready. I was probably somewhat like Jack was at first with you. After about a month I got a part-time job in a research lab at City Hospital. Nothing much, cleaning up mostly. It was good, though, because I saw so many faces, especially in the lunchroom. People tend to be more open around a hospital environment than in most other situations. Their expressions are more definite. It was helpful to me. All of that. And the hours let me paint. Tom was working on his dissertation. It wasn't until he'd handed it in that he understood how few people would read it. He'd convinced himself he'd been composing a book, and it had turned out to have been an exercise. A way for his graduate committee to decide whether he'd acquired academic disciplines, more than their being concerned with what he'd written. That was hard on him. Very hard on him. So much work. So few rewards.... Anyway, he got a teaching position out of it. In Wisconsin. That's what dissertations are for, really. Jobs. For awhile I thought I'd go with him. But I was afraid it would work out to be his career that mattered, basically, to both of us, even though neither one of us wanted that to happen. So he left. And I stayed."

"You were still at the hospital?"

"Yes, but that didn't last long. I'd forgotten how much difference it makes with someone else sharing the rent; and I moved a couple of more times...I wanted to find out what offices are like, what people do in them, so I signed on with a temporary agency, like you did. I think they're better for women. It's strange. Economic discrimination reverses at the bottom levels. I was working a few days and painting a few. My life looked like a hyperbolic curve. Or a parabolic. I don't know which. But...whichever it was, C. J....that was the year I learned how to make jumps in concentration from job to painting; and I got a lot better at observing people without interfering with them. I didn't have to worry much anymore about all the things that have to be done to keep up an apartment. Tom came back in June. Feeling that he'd been the kind of teacher who tries to get the students to do what he should be doing himself. After they graduate. He'd been impressed by how much advertising had affected the people in his tutorials; and he wanted to combine what he knew of art with magazine layouts and billboards, some television, too. So he hired himself out as an advertising consultant. We moved in together again. And we'd discuss everyone he was meeting. Another branch of the city I was storing up information about. We lived together for three years."

"Did you get to paint all that time?"

"Oh, no. He wasn't paying any of my bills. I worked forty-hour weeks two or three months, then painted, then worked again. I found that better than trying to do both things at once. And, too, I always painted some at night when I had a job. I was a secretary for a bus company. And a waitress. An assistant in an architectural firm...The object was never anything but to combine seeing as much as I could with saving as much money as I'd be able to get my hands on." She poured herself another glass of water and continued, "Growing together can be difficult sometimes, C. J. One of us would want to make a change that involved something the other one had depended on...And there were the days that seemed like boredom. Both with Tom and the painting. But it didn't take me long to appreciate that those often had been times of gathering strength. We'd come back to each other, or me to painting or him to his work, on new planes—higher ones."

"I know what you mean," said C. J. "There'll be the empty spaces with Jack. One of us'll start to wonder why we ever left here...You have to move on through those moods, like dormant plants, staying quiet until you're fairly sure again why you're where you are."

"The times stopped being able to be quiet, though, for me, C. J....Tom and I had a son."

"Leah!" C. J. exclaimed. "That's...my God, I don't know what to say!"

"His name is Chuck, C. J.," said Leah calmly and with exaggerated distinctness.

"Chuck."

"Chuck. That's what it says on his birth certificate. Chuck Miernan Tetrao."

"Where is he, Leah?"

"With his father right now. In Michigan."

"How old is he?"

"Three. He was born on July 7, 1970."

"Three...."

She held her water glass up to the light, looked through it, and then said, "Tom left for Michigan in June of '72. He went back to teaching. I was alone with Chuck. We wanted it that way. It was that we both had to do our separate work, not that we stopped caring about each other...Teaching art and doing it just cannot be combined. They cannot. It's like trying to mix the past with the future. And Tom understood that...Latching onto this place was a needed miracle, though, C. J. Chuck was with me until last April. I got work with an insurance firm.

Piecework. Typing and filing. Some correspondence. Proofreading. But I could do most of it here. So I was around Chuck almost every bit of the time. I'm still with the same company. I don't know how long it will last, but it's enough for now. It helps me keep out of a state where I'd be completely without human contact. Tom had things settled enough so he could take Chuck for awhile. I don't think we'll ever have any problems sharing the expenses or the time. I had to be sure of that before I knew I could have a child. And also there aren't as many raised eyebrows as there would have been ten years ago at the two of them being together." She started to clear the table and added, "As far as work goes, my thoughts and my hands have finally developed a coordination I can count on. I can get outside myself what I want to. I think I went through something like what you did with words, C. J. Remember? You used to have so much trouble."

"Yeah, even when I'd have every sentence mapped out, they'd end up said so unlike what I'd meant that sometimes what I'd been thinking and how I was talking were two opposite things. It took a long time to get so I was anywhere near comfortable with it all, that's for sure…But, Leah? Chuck and school. How're you going to deal with that?"

"I don't know. Neither does Tom. I'm sure I'm going to have to be an intermediary between him and the—oh, you know, C. J.—the contradictions he won't be able to help being exposed to. The 'I must pretend I do not feel what I feel's becoming the 'What do I feel?'s becoming the 'I know I can't feel what I'm seeming to feel and don't agree with what there's supposed to be no doubt I've accepted's. I'd hate to have him be forced into making all the standard numbed acceptances of so many incongruities that by the time he's eighteen he'll not notice the inconsistency of probably being expelled for saying an expletive at the same time he's expected to be registering for the draft!…The contradictions are going to be there, but I want him somehow to get skilled at sorting through them…I shouldn't start in on that, though. I expect we're agreed…. Want some pistachio nuts?"

"Sounds just right…"

"C. J., I've been meaning to tell you that I've got the papers set up to sell the paintings," said Leah, as she put a bowl of pistachio nuts on the table. "A business license, resale rights, copyrights. It'd be nice someday to be able to use the word *work* for some of what I do, at the same time that I'm talking about what I'm paid for. It's one of those terms that currently has to slip around my tongue in a fairly muddled kind of way. But where what I paint goes is important to me. It isn't only a money transaction. I give things away if it's to the right person. I hope the style of the work itself is going to guide me to buyers eventually."

"Six years isn't that long a time."

"Not for anything like painting, it isn't," Leah replied, adding, "Let's go back to the floor, all right? Did you have enough to eat?"

"At least enough...And there toward the end I was even getting the stirring down."

"It amazed me you hadn't had fondue before. We used to have them at home whenever there was the slightest hint of some reason to celebrate. We'd sit around the table for hours."

"Yeah, the...Yeah, I haven't been so relaxed in I don't know when," said C. J. "Anything you want me to carry over?"

"Oh, yes, the pistachio nuts, would you? We can just throw the shells on the floor. It's an easy floor to clean."

"That's the first thing I thought of when I saw it...."

Unspeaking, they sat on the floor for nearly a minute; and then Leah said, "We're either going to talk now or in the morning. It should be now. It'll be better."

Exhaling a lengthy sigh, C. J. secured his hands beneath his thighs, curled his back, and angled his eyes toward the easel.

"You're thinking it might have been me with you all this time," Leah continued.

"Or part of it, yes."

"You came here wondering whether you would stay on. Whether I would go away with you."

"Yes."

"Does Jack know that?"

"I told him as soon as I knew I was going to Boston I might not be coming back to Wyoming."

"Well, you're right, C. J....You know you're right...It might've been me. We all understood when you said you were leaving that you would've left with me instead of with Jack. You would've left with both of us. You would've left alone. But you would've left."

"That was the only choice I saw."

"It was what was outside us that decided how it turned out. Not us. I had to stay in one place. I had to be around people. I still do. I can't change that...Now we're almost where we were then. Only more so."

"It was chance," said C. J. "Whatever the alternatives might have been, we couldn't set them out and...We couldn't consider them. None of us knew how to then."

"No. No, we didn't."

"But we should be able to do that now."

"It's too late for that, C. J. We're too settled into who we've become."

"I never knew whether to write you or—"

"Oh, don't ever suspect I've been telling myself you've neglected me," Leah interrupted.

"I wasn't sure how you..."

"Even the distance was a help, in a way. Even the time. It's been a getting ready. Another reason for keeping on...It hasn't been a question of neglect. It's...I'll tell you exactly what I feel, C. J. It's very simple, and it's going to require just a few distinctions...You and Tom are...In a lot of ways you're as unlike each other as Jack and I were.... That's the truth, C. J. ...But what I feel for each of you, different as you are, when I add it all up and weigh it— and, oh, I have done that—but it's so similar it seems pointless to me to try to compare it. Even so, I can't live with either one of you. I mean that."

"But, to be alone..."

"Is what I'd rather be," Leah said, stretching her arms behind her, leaning on her palms. "It's unusual, it might be *very* unusual, I mean to have come as far as we have with each other, C. J. To know each other as well as we do. To have kept up with each other. But love involves more than time. It involves being together. What's outside of people lets the being together happen or prevents it from happening; and when two people can stay with each other for a time, going on, even without the supports that other people, perhaps, should have granted, that's when caring can become love. It's the years together coupled with caring that make what I mean by love. The being almost constantly in sight of each other. Love has to be only between two people. It's too complicated for more than that. Any two adults, yes! But two people together through time! It can't be you, C. J. And it can't be Tom either. There's the caring for you both, but there can't be the being together. The circumstances wouldn't let us be ourselves if we were together. I am going to be alone, or it's going to be...another person. That's how it is. I'm certain of that. And I cannot use the word *love* without the years."

"What word, then? What, Leah? Is *caring* enough?"

"All I can say is that it's a small jump from what I mean by *caring* to what I mean by *love*. It's a small distinction, but it's definitely fundamental...Yes, C. J. Yes, let's let *caring* serve for what we have together and go on with that. However we can. However we must. It's a bit of clarity. At least, if we look at it that way, what we do, we'll do because of what we feel rather than...rather than because we're trapped in all the conventions that depend on lying and denial and compulsion."

"Caring, then," said C. J. "Caring."

"Very slowly," said Leah. Then she laughed and added, "Look at it this way, C. J. You're older than I am...so we've been living together ever since I was born!"

2

She was sitting up when he awoke. He stroked her back and gazed at the early morning blues through the skylight above the bed.

"I had a long dream," he began. "...I was on something like a merry-go-round. All of the people I've ever known—or known of—were on it, too. Everyone, at some point—not in time—there was no time—everything that would ever happen had happened—but, still, everyone at some...point...would be everyone else.

"It was as if each wooden horse held someone and each person took a turn at every place on the ride.

"And I had a vision that stayed the same. A vision of something like a piece of glass. Or a part of a puzzle. Always in front of me. I knew everyone else each had a different piece. And that at some moment on the ride—at some level—we would assemble our pieces into an enormous whole. Every piece would fit into every other one.

"What made the ride meaningful for me was waiting to find out how the pieces would fit together. And I knew the other people were waiting for that, too.

"Along the way I had yearnings of wanting to know how the piece that was my vision connected with someone else's. I'd look at each face, and I'd know they could tell that what I had, that my part of the puzzle, fit with theirs in a very important way. Wanting to find out how was enough to keep them on the ride. Just as it was enough for me. To experience the entire fitting-together was what we were assured of...

"When we were nearing the moment—the point—when the assembling was finally going to happen, I held out my...my fragment...my piece...and just as I did that, I lost sight of it and was watching instead the coming-together of all the other pieces. The joining. What I saw would have made perfect sense, would have symbolized perfection, would have been perfection, if only the one piece I'd had before had been there. But I couldn't find it or remember what it had looked like.

"Then the sort of gigantic puzzle with the missing piece went away, and I was in complete darkness. Black. Floating. Knowing I was getting ready to become another rider with another piece in front of me. Right as the darkness was ending, I understood that the fitting-together was everything I had expected it to be. And that someone or something did experience it. Whole. The maker, maybe. Or somehow the puzzle itself. But that I, as each person, would always have only a view of one, little piece and a view of the assembling of all the other pieces.

"The sense of the two experiences—not how any of it looked—but the sense of the one piece and of all the pieces with one missing had been identical. And I realized they'd always be identical, at the same time that I realized there was no way to get off the ride. Thinking of being on it by choice would always be an illusion. The expecting to see the finished putting-together would always be another illusion. Except for the times of darkness in between, when I'd...wait.

"I'd always been on the same ride and always would be. Each trip living a different life. It made no sense to wonder how many times I'd taken the ride, because the entire framework had no beginning and no end.

"As it was all starting up again, the idea of eventually being able to have a view of the completed puzzle came back to me, along with a sense of the value of being on the ride. And I began to forget that the only reward always would be the happiness at that one little point of reaching-out of whatever piece I'd have, holding it out and not being able to remember I was right away—every trip on the ride—going to lose it...

"I was seeing what figure I was on and what the vision of my new piece looked like, when I woke up."

"The reaching-out," Leah said, her fingers wiping sleep away from her eyes, "sounds like the last trace of hope. When all other hope has gone. If it goes, there won't be any more. But...so far...it's what sustains us."

"Yeah," C. J. said. "But it probably can't go. If it goes, we do, too. And if we go, it may somehow stay on. To ask whether it's wrongfully convinced itself of its own ability to last is a hopeless question. Lots of other hopes have already been taken away by questions like that."

"Sometimes..." Leah said. "Sometimes...life can be a trifle bit absurd!"

"But just sometimes."

"Just sometimes."

"I wish," C. J. said resolvedly, "there were more people could look at your work, Leah."

"I know. I know. I suppose most of it will be seen. In time. I...No matter what happens, I'll keep on...working. Even if it gets to where I have to have five tubes of pigment and one canvas and have to scrape off whatever I've painted so I can begin something else. It's the activity itself...That's...that's enough. C. J., I...C. J., would you go? Would you go now?"

Nodding only once, he got up out of bed and dressed.

While he was buttoning his shirt, Leah went to the closet and pitched his coat to him. "You can open the two locks by hand from this direction," she said, as he started for the door.

"C. J.?"

"Yes?"

"Remember that kite you flew in New Haven? The one with the stamp on it? The one you let go?"

"I remember."

"Do you still expect—just sometimes—to find out who found it? If anyone ever did?"

C. J.'s face became somber; and very slowly he said, "I'd considered so much, when I let go of that kite...the sun, the angles of reflection, the schedules of planes.... but later on, I realized there was a lot I hadn't considered, too...like how that string could've gotten in the wheel of a moving car, and how the aluminum foil could've disoriented a driver on a highway...It wasn't as reckless as they say people were during the first atomic bomb tests, taking bets on whether that one explosion would start a chain reaction that'd end all our lives. But, still, what I did was too reckless to warrant being repeated. And the possibility of repetition is a major part of any good experiment.

"Anyway, after that kite seemed to disappear that morning, I kept watching the sky. The whole sky, I mean. I remember I felt like I was hardly even blinking. And I started thinking still-just-waking-up stuff like, 'Is the sun a kite let loose from…somewhere else…a long time ago? Did I just somehow start a sun I've lost?….Has the sun eclipsed that kite?'

"…Then, after awhile, ten minutes or so, I saw a point of light again. Falling this time. And I started running toward it. Nobody else was on the streets yet. Even by that time, it was only a few minutes past dawn….

"The kite finally landed in a slushy puddle on a sidewalk at the edge of New Haven. I went over to it, peeled off the stamp, tore the stamp into pieces I tossed like confetti onto the mud, and walked back to my room."

"So you left the kite where it landed," said Leah, intently, smiling a prologue to good-bye.

"It was too broken to fly again," said C. J. sighing. "I didn't want to move it. I felt like I'd been on a desert island and had sent out a message in a bottle the tide hadn't taken at all but had only brought back to me." Hesitantly he added, "We'll…keep on with each other."

"Oh, yes, we will," Leah answered reassuredly. "I'd like Chuck to come visit you for a while. When he's old enough."

"By then I might've met somebody I'd have a child with myself. Chuck could baby-sit…."

"It's never too late, they say. "

"I expect they're right about that these days….I…my…my…sexuality, Leah…I didn't totally choose it. I was partly forced into it…by what feels like was…the whole world I encountered. I don't think I'm living out what the nature of the human race really is, even though a few authorities are saying we're all inherently bisexual. I mean, I think some people are inherently ready to have sexual experiences only to allow children to …be conceived and…be cared about right. And that's fine with me."

"There are such differences in people, C. J.! Such differences that don't have to be divisive, really. I mean, if they…harmonize with…the constructive ways we're all the same."

"Yes. I…Leah, I…There's one thing more I have to say."

"What?"

"You'd better get ready."

"All right," she said. "Ready."

"No, you'd better get readier."

"Readier."

"It's that I'm Christopher Jeffrey now."

Leah took a step forward and quickly said, "You're not Chris."

"No."

"And you're not Jeff."

"No."

"Christopher Jeffrey."

"Christopher Jeffrey."

"Good-bye, Rongo," she said, smiling.

"Good-bye, Leah," he answered rapidly; and then he was through the doorway.

After walking several blocks to the Charles Street subway station, he paused to recall the expansive view he had often admired as a boy. Momentarily, he considered what direction he wanted to go, decided on Harvard Square, went through the proper entrance, changed his mind, paid an additional fare, and entered a subway headed for Park Street.

Then, having left the subways and agilely loped to the ticket line at a railway terminal, when it came his turn at a booth for purchasing, he shook his hair away from his eyes and said, his manner assured, his voice genial, "A ticket for one, please. Wyoming. Cheyenne. One way."

Simultaneously, Leah in her home/studio was looking at the unfinished painting she moments before had turned away from the wall; it was a realistic portrayal, so far, of both her son, Chuck, and his father, Dr. Tom Miernan.

Moving they were toward that sun, Leah thought. 'And then, that sun...turned...

'And on he flew.

'Until safely he reached land.

'Contained.'

About the Author

Roger Burkholder has spent much of his life several miles from the official headquarters of central power over the nuclear weapons of the United States. He is dedicated to nonviolence.

GOSHEN COLLEGE GOOD LIBRARY

3 9310 07030748 4

DATE DUE

7/8/02			
SEP 0 1 2008			

Demco, Inc. 38-293

9 780595 002573